COPYCAT

Alex Lake is a British novelist who was born in the North West of England. *After Anna*, the author's first novel written under this pseudonym, was a No.1 bestselling ebook sensation and a top-ten *Sunday Times* bestseller. The author now lives in the North East of the US.

@AlexLakeAuthor

Also by Alex Lake

After Anna
Killing Kate

COPYCAT

Alex Lake

HarperCollins*Publishers*

HarperCollins*Publishers* Ltd
1 London Bridge Street,
London SE1 9GF

www.harpercollins.co.uk

First published by HarperCollins*Publishers* 2017
1

A catalogue record for this book is available from the British Library

ISBN: 978-0-00-819974-6 (PB b-format)
ISBN: 978-0-00-824026-4 (TPB)

This novel is entirely a work of fiction.
The names, characters and incidents portrayed in it are
the work of the author's imagination. Any resemblance to
actual persons, living or dead, events or localities is
entirely coincidental.

Typeset in Sabon LT Std by Palimpsest Book Production Ltd, Falkirk, Stirlingshire
Printed and bound in the United States of America by LSC Communications

For more information visit: www.harpercollins.co.uk/green

To Mum and Dad, who taught me the magic words: 'Of course you can'.

PART ONE

Ten Years Earlier

The first time someone said that Karen was gone for good was during the week after she disappeared. People – mothers – didn't just leave their kids without warning for days on end, unless there was something wrong. Very wrong. Depressed, maybe, after the birth of her second child. Or unhappy in her relationship. Her boyfriend was not a local, and he was a few years older than her. Who knew what went on behind the closed doors of their house?

Not Sarah Havenant, or any of her friends, although they were the last to see her. It was the day Sarah moved back to Barrow, Maine, after four years of college and then four more of medical school, ready to start her residency at the local hospital, and she and her friends had gotten together in a bar. Reconnect. Catch up on old times. Talk about what was to come.

Sarah, Jean, Franny, Luke. The old gang, at least the ones who were still around.

And Karen. Karen, mom of two boys, a three-year-old and a one-year-old. Karen, who was now missing.

Sarah didn't remember Karen leaving the bar. It was sometime before 2 a.m., which was the time she had staggered into a cab with Franny and Luke. Alec – a guy they had bumped into – had offered to drive but, drunk as she was, Sarah had been sensible enough to turn his kind offer down.

Franny and Luke didn't remember seeing her leave either, and neither did Jean, who had left early; she worked on an organic farm in the summers and had to get ready for the farmers' market the following day.

But sometime in between Jean's early departure and 2 a.m., Karen had left too.

Although, as it turned out, vanished was a better word.

The next day, Sarah had run into Karen's boyfriend, and father of her two sons. She didn't know him – they'd met briefly once or twice when she was back in town – and he'd asked if she knew where Karen was.

Sarah shook her head. *Is Karen OK?* she said.

She didn't come home last night, he replied. *I woke up around four with this guy* – he was with his sons and he kissed the one-year-old on the top of the head – *and she wasn't there. I called her cell but there was no answer.*

He'd called around. Tried the local hospital. But there was no trace of her.

At some point in the night, impossible though it seemed, she had disappeared.

And, with nearly a week gone, it looked like she wasn't planning on coming back anytime soon.

1

Sarah Havenant glanced at her phone as she walked to Examining Room Three. She was expecting a message from Ben, her husband, telling her whether he could pick up their son, Miles – a mere seven years old but, all of a sudden, every bit the rebellious teenager, which was a surprising and unwelcome transformation – from the farm camp where he was spending a week of his summer vacation. If not it meant she would have to leave the Barrow Medical Center as soon as she finished work and head over there to get him, which would mean no stop at the gym on the way home and no workout.

And today, more than most days, she needed a workout, because she had just come from a patient who Sarah had told, sitting there in the examining room, that the results of the tests she had been for were not good; in fact, they were awful, and, given the particular form of cancer she had, it was probable her life expectancy would be measured in months and not years.

The patient – Amy, she was called – had left almost without a word. Her husband was with her; he had started asking questions, but Amy had stood up and shook her head and

5

told him they could get more details later, but right now all she wanted to do was leave.

I want to go and see Isla, she'd said.

Isla, her nine-month-old daughter. A daughter who would, barring a miracle, shortly be motherless.

So she needed the gym. And then she would go home to Ben and Miles and five-year-old Faye and two-year-old Kim and a meal and then stories and bathtime and bed. And she would make sure to say a prayer of thanks – even though she was not religious in any way – for her family.

But there was no message from Ben. There was, however, a Facebook friend request, from a name she hadn't thought of for a long time. A decade, at least.

Rachel Little.

Who was not *really* a friend. She'd been at Barrow High School with Sarah, but she'd not been part of Sarah's circle. She'd not been part of anyone's circle, really. She didn't fit; high school was carefully stratified into tribes – jocks, cheer squad, chess club – and Rachel was into tarot readings and the occult and weird food fads. It probably wasn't true, but Sarah remembered her eating and drinking nothing but home-made vegetable juices, which she enthused about to anybody who would listen.

Rachel had been tall and long-limbed, but not in a graceful way. In a not-quite-in-control of her hands and feet way, and her hands and feet were prominent, because she always wore pants and long-sleeved shirts – never dresses or skirts or tank tops or T-shirts – and they were always too short for those long, gangly limbs.

But still, she was nice enough, and it would be interesting to see what she was up to. That was one of the great things about Facebook. You could keep in touch with lots and lots of people in a non-committal way. Ben thought it was a waste of time – he'd deleted his account a few months back – but

Sarah liked it. She liked people, and she was interested in their lives.

She paused at the door to Examining Room Three – inside was her last patient of the day, a hypochondriac man in his early forties who enjoyed splendid good health but was convinced he was dying – and opened the friend request.

Hi Sarah! It's me, Rachel! Recently got on Facebook (a bit late but you know me – not exactly with it!) and thought I'd look you up. Hope you're well. I'm in the process of moving back to Barrow so maybe we'll catch up. One question – is this the right account for you or is it the other one (with your name and photo on)?

Sarah frowned and typed a response.

Rachel! Would love to catch up. At work or I'd write more. And I only have one account – this one!

She sent the reply, walked into Examining Room Three, and forgot all about it.

Ben, it turned out, was able to pick up Miles. His message – OK re: Miles – was typical of him. He treated email and text messages as vehicles to pass on the maximum of information with the minimum of words. He claimed it was because he was British and didn't believe in idle chat, but Sarah thought it was really because he harbored some vague idea that the more words you wrote, the more the message could cost. Either way, Miles was taken care of, so she stopped at the gym on her way home and joined, a few minutes late, a spinning class. Afterwards, she walked outside with Abby, a marketing graduate in her mid-twenties who had played lacrosse in college and who took, it seemed to Sarah, a too

7

obvious pleasure in out-spinning the late-thirties moms and retirees who made up much of the gym-going population of Barrow.

'Ugh,' Abby said. '*So* hard. My thighs were burning. She's the best instructor.'

She was Tanya, a woman who was a few years older than Sarah but who had a body that, as a doctor, Sarah considered to be a marvel of medical science. She did the class with her charges but, when they were dissolving into puddles of their own sweat, she was untroubled. And, as she spun, she would shout out what to do next. The fact she was capable of rational thought was impressive; that she could speak was amazing; that she could shout was beyond belief. Although it was ridiculous – she was a thirty-eight-year-old mother of three with a husband with whom she still had an active (and not unadventurous) sex life – Sarah had, she realized, a bit of a crush on Tanya. Not – she didn't think – in a sexual way, but in a I-want-to-be-this-person way. She was awestruck by Tanya, and found herself wanting to impress her with her spinning skills, a mission which was likely to result only in Tanya wondering why Sarah was so easily reduced to a red-faced and panting wreck.

'She *is* phenomenal,' Sarah said. 'I don't know how she does it.'

'Lots of hard work,' Abby said, with the literal-mindedness of the young. 'There's no secret sauce that gets you in shape.'

'I guess so,' Sarah replied, wishing there was a secret sauce that got you in shape. She took her phone and car keys from her bag. 'See you next time, hopefully.'

'I'll be here for Thursday's class,' Abby said. 'See you then.'

Sarah nodded and opened her car door. She put the keys in and started the engine. As she waited for the air-conditioning to kick in she looked at her phone.

There was a new message from Rachel.

Great! I'll let you know when I'm back in Barrow. And here's the other account in your name! It's definitely you!

There was a link. Sarah tapped it with her forefinger and it brought up a Facebook account.

She frowned. It was her name. Sarah Havenant.

She scanned the page. Married to Ben. Mother of three kids.

And the profile photo was of her. She was smiling and looking straight at the camera, standing by an ice rink they had skated at a lot last winter. She remembered that particular day: she was wearing the coat she'd bought at one of the outlet stores in Freeport. It was made from some new material – super lightweight but super warm – and she'd been struck by how much she wished they'd had things like this when they grew up; most of her childhood winters had been spent wrapped in so many layers it made movement practically impossible.

But it was all irrelevant. The question was, why the hell was there a Facebook account purporting to be her? And, more to the point, who had set it up?

She scrolled down.

And froze.

The most recent post was from *that morning*. It was a photo of Miles, Faye and Kim sitting on a beach towel eating peanut butter sandwiches, and it had a caption:

Turns out Kim likes sand sandwiches. Thanks to her older siblings for putting the sand in her sandwich and helping her discover this!

Sarah stared at the screen. This was not some random photo of her at an ice rink six months ago. This had happened *yesterday*.

9

They had been at the beach, and, at lunchtime Miles and Faye – it was more Faye, in truth – had told their youngest sibling the reason they were called sandwiches was because they had sand in them, and, desperate for attention, Kim had nodded agreement. Smiling, they had spread mayonnaise on bread, sprinkled it with a liberal dose of fresh, warm sand and handed it to her.

Mmm, Kim said, as they encouraged her to eat it. *I love sandwiches.*

But no one else knew about it. They had come home late in the afternoon, and, once the kids were in bed, Sarah had spent the rest of the evening getting ready for work.

Slowly, she began to scroll through the rest of the post.

2

She could not believe what she saw.

The next post was a photo of her and Ben on a date a few weeks earlier at a Japanese restaurant. They were sharing a sushi boat and a bottle of white wine; the photo had been taken from behind Ben and she was listening to him, her right hand resting on her glass. The caption read:

Date night with my wonderful husband. We need to do this more often!

It was, she realized, exactly the sort of banal post she would have written.

Except she hadn't. Someone else had. And they had done more, many more.

A photo of her in a Greek wine bar in Portland with Toni and Anne, her two best college friends, on a night out in early spring. Caption: Girls night! Yay! A photo of her and Jean, a teaching assistant in the local kindergarten who Sarah had known all her life, after a 10k race they'd run in April. It had rained nonstop throughout, an old-fashioned down-pour, and they were dripping wet, and grinning. Caption: Bit rainy but no problem. My delightful British husband said before we set off 'Nothing to worry about. This is just drizzle back home.' He then proceeded to pull out his golf umbrella, hand warmers and flask of hot tea.

Ben *had* said those very words, then waited at the finish line under his umbrella, sipping his drink.

Holy shit. What was this? What was this and who had done it?

It got worse.

A photo of Faye's pre-school production of *The Giant Turnip*, Faye at the left of the stage dressed as a carrot.

A photo of the kids building a snowman on the town square.

A photo of Sarah sipping hot chocolate in the Little Cat Café, a sheaf of papers on the table in front of her. She'd been researching an article and had gone to the café to arrange her thoughts.

A photo, from February, of her new kitchen, installed over the winter months.

Caption: Finished! I love this!

A photo which had been taken inside her house.

The air-conditioning in the car was now fully up and running, cold air flowing from the vents and washing over her, but she barely noticed it. She had goose pimples up and down her arms and legs, but it was not the cold air raising them. It was not the cold air chilling her.

It was the photos. Of her, of Ben, of her house.

Of her kids.

Who was doing this? It had to be someone who was at all these places, someone who was at the beach yesterday and out on date nights with her and there when she was with her girlfriends and at Faye's pre-school performances.

There was no one. Not even Ben.

And why? Was it some kind of a joke? Maybe all her friends were in on it – which would explain how they had so many photos – but why? What did they get from it? And why do it for six months without telling her? Why do it at *all*?

It made no sense.

Worse, she thought, *a cruel trick by my friends is the best explanation I can hope for. I have no idea what the alternatives are, but I bet none of them are good.*

She looked back down at her phone and scrolled through the photos. This was not her friends. A joke at *her* expense – perhaps a fake Facebook account in her name in which she made off-color jokes or revealing admissions about her sex life – was just about possible. Toni had been a bit of a prankster in college – calling for pizzas for other people's houses, that kind of thing – and, although she had mostly grown out of it, she still retained part of her juvenile nature. She always would. It was in her blood. Her father and two elder brothers never stopped playing tricks on each other, Toni and her long-suffering mom. The first time Sarah had stayed at their house on Cape Cod, in the summer of their freshman year in college, Marty, Toni's dad, had made boiled eggs for breakfast, serving them in dainty porcelain egg cups with neatly sliced toast glistening with butter besides them.

Eat, he said. *It's my specialty.*

Boiled eggs aren't much of a specialty, Dad, Toni replied, still sleepy.

These I call Marty's Boiled Eggs Surprise, he said. *Dig in.*

Sarah tapped the shell with her spoon. It cracked and she pulled it away. For a second she didn't understand, then she looked up at Marty – he insisted she call him Marty and not Mr Gorchoff, which made her feel grown up and a bit uncomfortable at the same time – and told him the egg was empty. It was a hollow shell.

That's the surprise! he said. *Your egg's not there.*

He passed her a mug of coffee. She took a sip, and then another – it was a wonderful, heady brew – then glimpsed a sudden blaze of color among the brown, muddy coffee, which disappeared when she held the coffee mug upright.

She tilted it again, and there it was.

An egg yolk.

Mr Gor— Marty, she said. *There's an egg in there!*

That's the other part of the surprise, he said. *But don't worry! They're organic!*

She had spent the rest of the weekend in terror of the next little 'surprise', but mercifully she had been left alone. Toni, however, had grown up being constantly subjected to pranks which were a touch cruel and more than a touch irresponsible – so it was not impossible she would have set up a fake Facebook account in her friend's name.

But not one with Sarah's kids on it.

Like most of her mom friends, Sarah was a little tentative about putting photos of her children up on the Internet, whatever Facebook said about privacy, so she restricted access to her account to only her friends, and then she was careful about what she put up there.

But this account was public. These photos were there for all the world to see. And even Toni would not have gone this far in the service of some prank.

Which left who? Ben? He'd have access to the photos – he could get them from her phone – but she couldn't imagine him doing it. He'd have to have set it up on his work computer and then made sure she never saw any of the notifications and emails that would come in. She often used his phone, and – she wasn't proud of this, but it was true nonetheless – gave his emails and text messages a quick scan. They were reassuringly boring. Stuff from his colleagues about operating committee presentations and legal reviews and seeking board approval and texts from his friends about where to watch the game and whether they had a pass from the wife to go out.

No, if it was Ben, he would have had to employ a level of deception she did not think he had in him, not least because his utter cluelessness about how computers worked would have to be a long-standing deception requiring a level of acting talent she was pretty sure was beyond him.

Pretty sure. But you never really knew. You heard of stranger things in marriages.

She shook her head and dismissed the thought. There was no way this was Ben.

But then who? Who the *fuck* was doing this?

3

So, she has found it, finally. It has taken a while. It has been there for six months, a piece of bait, dangling in the water. But she has not sensed it until now. Not been aware of its presence. She is not the most observant of people – surprising, for a doctor – which works against her. It makes it easier to do a thing like this.

Obviously she does not Google herself. That is a mistake. It's always a good idea to know what is out there, to have the best available information, to know what your enemy knows. But then, if you don't even know you have an enemy, why would you bother?

She will be wondering who did it, who put these photos up there, and she will be asking herself why, but she will not figure it out. Her mind does not work in such a way. She sees no reason why anybody would do this to her. She doesn't even know *how* they would do it, although the who and the how are closely related. Understand one, and she will understand the other.

But she will understand neither.

Not, at least, until it is too late.

Because this is only the beginning. This Facebook account

16

is merely the hook that lodges in the mouth of the fish. The fish thinks the hook is its only problem, thinks that if it can only get rid of it, then all will be well again in its world.

But it is wrong. Because the hook is attached to a line which is attached to a rod which is held by a hand. And the hand is controlled by a mind, a mind which has been waiting and watching and plotting the best time and place and method to catch the fish.

And so the fish struggles to free itself, but all it manages to do is to embed the hook deeper. And as it continues to wriggle and fight it uses up its supplies of energy until it is too exhausted to continue, and then its struggles wane.

And the hand senses it, and begins to wind in the reel . . .

So far she has only felt the prick of the hook in her cheek. The rest – the struggles, the fight, her eventual destruction – is yet to come.

Fun. This will be fun. Fishing always is.

Revenge always is.

4

Sarah parked next to Ben's car – a dark blue (night mineral blue, according to the salesman who had sold it to them when Miles was an infant) family sedan. America's favorite: a Toyota Camry. Sensible, reliable, fuel-efficient, strong residuals. And needing to be replaced, soon.

A few weeks back, Ben had mentioned getting a convertible to replace it.

OK, but get one with five seats, she said.

They don't make them with five seats, he replied. *The roof has to fold into the body of the car so it reduces the space available for a back seat. It's normally two at most.*

She looked at him, her expression a mixture of amusement and incredulity. *But we have three kids, Ben. What's the plan? Make Miles ride his bike?*

We have your car if we need to go somewhere all together, he replied. *I only really drive this to work. And it'd be nice in the summer to have the top down.*

But what if you do need to take all three? What if I'm away for the weekend and something happens?

I'd get a cab, he said. *And you can always think of reasons why we would need two big cars. But most of the time we don't.*

Fine, she said. *If that's your priority.*

It's not a question of priorities, he replied. *I'd simply like to have a convertible. But never mind. Perhaps it's a stupid idea. Early onset midlife crisis.*

And they left it there. She felt bad about having dented his dream; in truth, she wasn't sure why she didn't want him to get a convertible. It would have been nice for her to drive it, too. It was simply . . . well, it *did* reek of a midlife crisis. In some vague way she found it a threat, a sign he was making decisions based on his own needs and not the needs of the family. Anyway, she'd tell him to go ahead and get his convertible. She'd be happy for him. At least, she'd try to be.

That was for later. For now, she was glad his current car was there. It meant he was home.

Ben was sitting on the couch, Kim on his lap. He was reading the book of the moment, *Hairy Scary Monster*, which Kim demanded incessantly. Ben was a very patient dad – it was one of the things Sarah loved about him – but even he would balk at the seventh or eighth reading of the same kids' book during the same bedtime.

'You're reading *Hairy Scary Monster*,' Sarah said. 'Imagine.'

'Only the second reading today,' Ben said. 'So it still retains that fresh feeling common to all great literature.'

'Daddy, read,' Kim said. She fit the profile of a third child exactly: with two older siblings she had learned to fight for her fair share of whatever commodity was up for grabs – attention, cake, time on the trampoline. She was desperate to be in the gang, whatever the cost, which was what had led to the sand sandwich episode on the beach.

'Hey,' Sarah said. 'Something pretty weird happened today.'

'At the clinic?'

'No. I got a friend request from someone I went to high school with. She's moving back to Barrow.'

'What's weird about that? Plenty of people move here. I moved here from London.' He grinned at her. 'But then I had a good reason to.'

'That's not the weird part.'

'Daddy,' Kim said. 'Read!'

'One moment, petal,' Ben said. 'Mummy and I are talking. So what was the weird part?'

Kim grabbed her dad's hand and put it on the book. 'Read!' she said. 'Read *Hairy Scary Monster*.'

Ben rolled his eyes. 'Can we talk about this later?' he said. 'I don't think Kim is too keen on having her story interrupted.'

It was nearly nine o'clock by the time they got round to talking about it. As she was putting Miles to bed he started telling her about farm camp – they had washed a pig with a hose and he was wondering whether they could get a pig as a family pet. Sarah explained that pigs weren't really pets, and they didn't have time to take care of one, but Miles demurred: *he* would take care of it, he insisted. And not only would he look after it night and day, he would do lots of jobs to earn money to buy it fun toys.

Let's start with a pet which is a bit less ambitious, Sarah told him. *Like a goldfish.*

Or hairless rats, Miles said. *Anthony has hairless rats.*

Sarah shook her head. She'd seen those hairless rats; she wasn't squeamish – she was a doctor – but they were not the most beautiful members of the animal kingdom.

Goldfish, she said. *And if you can take care of those, maybe a hamster.*

And then a pig? Miles said.

Maybe then a pig, Sarah said, confident they would never make it to that point.

Downstairs, she poured two glasses of wine. Ben was on the couch, his laptop open on his knee. She handed him a drink.

'Work?' Sarah said.

'Cleaning up email,' Ben said. 'No big deal.'

With Ben it was never a big deal. He was a lawyer and she knew he had some stressful cases, but he never brought it home.

There's no point worrying about work, he'd say, adding his favorite quote: *'worry is a dividend paid to disaster before it's due'. You spend your time thinking about things that might never happen. It's pointless. If it happens, figure it out. If it doesn't, don't worry about it.*

And he didn't. Which was one of the things Sarah – who did worry, who had always worried, to a fault – loved about him.

'So,' she said. 'Miles wants a pig.'

'Presumably his desire for a pig is not the weird thing you mentioned earlier? Because it seems exactly the sort of thing Miles would want.'

'No. I'll show you the weird thing.' She picked up her phone and opened the fake Facebook account. She passed it to him. 'Take a look.'

He scrolled down the screen. 'I don't get it,' he said. 'What's weird about this? I know I don't use it, but isn't this what Facebook is for? Sharing photos? Telling people that you have alfalfa sprouts in your smoothie?'

'It is. And I'm amazed you know what an alfalfa sprout is.' She paused. 'But this isn't my account.'

Ben frowned. 'What do you mean? The photos are of you. And the kids.'

'I know. But I didn't know it was there until today. Rachel, the friend who sent a friend request, asked me which account was mine. I hadn't set eyes on it until then.' She took the phone and switched to her account. 'This is me. The real me.'

Ben looked at the screen for a few seconds, then put the phone on the couch next to him. 'So who set it up?' he said.

21

'That's exactly what I want to know,' Sarah replied. 'I have no idea.'

Ben stared at her. 'This is weird,' he said. 'But let's think about it logically. Who *could* have set it up?'

'I don't know. No one.'

'It would need to be someone who was at those places. And there aren't many photos. About eight, in total? So it wouldn't be too difficult to do.'

'But no one was at all those places.'

'Maybe it was someone who has access to your phone,' Ben said.

'But I didn't take all those photos. Like the one of me and you at the Japanese restaurant. It looks as though it was taken from somewhere inside. It wasn't me who took it.'

'So either it was someone who happened to be at all those places, but who would have had a good reason to be there so you wouldn't have noticed anything out of place, or it's someone who knew you would be there and went – surreptitiously – to take the photos.' He raised his hands in mock fear. 'Which would mean you have some kind of stalker.'

'Ben!' Sarah said. 'Don't joke about it! It's not funny!'

'Sarah,' he said. 'I don't think you have a stalker.'

'Maybe not. But no jokes.'

'OK,' he said. 'No jokes. But let's see if we can narrow it down. Let's start with the most recent photo. We'll remember that best. Who was at the beach yesterday?'

'Lots of people. It was a hot Sunday in summer in Maine. Everyone heads to the water.'

'Let's list them.'

'Mel was there, with Anthony and James. I think I saw Bill, her husband, as well. Then there was Jean and her two kids. Lizzie and Toby were there with their girls. And I saw Miles's kindergarten teacher. She was at the other end of the beach to us.' Sarah shrugged. 'There were lots of people.'

Ben puffed out his cheeks. 'All I can think is, it's some kind of a joke,' he said. 'Someone's winding you up.'

'It's a possibility,' Sarah said. 'But there's still the question of who would do such a thing. Whoever it was would have to have been in all those places.'

'Not necessarily. It could be a few of your friends. They could have shared photos with each other.'

'I suppose,' Sarah said. 'But it seems a very elaborate trick.'

'Well,' Ben said. 'I wouldn't worry—'

Sarah's phone buzzed. She looked at the screen and held up her hand to silence him.

There was a notification. From Facebook.

She opened it, and blinked. She did not believe what she was seeing.

'Holy shit,' she said.

'What?'

'It's a friend request.' She looked at her husband. 'From me. From Sarah Havenant. From the fake account.'

5

Friend Request: Sarah Havenant. Confirm / Delete.

Sarah knew it was nothing, just digital information rendered into text by some software, but that didn't stop her from feeling very disoriented. It was odd to see your own name and photo asking you to be a friend.

I'm *Sarah Havenant*, she thought. *Not you. Not you, whoever you are.*

'Can I see?' Ben held out his hand for the phone. He stared at the screen. 'This is weird,' he said. 'Really weird. It's got to be some kind of a joke. There's no other explanation.'

There was a confidence in his tone which Sarah found reassuring. Ben was quick to analyze a situation – a legal case, a friendship, a problem with the kids' behavior – and quick to understand what was important, which gave him a sense of clarity in the stages before the facts came in. It was how they had got married. They met in a club in London when Sarah was at a work conference there, and they'd kissed. Nothing more had happened that night, but they'd arranged to get together before she left. It turned out 'before she left' meant the next night, and the next, and the next. The last night she was there he told her they were going to get married.

She had laughed. *It's a bit early for a wedding, isn't it?*

Take it the right way, he said. *It's not a proposal. It's a prediction. I can tell. I get the same feeling at work. We have some case come in and there are all kinds of competing opinions and contracts and noise and I look the guy in the eye and know he's a crook. Which is the only important thing to know. And it's the same with you. The only important thing is that I already know we're getting married. The rest is merely details.*

But I live in Maine. I'm at the beginning of a residency in a hospital in my hometown. And I'm only here until tomorrow.

Like I said, he replied, *mere details. They can work themselves out.*

And they did. The next day she decided to change her flight and stay on a while. They went to Stonehenge and Edinburgh and Durham and Hadrian's Wall and then she really *had* to go home.

Once she was back in Maine, they had a long-distance relationship, a kind of relationship which she had always been convinced would never work, but in this case, it did: and it did because of Ben and his certainty. He called almost every day, visited once a month – he always came to her – and then, nine months after they met, he asked her to marry him.

Are you sure? she said, aware this was not the normal response.

Yes, he said. *I'm always sure.*

And it was this certainty that had led them to get married and for him to give up his legal career in London and move to Maine and have kids. It was a powerful force, his certainty, and she found it, in truth, a little frightening. It was fine

25

when it was working in the same direction as her, but she had wondered, more than once, what would happen if it started to work in a different direction. One day he might decide their marriage was over, might analyze their situation and decide it was hopeless, and then his certainty would take him inexorably away from her.

But for now she was glad he had decided this Facebook account was nothing more than a joke. She only hoped it was true.

'Have you talked to anyone else about this?' he said. He had a thoughtful look on his face, as if something had occurred to him.

She shook her head.

'No one at all? No one knows you found out about this?'

'No one. Why are you asking? What are you getting at?'

'The timing,' he said. 'It's a bit – well, it's a little bit odd, don't you think?'

'The timing of what?'

'The friend request from the other Sarah Havenant. It's odd it should come in now, on the same day you found out about the profile. I mean, it's been up there a while. Why today? It's quite a coincidence, if indeed it *is* a coincidence.'

Sarah's stomach tightened. 'You think it's not a coincidence? Someone knows I found out, and that's why they sent it?'

'Maybe,' Ben said. 'But it helps, right? Figure out who could know you got the friend request and you know who sent it.'

'No one knows,' Sarah said. 'How would anyone know?'

'What about the person who told you there was another account in your name? What was her name?'

'Rachel,' she said. 'Rachel Little.'

'Maybe it was her. She'd know you'd found the account, since she told you about it.'

'No,' Sarah said. 'It can't be her. She's not been in Barrow for years.'

Ben shrugged. 'Ask her.'

'Maybe I will. But first I need to speak to Jean.'

6

Jean lived on the next street. To walk on the road was about a half mile, but there was a path through the trees which connected their backyards. Sarah called on her way along it to let her friend know she was coming.

Thankfully, Jean was still up. Even though it was only half past nine, that was not a given: she was a single mom with two adopted kids, so early nights were the norm. Her former husband – father of the two kids she had adopted – had died three years ago in a hit-and-run car accident. They never found the driver; there was a stolen car, abandoned a few miles away with a dent in the hood, a web of cracks in the windshield, and an empty bottle of whiskey in the footwell. There was also a syringe on the passenger seat.

The car had been stolen from the Rite-Aid car park in Barrow; the cops had CCTV footage of it leaving the car park but they could not identify the driver, who was wearing a hooded top. They assumed it was a petty thief looking to make a few bucks for their next fix of heroin, which was the drug of choice in Maine for those who could not get their hands on prescription opiates.

She'd had a rough time of it, Jean, but she was one of

those people who somehow managed to carry on. Even after Jack had died, she'd tried to focus on the positives. She'd said to Sarah that at least she had the kids – she couldn't have any of her own – so they would be her family for the rest of her life.

They were lucky to have her as a mom, Sarah replied. *As she was to have her as a friend.*

Sarah opened the back door and walked into the kitchen.

'Hi,' Jean said. She was making sandwiches for her sons' lunches. 'What's up?'

'Well,' Sarah said. 'It's been one of those days.'

Jean raised an eyebrow. 'Oh?'

'Did you hear about Rachel Little?'

'Coming back to Barrow?' Jean nodded. 'She sent me a friend request.'

'Me too,' Sarah said. 'Anything weird about yours?'

'No,' Jean said. 'What do you mean, weird?'

'Well, she asked me which was my true profile.'

Jean pursed her lips and frowned. 'I don't get it.'

Sarah passed her phone to Jean. 'She meant this.'

Jean put the knife down and swiped her finger over the screen. She studied it for a few seconds.

'Holy shit,' she said. 'What the hell is this?'

'That's my question. And ten minutes ago I got a friend request. From this fake account. So someone knew I'd just found out about it.'

'Oh my God,' Jean said. 'Who would know? And who was at all the places the photos were taken?'

'Nobody I can think of,' Sarah said. 'Other than me.'

'Right. And it wasn't you.'

Sarah paused. 'Ben thought it might be Rachel. She knew I'd seen the account, because she alerted me to it.'

'I guess,' Jean said. 'But I don't know how it could be her. How would she have got the photos? She'd need to have

29

been around Barrow for the last six months, which rules her out. She's been on the West Coast.'

They looked at Rachel's profile to check; she had been working as a psychologist in San Diego, specializing in grief counseling and post-traumatic stress disorder. It made sense; there was a large military presence down there. That was all there was, though: her profile was only a few weeks old.

'She's new to Facebook,' Sarah said. 'So it could all be bullshit she put on her profile, when all along she's been much closer to home.'

'Maybe,' Jean said. She looked doubtful. 'But it seems a bit of a stretch. And you still have the question of why she would be doing this. You guys got along OK in high school, right?'

'More or less. She was pretty quiet. I didn't have much to do with her.' Sarah paused. 'Although there was one time we were kind of at odds, over that guy Jeremy.'

Jean nodded slowly. 'I remember,' she said. 'Sort of. But it was no big deal, right?'

Jeremy had showed up in their sophomore year of high school. He'd come from somewhere in California and he was a new and exotic addition to their lives. He surfed – at least he said he did – talked with authentic West Coast slang about all the grunge clubs in Seattle he'd been to, and wore clothes that Sarah and most of her friends had only seen on MTV.

A week or so into the school year he had asked Sarah out for coffee. She went along; he was funny and charming, but underneath all the clothes and surface cool she realized he was terribly immature. She doubted the truth of most of his stories, and so, after a few more dates, she told him she was no longer interested.

Before she did so, there had been an odd encounter with Rachel. After school one day Rachel had grabbed her elbow

30

and steered her into a classroom. She looked exhausted and on edge, and she asked Sarah what was going on with Jeremy.

Nothing much, Sarah replied. *He's nice but there's no spark.*

Rachel had tears in her eyes when she spoke. *Then leave him for me,* she said. *Leave him for someone who cares.*

Before Sarah could reply the door opened and one of the teachers – an English teacher called Mrs Coffin – came in, and Rachel scuttled away.

As far as Sarah knew, she and Jeremy never got together, and in any case, six months later Jeremy was gone, his dad's job transferred back to the West Coast. Until now, Sarah had never thought of him again.

But all that was nothing to do with this. It was years ago, and it had been irrelevant even back then.

'I think it's all a coincidence,' Sarah said.

'So whoever's behind this just happened to send it today?' Jean replied. 'Bit weird.'

'I hope so,' Sarah said. 'Because the alternative is someone's watching me.'

She poured a glass of wine; Jean didn't drink a great deal but she had half a bottle someone had left after a cook-out at the weekend. She stared at the red liquid, looking at her distorted reflection. It was ridiculous. Either this was some kind of elaborate joke or Rachel Little was doing it or there was some fucking stalker out there, but whatever it was, it was crazy.

And it had been going on for six months. For six months someone had been on Facebook, pretending to be her. The more she thought about it, the more scared she became.

'Who's she friends with?' Jean said. 'The fake Sarah? Who's been looking at her posts?'

'I checked,' Sarah said. 'A bunch of random people; no one we know. You know how Facebook is.' Sarah shook her head. 'Which means this is purely for me.'

Jean smiled, but they had been close friends long enough for Sarah to recognize it as a smile she was forcing on to her lips.

'It'll be fine,' she said. 'Soon we'll be looking back at this as some weird shit that happened in the past.'

'I hope so,' Sarah said. 'I really hope so.'

7

This is all part of the plan. She is confused, naturally. She starts to question things. People. Friends. Events. She wonders what happened. She wonders whether there is a link between the friend request from her fake self to her real self and the fact it came on the same day she discovered her fake self. She considers there must be. But what? And why? And who? She cannot work this out, so she will think it might be a coincidence. And this thought will be nice and comforting and so gradually she will let this thought become her explanation.

A coincidence. Yes, it is a coincidence. The alternative – a stalker, watching her, hidden in the shadows – is too awful to contemplate, so a coincidence it is.

But she is wrong. She has been watched for a long time. Watched until she found the Facebook account.

Finally. For now, after all the planning and waiting and watching, it truly starts. It has been a long time in the weaving, this tangled web. And now she has taken one thread of it, and she will start to pull.

She will pull and it will unravel in ways she cannot imagine. For there are many threads. And as she thinks she is making progress, as she thinks she is figuring this all out, she will discover the truth.

In untangling the web, she has merely become trapped in it. Stuck fast.

A fish in a net. And the more she struggles, the tighter it will grip her.

Until there is no way out.

8

Sarah lay in bed, eyes open. She had got back from Jean's house at eleven and had struggled to fall asleep. Now, after not much more than four hours of fitful sleep, she was awake.

Wide awake. Too much wine had given her a headache and, although the ibuprofen she had taken had dulled the pain, it was not much use in calming the other problem with her head, namely the questions rolling around and around in a futile search for answers. She wanted to know who was behind this, and why.

And she wanted to know if it was dangerous. Because it certainly felt like it could be. Whoever had done this had been at her daughter's pre-school. In a restaurant with her and Ben.

They had been in her *house*.

She felt her chest tighten and she inhaled deeply, held her breath, then slowly exhaled.

Not this, she thought. *Please, not this.*

It had been a few years since her last anxiety attack, since the last time her mind had run away with itself and sent her fight-or-flight reflex haywire, leaving her short of breath, dizzy, heart racing and gripped by a powerful nausea. It had felt like she was having a heart attack, or, on occasion even worse: she'd felt like she was dying.

And, at times, she'd caught herself thinking maybe she would be better off dead. The panic could start at any time. In the car, in the supermarket, at work. She lived in a debilitating fear, and she wasn't sure she could go on.

She had always been anxious, but what made the panic attacks even harder to bear was that they had started in earnest when Miles was born, and so she associated them with him. This in turn made her feel guilty, which triggered the panic.

Ben had been very worried – this in itself was a big deal, which made her even more anxious – and had spoken to some of the other doctors about possible solutions. In the end, Sarah had seen a colleague who had given her some coping strategies – deep breaths, positive thinking, exercise, and, initially, medication. She had, mercifully, managed to avoid them since.

But the threat of their return had been in the background; they were gone, but there was always the lurking thought: *only for now*.

And, right on cue, here they were. Hands shaking, heart skipping out of control, she sat up, her head against the cool wall. Next to her, Ben snored gently.

There was no point trying to go to sleep. She swung her legs over the side of the bed and went downstairs.

She was watching the local news when the door to the living room opened. It was Ben, hair tousled, in his boxer shorts.

'You're up early,' he said.

'You too,' she replied. 'You should go back to bed.'

'I can't sleep when I know you're down here.' He sat beside

her and took a swig from her coffee, then began to massage her shoulders. 'You OK?'

'I guess. But this Facebook thing has freaked me out. I can't stop thinking about it. I felt like I was going to have a panic attack. You know, like I used to.'

'Hmm,' he said. 'Not good.'

The pressure from his fingers intensified. It felt wonderful, and she leaned against him. His left hand slid forward, over her shoulder and on to her breast.

'Hey,' she said. 'I thought this was a back rub?'

'I never said so,' he replied. 'And I think you need to take your mind off all this Facebook nonsense.'

'A back rub would do the trick,' Sarah said. She leaned back and kissed him. 'But maybe something else would be good, too.'

The sex distracted her, but as she sat and ate breakfast with Miles, Faye and Kim – Ben had gone to work – the questions came back: Who was it? Why? And with them, the anxiety. It was awful; she had an all-pervading sensation of impending doom which occupied most of her attention. For everything else, she was going through the motions, almost mechanically. She felt disengaged from her kids, her home, everything.

Work helped, a little. When she was with the patients, she was focused on them, but whenever she looked at her phone she got a kind of low-grade jolt of worry, a shot of fear that there would be a message, another friend request, or some new, unwelcome contact from the other Sarah Havenant.

But there was nothing.

At eleven forty-five she saw her last patient before lunch.

She looked at the schedule: Derek Davies. His last visit to her office had been less than a month ago; he had been complaining of back pain, but she had been unable to find anything wrong. She opened the door to the examining room and walked in.

'Mr Davies,' she said. 'How are you?' She logged on to the computer and brought up his notes. It was the fourth time he'd been in the last few months, each time with a different complaint, and each time she had found nothing to be concerned about. 'Is it your back again?'

He shook his head. He was in his mid-fifties, and drifting toward obesity. He was wearing a crumpled shirt with grease stains on the collar. 'It's my leg,' he said. 'I get a pain all down it.' He pressed the side of his left buttock. 'It starts there.'

Sarah nodded. 'How long's it been bothering you?'

'Two weeks. It's very painful. I called for an appointment but there weren't any.'

'Really? Normally we can fit someone in at shorter notice.'

'I wanted to see you. And you had no availability.' He smiled at her, his teeth a little yellow. 'You're very popular, it seems!'

'Well, that's nice to hear,' Sarah said. 'But all the doctors here are equally as capable as me. You should see one of them if there's a hurry.'

'I like to see you. I don't like change.'

'So,' Sarah said. 'The pain. Is it worse at certain times of the day? Or during certain activities?'

'When I'm driving,' he said. 'Or sitting for long periods.'

'Do you sit for long periods?'

'Sometimes.'

'Do you work, Mr Davies?'

'Derek,' he said. 'Call me Derek. And I used to work. I was a finance clerk, but I lost my job at Christmas.' He shook his head. 'Can you believe it? They fired me at Christmas.

38

I've not been able to find a new job since. No one wants someone my age, not these days. They want kids.'

It was, she thought, an explanation for his numerous visits to the doctor's office. He had too much time on his hands and needed something to do. She glanced at his hand; no wedding ring. Perhaps he also needed company.

'Well,' she said. 'It sounds like sciatic pain. The sciatic nerve runs down your leg and it can become irritated if the muscles in your hip and leg get too stiff. I'm going to suggest some physical therapy. The PT will give you some stretches, which should help. Do you get much exercise, Mr D— Derek?'

He shook his head.

'Do you have hobbies?'

'Computer stuff, mainly. I like some of the games. You know Minecraft?'

'I've heard of it,' Sarah said, even though she hadn't. 'But I'm not familiar with it.'

'You build worlds,' Mr Davies said. 'Which you control.'

'Sounds fascinating. Do you spend a lot of time playing it?'

'You don't really play it. It's about the world you create. You're like a puppet master.'

Sarah had an image of him staring at his computer in the dark, his face illuminated by the glow from the screen as he built and managed his imaginary world.

'Well,' she said. 'You might want to limit the time you spend sitting down. Maybe take a walk every day for thirty minutes, or even two walks.'

He frowned. 'Is that all?' he said. 'You don't want to take a look?'

'I'm not sure what I would see,' she replied, and smiled. 'The receptionist will make your PT appointment.'

* * *

39

At lunchtime she drove to the pet store. The man behind the counter led her to a large tank filled with hundreds of goldfish.

'Fifty cents apiece,' he said. 'You'll need a tank and some food, as well as a bottle of the anti-chlorine stuff. Tap water has chlorine in it; it needs to be neutralized or it'll kill the fish. We can drink the stuff but a fish can't.' He shrugged. 'Go figure.'

In total it was nearly twenty dollars. A fifty-cent fish with a nineteen-dollar tank. The man laughed when she pointed it out.

'Yeah,' he said, 'but if the fish dies, it's only another half-dollar to replace it.'

'And they all look the same,' Sarah said. 'So the kids will never know it's a new one.'

The man gave her a strange smile. 'You'd think so,' he said. 'But it turns out kids always know. In my experience they pay attention to the details much more than we do. They can tell the difference between one fish and another pretty darn good. Best to come clean, tell 'em the fish died, and let 'em pick another.'

'Well,' Sarah said. 'Either way, it's still only fifty cents.'

'That, ma'am, is the truth,' the man said. 'Now enjoy your fish.'

On the way out, the man had told her to fill the tank, then put the fish – keeping it in the plastic bag full of water he had put it in – in the tank, so the water in the bag and the water in the tank could come to the same temperature. Then, after a few hours, she could pour the fish into its new home.

She didn't want to do this at work, so she stopped at home and followed his instructions. On the way out, she waved to the fish. It already felt like one of the family. The kids were going to *love* it.

That evening, as she was leaving work, she got a notification on her phone informing her she had been tagged in a post. She tapped on the link.

It was in a post from Sarah Havenant. The Fake Sarah. No photo this time; just her name, as part of a new post.

A post which read:

Got my goldfish! She's a beauty!

Sarah stopped at the front door of the medical center. Her head spun and she felt close to passing out. She sat on one of the benches by the door. Before smoking was entirely banned on the premises it was where smokers had sat, and it still had faint traces of the acrid smell of cigarettes.

June, one of the nurses, tapped her on the shoulder.

'Are you OK, Dr Havenant?'

Sarah nodded. 'I'm fine. Thanks.'

'Are you sure?'

'Yes. I didn't have lunch. Low blood sugar.'

The nurse walked into the medical center. When she came out she was holding one of the lollipops they gave to kids.

'Here,' she said. 'Have this.'

Sarah sat in the car. She was cold, her mind blank.

There was no doubt now. Whoever this was, they were doing it to get her attention.

They were fucking with her. They were deliberately trying to mess with her head.

And it was working.

Worse, they knew she had been to the pet store. They had been there and seen her walk out with a goldfish in a bag.

Whoever was doing this was watching her.

Hands shaking, legs weak, she started the car. She had to get home, and she had to get there immediately.

9

Ben's car was in the driveway when she pulled up. She could hear the kids playing in the backyard.

She went into the house and walked through to the kitchen. Ben was closing the oven door.

'Baked potatoes,' he said, and smiled at her. 'I'll make some burgers on the grill.'

'I didn't know we were having burgers,' Sarah said.

'I needed to distract the kids,' Ben replied.

'What do you mean?'

'We had a bit of a nasty surprise when we got home.'

Sarah's mouth went dry. She felt the blood rush from her face. What now? What had Fake Sarah done now?

'What kind of surprise?' she said, her voice little more than a croak.

'Are you OK?' Ben said.

She wasn't, but she nodded. 'What surprise?'

'There was a dead fish floating in a bag,' he said. 'At first they were excited when they saw it, then they started to ask why it wasn't swimming. They figured it out pretty quickly. Faye had a bit of a meltdown. Hence the burgers. I promised bacon and avocado on top as well.'

Sarah relaxed, a little. 'A dead fish is all?' she said. 'I thought – I thought it might be worse.'

'Worse?' Ben said. 'Why were you expecting worse?'

The skin around Sarah's eyes tightened and she felt her mouth begin to tremble. 'It – it happened again,' she said. 'A post. About the goldfish.'

'On the fake Facebook account?'

She nodded. 'They posted about the fish I bought at lunchtime.'

Ben straightened. 'They did? How did they know?'

'I don't know. They must – they must have been following me.'

'Shit,' Ben said. 'If this is someone's idea of a joke, then it's not funny.'

'It's not a joke, Ben. None of my friends would do this.'

'Then who?' he said. 'Who would have been following you?'

'I have no idea.'

She called Toni when the kids were in bed.

'Hey,' Toni said. 'How are you?'

'Good,' Sarah said. 'Well, kind of. But I'll get to that in a bit. How are you holding up?'

Toni had separated from her husband, Joe, six months earlier and was in the process of getting divorced. They'd met when she was thirty-two and she had married him despite her – and her friends' – misgivings. He was tall, good-looking, well-dressed and had a whiff of the snake-oil salesman about him. It was his shoes which had put Sarah off: every time she saw him he was wearing a new pair, and they were always meticulously shined or brushed or cleaned. Ben had good shoes, solid English brogues from Church's or Loake, but they had a reassuringly scuffed appearance. From time to time he polished them, but only when necessary. He didn't

44

want to polish them; he had better things to be doing. But Joe must have spent hours on his shoes and clothes and hair. It was, as far as Sarah was concerned, a bit suspicious. It couldn't all be for Toni's benefit.

And it turned out it wasn't. Joe was having a series of affairs with women who worked in his office. One, Toni might have forgiven. Six or seven was too much.

'The divorce comes through in a fortnight,' Toni said. 'Can't wait.'

'It'll be good to get it over with. You been busy?'

'Oh yeah. My life is a laugh a minute. All I need is to get all the hot twenty-six-year-old firemen to leave me alone so I have time to write my novel and then I'll be OK. But enough about my amazing life. How are you?'

'Well,' Sarah said. 'There has been some weird stuff going on.'

'Don't tell me Ben is having an affair. I couldn't take it. Not Ben. He's too boring.'

'He's not boring!' Sarah paused. 'OK, well maybe. But no. It's not an affair. It's – there's a Facebook account. In my name. It's easier if I send it to you. Let me know when you have it.'

She messaged a link to Toni.

'Here it is,' Toni said. 'I'll bring it up.' There was a pause. 'OK, got it on my screen now. There you are, posting stuff. What's the big deal?'

'The big deal is, it wasn't me who posted it. Any of it.'

'What do you mean? These are your photos. There's one of us in Portland with Anne.'

'I didn't post them,' Sarah said. 'That isn't my account. It's someone else's, someone who has been posting photos of me, under my name. And there's one from inside the house.'

There was a sharp intake of breath.

'You didn't do this?' Toni said. 'This is crazy.'

'It isn't' – Sarah hesitated, but she had to ask – 'it's not you, is it?'

'What? Why would it be me?'

'You do have a track record of pranking people, Toni.'

'Yeah, but firstly that was when we were in college. And secondly, even I would never come up with a prank like this, let alone be able to do it. I mean, where would I get the photos?'

'You could have asked other people.'

Toni laughed. 'Look, Sarah,' she said. 'Let's put this one to bed, once and for all. I had nothing to do with this, OK? And in any case, my pranks were funny—'

'I wouldn't say funny, exactly,' Sarah interrupted.

'Well, at least harmless. And this is neither. This is creepy. Very fucking creepy.'

This was not what Sarah had been hoping to hear. She had been hoping – although, looking back, it was probably a vain hope – Toni would say, *Yeah, it was me* or *don't worry, it's a thing millennials do to tease people*, but instead, she was agreeing.

'I know,' Sarah said. 'I'm worried.'

'Have you called the cops?'

'You think I need to?'

'I don't know. It can't hurt. And you could tell Facebook. Contact somebody there and ask them to take the profile down.'

'Would they do that?'

'Probably not. They'd cite freedom of speech or whatever to justify their unwillingness to lose a user, but you might as well ask the question.'

'OK,' Sarah said. 'Thanks for the suggestions.'

'No worries. And keep me posted, OK?'

Sarah ended the call. Ben appeared in the doorway to their bedroom.

'How was Toni?' he said.

'Good. The divorce is nearly done.'

'What did she think about Fake Sarah?'

'She suggested I contact Facebook and ask them to remove it, and also call the cops.'

Ben wagged his head from side to side. 'I'm not sure what the cops will do,' he said. 'There's not really a crime for them to investigate. But you could try.'

'I will,' Sarah said. 'I'll do it in the morning. I need to go to bed. I barely slept last night.'

She didn't sleep much better that night. She got out of bed early and decided to start with Facebook. The police could wait; there was no point calling them at this time anyway as they would hardly rush over because of some Facebook account, and besides, she didn't particularly want them showing up at her house at 7 a.m. She preferred to be dressed and showered before a face-to-face meeting with a police officer.

She logged on to her account and looked for some contact details. Under 'More' there was an option for 'Help and Support'; she clicked and a link appeared for reporting abusive content. She was about to follow it, but she stopped herself.

Was it really abusive content? She wasn't sure it was. It was weird and unsettling, but it wasn't abusive, or obscene. It was merely photos. She needed to think about how she was going to approach this.

She decided to take a look at the fake account so she could tell Facebook exactly what was going on. She could gather her thoughts, and at the same time see if anything new had been posted.

She clicked the link.

It wasn't there.

She searched Facebook for *Sarah Havenant*.

There was her account, and there was another Sarah Havenant, but she was a teenager from Ohio.

The profile had been deleted, so now there was nothing to show the cops or to write to Facebook about.

She felt a momentary surge of relief, but it was quickly replaced with a nagging unease. Maybe, just maybe, this was the end of whatever had been going on.

And maybe it wasn't.

10

She will look, today, at the account. Maybe she will wake up and decide not to, decide she is going to ignore it, but eventually she will want, *need* to look, like a drunk who wakes up with all the best intentions – *I will not drink today, I will not* – but then as the day goes on and all the old feelings and insecurities come back, the glass of beer or wine or vodka starts to look more and more appealing.

And then you're drinking it, and you hate yourself, but at least you scratched the itch.

When she gives in, though, the account will not be there. It is unlikely – but possible – Facebook would take her seriously and help her trace it, although they would find it hard to locate the owner even if they did. So it is better to close off that avenue before it becomes a problem.

And the account itself is not important. It's merely the hook.

And the fish is hooked now.

Well and truly hooked.

11

In the evening Sarah googled herself again; in the morning she repeated the exercise. She was there – her MD page, some records from 10k and half-marathon races she had run, a photo of her and Jean at a charity dinner that had made it into the Portland newspapers – but there was nothing from her doppelgänger.

The other Sarah Havenant was nowhere to be seen.

She wondered whether it was an error of some kind in Facebook itself, a bug in the code that created shadow profiles then shut them down when it realized they were there. It was unlikely, but so were the alternatives.

Either way, it was gone.

'So,' Sarah said. 'What are you going to call it?'

'Is it ours?' Miles asked.

'Sure,' Sarah said. 'All yours.'

'And we can call it what we want?' he said.

'As long as it isn't rude, then yes.'

She, Ben, Miles, Faye and Kim contemplated the new goldfish. It swam contentedly around its new home.

'I'm calling it Faye,' Miles said.

'You can't call it after your sister,' Sarah said. 'It's a fish.'

'I want it to be called after me,' Faye said. 'Faye the fish.'

'It'll be confusing,' Sarah said. 'Let's think of another name.'

'You said it's our fish,' Miles replied. 'And Faye's not rude, so if we want to call it Faye, we can.'

'He has a point,' Ben said. 'It *is* what you promised.'

'But then we'll have two Fayes,' Sarah said. 'And I don't want to.' What she was thinking about was the day – which was inevitable – when the fish died. She didn't want the words *Faye is dead* spoken in the house, even about a pet fish.

'But it's ours!' Faye said. 'Mommy, we're calling it Faye. And you can't stop us.' She turned to the tank. 'Hello, Faye,' she said. 'That's my name too.'

'There you go,' Ben said. 'Faye the Fish it is.'

Rachel Little, it turned out, was coming back to Barrow later in the week. She sent Sarah a message to let her know, and to ask whether she wanted to meet up over the weekend.

Sarah didn't, particularly, but it was hard to say no, so she suggested a coffee on Saturday morning at the Little Cat Café.

I'll have my youngest with me, she said. *Hope it's OK.*

Kim? Rachel replied. *Fine. Would love to meet her.*

Sarah was jarred by the fact this stranger – because Rachel was a stranger, after all these years – knew her kids' names, and she almost cancelled, but she reminded herself that, had it not been for the fake profile, she wouldn't have noticed that someone knew what her children were called. The information was out there for anyone to see, after all.

A *lot* of information was out there for anyone to see.

We'll be there, she replied. *And welcome back.*

'Sarah?'

The voice came from behind her and she turned to face the speaker. At first she did not recognize Rachel. The last time she'd seen her – twenty years ago – she'd been tall and gangly and wild-haired and badly dressed, but now she was totally different. She was wearing a pair of flat-fronted linen pants and a sleeveless olive blouse, her hair – tinged with auburn – was long and luxuriant, and her skin glowed with a West Coast tan.

But those were outward changes; what Sarah noticed most was how much more at ease Rachel was. As a teenager she'd seemed a bit lost, a bit unsure of her place in the world. Now it was obvious she had grown into herself; all the awkwardness was gone, replaced by a calm elegance.

'Rachel,' she said. 'How are you? It's great to see you.'

'I'm well. Glad to be back in Barrow.' Her voice was different too. Fuller, more mature. Less reedy than Sarah remembered. 'You?'

'Despite college and medical school, sometimes I feel like I never left! But I like it here.' Sarah gestured at Kim, who was playing with some wooden trains at a toy table in the corner of the café. 'It's a great place to raise kids.'

Rachel's smile faded for a second; she brushed her stomach with her hand. It was a gesture pregnant women often made, and Sarah wondered whether she was going to tell her she was expecting, but Rachel simply nodded agreement. 'Where will you be living?' Sarah said.

'Gold Street. I rented an apartment there. I'm looking for a place to buy, eventually.'

'A lot of houses don't make it on to the market,' Sarah said. 'There's a lot of private sales. Barrow's become quite a popular place for people to live. Lots of families move back here – good schools, low crime. And there's the college.'

Barrow was home to Hardy College, a small, liberal arts college which had invested heavily in the town.

'I know. I spoke to the realtor and she was bemoaning

the fact,' Rachel said. She smiled. 'But something will come up. It always does. There's no point worrying.'

'You sound like my husband, Ben. He always says worry is a dividend paid to disaster before it's due.'

'I like it. Where does it come from?'

'I think it's from one of the James Bond books. Not exactly Gandhi.'

Rachel laughed. 'Well, it's true all the same. Even James Bond has life advice for us.'

'Anyway,' Sarah said. 'I'll ask around about any houses coming up for sale.'

'Would you?' Rachel said. She sounded genuinely touched. 'That's so generous. Thank you.'

Kim toddled toward them. 'Mommy,' she said. 'Can I have some water?'

'Of course.' Sarah handed her a plastic cup. 'This is Mommy's friend, Rachel.'

'Hi,' Kim said, her voice muffled by the liquid.

Rachel leaned forward, her hands on her knees. 'Hello,' she said, her voice low and soft. She was smiling, and taking time with her movements. 'Are you Kim?'

Kim nodded, a matching smile on her face.

'I'm Rachel.' She held out her hand, palm upward, and Kim placed her hand in it. Rachel gave it a gentle shake. 'It's very nice to meet you.'

Kim gave a little giggle, then buried her face in Sarah's hip.

'I think she likes you,' Sarah said. 'She's come over all bashful. It's not like her at all. She's normally all up in people's faces. It's the fate of the third child. They have to fight for everything.'

'I know,' Rachel said. 'I was one myself.'

'Were you?' Sarah didn't recall her having siblings, but then she didn't know much about her home life at all.

'Yes. The others were older, though. I had two brothers. Brian and Vinnie. Brian was six years older and Vinnie eight.'

'I don't remember them.'

'They weren't around much. Vinnie went into the army and Brian didn't really . . . he kind of kept himself to himself.'

'So what are you planning to do?' Sarah said. 'You're a therapist, right?'

Rachel nodded. 'I'm going to do the same here. I've not got anything in place yet, but I will.'

'I might be able to help there, too,' Sarah said. 'I'm a doctor. Family medicine, mainly. Let me know when you're ready and I can put you in touch with some people who might be worth talking to.'

Rachel shook her head, as though disbelieving. 'You're so kind,' she said. 'So welcoming.'

Sarah felt a little discomfort at her gratitude. 'It's a small town,' she said. 'Everyone wants to help.'

'I guess so,' Rachel said. 'I guess I'd forgotten Barrow was like that. Makes my decision to come back all the better, I suppose.'

12

Sunday was forecast to be hot, up in the high eighties and humid with it. It turned out to be even hotter, and in town it felt worse: claustrophobic and suffocating. Along with the rest of the population of Barrow, Sarah and Ben headed to the beach.

It was a thirty-minute drive up the Phippsburg peninsula and by this point in the summer they had the trip down, as Ben would say in one of his incomprehensible British expressions, to a tee. Shovels, kids' wetsuits, beach chairs, umbrella: all their beach stuff was put in the car in June and remained there until September. The only thing they had to add was dry towels, a cooler full of snacks and drinks and the kids themselves. Which was good, because on a day like this the beach filled up. Anyone who arrived there after around 10 a.m. would be facing a full car park and a return trip to the heat of town.

They pulled up alongside Jean's battered minivan, the sandy gravel crunching under the tires.

'I don't know how she does it,' Ben said. 'I mean, wrangling our kids is hard enough with the two of us. She's alone. It's amazing, frankly.'

'She's super-organized,' Sarah said. 'She has to be. The laundry alone – it's frightening. She showed me her system for getting it done: each kid has a basket which they put their dirty clothes into. They fold up any that can be worn again and put them away. Immediately after bedtime she puts a load in the washing machine, then puts them on the drying rack before she goes to bed.'

'There's the difference,' Ben said. 'Her kids don't throw everything all over the place. She has some *discipline*. I wish I knew her secret.'

'I don't think there's a secret,' Sarah said. 'She's always busy. Washing clothes or making lunches for the next day or preparing her schoolwork.'

'It's impressive.'

'It's funny. In high school she was a hot mess. Not that we said "hot mess" back then.'

'In what way?'

'Oh, you know. She didn't have her shit together.'

That was a bit of an understatement. In their senior year Sarah had a car – a Toyota Corolla – and used to pick up Jean, as well as two other friends, Katie and Emily, on her way to school. Jean was never ready, and, when she did appear, she had invariably forgotten her purse or books or homework, so they'd have to go back for whatever was missing, and then it would be a mad scramble to get to school before the tardy bell made official their lateness. And lateness wasn't all; she studied for the wrong exams, showed up at the wrong time or not at all for her summer jobs, and lost her purse or bag or ID almost every time they went out.

Her parents didn't help. They were very strict and very private; whereas Sarah and Katie and Emily's parents used to chat to the girls or drive them places, Jean's never did. Often they refused to let her join her friends after school or on the weekends – on one occasion, Jean more or less

56

disappeared for three weeks – but when they asked Jean why she'd been grounded, she shrugged and said her parents thought she was letting them down with her poor performance and she needed to focus more. Jean claimed it didn't bother her, but Sarah could tell she was putting a brave face on what must have been a deep hurt.

And then she had met Jack. He already had kids; Jean could not have her own – which was another tragic story she managed to cope with – and she always said it was a blessing she met Jack and got a husband and family all at the same time. She didn't say it, but Sarah was pretty sure she wanted a family so she could put right some of the wrongs of her own childhood.

And Sarah suspected there were plenty more of those than Jean had shared.

She may have told Katie more. Katie and Jean had been friends since they were born – their moms met on the maternity ward – and they had a special bond. Like lots of groups of friends, the friendships weren't equal; for them, it had been more like two groups of two. Jean and Katie, Sarah and Emily.

Sarah missed Emily. She had moved to the Pacific Northwest – Oregon, somewhere – and they kept in touch via Skype, but it wasn't the same. As for Katie, no one knew where she was. She'd gone traveling in her early twenties, and they'd lost contact with her.

So, even though they had not been the closest of the friends in their group, Sarah and Jean were the only ones left, and Sarah was glad to have her in her life. Her college friends were great – in some ways she preferred them – and they had shared some wonderful times, but there was a special quality to her friendship with Jean. It went back so far, and they knew each other so well. With her college friends, she had taken care to present her best self. She was almost an adult when she met them, and she knew who she was and who she wanted to be. She had a self-image, and she wanted to make sure others shared it. Jean and Katie and Emily, on the other hand, had seen her at her worst: screaming at her mom, stealing another girl's boyfriend, and on one occasion – Sarah still felt guilty about this – bullying a girl she didn't like until the girl's parents called the school. Jean was more like a sibling than a friend. However close she got to other people, they would never know her like Jean did.

'Well,' Ben said. 'With those kids, she has to have her shit together now. No choice.' He opened the car door. 'Let's get on the beach.'

13

Jean was sitting on a beach towel, deep in conversation with another woman. It took Sarah a moment to recognize who it was.

Rachel.

A few yards in front of them, Jean's two kids – Daniel, thirteen, and Paul, ten – were digging a hole in the sand. Miles, Faye and Kim sprinted over to them and added their labor to the hole-digging project.

'Hi,' Sarah said. 'Mind if we join you?'

'Of course not,' Jean said. 'We were hoping you'd show up. Ben, have you met Rachel?'

Ben shook his head. 'No, but I've heard a lot about you.' He held out his hand for her to shake. 'Pleased to meet you.'

'You too,' Rachel said. 'It's a pleasure. And what a beautiful day.'

'Look at them,' Ben said, nodding at the children. 'It's amazing. I can't get them to help me with anything in the garden – weeding, raking leaves, picking up twigs or acorns from the lawn – but they're happy to spend hours on the beach digging a pointless hole.'

Jean laughed. 'They're hoping to build a wall of sand in front of it so they can defend it from the waves.'

'They'll be waiting a while. The tide's going out,' Ben said. He unfolded two beach chairs and passed one to Sarah. 'Can I offer anyone a seat? I'm happy to sit on the sand.'

'I'm fine,' Jean said. 'But thank you for asking.' She looked at Sarah. 'The perfect English gentleman.'

'We're brought up that way,' Ben said. 'Manners beaten into us at every turn by cold, unfeeling matriarchs.'

There was truth in his joking. He didn't see his parents often, and when he did they had a very formal relationship. Sarah sensed that he and his father, Roger, were – in a reserved, English way – pretty close, but he and his mom – Diana – were distant. He didn't often talk about his childhood, and his mom rarely figured in the stories. When she did, her appearances were limited to the fringes – *She dropped me off at boarding school* or *She didn't approve of me and Dad going fishing; she thought it was a waste of time* or *Pubs were for drunks and commoners, so on the few occasions we went out for dinner at one it was just me, Dad and my brother, Sam.* Diana didn't seem part of his life; it was as though he didn't particularly know her. Which was in part because Diana Havenant was almost unknowable. She didn't say a great deal – the longest one-on-one conversation Sarah had ever had with her probably ran to no more than three minutes of polite small talk – and it was invariably critical or damning with faint praise. *Barrow*, she had said, on her one trip to visit them in Maine, was *very nice.* Sarah had been surprised to hear such unqualified praise, but then she had added:

. . . for those who like that kind of thing.

Sarah, who normally resisted the temptation to argue with her mother-in-law, had risen to the bait. She felt she had to: Barrow was her hometown, the place she was raising her family. If Diana thought there was a problem with it, them, it was, in her mind, a direct comment on her parenting.

What do you mean, 'that kind of thing'? she'd said, struggling to keep her tone light. Next to her, Ben stiffened.

It's hardly London, is it? Diana replied.

No, Sarah said. *But I'm not sure I understand what you're getting at. Lots of places aren't London. Paris, for example, isn't London. Neither is Buenos Aires.*

Quite, Diana replied. *What was it Johnson said? When a man is tired of London he is tired of life?*

Was he a Londoner, by any chance? Sarah asked.

I think he was pointing out how London offers such broad horizons. Which is a good thing. Other places – by which she clearly meant Barrow – *are a little less stimulating for young minds.*

It was clear she felt her son had made a mistake in leaving the cultured shores of the UK for the barbarian wastes of Maine. She probably felt he had made a mistake in marrying Sarah, too. For years Sarah had worried that at some point Diana would convince Ben to move them all back to the UK – or Ben and the kids, at any rate. She doubted Diana would have been bothered if he left his wife behind – but Ben had reassured her his mother would never attempt such a thing, and if she did, it wouldn't work.

Over time, Sarah had come to believe him, but the lurking fear that Diana might one day try to win her son back never fully left her.

Sarah sat down beside him, her feet sinking into the hot sand. She took a deep breath, reveling in the briny tang of the ocean.

'I'm not sure those matriarchs did such a good job with you,' she said. 'My perfect English gentleman who wants to buy a convertible which only half the family can fit into.'

'Four-fifths of the family,' Ben said. 'I was planning on getting a four-seater. I suppose I could get a two-seater, which would only be two-fifths of the family. But not half.'

'Sounds fun,' Jean said. 'I can see you, top down, wind rushing through your hair— '

'More over my scalp,' Ben said, rubbing his thinning hair. 'But I get what you mean.'

'You'll have to take me for a spin,' Jean said. 'I'm not sure I've ever been in a convertible.'

'Thanks, Jean,' Sarah said. 'I was hoping you might *dis*courage him!'

'Oh,' Jean said. 'Seemed like a good idea to me.'

Miles detached himself from the group of hole-diggers and walked over.

'Do we have any snacks?' he said.

Sarah put on an expression of shocked disbelief, although it was only partly put on. Her kids' capacity for asking for food was a constant source of amazement for her. 'We've hardly been here five minutes,' she said. 'You had breakfast an hour ago.'

'I know,' Miles said. 'But I'm hungry.'

'You can't be,' Sarah said. 'Go and dig a hole. Work up an appetite.'

'I already have an appetite.'

'No,' Sarah said. 'It's too early for lunch.'

'Just a snack.'

'No, Miles.'

His face hardened and she saw he was not going to back down. Well, neither was she. He didn't need to eat again.

'Mom,' Miles said. 'You can't starve me.'

'I'm not starving you.'

'I want some food!'

Ben stood up. 'I tell you what,' he said. 'Let's go to the rock pools. You have a quick snack before we go and then when we get back we can have some lunch. Off you go and see if anyone else wants to come.'

Miles paused, then nodded. He ran over to the rest of the kids.

'Ben,' Sarah said. 'I told him no. And now you're giving him a snack.'

'I haven't given him anything,' Ben replied. 'Not yet. And he'll forget. He needed diverting, that's all. He eats when he's bored.'

Ben was good at avoiding conflict; he had the ability to sidestep it. Perhaps he had learned it during a life with Diana.

It turned out all five kids wanted to go.

'Right,' Ben said. 'Let's get moving.'

'What about my snack?' Miles asked.

'I'll bring it with me. Everyone get water shoes on.'

'Are you OK taking them all?' Jean said. 'That's a lot of kids.'

'I think so,' Ben said. 'Hopefully I won't lose any.'

'I'll come with you,' Rachel said. 'Keep you company. I love rock pools.' She stood up. She was wearing a dark red bikini, and she had not put on any weight since high school. She pulled on a T-shirt. 'OK, kids. Let's go.'

Ben looked at Sarah. 'Want to come?'

'Or sit here for an hour in the sun with Jean and have no kids to worry about?' Sarah furrowed her brow, pretending to think hard. 'Maybe I'll stay.'

She watched as the kids sprinted along the beach, Ben and Rachel walking behind them. When they were about thirty yards away Rachel turned to Ben, nodding with laughter, which carried on the breeze to Sarah. It was a full, *you're-a-really-funny-guy* laugh; whatever Ben had said had really amused Rachel, or at least, Rachel wanted him to think it had. Some dry, sardonic comment about the convertible, maybe. She'd ask Ben when he got back.

Jean had noticed too. 'Must have said something funny,' she said.

'Yeah. Not like Ben.'

'He's amusing enough, in his goofy way.' She reached into her cooler and took out a can of seltzer water. 'Want one?'

Sarah was about to say yes, when she heard someone call her name. She looked up, and a couple were walking toward them. The woman waved to her.

'Who is it?' Jean said.

'Becky and Sean,' Sarah replied. 'You remember them?'

Jean shook her head. 'Not sure I do.'

'They were at our house last Christmas. At the party we had. Sean had not long moved here.'

Jean nodded. 'I remember now. Didn't you set them up with each other?'

She had. Sean – a doctor at their practice – was new in town and she had invited him to the party so he could meet some people. Specifically, she wanted him to meet Becky, who had recently broken up with her boyfriend.

She introduced them, and they had hit it off, so much so that no one had seen much of them since.

They walked over. Sean was tall and lean, his stomach flat.

'Hi, Sarah,' he said. He held out a hand to Jean. 'I'm Sean. We may have met?'

Jean shook his hand. 'I think so. At Sarah's house, maybe.'

'Oh, yeah,' Sean said. 'At Christmas, right?'

'Yes,' Jean said. 'Nice to see you again.'

'You too,' he said, then turned to Becky. 'Shall we tell them?'

'Tell us what?' Sarah said.

Becky put her hand around Sean's waist. 'We have some news.'

Sarah glanced at her hand; there was no engagement ring. Her gaze flickered to Becky's stomach.

'What kind of news?' she said.

'We're pregnant,' she said. 'It's early days yet, and we're not telling too many people, but since you're the reason we met, we thought we'd let you know.'

Sarah laughed. 'Wonderful news!' she said. She glanced at Jean. 'And don't worry. We'll keep it to ourselves. I'm so glad for you both! When's the baby due?'

'February,' Sean said. 'We can't wait. And thank you for your matchmaking. It's the best thing that ever happened to us.'

Sarah looked at Jean, and grinned. 'My pleasure,' she said.

As Becky and Sean walked away, Jean handed Sarah a can of seltzer water.

'God,' she said. 'I find it so annoying.'

'What?' Sarah said. 'That they're having a baby?'

'No, of course not. It's when people say "we're pregnant". It's the woman who's pregnant. There's no "we" about it.'

'Well,' Sarah said. 'I think we can forgive them. And I have to say, I take a bit of extra pleasure since it was the result of my matchmaking efforts. They seem really in love.'

'They do,' Jean said. 'And by the way – next time you have an eligible bachelor show up, send him my way, would you?'

'Sure,' Sarah said. 'You're next on my list.'

'Thanks,' Jean said. 'Hey, I meant to ask. Did anything come of the Facebook thing?'

Sarah felt the warm glow fade from the day.

'No. The account was shut down. But not before one more post.'

'Oh? What about?'

'I went to buy a goldfish at lunchtime. Sometime in the afternoon there was a post about it.'

Jean shook her head. 'How would they know?'

'I've no idea. I've been thinking about it a lot. I'm not even sure who would know. Someone would have had to follow me.'

'Who?'

'A patient, maybe?' Sarah said. 'Someone who I'd seen?'

'Which is half the town,' Jean replied.

'There was one guy who I saw yesterday. He was a bit weird with me. He'd waited for two weeks to get an appointment, and there was nothing really wrong with him.'

'You think he followed you?' Jean looked doubtful.

'I don't know. I doubt it. But he *was* my last patient before I got the fish, and it's not the first time he's been in. It's like the fourth appointment he's made since Christmas.'

'Odd,' Jean said. 'What I can't figure out is who *could* be doing it.'

'I know,' Sarah said. 'That's the mystery.'

Rachel raised an eyebrow. 'One person who it could be – and I'm not saying it is or even that I think it would ever be – is Ben.'

There was a long pause.

'I don't think so, Jeannie,' Sarah said. 'I mean, it's possible. But Ben?'

'I agree. I'm only saying he would have known, and had access to the photos.'

'I know. But why?'

'I don't know. But stranger things have happened. You remember my husband, right? None of us saw *that* coming.'

'True. But I don't think so. And the account's gone now. It was probably some mistake.'

'I hope so,' Jean said. 'I really hope so.'

14

A beach day. Soaking up the rays with the family. Those three beautiful children. Her sturdy British husband with his pale skin and emerging pot-belly and baffled expression.

She loves them. They are the most important thing in the world to her. Nothing unusual. For most people all around the world, it's true.

Not for everyone, though. She will find out about that later.

But for now she is happy. The weird thing with Facebook has gone away. It is still a worry, of course it is, but at least it has stopped. It's like a rainstorm you drive through: once it's behind you, it's still there, but in the rearview mirror. It is *receding*. A shadow. No longer a problem.

But it can come back. The weather can change. The wind can switch direction. So you better not take your eye off of it for too long.

But people do. It is what she will do. It is natural. The strange thing happens, the surface of the pond is disturbed, but then the ripples vanish, and the water settles and all trace of them is gone.

Out of sight, out of mind.

But whatever caused them is still there, under the black water. Maybe a long way away, deep and safe.

Or maybe just below the surface . . .

So she is enjoying her beach day with her loving family. The family at the center of her life. The family she does it all for.

The family she barely deserves.

The family she will lose.

15

Sarah was finishing a quick coffee in the break room at work when her phone rang. It was Anne, her college friend. She was due to see a patient in a few minutes, but she picked up the phone.

'Hi,' she said. 'How are you? I have an appointment coming up, so I can't talk for too long.'

'I'm good,' Anne said. 'Enjoying summer. It's been lovely up here.'

'Up here' was Burlington, Vermont, where Anne was a high-school science teacher. She was married to her college boyfriend, Don; they'd had kids early. Melanie, who was ten, and Parker, who was eight.

'I wish I had your holidays,' Sarah said. 'It must be amazing.'

'Mel's at her first sleep-away camp this week, and Parker's always with his buddies, biking round the neighborhood. Don's working, so I have a lot of alone time.'

'God, stop. You're making me jealous.'

'It *is* nice,' Anne said. 'But I do miss the days when summer was me and the kids hanging out by the lake or in the back-yard. It feels like they're growing up too fast. In eight years we'll be dropping Mel off at college. I'm already traumatized by the mere thought of it.'

'I know. It goes so fast.'

'Anyway, I was chatting to Toni yesterday. She paid us a visit.'

Sarah couldn't help the small twinge of resentment that flared at the news Toni and Anne had got together without her; without even informing her. She wouldn't have been able to go, but it would have been nice to have the option. It was stupid, she knew, but it did feel as though she had been left out.

'Oh,' Sarah said. 'I spoke to her the other day.'

'She mentioned it. She told me about the weird Facebook thing. Is everything OK?'

'Yeah,' Sarah said. 'I think so. The account has gone now.'

'Right,' Anne said. 'I was wondering where it was. I had a look, and I couldn't find it.'

'I think it may have been some kind of Facebook error,' Sarah said. 'They have access to so much of your data, who knows what can happen? I was going to send them a note to ask, although I'll probably never get around to it.' She glanced at the clock on the wall. 'I have to go, but it was great to talk to you. I'll call you one evening?'

'OK. And let's get together this summer. It's been too long.'

'Way too long,' Sarah said. 'We'll find a date.'

She cut the connection and put her phone in her bag. As she did it buzzed. It was a text message from Carla, a friend with a son and daughter who Sarah had used to hang out with often. She didn't see her as much since Miles and Ricky, her son, had started kindergarten; they were in different school systems so their orbits drifted apart. Still, they liked to get the kids together sometimes and arranged periodic play dates.

Hi, it read. Are you running late?

71

Sarah frowned. She hadn't planned to meet Carla today. She had to see her patient, but she texted back, quickly.

For what?

The answer arrived seconds later.

The play date. I'm at your house with Ricky. No one's here.

Sarah felt a slow churn in her stomach. The taste of the coffee soured in her mouth. She hadn't spoken to or emailed or texted Carla in a week.

Which meant this was not a simple mix-up. It couldn't be.

Did we plan a play date? I'm at work. Miles is at camp.

The dots signifying a reply was coming scrolled across the bottom of the screen.

Really? We emailed about it last night. You said to come at ten.

She hadn't sent any emails the night before. She'd come back from the beach, fed the kids then curled up in front of a movie once they were in bed. And even if she had emailed Carla, she wouldn't have arranged a play date, for the simple reason she was at work and the kids were either at camp or in day care.

She checked her phone. Nothing to Carla in the sent email folder. Which meant, unless Carla was making it up, someone else had emailed her.

Someone claiming to be Sarah.

She felt faint, dizzy. It was an effort to focus. Hands shaking, she typed a reply.

72

Sorry. I think I have an idea what happened. Can I see you at noon? I'll be free for lunch then.

Sure, Carla replied. Call me.

Sarah shook her head. That wouldn't do.

Can I see you? Sorry to be a pain, but you'll understand.

Carla's reply hinted at a little irritation.

I have a gym class starting soon. But I could meet around 12.20?

Sarah accepted. It would be a short lunch, but she needed to see her friend.

In the end Carla showed up at the Little Cat Café at twelve thirty. She was wearing yoga pants and a finishers' T-shirt from the 2014 Lobsterman Triathlon. She looked – post-exercise – in a good mood.

Sarah waved at her and pointed to the cup of coffee – a skinny cappuccino – she had ordered as a peace offering. There was also a blueberry smoothie on the table.

'Where's Ricky?' Sarah said. 'I got him a smoothie. Help him get over the missed play date.'

'He went to Logan's house,' Carla said. 'Sandy' – Logan's mom – 'had mentioned Logan was free, so I gave her a call.'

'Sorry about earlier,' Sarah said. 'But it's not what you think.' She leaned forward. 'Is there any way I could see the messages you got from me?'

Carla frowned, puzzled by the request. 'Why? You sent them.'

'I don't think I did. Can I see them?'

'Are you OK, Sarah?'

Sarah nodded. 'Fine. But let me see and I'll explain.'

Carla tapped her code on to the screen and scrolled through the messages. She handed the phone to Sarah.

There they were. Three messages, in a thread titled *Play date?*, all from Sarah Havenant. Sarah opened one and looked at the email address.

It was her name, but it wasn't her account. It was Gmail, and Sarah used Outlook.

'I don't believe this,' she said. 'This is a fake email account.'

'What do you mean?'

'I mean someone set this up and is impersonating me. My email address is Outlook, not Gmail. It's easy to establish an account and set the name to show as whatever you want. So all you see is the name Sarah Havenant, and unless you bother to look at the address you wouldn't know it wasn't from me.'

Carla shook her head. 'So you're saying someone set up an email account in your name so they could fake a play date? So they could piss me off? They must have known you'd find out.'

'I don't think they minded getting caught,' Sarah said. She was feeling very calm, almost like she was observing herself. It was a form of shock, she realized, her body's way of stopping her going into a full-on panic. 'I think getting caught was the point. This is not the first time this has happened.'

'Are you kidding? What's been going on?'

'There was a Facebook account,' Sarah murmured. 'I thought it had gone away.'

'What kind of Facebook account? What's wrong with a Facebook account?'

'It was a fake one,' Sarah said. 'In my name. With photos of me and Ben and the kids and the house. Recent ones.' She looked at Carla, blinking. 'Someone's fucking with me, Carla.

74

I don't know why, and I'm scared.' She pushed her coffee across the table. 'Very scared.'

'I'm sure it's nothing,' Carla said. 'Just a joke or . . .' she paused, at a loss for words, then finished, limply. 'Or something.'

Sarah didn't reply. She looked around the Little Cat Café. There were couples, young women with laptops, college-age boys with books and iPads. Was it one of them? Was it someone who was here, now, in the café?

'Hey,' Carla said. 'I need the bathroom. I'll be right back.'

Sarah watched her walk across the room. It was as though she couldn't wait to get away from her, as though she thought Sarah was contaminated, dangerous, spoiled goods. Well, when she got back, Sarah would tell her she had to be back in the office, release her from her obligations.

A few minutes later the bathroom door opened and Carla came out. Her face – summer-tanned when she went in – was chalk white.

She walked over, her phone in her hand.

'Did you . . .' she said. 'Did you send this while I was in the bathroom?'

'No,' Sarah said. 'I didn't send anything. What is it?'

She handed her phone to Sarah.

There was another message in the thread. Another message from Sarah Havenant.

Where were you? Miles was disappointed you didn't show up.

'He's at camp,' Sarah said. For some reason – perhaps, she thought, to maintain her grip on reality – it was important to her to state the facts. 'Miles is at camp.'

'This is fucking weird,' Carla said, her voice loud enough that a few other customers glanced at her. She lowered her tone and stared at Sarah. 'Very fucking weird.' She looked at Sarah. 'Should I reply?'

'No,' Sarah said, quickly. 'No. There's nothing to reply to.' She hesitated. 'This isn't a message to you, Carla. It's a message for me. It's a message to let me know this isn't over, after all.'

'Should I delete it?'

Sarah shook her head. 'No. Would you forward it to me? Thanks. I have to go. I need to call Ben.'

16

The worst thing about this was that it was everywhere, and it was nonstop.

When she was twelve, Sarah had drawn the attention – for some reason she still did not understand – of a girl, Donna, in the year above her at Junior High. Donna had made her life a misery; she was much more physically developed than the rest of her class and everyone, boys included, was terrified of her, so when she cornered Sarah at break time and explained to her why she was a worthless piece of shit and a slut – Slutty Sarah, she called her, a name which Sarah did not even fully understand – then punched and kicked her, no one did anything to stop her.

Although even if they'd wanted to they couldn't have: the arrival of Donna was like a shark showing up among a bunch of swimmers – everyone's first thought was to hope it wasn't going to choose them as its prey, then, once it hadn't, their main concern was to get out of the water.

So Sarah did the only thing she could. She watched out for Donna and, if she saw her – at school or out in the neighborhood – she fled. It was simple: when the threat showed up, she did her best to get away. Eventually, Donna forgot about her and life went back to normal.

Ironically, Donna was still part of her life. Her former tormentor was now a patient of hers who had chronic GI problems, but despite the fact Sarah was now thirty-eight and a mother of three and a successful physician, she still felt a tiny flutter of panic – *run*, it said, *run* – when she opened the door to the examining room and saw Donna sitting there.

This, though, was different. The threat from Donna was easy to identify: no Donna, no threat. But this – it could come from anywhere. An email, a Facebook message, a phone call: she was constantly waiting for a message from someone claiming to be her. Claiming to be Sarah Havenant.

Worse, she had no idea who it was, or what they wanted. Was it simply a latter-day Donna, getting kicks from causing other people pain? Or was it more sinister? She didn't know, didn't have any way of knowing, and she felt unmoored by the constant churning of her thoughts.

She stopped at Jean's house on her way back from work. In the kitchen, Jean and the kids were making dinner. Daniel was washing carrots and passing them to her so she could chop them. Paul was tidying up.

'I don't know how you do it,' Sarah said. 'My kids would be causing chaos. Yours are so helpful.'

'Great parenting,' Jean said, and shrugged. 'Or I just got lucky.'

'Well, if you have any tips, please pass them on.' Sarah caught her friend's eye. 'Got a minute?'

'Sure.' Jean put the knife down and walked into the living room. 'What's up?'

Sarah pursed her lips. 'It happened again.'

'The Facebook thing?'

Sarah nodded. 'But not Facebook this time. An email. To

Carla, arranging a play date. Carla showed up at my house but – of course – there was no one there. So she texted me.'

'Holy shit,' Jean said.

'I know,' Sarah said. 'I don't know what to do. When it was just the Facebook thing it seemed' – she paused – 'it seemed like it might be harmless. Some online, virtual stuff. But this is more serious. It's real. And it's here. It's my friends, showing up at my house.' She shuddered. 'It's so *personal*.'

'It does seem to be,' Jean said. 'Which is why I think you should call the cops. Talk to them. They might know what to do.' She tapped her fingers on the cutting board. 'I'd ask them if they think there's any threat. And if there is, you might want to think about the kids.'

The kids. *Her* kids. The idea that this might affect them was unbearable. Sarah's heart rate increased and she felt dizzy. Her vision blurred, and she leaned against the wall. She took a deep breath, then another, then another.

'Are you OK?' Jean said.

'I need to calm down,' Sarah said. 'I haven't had a panic attack for a couple of years, but all this worry is bringing them back. I nearly had one the other day.' She inhaled deeply. 'God, this is the last thing I need.'

'I'm not surprised you're having them again,' Jean said. 'I would be. But you should definitely talk to the cops. It'll make you feel better.'

Ian Molyneux – Lieutenant in Barrow PD and high-school friend of Sarah's – arrived shortly after 8 p.m.

Sarah opened the door and led him into the living room. She pointed to an armchair.

'Take a seat,' she said. 'Good to see you. Beer?'

'Since I'm off-duty,' Ian said. 'Why not?'

Ben came into the room. 'I'll get them,' he said. 'IPA OK, Ian?'

'Perfect.' He looked at Sarah. 'So,' he said. 'You mentioned there was a problem you wanted to talk about?'

'Yes,' she said. 'It's kind of unusual. I was wondering whether you would have any advice.'

'I might,' Ian said. 'Try me.'

Sarah outlined what had happened, from the Facebook posts to the fake emails to Carla. As she was finishing, Ben came in with three bottles of IPA.

'Thanks,' Ian said, taking a swig from the bottle, then setting it down on the table in front of him. 'It is pretty unusual,' he said. 'I can't say I've ever come across anything quite like it.' He paused. 'The closest thing would be a stalker, or an online troll abusing you. We can deal with both of those – it's not necessarily easy, but there are things we can do. Court orders restricting someone from coming within five hundred feet of you, that kind of thing. If someone's abusing you online, you can report it to the Internet company, or block them. And mostly cyber abuse turns out to be some keyboard warrior working out his or her frustration at their shitty lives. They're happy to abuse people behind the safety of their screen, but if they met their target face to face they'd run a mile, although from time to time it can be more serious.' He paused for another sip. 'The problem is that this is different. We don't know who's doing it.'

'Right,' Ben replied. 'The only name we have is Sarah Havenant, which isn't really much help. It could be *anyone* doing this, which makes it hard to deal with.'

Ian looked at Sarah. 'Do you have any ideas who it might be? Think who would *want* to do it. And then who would be *able* to do it.'

'I tried,' Sarah said. 'But I can't think of who would want to do this. And then there's the practicality. No one was at all of the places in the photos. At least, I don't think there was anyone.'

80

Ben sat forward. 'One question we should ask is *cui bono*? Who benefits? Who profits? When there's not an obvious motive for an action, figuring out who benefits from it might reveal who's behind it.'

Sarah thought for a few moments. Who did benefit? No one was getting richer. No one was getting *anything*, other than her, who was getting freaked out. So the question was, who would want to freak her out?

And she couldn't think of anybody.

'Has anything changed recently?' Ian said. 'At work? New colleagues?'

Sarah shook her head. 'Apart from the return of Rachel Little, nothing's new.'

Ian frowned. 'Rachel Little from high school?'

'The same. She was out west, and now she's back. In fact, it was her who told me about the Facebook profile.'

'Hmm,' Ian said. 'Interesting.'

'You think it could be her?' Ben said. 'She seemed harmless enough when I met her.'

'She was a bit of an oddball, back in the day,' Ian said.

'She's changed,' Sarah said. 'Grown up. Like all of us.'

'It could be her,' Ian said. 'It's not obvious why she would suddenly be doing this, twenty years after we last saw her, but it is a coincidence that she happens to return right when this is going on.' He shrugged. 'Coincidences happen, though.'

'Is there anything you can do?'

'I can look her up,' Ian replied. 'See if there's anything unusual. I'll let you know, if there is.'

'And what should we be doing?' Ben said. 'Anything specific?'

'Be vigilant,' Ian said. 'Sarah – if you go somewhere alone, make sure Ben or someone else knows so they can check you got there. Lock your doors and windows at night.'

'And the kids?' Sarah said. It was hard to believe she was

having to question whether the safety of their children was in any way compromised. 'Miles and Faye are in camp. Kim's at day care.'

'You could mention this to the camp leader and ask them to keep an eye on the kids. Likewise at day care. But they should have security practices around supervision and pickup.'

'You don't think we should pull them out?' Ben said.

'You could,' Ian replied. 'That's a matter for you.'

'But then what?' Sarah said. 'They're stuck in the house all day while their buddies are out doing stuff. And we have to work. We'd need a small army of babysitters.'

'Who are probably less qualified than the professionals to take care of them,' Ian said. 'If there was a threat to your kids, I don't think they'd be particularly safe in the care of a bored teenager.'

'Then we leave them in,' Ben said. 'For now. And you'll look into Rachel, correct?'

'Correct,' Ian said, and got to his feet. 'Thanks for the beer. I'll inform the station. If you call for some reason, they'll know there's been something going on. And good luck.'

When Ian had left, Ben sat next to Sarah on the couch. He put his arm around her and pulled her close to him. She pressed her cheek against his chest and closed her eyes. She loved Ben in a way which she had not understood was possible until she had met him; she'd had a boyfriend in high school and then a couple in college who she had thought she was in love with – and maybe she was, in a way – but she had felt apart from them, in some important sense. She had liked them, admired them, had great, passionate sex with them, but she had always known she could live without them.

With Ben it was different. It wasn't that he was better than them, necessarily – no doubt they were loving, responsible fathers and husbands themselves – but she and Ben fitted. They'd met and clicked, right away. They worked. They were happier together than apart: it was, in many ways, as simple as that.

And the feeling had never gone away. There was a strange paradox at the heart of it: she felt totally comfortable with him, trusted he loved her whatever she did, yet at the same time she still wanted to impress him, still wanted to show him she was a strong and intelligent and beautiful woman who merited his ongoing love and attention. She didn't resent the feeling, because she didn't think she had to do it. He made it clear he loved her whatever – even when she was an exhausted new mom screaming at him because she was scared and tired and lost and he was there so he was the one she was going to take it out on, or when she'd had a bad day and her nasty side – and she did have a nasty side – was on full display – she never felt his love for her was at risk, because she knew he felt the same way she did: they were lucky they had found each other, and when you got lucky you made sure you didn't waste it.

And right now she needed the man she loved more than ever.

'We'll work this out,' Ben said. He was unsmiling. 'And when we do, whoever did this will regret it.'

It was unusual for him to be angry; normally he was more sanguine. When they were younger – it didn't happen so often now – and other guys chatted her up at bars, or weddings, or parties, he didn't get mad, didn't threaten them or glare at them. He left her to deal with it, and, if she mentioned it, he smiled and said other guys could talk to her all they wanted. He was the one going home with her. He was the one who'd be having breakfast with her. He was the one who bought her the sexy underwear she was wearing and who would be taking it off in the not too distant future.

At most – if he felt she was uncomfortable – he would wander over, and introduce himself. Shake the guy's hand, then apologize for interrupting, and tell her the mother-of-the-bride wanted to talk to her, or he wanted to introduce her to a work colleague who was about to leave, or say their taxi had arrived and it was time to go. She loved his confidence, his assumption that his position was not threatened by these half-drunk sleazeballs on the prowl at parties.

She'd asked him once, after a glass of wine too many, *What if it wasn't a sleazeball, but some handsome, charming guy? Would you be threatened then?*

He'd laughed. *I'd be fine. If you were interested in handsome, charming men you wouldn't be with me. But you are with me. So I assume you're interested in guys who are like me. And I'm the person who's most like me that I know. So – logically – you're never going to find someone more like me than me, which means I have nothing to worry about.*

She shifted closer to him on the couch.

'How will we find them?' she said. 'I have nowhere to start.'

'I was thinking about that. It has to be someone you know. I mean, in theory it could be a complete stranger, but I don't see how. And if it is someone you know then maybe we can work it out. Or narrow it down.'

'Right,' Sarah said. 'I suppose. But I've been trying, and getting nowhere.'

'What if you missed someone? What about an ex-boyfriend? One of them might hold a grudge.'

'But why now?'

'Who knows? Maybe they got divorced. Or developed a drug problem. Or decided to fuck with you. What about the guy you dated in college? He was a bit intense, as I recall.'

'Matt?'

'I think so. The one who tried to sabotage our wedding.'

84

She'd forgotten about him. She smiled, although it hadn't been funny at the time. She'd dated a guy from Cape Cod, Matt Landay, for a semester in her sophomore year of college. He was not really her type – a jock with rich parents and a frat boy attitude to match – but there had been some chemistry between them, and in the spirit of youthful experimentation, she had started a relationship with him. He was only the second man she had slept with, and they had a *lot* of sex, but by the time the semester ended she was bored of him. She didn't bother breaking it off; she just went home for the summer and, in the days before cell phones and text messages, forgot about him.

He didn't forget about her, though. A week into the vacation he showed up in Barrow, in his parents' convertible BMW, and knocked on her door.

She was surprised, and not pleased, when she opened it to see him standing there in his khaki shorts, linen shirt and Oakley sunglasses.

It took her two days – and a fictitious weekend away with her friends, which she told him she wanted to cancel but couldn't – to get rid of him. It was awkward, and uncomfortable, and they only had sex once, in silence.

She thought he would get the message, but the next week he called and informed her he was thinking of coming back. She asked him not to; he insisted.

You're my girl, he said. *I want to see you.*

She wanted to say *I'm not anybody's girl*, but instead she told him she was enjoying time alone and planned to go on doing so.

For how long? he said, a note of desperation in his voice.

I dunno. All summer, maybe.

He was silent. *No*, he said, finally. *No way.*

Matt, she said. *It's up to me.*

No, he said. *You're my girl. You are.*

So this time she said it: *I'm nobody's girl, and I don't want you to come to my house.*

He started to plead, but she hung up.

Two days later she was coming back from the beach with Jean. They pulled into her street and there was a red BMW convertible in her driveway. Leaning on the hood, his back to them, was Matt.

She told Jean to keep driving. When she got home in the evening he was gone. Her mom gave her a wry smile.

Be careful, she said. *These young men can get carried away.*

He didn't show up again. He didn't even call, and back in college, he avoided her. It was about a month later that Toni suggested they go out for a coffee.

I think you need to talk to Matt, she said.

No thanks, Sarah replied. *I've been enjoying not talking to him.*

Well, you might have to. Toni paused. *He's been saying – well, he's been telling people the reason you guys broke up is because you're crazy. He's saying you stalked him during the summer and you cried if he tried to do anything without you. He's also spreading a rumor you're a nymphomaniac, although he's claiming it could be because he's so good in bed.*

So Sarah did talk to him. She explained that whatever respect she'd had for him was gone forever. And she asked him to tell everyone that his explanation for their break-up was lies.

He refused, and it was the last time she had any contact with him.

Until the week before her wedding, when an email arrived. Matt had learned she was about to get married and, as a result, would be lost to him forever. He had always loved her, he claimed, so, in a last-ditch attempt to salvage their relationship, he was letting her *know* he loved her.

I only spread those rumors when we broke up because I was hurt, he added, in his email, as though his being hurt justified anything. *I'll always love you, Sarah, and if you want to change your mind I'll be waiting.*

She didn't want to. She let him know this – and not too gently – and suggested he not contact her again. At the time she had been a bit shaken up – she had no idea he still held such an intensely burning candle for her, and she couldn't believe he thought his plan might work – but looking back, it was quite amusing.

Unless the candle had not gone out, and he was impersonating her on Facebook and email.

'You think it might be him?' Sarah said.

'You'd know. From what you told me, he was a bit on the possessive side.'

Sarah nodded. 'OK, I'll ask around. See if anyone knows what he's up to these days.'

'Good,' Ben said. 'Sounds like a plan.'

17

She is looking for answers. Trying to think who might be behind this. She is worried; the events themselves are harmless, nothing more than digital information on the Internet or in a message, but it is what lies behind that bothers her.

What lies behind – what *might* lie behind – is what causes the fear.

The fear that this cyber threat will become a *real* threat. A *physical* threat. And so she thinks of stalkers and killers and kidnappers.

But – as so often – she is missing the point.

What lies behind is not a physical threat.

It is *much* worse.

Why is a man able to kill – with ease – a lion? *All* lions, if he wishes? Or sharks. Elephants. Dinosaurs, if they still existed.

It is not because of *physical* strength. If all we had to go on was physical strength, mankind would be in the middle of the food chain, somewhere around a cow or dog. Mankind would not be close to being the apex predator.

But mankind has something the others don't.

Intelligence. The ability to use tools, to co-opt nature to

serve his ends. To make spears and then guns and then missiles.

And then to use them. To outwit and outthink and out-plan our prey. To lay complicated traps for them. The knife or the gun is merely the tool chosen to finally dispatch the target.

It is the same here. Facebook, emails, text messages. They are merely digital signals, but the truth – the truth will rip out the very heart of her life.

And when it comes she will realize there is nothing she can do. There is nowhere she can turn. No safe place she can run to.

This is everywhere. Always, and everywhere.

She is about to find out that she is helpless.

She is about to understand there is a superior intelligence at work. A superior intelligence which has taken an interest in her world. More than an interest: a stake. A *controlling* stake.

This is a takeover bid, one company buying another. In this case, against its wishes.

A hostile takeover, they call it.

A hostile takeover that has been coming to her for a long time.

A very long time.

18

Sarah looked at her schedule for the day. Her first appointment was with Margaret Bergeron, a retiree who was complaining of dizziness and faint spells. Sarah ran through the potential causes – from the harmless – tiredness and eye strain – to the more worrying – depression, maybe – to the seriously troubling – a brain tumor – and got ready to go and see her.

'Dr Havenant?' The receptionist, Dora, intercepted her.

'Yes?'

'We had a cancellation. Mrs Bergeron called and said she feels better. I told her to call back if anything changes.'

'Oh. Is the next patient here?'

'Not until twenty past. But Mr Davies has arrived. He left a message to let him know if a slot opened up. We called and he's available.'

Sarah nodded. She felt light-headed; the first fluttering of panic rose in her chest. She took a deep breath. This was simply her body over-reacting, the adrenal glands producing too much adrenaline in response to a perceived threat that was not really there.

At least, this was what she told her patients about anxiety attacks. But what if the threat was real? What if Mr Davies –

'call me Derek' – was the person behind all the emails and Facebook posts?

Then it was an appropriate response.

Which made it worse.

'Are you OK?' Dora said. 'You look a little pale.'

'Fine. What is Mr Davies here for?'

'Sciatic pain.'

'Did he see the PT?'

'I don't know.'

Sarah nodded. 'OK. Send him in. Thank you, Dora.'

'So, Mr Davies. You're still having the pain in your leg?'

'Derek, please. And yes. It's getting worse.'

'I see. Did you visit the physical therapist?'

He nodded. 'She gave me some exercises to do. Stretches. They don't work.'

'Did you follow her instructions?' Sarah said.

'Yes. But it didn't help.'

'You might need to give it more time.'

'My ankles hurt as well,' he said. 'They tingle.'

'Both of them? Or only the left?'

'Both. But the left more.'

Sarah stood up and moved toward the bed. She felt him watching her. She swallowed, fighting the feeling of panic. 'Could you hop on here for me and remove your shoes and socks?'

Derek Davies perched on the bed. He took off his shoes – scuffed leather walking shoes – and pulled the stained white exercise socks off his feet. They gave off a rotten smell; Sarah snapped on a pair of surgical gloves.

She sat on a stool and took his left foot in her hand. The toenails were thick and yellow; up close the smell was even worse. Some athlete's foot between the toes, dry skin on the top of the foot. She paused, and looked at his ankle. It was slightly swollen, and there was a dark, mottled spread of veins covering it.

Sarah took a metal pin from a tray on the table. She pressed it into his swollen flesh.

'Does this hurt?' she said. She did it again.

'A bit. Should it?'

'Mr Davies,' Sarah said. 'Have you been tested for diabetes?'

'No,' he said. 'Do I have it?'

'It's a possibility. Often diabetes can cause swelling or bruising in the foot, along with loss of sensation. I'm going to have you do some bloodwork.'

He looked at her, a little startled.

'I didn't expect that,' he said.

'What did you expect?'

For a moment he looked puzzled, almost caught out, then he shrugged. 'I'm not sure,' he said. 'Is it serious? Will I have to come to see you often?'

His expression grew intense, hungry almost, and her heart began to speed up.

'Properly managed, it should be fine,' she said, her words coming quickly. 'We can work with you on how to deal with it.'

She was breathless, and her face felt hot. Derek Davies leaned forward.

'Is everything OK, Dr Havenant?' he said. 'You seem upset?'

He reached out his hand as though about to touch her forearm and she shrank back.

'Fine,' she said. 'I'm fine.' She got to her feet. 'See the receptionist on the way out,' she said. 'She'll arrange the bloodwork.'

19

For once, Sarah was early for camp pickup. After Derek Davies had left she had moved the last appointment of the day, anxious to get home.

She pulled into the gravel car park of Mitchell Field, the oceanside location of Faye's Nature Discovery Camp, and squinted; the sun was reflecting off the water of the Harpswell Sound and she had left her sunglasses at work. She grabbed a baseball cap from the passenger seat – an old green John Deere one they had picked up somewhere, which said 'Owners' Edition' on it, a fact which Ben claimed won him friendly and respectful nods from farmers and other owners of John Deere farm equipment – and got out of the car.

She was the first parent there, and the kids had recently returned from their activities. They were all changing into their normal shoes – they'd been on a beach – under a canvas awning.

Sarah headed for Marla, the camp leader. She wanted to let her know to be extra-vigilant when it came to Faye. She wasn't sure how she would broach the subject – she didn't want to sound over-dramatic in case Marla got spooked and asked her to remove Faye from the camp entirely, but at the same time she had to say something.

'Hey, Marla,' she said. 'How's camp?'

Marla was bent over a trestle table, working her way down a list. It was a second or two before she looked up.

'Oh,' she said. 'Sarah. I wasn't expecting to see you.'

Sarah frowned. 'Why not?'

'I thought you were out of town.'

'Out of town? Why would I be out of town?'

'Because of your dad.'

'What about my dad?'

Sarah's throat tightened. It was happening again. She rested her hands on the table to steady herself.

'His illness.'

'My dad's dead,' Sarah said.

'Oh,' Marla said. 'I'm sorry. It must have been a shock. So sudden.'

'He passed away four years ago,' Sarah said.

A shadow crossed Marla's face. She was new to Barrow, a recent transplant from Boston looking for a slower-paced existence for her kids. As a result she did not know the ins and outs of the lives of other Barrow residents; most people would have known that Sarah's dad – a former mayor – was no longer around.

'I don't understand,' Marla said. 'Your email—'

'Could I see the email?' Sarah said.

Marla passed her a phone. 'There,' she said. 'See?'

There was, as Sarah knew there would be, an email from Sarah Havenant. Gmail, not Outlook.

Hi Marla, it read. Sorry to do this so late but my dad had a bad fall and broke his hip. I need to go visit with him. My mom needs help. Can you send Faye home with her uncle? He's called Tim, and he'll be coming to pick her up after camp. Any problem, give me a call. You have my cell, right? S.

94

Sarah fought the urge to throw up. She glanced up at the entrance to the field, half-expecting to see a car pull up and stop, a man looking out at her and realizing his plan had failed, then driving off. What would she do? Give chase? No – she'd call the cops and tell them to stop him, somehow. Stop Uncle Tim, the man who was going to abduct her daughter.

Thank God she'd been early. If she'd been late, as usual . . . she pushed the thought away.

'Sarah?' Marla said. 'What's going on?'

'I don't know,' Sarah said. 'I honestly don't know.'

'Is this email a fake?' Marla said.

Sarah nodded. 'Yes,' she said. 'It is.'

'Someone was *impersonating* you? Saying Faye's *uncle* would be coming to get her?'

'She doesn't have an uncle,' Sarah said. 'There is no uncle. Whoever was coming was nothing to do with her or her family.'

Marla – who was tanned from the weeks outside – went totally pale. She clapped her hand to her mouth.

'Oh my God,' she said, in a low voice. 'I don't believe it.'

This kind of thing doesn't happen here, she was thinking. Sarah could see it in her expression; there was a look in her eyes that was both shocked and disillusioned. *This kind of thing doesn't happen here. We moved here for that reason.*

Except this kind of thing did happen here, clearly.

'I'm sorry,' Sarah said.

'No!' Marla replied. 'Don't apologize. *You* have *nothing* to apologize for.'

'I know, but you don't need this at your camp.'

'It's fine,' Marla said, even though it wasn't. 'We should call the cops. Whoever it is may still show up.'

Sarah nodded, but she was pretty sure that, even if they did come, they would turn away as soon as they saw her.

Marla reached for her phone; Sarah listened as she explained what had happened.

'They're going to send someone,' Marla said.

'I think I'd like to take Faye now,' Sarah said. 'I don't want her to be here when the cops show up. Could you ask them to come to the house? I can talk to them there.'

'Of course,' Marla said. 'I'll go and get her.'

'It's fine. I will.'

'OK,' Marla said. 'And – will you be bringing her tomorrow?'

Sarah shook her head. 'I don't think I will,' she said.

Marla, Sarah saw, was more relieved than anything. She didn't blame her.

20

Ben was already back – with Miles and Kim – when Sarah got home. She opened the rear door of the car and followed Faye into the house.

'Hey,' she said, the brightness in her voice and the smile on her face entirely and obviously forced, a fact which caused Ben to look at her with a frown. 'Who wants to watch a TV show? And have pizza for dinner?'

Miles stared at her. 'Really? On a weeknight?'

Miles loved watching TV to the point of obsession. Sarah, like most parents, looked for clues in her children about the adults they would grow into. Whether they were relaxed, or quick to feel and show emotion; whether they were happier in company or alone; whether they were naturally considerate of others or whether they were self-centered. And then, if she saw a trait emerging she didn't like, she would seek to correct it, by modeling the behavior she wanted to encourage. It was useful for her also; on a number of occasions she had seen Miles get unreasonably anxious about being late for school or a birthday party, and had mentioned it to Ben.

Gets it from his mum, he said.

Really? she replied, although she knew it was true. She

hated being late, with an almost physical intensity, and always arrived on time. A 7 p.m. party invite meant, for her, a 7 p.m. arrival. Likewise, if she invited people over to eat lunch at 1 p.m., the lunch – hot and delicious and rapidly losing both qualities – would be ready at 1 p.m. She hated watching the clock tick from five after to ten after to quarter after, the food getting colder and colder and her mood worse and worse.

So she had forced herself to relax – if you could force yourself to relax – and she thought she was a bit better these days. Not much, but better.

However pleased she was to be modeling this more relaxed behavior to Miles, she was less keen to accept the other trait she saw developing in her son: he was a TV and computer game addict. He would, if allowed, sit for hours staring at the screen, and so they limited screen time to weekends. She was sure he would spend most of his college days batting aliens or driving stolen race cars, but while she could she was going to limit it.

So the offer of a TV show on a weeknight was a big deal.

'Yep,' Sarah said. 'You can watch a show tonight.'

'Anything we want?' Miles said.

'Anything appropriate for Kim,' she replied.

'Aww,' Miles said. 'But those are baby shows.'

'Do what you always do, Miles,' Ben said. 'Watch five minutes of *Daniel Tiger* and then turn on some violent cartoon when Mum and I aren't paying attention.'

'Oh,' Miles said. 'OK.'

'I'll call for pizza,' Sarah said. 'You guys go and settle on the couch.'

'Well,' Ben said, when the kids were gone. 'Very unusual. What's going on?'

Sarah pulled a chair from under the dining table and sat down. Her legs were suddenly weak; now the kids were out of the room there was nothing to keep her occupied and stop her emotions from taking control. Nothing to stop the feeling of sheer terror that gripped her every time she thought of what had happened.

'Sarah?' Ben said. He crouched next to her. 'What's wrong?'

She gestured for him to sit.

'Marla got an email,' she said, her voice strained. 'At camp. It said Faye's uncle was coming to pick her up.'

'What uncle? She doesn't have one, at least not here. My brother's in London.'

'Exactly.' Sarah swallowed. Her throat was dry. 'Would you mind getting me a drink?'

Ben stood up. 'Of course. Water? Tea?'

'Maybe a real drink.'

'Wine. We have some white open.'

'Do we have gin and tonic?' Sarah said.

'No tonic. We have seltzer, though.'

'That'll do.'

He poured her a drink, then sat down again. 'So. This uncle?'

'Someone using my name – it was the Sarah Havenant Gmail account – emailed Marla and told her Faye's uncle would be coming to camp to pick her up since I had gone to see my dad.'

'Your dad's dead.'

'Marla didn't know. The email said this fictitious uncle would be there a bit early, and could she have Faye ready.' Sarah's lip started to quiver and she blinked back tears. 'I happened,' she said, her voice breaking, 'I happened, by chance, Ben, by dumb luck, to be there early, so it was me who picked up Faye, and not someone else.'

Ben stared at her. 'Are you serious?' he said.

Sarah nodded. She covered her mouth with her hand. 'She could have been taken,' she said. 'Our little girl. She could have been taken.'

'Fuck,' Ben said, his face pale. 'Fuck. What do we do?'

Sarah shook her head. 'Talk to the cops. We need help.'

The pizza arrived shortly after Ian Molyneux showed up, this time in uniform. He refused a slice and patted his stomach.

'Might as well strap it to my waist,' he said. 'Older I get, easier it is to put it on and harder it is to take it off.'

'Thanks for coming at such short notice,' Sarah said.

'No problem. So, what happened?'

'This was sent to Faye's camp counselor.' Sarah handed him her phone and showed him the email Marla had forwarded to her.

Ian read it. 'I thought your old man was— I thought he passed away?'

'He did. The email isn't from me.'

'It's another fake email,' Ben said. 'This doesn't feel like a prank anymore. If it ever did.'

Ian passed the phone back to Sarah. 'No,' he said. 'It sure doesn't.'

'So,' Sarah said. 'What do you think?'

'I think I need to talk to some folks,' Ian said. 'Find out if this has happened anywhere else. It's possible there might have been similar situations in other places. Attempted abductions that follow this pattern.' He paused. 'Although I don't see why anyone would bother with the Facebook stuff. All it does is draw attention. But then, who knows with these people?'

These people, Sarah thought. The way he said it made clear that in his mind *these people* were the crazies, the psychopaths, the murderers and rapists. And now *these people* were in her and her family's lives.

'And if there aren't other cases like this?' Ben said.

'I dunno,' Ian said. 'We may be able to trace something. The Internet companies have a lot of data. They don't always

100

like to share it, but if there's a threat to a kid involved – well, they might be more willing. They're parents, too. Some of 'em, at least.' He took out a notebook. 'Old school way,' he said. 'Can't break the habit. What was the name of the woman who got the email?'

'Marla Niles,' Sarah said. 'I can give you her details. Are you planning to talk to her?'

'Someone will. They'll want to see the original email.'

'OK,' Sarah said. 'I'll let her know the cops will be in touch.'

'Actually,' Ian said. 'It would be better if you didn't.'

'You think she's a suspect?' Sarah said. It was hard to imagine that Marla would have sent herself the email; after all, she could hardly pick up Faye from her own camp.

Unless, of course, she was working with someone, and the email was cover. Sarah pictured her talking to the cops, Faye long gone.

I didn't know her dad was dead. I'm new in town. I thought it was really her uncle.

She stopped herself. It was ridiculous. Marla wasn't involved.

Unless she was. That was the thing with this situation: since there were no suspects, everyone was a suspect.

'OK,' she said. 'I won't say anything.'

'Thanks,' Ian said. He paused. 'I shouldn't share this, but I looked into Rachel Little.' He glanced at Ben; clearly the presence of a lawyer was unsettling him. 'We're friends, though, right?'

'Right,' Sarah said. 'And I get it. You never said nothin'. Did you find anything out?'

Ian shook his head. 'Nothing striking. She has no criminal record. Seems to have been living in San Diego until she moved back here. She was married, for a couple of years. Got divorced six months ago.'

'Maybe she moved back because of the divorce,' Sarah said. 'Although she didn't mention it.'

'No kids?' Ben said.

'No,' Ian said. 'Not that I know of, anyway. She changed her name back to Little. She was Landay, Rachel Landay. Her husband was from this side of the country. Connecticut.'

Sarah tensed. She leaned forward.

'Not Matt Landay?' she said.

Ian looked up at her, his eyes narrowing. 'How did you know?'

'I knew a Matt Landay from Connecticut. Our age. It's an unusual name.' She glanced at Ben. 'I dated him in college. He was – he was a little obsessive.'

'You think this is the same guy?' Ian said.

'I don't know,' Sarah said. 'I'll give you his details.'

Molyneux nodded. 'OK. I'll look into it.' He frowned. 'I'll let you know as soon as I find anything out. In the meantime, be in touch immediately if anything happens. You can call 911 or the station, but you have my cell phone if you need it. It's always on and I live close by. Hopefully there's no need, but just in case.'

'Thank you,' Sarah said. 'That's very reassuring.'

'All part of the job,' Ian said. 'You guys take care.'

21

Sarah didn't want to be in work, and in all honesty she probably shouldn't have been. She was hardly her best self; she'd been distracted all morning. But she'd had no choice. The practice couldn't get a replacement until the afternoon, so Ben was home with the kids and she was here for half a day. But her mind was not on her work.

It was on the person who was masquerading as her. Who had been sending emails in her name. Who had been taking photos of her and her family.

Who had been planning to kidnap her daughter.

It was a struggle to stop the panic – the tightness in her throat, the shortness of breath, the waves of dizziness – from overwhelming her. She knew it was, in part, her body over-reacting; she'd learned that as a doctor, but also from her own experience of anxiety attacks, when her mind would run riot at the most ridiculous things – once, she had ended up sitting on a park bench deep-breathing to get herself under control because she had been worried an airplane might fall out of the empty blue sky and kill her and the kids.

It wasn't a rational response to a clear threat.

Except this time, maybe it was. This time there *was* a threat.

She looked at her schedule. Next up was Becky. The notes said she was complaining of nausea and sleeplessness. Well, she was pregnant.

Sarah went into the examining room. Becky was standing up, her arms folded across her chest.

'Becky,' Sarah said. She studied her for a few moments; she looked dreadful, her eyes ringed with dark circles and her face thinner than Sarah remembered. She sat down and gestured to the empty chair opposite her. 'Take a seat.'

Becky ignored her.

'How are you?' Sarah said. 'Is everything OK?'

Becky nodded, twice, shifting her weight from foot to foot. She seemed unable to look Sarah in the eye.

'Why don't you sit down? Tell me why you came in today?'

Becky hesitated, then moved toward the chair. She sat down, her arms still tightly folded.

'The notes say you've been suffering from nausea and sleeplessness?' Sarah said. 'Could you give any details?'

'It's bad,' Becky said, her voice barely audible. 'I don't sleep more than an hour or two a night. And I feel sick, all day.'

'Have you vomited?' Sarah said. 'Or is it only the feeling?'

'Once or twice,' Becky said. 'But it's mainly the feeling.'

'That *is* fairly normal in pregnancy,' Sarah said. 'As is insomnia. Your body is going through a lot of changes – physical, hormonal, emotional – and a reaction is common. Even quite an extreme reaction, like this seems to be.'

'It's more than that,' Becky replied. 'A lot more.'

'Oh?' Sarah said. 'Like what?'

'I feel – it's hard to describe – but I feel smooth,' Becky said. 'Like I can't get hold of anything, can't get any grip. Sometimes I feel like I'm in a bubble. Other times I don't feel anything. And I feel the same way about the baby.' She started to cry. 'I don't feel happy or excited. I feel empty. And that

104

makes me feel awful, like I'm already a bad mom. And then I think I don't deserve this amazing gift, like I'm ungrateful, and I start to worry it'll be taken from me.' She paused. 'I'm worried I'll lose the baby, and it'll be my fault.'

Sarah handed her a tissue.

'It's very hard to deal with,' she said. 'But even this kind of thing is not uncommon. It's hard to over-estimate the effects of pregnancy on mood, behavior, appetite. It's a massive thing for the body to go through.'

'But it started before the pregnancy,' Becky said. 'It's been going on for months. I've felt numb and stupid and worthless for months and I want it to go away!'

'When did these feelings start?' Sarah said.

'Around Christmas, which is crazy because that's when I met Sean. I feel so guilty. I have all this wonderful stuff in my life, and all I can do is complain.'

'You're not complaining.' Sarah caught Becky's eye. She held her gaze. 'Have you considered that you might be depressed?' she said. 'It would explain a lot of this.'

'But why?' Becky said. 'What have I got to be depressed about?'

'It doesn't always works like that,' Sarah said. 'Think of it like an illness. You don't need a reason to catch a cold; it's a virus. Part of the problem with mental illness in general is the way people look on it as some kind of failing on their part, but it isn't. It's a chemical imbalance in the brain.'

'I know,' Becky said. 'But what am I going to do?'

'We could try you on some medication,' Sarah said. 'Other patients have found that effective.'

'I'm not sure,' Becky replied. 'I don't think – I mean, is there another way?'

'Would you like me to refer you to somebody? A therapist? They might be able to help.'

Becky paused. 'I'm already seeing someone.'

'Oh? Good. You could ask them about medication?'

Becky shook her head. 'They said it wasn't necessary to take medication. There are strategies for coping.'

'Could I ask who you saw? Was it a medical professional?'

'I don't know their qualifications.'

'If you give me their name, I might know them. You don't have to, of course. So no pressure.'

Becky nodded. 'I've been seeing a woman called Rachel Little.'

Sarah hesitated. She hadn't been expecting that name. It seemed to crop up everywhere.

'Do you know her?' Becky said.

'I do,' Sarah said. 'I've known her a long time. Since high school.'

'Oh,' Becky said. 'Good.' She clearly took the length of Sarah and Rachel's acquaintance as a positive sign; Sarah did not feel like correcting her, even though she had no professional knowledge of what Rachel did or how effective it was.

'Well,' Sarah said. 'If anything changes, get in touch, especially if it gets worse.'

Becky stood up. She held out her hand for Sarah to shake; it was an oddly formal gesture.

'I will,' she said. 'Goodbye.'

22

There she goes. Making her way home to the family she does not deserve. To the family she will lose, when she is finally destroyed.

And she will be destroyed. She has no idea she is hated as much as she is; she has no concept she *could* be hated like this. She is a good person, a doctor, and mother, and dutiful, loving, loyal wife.

Although there was that incident with the handsome physical therapist a few years ago. She thinks no one knows – and if anyone did, they will by now have forgotten – but this is a small town and word spreads and people have long memories.

She has forgotten, more or less. It wasn't much, after all. A handful of dates, one of which ended up with a hurried, guilty coupling at his house.

And she had an excuse: she was going through a difficult time. Depressed? Perhaps not. But anxious? Most certainly. And lost? Without any doubt. Lost and grasping at straws. And the physical therapist – Josh, was his name – was one of those straws.

He'd recently started working at her medical center. She

went to see him because of back pain and difficulty breathing. Tightness in her ribs, brought on, she thought, by the anxiety that plagued her, woke her in the night and left her reeling, dizzy and unable to think straight during the day.

He made her feel better. Safer, more secure. Gave her stretches and exercises. They helped; they were the only thing that did, and she mistook her gratitude for something else.

He didn't. He saw it for what it was. An opportunity for some sex with a desperate housewife. He liked that kind of thing.

But after their first, fumbled time together she realized her error. Broke it off. Went back to her family and husband.

Didn't tell him, of course. Didn't feel she needed to: it was an honest mistake. She is a good person. Not a slut. Not the kind of person who sleeps with handsome physical therapists called Josh on a whim. No: she told herself it was part of her sickness. A symptom of the malaise which plagued her. And now it was gone. No need to tell Ben and make it worse than it needed to be.

After all, she felt – weirdly – better. Relieved she had got away with it. Newly grateful for her beautiful son and loving husband.

And other than one little slip-up – and we all deserve *one* slip-up – she's blameless. So no one could hate her. How could they? What is there to hate? She is safe in the knowledge that, whatever else might befall her, no one could be so filled with disgust and hatred for her that they would want to bring her down from her lofty perch and destroy her utterly.

This certainty is her downfall.

Because she is wrong.

Totally wrong.

23

As she drove home, Sarah could not shake the meeting with Becky from her mind. She was clearly suffering from either the beginnings of depression or depression itself, and it had started six months ago.

When Sarah introduced her to Sean.

Which happened to be when the Facebook account had been set up.

And unlikely as it was that Becky was involved, it was an odd coincidence, and right now, with everything else going on, anything odd – even slightly odd – stood out.

Was Becky involved? Sarah couldn't see how, or why, but it was at least possible. And she was seeing Rachel Little, which was another coincidence. As was Rachel Little's divorce six months earlier. She was the one who had alerted Sarah to the existence of the Facebook account, right before she moved back to Barrow.

And now she was Becky's therapist. Sarah could imagine the scene, Rachel sitting, arms folded, brow furrowed in a look of deep, sincere concern for her new patient.

And do you think these feelings are linked to meeting Sean? Weren't you introduced to him? Match-made, so to speak?

Yes, by Sarah Havenant.

And perhaps, in some weird way, Becky blamed Sarah for the depression, and Rachel was using that to get her to set up fake Facebook accounts and invite Sarah's friends' kids to fake play dates, or invent a fictitious uncle who was supposed to pick up Faye from camp.

But why? Why would Rachel do it?

Because she wants your kids, Sarah thought, and a chill went through her. The thought had come unbidden, surfacing from her subconscious like a whale breaching. Like the truth emerging.

She shook her head. It didn't make sense. If she wanted Sarah's kids – and why she would want hers over someone else's was a mystery – why do all this? All it did was attract attention, which was the last thing a kidnapper wanted.

It didn't make sense. None of it made any sense.

And that made it all the more threatening.

She pushed open her front door. It opened a few inches, then stuck. She pushed again; it gave a little – as though it was pushed up against something soft – but wouldn't move.

She shoved harder, panic gripping her, and the door flew open.

Skidding to a stop in the middle of the hall was one of Ben's New Balance running shoes. The toe was compressed; it must have been wedged under the door, out of its normal home in the boxes by the door.

It wasn't the only thing out of place.

Most of a wooden jigsaw puzzle was strewn across the floor, mixed in with what looked like hundreds of Lego pieces. The book Sarah had been reading was open, face-down, spine bent, in the doorway to the kitchen, and there were Pokémon cards *everywhere*.

She walked into the kitchen, where the scene was repeated.

110

'Ben?' she called. 'Are you there?'

The back door opened and he walked into the house. He was dripping wet, and grinning.

'What's going on?' she said.

'Water tag,' he replied. 'I started off with the hose but somehow the kids ended up being the ones doing the spraying. Miles, mostly. Saves me having a shower before I head into the office.' He looked at his clothes. 'Although I think I'll need to change.'

Sarah bit back her anger. He was off to work, leaving her to clean up this mess. No doubt the kids were equally soaking, which would mean yet more laundry.

'Have the kids had lunch?' she said.

Ben shook his head. 'I was planning to feed them but we got carried away.'

'Did you go to the store? We don't have much in.'

'No.' His expression had changed, the smile replaced by a wary, conciliatory look. 'I can go on the way home, though.'

'Doesn't help me now, does it? I've been at work all morning and now I come home to this,' – she swept her hand behind her, indicating the mess – 'and nothing for the kids to eat.'

'I'm sorry, darling. It's a summer's day and we were messing around.'

'Well, I'm glad you had fun.' She could hear the sarcasm in her voice; it was unpleasant and she didn't like it, but she couldn't help the rising tide of emotion. 'Off you go to work. At least now there's a grown-up in charge.'

His expression changed again; this time the conciliation was gone, replaced by a mounting anger.

'Look,' he said. 'I know it's been a stressful few days, but don't take it out on everyone else. We were only having some fun.'

'That's got *nothing* to do with it!' she shouted. 'I come

111

home to a dump, hungry kids and an empty kitchen, and all you say is "We were only having some fun."' She glared at him; he backed away. '*That's* what this is about,' she said. 'Not the last few days. So don't make excuses.'

'Fine,' he said. 'I'm going to get changed. And on the way I'll pick up the toys. Should take me – oh, five minutes? And I'll call for a pizza, which should take care of lunch.' He folded his arms. 'You don't think you may be over-reacting, do you? A little?'

She wanted, at that second, to sink her nails into his cheeks and claw them off. Before she could, he turned and went upstairs.

24

Sarah handed Jean a mug of coffee and sat down. They were sitting out in the backyard on Sarah's favorite chairs – two Adirondacks she had bought the previous summer. They were expensive, but she had wanted them for a while, and the year before she had finally pulled the trigger.

'Did Kim go down OK?' Jean said.

'After a struggle.' Kim's afternoon naps were becoming less regular; the other two had slept more during the day, but she fought it, aware that her elder siblings were having fun elsewhere. Which was perfectly reasonable; at that moment Miles, Faye, Daniel and Paul were throwing themselves along the slip 'n' slide.

'Thanks for coming,' Sarah said. 'It's so much easier when the kids have friends to play with.'

'No problem,' Jean replied. 'Mine aren't in camp this year anyway, so I'm always looking for something to do with them.' She shook her head. 'Camps are so *expensive* now. It wasn't that way when we were kids.'

'The Rec Camp where we went was free,' Sarah said. 'Although it was a bit crappy. It was in that windowless basement, remember? It felt like a prison.'

'But we had fun,' Jean said. 'Kids do.' She looked at Sarah. 'Are you going to send yours back to camp this summer? After the email?'

'I'm not sure,' Sarah said. 'I want to – I want everything to be normal – but I'm not sure I can. I'm not sure I'll be able to. I'd spend the whole time worrying about them.'

'I would too. I'd be terrified.'

Sarah massaged her temples with her forefingers. 'I don't get it,' she said. 'I don't understand what's going on.'

'It's got to be some sick joke,' Jean said. 'I don't see what else it could be.'

'But who?'

'A patient, maybe? Someone you upset in some way? Maybe you wouldn't give them oxy?'

'There was a patient today,' Sarah said. 'It was a bit weird.'

'Oh?'

'I can't say too much, but – well, she'd was quite depressed. It began six months ago. I offered her medication but she declined, so I suggested a therapist, but she'd already contacted one.'

'So far, this doesn't sound at all strange, Sarah.'

Sarah leaned forward. She was aware this was a breach of patient–doctor confidentiality, but it felt important to share it.

'She's been seeing Rachel Little.'

Jean frowned. 'And you think that's relevant?'

'It's a coincidence, at least.'

'I don't know,' Jean said. 'It's pretty thin.'

'It is,' Sarah said. 'But it's something. You want to stay and eat? I can call and ask Ben to pick up stuff for the grill. If he answers my call.'

'Why wouldn't he?' Jean asked.

'I snapped at him earlier,' Sarah said. 'When I got back the house was a mess and I kind of lost it.'

'You've got a lot on your mind.'

'That's what he said, which made it worse. But you're both right. I'll say sorry. And I can text him, so if he doesn't answer, he'll still get the message. And the apology.'

'It's fine,' Jean said. 'I need to get back and feed the kids. I've got a babysitter coming at five thirty.'

'Oh?' Sarah said. 'Going out?'

'Yep,' Jean said. 'On a date.'

'A date?' Sarah said. 'Who with?'

'It's kind of embarrassing.'

'No it isn't. Well, it might be. But tell me anyway.'

'You know Clara, from the school?'

'The receptionist?'

Jean nodded. 'She has a friend called Carl who's recently moved to Lewiston. He's setting up a business there in the old mill. The one that's being redeveloped.'

'Doing what?'

'I don't know. Clara said, but it wasn't clear. She mentioned IT networks, which didn't really help.' Jean gave a bashful smile. 'She set it up. Kind of a blind date.'

Sarah grinned. 'Great! And a blind date. That's pretty brave.'

'We're meeting for a coffee downtown. Early evening, no pressure. Clara suggested dinner, but a meal could last hours. Don't want to be trapped if he turns out to be a weirdo.'

'Does she know him?'

'She does. He was friends with her brother. She says he's a good guy.'

'I guess you'll find out. Divorced? Kids?'

Jean nodded. 'Divorced, yes. Kids, no.'

'Perfect,' Sarah said. 'He sounds lovely.'

Jean rolled her eyes. 'How does he sound lovely? He's a divorced IT nerd. So lovely maybe isn't the word. But it's worth a shot, although I'm kind of nervous. I've forgotten how to date. It's been a while. Apart from that *disaster* with the college professor, it's the first date since Jack died.'

Sarah laughed. 'The professor was a piece of work.'

That was an understatement. He and Jean had met when Hardy College was organizing students to volunteer in local schools. He'd asked her out and they'd gone on a couple of dates; after the last one she went back to his house – *full of models and jigsaw puzzles*, she told Sarah, *wall to ceiling, complete, in pieces* – and they kissed, despite the fact Jean was already having second thoughts.

Then he asked me if I could meow, Jean said, *and gently scratch his face. He told me to imagine I was a gentle cat who loved her owner but might bite him if he was naughty.*

And did you? Sarah asked, over a Mai-tai in a local bar.

No! Jean said. *Although I might have, for the right guy. But not for him. I made my excuses and bolted.*

'This one'll be fine,' Sarah said. 'Unless he has a thing for dogs.'

'Thanks,' Jean said. 'I feel so much better now. Although all I really need is someone who doesn't care about all the baggage I bring.'

'It's not *that* bad,' Sarah said.

'You don't think? Widow, two kids from her dead husband's first marriage, infertile, no money, getting a bit on the fat side, constantly exhausted?'

'Yeah,' Sarah said. 'But for the right guy, you'd be prepared to act like a playful but latently aggressive cat. Which *has* to count for something.'

'Well, if you put it in those terms,' Jean replied. 'I'm a great catch.'

'You are a great catch,' Sarah said. 'And not only because of your cat impersonation skills.'

Jean stood up. 'Could have done with someone like Sean.

But Becky snapped *him* up. Anyway, it's time for me to go.'

Sarah smiled and hugged her friend. 'Good luck,' she said. 'And I expect a call later with all the juicy gossip.'

25

Sarah woke early the following morning. She checked her phone; no message from Jean. She'd call later to find out about her blind date. Then she opened her email; some spam, but nothing else.

Nothing from an email account set up under the name Sarah Havenant.

It was crazy: every time she checked her email there was a moment when she felt her heart had stopped, when a little shot of adrenaline put her on alert, in case there was something new, something sinister and weird in there.

And then, when there wasn't, she relaxed. The fact it was a relief not to have an email from someone posing as her showed how very fucked up this had become.

There *was*, however, an email from Ian Molyneux.

Sarah – I ran Matt Landay. I think he's in the clear. He's been in Dubai working on some finance deal for the last three months. Anyway, I'll keep you posted.

She wasn't convinced. It was conceivable that Rachel and Matt had met and married – they were part of a group who had attended liberal arts colleges in New England at the same time, and there would have been plenty of opportunities for them to meet – but it seemed ominous that six months ago Rachel Little divorced him and all this started.

Matt could be doing this from Dubai. He was smart enough. She'd tell Ian not to cross him off the list just yet.

She put her head back on her pillow and closed her eyes.

Next to her, Ben stirred. He opened one eye and looked at her.

'Everything OK?' he said.

'Yes,' she replied. 'Woke up early.'

'I was dreaming of you,' he said. 'Of us.'

'Oh? What were we doing?'

His hand snaked across the bedsheets and on to her hip. He pulled her toward him then rolled on top of her.

'This,' he said.

It was another hot day, and they were planning a trip to the beach. Ben sat by the door, pulling on his running shoes.

'I'll be back in thirty minutes,' he said. 'And then we can go. I'll pack some food if you get the kids ready.'

'Sure,' Sarah said. 'I need to run this weekend, though. Maybe tomorrow morning.' This was part of the dance of their married lives: you run now, I run later. Quid pro quo. If he got to do an activity, then she did too. Sometimes, to make sure they were equal, she did things she didn't really want to. He went out with the boys – which was pretty rare – and she would go out with the girls, even if she was wiped out and mainly interested in an early night.

'You got it,' he said, in his fake American accent, an accent that still sounded, after years in the US, like a Welsh cowboy. He kissed her. 'Back soon.'

As he left, her phone buzzed. She glanced at it, the little shot of nervousness coursing through her before she saw it was Jean.

119

Went well. Sorry I didn't call last night. Got home later than expected!

Sarah typed a reply.

omg. Sounds like it went really well. What happened?

He's nice. Cute too. I'll tell all later. What are you guys doing today?

Going to Crescent Beach. See you there?

So Jean had a boyfriend. Maybe, at least. It was great news. She'd had a tough run over the years, from her over-strict parents through having to get an abortion at eighteen and then later the loss of her husband. She deserved some happiness. Sarah went to find the kids' beach clothes with a smile on her face; things felt faintly normal, for a change, and at least someone was having some luck. Her mood – tense, anxious, low – lifted for the first time in days.

She only hoped it would last.

26

Getting a seven-year-old, five-year-old and two-year-old into beach clothes – shorts and T-shirts, nothing more – should not have been this difficult. It should not have required nearly forty minutes of polite requests, desperate cajoling and finally flat-out shouting to get it done.

How was it that Miles, who was seven and perfectly capable of dressing himself, was walking around naked half an hour after she asked him to put his clothes on?

I can't find them.

I put them by your bed.

Oh. Thanks, Mom.

Then five minutes later:

Miles! Why are you not dressed?

I don't have my clothes.

I told you! They're by your bed!

No they aren't! I looked.

Then she went upstairs and there they were, right in front of him, which she pointed out to Miles.

Oh, he said. *Those clothes*, with the emphasis on *those*, as though she had cleared up some great mystery and his inability to recognize the clothes he went to the beach in every weekend when they were right in front of his face was perfectly reasonable.

Miles, though, was one thing. He was simply incapable; the only explanation for Faye was that she was being deliberately obstructive in an attempt not to have to go and play with her friends by the ocean, a place which, when it came time to go home, she would scream blue murder about having to leave.

And Kim. Getting her out of the door was like trying to empty a swimming pool with a colander. A *leaky* colander.

But forty minutes later it was done. Three kids, dressed and ready. Smiling and enthusiastic about a trip to the beach. The only victim was her sanity. In moments like this she wondered whether she was a particularly incompetent mother or whether her kids were particularly difficult to herd.

Or maybe all kids were like this. If so, she shuddered at the prospects for the human race.

'Hey.' The front door opened. Ben stood there, dripping sweat. He ruffled Miles's hair. 'Nice job,' he said. 'They're ready.' He was holding a parcel in his hand. He handed it to Sarah. 'This came. It's for you. Did you pack lunch?'

Sarah didn't reply. She was staring at the box. It was from Amazon, addressed to her.

She hadn't ordered anything.

Which meant it was a surprise gift. And right now she didn't want any surprise gifts.

'Sarah? Did you get lunch packed?'

She looked up at Ben. 'No,' she said.

'OK. I'll grab some stuff for sandwiches.' He paused. 'Are you OK?'

'Fine,' she replied.

'Is there a problem? With the parcel?' Ben glanced at the kids then took her by the elbow. 'Come and help me with the lunch,' he said. 'We can talk in the kitchen.'

When they were out of the kids' hearing, he took the box from her hands.

'What is it?' he said. 'What did you order?'

'I didn't order anything,' Sarah said. 'I don't know what it is.'

Ben paused; he looked at her and for a moment there was a serious, concerned expression in his eyes, but then he shrugged it away.

'You probably don't remember,' he said. 'I do that all the time.'

It was an act, Sarah knew, an act designed to pretend this was not what it was going to turn out to be. To panic, to worry was to admit this was real, and Ben was not ready to take that step, not yet.

But it *was* real. She knew it. She knew she had not ordered anything from Amazon and then forgotten it, and she knew Ben did *not* do it all the time, whatever he said to reassure her.

'Are you going to open it?' he said.

She didn't want to. She didn't want to know what was in there. She wanted it never to have arrived.

'Here,' he said. 'I'll do it.' She handed him the box and he hefted it in his hands.

'Books,' he said. 'I think it's books. You ordered a book and forgot. Probably some medical thing. Or maybe one of your doctor friends sent it.'

'Maybe,' Sarah said. 'Why don't you take a look?'

He pressed a nail into the corner of the tape – *Amazon Prime*, it said – and slit it. He tugged open the cardboard flaps and reached inside.

A layer of air-filled plastic packaging materials. Then paper. Books. Two of them.

He pulled them out. She read the titles, and gasped.

27

She took them from him and stared at them.

The title of the first one was bad enough: *Coping With Depression* by some MD trying to make a few extra bucks.

The second was awful.

Living with Bipolar: Family Strategies to Cope with a Bipolar Parent.

She hadn't known this was a topic to warrant a book being written about it, but it seemed it was.

She threw the books on to the kitchen counter. She didn't even want to look at them. There was a sheet of letter paper in the one about depression. As the book landed it fell to the floor.

Ben picked it up. 'Oh,' he said. 'I thought this was an invoice, but there's a message.' His eyes scanned it, and the serious, concerned expression came back on his face. 'Holy shit,' he said. 'You better read this.'

'Do I have to?' Sarah said.

'I think you should.'

He offered it to her and she took it from his outstretched hand.

Dear Sarah. I hope you enjoy this gift. The first step in accepting help is recognizing you need it. You know you need it, but you will not admit it to yourself. So you have taken the unusual step of sending yourself the books you need to start your journey of recovery. The contents of one of these books – the one on depression – will, as a doctor, be familiar to you, but I think a little refresher will help. The second book is a warning: if you do not start to help yourself, then this is where this might all end, which would be terrible for your family.

Enjoy! Yours, Sarah Havenant.

'Ben,' Sarah said. 'Ben, what is this?'

Ben picked up her phone. He tapped on the screen.

'What are you doing?' Sarah said.

'Opening the Amazon app,' he said. 'I want to see if this came from your account.'

'It didn't!' Sarah said. 'I would know if I'd ordered these books! They're not the kind of thing I would forget!'

'Let's check.'

'Do you not believe me?' Sarah said. 'You think I'm lying?'

'I believe you. I just want to check.' He handed her the phone. 'Here. Log in.'

She shrugged and typed in her username and password. He wasn't going to find what he was looking for, but it would at least put a stop to this line of enquiry.

She tapped on her orders, and watched as a new screen came up.

And there it was. Ordered two days ago at 4.37 p.m. *Coping with Depression* and *Living with Bipolar: Family Strategies to Cope with a Bipolar Parent*, both sent from her account to her.

Her expression must have given her away, because when he spoke there was a worried urgency in Ben's voice.

'Sarah?' he said. 'What is it?'

'They're there,' she muttered, finding it hard to believe her eyes. 'They were ordered from my account.'

'Then . . .' Ben paused '. . . then you ordered them.'

'Or someone else with access to my Amazon account,' Sarah said.

'Like who?'

'There is no one,' Sarah said, and looked up at him. 'Other than you.'

'Right,' he said. 'And I don't even know your Amazon password. I have my own.'

'Which only leaves me,' Sarah said. 'And I didn't do it.'

'Then it's somebody else who has your password. Or guessed it. It's not too obvious, is it? Like MilesFayeKim?'

'It's RedFrontDoor,' Sarah replied. 'Because we have a red front door. Which I don't think is too obvious, is it?'

Ben shook his head. 'Probably not.'

'I don't know who this could be,' Sarah said. 'It's driving me mad.'

'That's one question,' Ben said. 'The other is why? Why *these* books?' He put his hands on her shoulders and looked straight into her eyes. 'Are you OK, Sarah? Is someone trying to send a message to you by sending these?'

'Maybe,' Sarah said. 'But I don't know what message. I'm fine. I'm totally fine.'

'Are you sure?'

'Of course I am. There's nothing wrong, Ben. I promise.'

From the look on his face, she did not think he was convinced.

28

She will have them by now. The books will be in her possession and she will be asking herself what they mean and who sent them, but she will not get answers.

She is floundering. Sinking. Lost. A fish on a hook, thrashing about.

She is not able to work it out for herself and she will not be told. Will not be given them for nothing.

Not yet.

Eventually she will, of course. Or this would all be pointless. It would also be no fun, but fun is a secondary consideration. The fact it is fun is a bonus. When she finds out who is doing this and why she will choke on her disbelief, but her terror is only part of the goal. It is nice to have, but not necessary.

And when she finally understands, she will understand one other thing as well.

She will understand that it is too late for her to do anything about it.

29

'OK,' Ben said. 'Time to go. Car's all packed.'

Sarah moved the mouse and clicked on her Amazon account. 'Hold on,' she said. 'I need a few minutes.'

'The kids are in the car and quiet,' Ben said. 'Which might not last, especially if we sit in the driveway for half an hour waiting for you.'

'I won't be half an hour!' Sarah said. 'I told you, I'll be a few minutes!'

'Can't it wait until we get back from the beach?'

Sarah closed her eyes and fought the rising anger. 'No,' she said. 'It can't.'

'What are you doing?'

'Nothing. Give me a few minutes and I'll be done.'

'Sarah,' Ben said. 'It's not—'

'Can you not hear me?' Sarah said, her voice rising into a shout. 'For fuck's sake, Ben! I told you I need some time to do this and then we can leave.'

Ben stared at her in silence. His mouth was a thin line. He nodded slowly, as though realizing something for the first time, and then turned and left.

Sarah went back to the screen. She felt bad, but this was important.

At least, she had thought it was. Now, though, after she'd screamed and sworn at her husband, it seemed less urgent.

But it was all she had. It was the only thing she could do to get control of the situation.

She needed to change her passwords. Email, Amazon, eBay, bank account, everything. Next was the credit card that had been used to buy the books. She would delete it from her Amazon account, and then she would cancel her Facebook account.

They were all going. The whole digital mess was on its way out. From now on she was buying things in shops and communicating face-to-face or by phone. Email was unavoidable, but she would tell everyone that whenever they got an email from her making any kind of arrangement – picking up kids, play dates, party invites – they were to call and check with her, verbal confirmation required.

It might not be perfect, but it was a start, which was why she had been so annoyed by Ben trying to stop her.

It took longer than she expected, and it was twenty minutes before she was done. She shut down the computer and grabbed her hat and sunglasses from the kitchen counter. She pictured herself getting in the passenger seat of the car and turning to the kids.

Sorry! she'd say, her voice bright. *Mommy had to do an important job. But how about we all get ice creams when we get to the beach?*

And then she'd look at Ben and he'd still be mad at her, but she'd put a hand on his thigh – high on his thigh so he understood the promise she was giving that she'd make it up to him later on – and say *sorry* to him too, and that would re-establish contact and it'd all be OK, ready for a fun day at the beach.

She closed the front door behind her and walked on to the porch.

She stopped.

There was only one car in the driveway. Ben's Camry.

Her car was gone. The SUV they used when they needed to travel as a family – for instance, when they went to the beach – was not there.

He'd gone without her.

She grabbed her phone and called him.

'Hi,' he said. 'What's up?'

'What's up? You left without me.'

'Just giving you the space you need,' he said. 'The kids wanted to get going, so after a few minutes waiting we decided to go.'

'Where are you?'

'Near Bath.'

'Are you planning to come back and get me?' Sarah said. 'I'd like to join you guys at the beach. I was hoping to have a family day.'

'I wasn't planning to,' Ben said. 'We're halfway there now.'

'Great,' Sarah said. She felt tears well in her eyes. 'Thanks, Ben. Thanks a lot.'

'Sarah,' he said. 'We waited for you. We wanted you to come. But you seem like you need to be alone. If not, come along. We'll see you at the beach.'

'OK,' Sarah said. 'I'm on my way.'

'Great,' Ben said. 'But take your time. Relax for a while, OK?'

Sarah decided to take him up on his offer.

It was – she had to admit – not unpleasant to drive on her own. The road was quiet and winding and surrounded by beautiful views of the ocean. She stopped at a pretty café in an area called Winnegance and ordered an iced coffee. It seemed ages since she'd been alone, on a weekend, in a café where she had nothing to do but relax. She was in no hurry to get to the beach – after all, Ben had left without her, so he could hardly complain – so she took her time over the coffee, then, when it was finished, ordered a lobster roll.

She was hungry, she realized. She hadn't eaten much the last few days and all of a sudden her appetite was back.

'A large roll?' the waitress said. 'Or small?'

'Large, please,' Sarah replied.

'With chips on the side? And a pickle?'

'Why not? Thank you.'

The roll, when it came, was enormous, lobster spilling over the sides of the toasted bun. She took a bite; it was every bit as delicious as it looked. No wonder Maine was famous for the lobster rolls; as a local she rarely had one, but she might have to introduce them into her diet more often.

God, it was good to have a moment to herself. She loved Ben and the kids, unreservedly and without limit, but a little distance – even this small amount – was a real treat. It relieved the pressure, and allowed her to get some perspective back.

She paid the bill – twenty-two dollars well spent – and got back in the car. It was going to be a fun day at the beach. She was going to bring her good mood and let it spread to all of her family, washing them in a golden glow.

She parked next to their SUV – the spot was open, which she took as a good sign – and walked the short path up the dunes that led to the beach proper. The smell of the ocean added to her good mood; it was invigorating and restorative.

At the top of the dunes she scanned the beach, looking for the large red umbrella she had bought earlier in the year. It was off to her left; she could see the kids digging a hole a few yards from the water's edge, and Ben, standing by the umbrella, talking to someone.

Someone in a blue bikini. They looked deep in conversation; from the tilt of her head she seemed to be listening intently to whatever Ben was saying.

She was wearing a red baseball cap so Sarah couldn't make out her face, but she didn't need to. She knew exactly who it was.

It was Rachel Little.

30

'Hi, Rachel,' Sarah said. 'Beautiful day. I didn't know you were coming.'

She didn't, and there was no reason she should have. Just as there was no reason she should be surprised to see Rachel here on such a hot, perfect Maine summer day. Where else would she go?

To Simpson's Point, or Reid State Park, or Popham Beach or one of many other coastal Maine locations within easy driving distance of Barrow, that was where. But she was *here*, and the sudden silence that had fallen when Sarah walked over to Rachel and her husband suggested they had been talking about a topic they did not want her to know about.

Maybe she was being paranoid. Probably she was. But nonetheless: as she had approached they had been deep in conversation, a conversation that stopped as soon as they saw her. Normally people would *continue* their conversation when someone new joined them.

Hey, how are you? We were talking about the new principal at the high school. Apparently she was an Olympic Swimmer in the 1984 games. Got to the final of some event.

Breaststroke, I think. But swimming's so complicated. There are so many events. You have to be a swimmer to tell them all apart.

And then the new person would offer an opinion and the conversation would continue.

Not in this case. Whatever they had been talking about was over.

Rachel smiled at her. It was a bland smile, almost deliberately expressionless.

'It's beautiful here,' she said. 'I used to come here as a kid with my family.'

'It's definitely the most family friendly beach,' Ben said. 'Popham is more spectacular, but it's harder to manage the children there, and there are some powerful currents in the water. This is much more self-contained.'

'We come here for the same reason,' Sarah said. She looked at Miles, Faye and Kim. 'Because of the kids. If it wasn't for them we might go elsewhere.'

If Rachel had picked up on her point – why are you here, at this family friendly beach, surrounded by kids, when you could be enjoying the splendor of Popham? – she didn't show it. Instead, she smiled.

'Well,' Rachel said. 'I was on my way to get a coffee when I saw Ben. Would you like me to pick one up for you?'

'No thanks. I had one on the way here.'

'Oh,' Rachel said. 'Well, see you later.'

As she walked away, her legs tan against the pale blue of her bikini, the muscles long and lean, Sarah felt disconcerted, as though there was something out of place in the exchange they had just had.

It came to her.

Rachel had not asked why Sarah had arrived late. No *busy morning today?* Or *Problems at work? I guess some weekends you're on call?* Those – or some variant of them – would

134

have been the natural questions to ask on a Saturday morning when a mom was not with her family.

Unless, of course, she already knew. Unless that was what she and Ben had so abruptly stopped talking about when Sarah showed up.

'Nice to see Rachel,' she said.

'Yes,' Ben replied. 'She's very pleasant.'

Sarah had learned over the years that Ben – in common with many of his countrymen – had the ability to answer a question with a pleasantry that could mean anything at all. The meaning of *She's very pleasant* ranged from *She's totally beneath contempt but I don't want to waste time talking about her* to *She's an outstanding human being but I don't want to talk about her anymore in case it gets awkward*. It was the same with other things he said. *I'm not sure I agree* could mean exactly what it said, or it could mean *Your opinion is utterly worthless but let's pretend it isn't*.

Sarah was in no mood to be fobbed off. She looked him straight in the eye.

'What were you guys talking about?'

Ben shrugged. 'Bits and bobs. Usual stuff.'

'It seemed rather an intense conversation,' Sarah said. 'More than bits and bobs.'

'It wasn't,' Ben said. 'I barely know her.'

'OK,' Sarah said. She was not convinced, not convinced at all, but it was clear Ben had his story and he was going to stick to it. 'Fine.'

The kids went to bed early. One of the benefits of a long day at the beach was that the fresh air and sun and swimming tired them out. It was a good feeling as a parent, to see your kids fall into a deep restful sleep, a smile on their faces, their limbs twitching as they dreamed of running around in tide pools and building sand castles.

Sarah took a bottle of white wine from the fridge. It was more than half gone; she'd opened it when they got home and had a couple of glasses. Ben had drunk a beer, which meant she was responsible for half a bottle already.

She'd have to slow down, but it had been that kind of day.

She went and sat next to Ben on the couch. He was watching a show about classic British sports cars.

'What a fabulous car,' he said. 'A Triumph Stag. My dad had one when I was a kid. Lovely looking thing.'

Sarah was not interested in classic British sports cars at the best of times; now she couldn't muster up even a polite comment.

'Ben,' she said. 'What were you talking to Rachel about when I showed up?'

He turned to look at her.

'Nothing,' he said. 'We were just chatting.'

'There was an awkward silence,' Sarah said. 'Which isn't what happens when people are just chatting.'

Sarah did not think Ben was having an affair. He was a deeply honest person; he didn't even like lying to the kids about the existence of Santa Claus and the Tooth Fairy, and when he did he got an odd, teacherly tone in his voice.

Why did you put that voice on? Sarah had asked him, once.

What voice? he said. *My voice was totally normal.*

So even if he was lying to her, she was pretty sure she'd be able to tell.

You never knew, though. She would have thought the same about herself, but she had managed to get involved in that awful, tawdry episode with Josh, and she had lied about it. Not in the sense of telling an untruth when asked, but in the sense of keeping it quiet.

She'd done a lot of thinking about what happened and what to tell Ben and she'd decided it was not worth breaking up her family over. It was worse than a one-night stand, certainly – there'd been a few dates and then the one occasion they'd slept together, an event which had been eminently unforgettable, as well as horribly awkward – but still not enough to put their marriage and family life at risk.

She'd also thought about *how* it had happened. Back then, she'd been in the throes of the worst of her anxiety attacks, prone to a sudden onset of dizziness and heart palpitations and nausea and blurred vision at any moment. On top of which, Faye was two and a lot of work and she was constantly exhausted. She often felt either desperate, or a passive, disinterested observer of her own life. It was this numbness that upset her the most; she'd felt unable to truly experience anything: no joy in her kids, no enthusiasm for her family life. The color and pleasure were gone from the world; the only intense experiences she had were the panic attacks, and those she hated, which was what the affair had been about. It wasn't about sex or lust, but about recklessness and danger and how it made her feel. It was a cliché but it made her feel alive again. It was like dancing in a rainstorm after a long walk through a parched desert. Which didn't make it any more forgivable, but it made it explicable. And the explanation was good enough for her.

So she'd kept her mouth shut. She hadn't been sure she would be able to, but it turned out she was. She didn't think Ben could, though.

He paused the show. On the screen a green convertible was frozen in the middle of a corner on a racetrack.

He looked her straight in the eye.

'I was telling her about the books—'

It turned out she was right. He *couldn't* tell a lie.

Sarah stared at him. 'Are you kidding? You told her they showed up at the house with a note from me – the fake me – to me?'

137

'No!' Ben said. 'Of course not! I was asking her about her job as a psychologist. She said she worked with people who needed therapy, so I asked if she'd *heard* of the books. I only wanted to see if she'd heard of them. Any information could help us figure out who sent them.'

'I can't believe you told her,' Sarah said. She took a swig from her wineglass. 'It's none of her business!'

'I didn't tell her anything,' Ben said. 'I asked about those books.'

'Oh, for fuck's sake, Ben,' Sarah said, aware of the ugliness in her tone. 'How could you be so naïve? She's a therapist; she'll know we have those books – why else would you be asking about them – and she'll think I need them. She'll think I have depression or a bipolar disorder. I'm a doctor, Ben, I don't need people gossiping about my mental health!'

'Sarah,' Ben said. 'She's your friend. She's not going to gossip. And she's a professional. There's patient confidentiality issues.'

'So you're her patient now?' Sarah said. 'Or is it me who's the patient? This is getting ridiculous.'

'I'm not her patient,' Ben said. 'And neither are you. And I didn't give anything away. I was only asking about the books.'

'So why the awkward pause when I showed up?'

There was a long silence. 'I think you may be reading a bit too much into this,' Ben said, his voice low and quiet. 'And I think you might want to take it easy on the wine.'

'Oh,' Sarah said, feeling her neck and face flush. 'So I'm an alcoholic now, too?'

'I didn't say that. All I said was, you might want to take it easy. I don't think it's helping.'

She stood up, taking care to do it as steadily as she could. 'I'll drink,' she said, 'what I damn well want.'

He nodded. 'OK. Enjoy it.'

She went into the kitchen. She stared out of the window, watching the trees sway in the breeze. Who was doing this? Who had sent the books? The only people who could have done were her and Ben. So was it her husband? Was he doing this?

It couldn't be. Ben would have to be someone so utterly different to the man she knew that she couldn't believe it was him. Which left her.

But it wasn't her. She wasn't doing all this. She knew she wasn't, and the only way she was wrong was if she was crazy.

And she wasn't crazy.

Her head was swimming, a combination of anxiety and alcohol. She tipped the wine into the sink and filled the glass with water. Ben was right; it wasn't helping.

Then she went upstairs to shower away the salt and sand of the sea and put an end to this day.

31

Sarah buried her head under her pillow. There was a buzzing noise in the room.

Probably one of the huge flies that made Maine their home during the summer. She tried to ignore the sound; despite dumping out the last glass of wine and replacing it with water she had woken up with a headache. Maybe a hangover, maybe stress: either way, the noise of the fly was not helping.

Damn, it was annoying. When Kim had woken up – she was an early, noisy riser – Sarah had nudged Ben and asked him to get up with her. He had, which meant this was a rare chance to have a lie-in.

Which was in danger of being ruined by this fly.

It was one of the mysteries of life: you could fall asleep in a noisy airplane or with the TV on, but one little buzzing fly was enough to destroy any chance of nodding off. It wasn't the volume, either: there was a particularly irritating quality about a fly's buzz.

She took her head from under the pillow. She was going to have to kill it if she was going to go back to sleep. She looked around the room; there was no sign of any fly.

But the buzzing was still there, and, she noticed, it was

constant. It didn't rise and fall or stop from time to time like a fly would. It went on, a constant drone.

And it was coming from outside the window.

She got to her feet and opened the blinds. The noise was definitely louder here. It seemed to be coming from above the house. She craned her neck to look up, but the roof of the house was in the way.

She pulled on a pair of shorts and a tank top and headed downstairs. At the bottom of the stairs there was a note in Ben's cursive script:

Taken kids to Little Cat for breakfast. See you there?

It sounded good. Coffee and a breakfast sandwich. She'd figure out what was making the buzzing noise then head down to see them all.

In the kitchen she opened the back door and stepped on to the grass. The buzzing was louder outside; it was definitely coming from above her. She looked up. The sky was blue and cloudless. She was expecting to see a plane or a helicopter, but there was only the unbroken summer sky.

And then it appeared.

A square white box the size of a paperback book moved slowly over the roofline and into view. There were four spinning blades – each like a helicopter rotor – keeping it up in the air.

She tensed. For a second she had a feeling this must be what it was like the moments before a military drone showed up and started firing at people: out of the blue a faceless machine appeared, close enough so you couldn't miss it, but high enough so there was nothing you could do about it.

It stopped directly over her head, and then started to slowly descend.

Sarah sprinted inside and slammed the door. She turned

the lock. The main panel of the door was glass and she pressed her face to it and looked upward, her ragged breathing fogging up the window.

The thing was still coming down. She watched as it descended until it was dead level with her head. It hovered, six feet from the back door, the four blades spinning, the buzzing much louder.

She stared at it. There was a kind of tube suspended from the main body. As she looked, it tilted until it was facing her.

It was a lens, she realized. This thing was carrying some kind of camera.

She was being observed.

The machine moved toward the door.

She screamed, and ran back from the window. She looked around for her phone then remembered it was next to the bed, so she bolted up the stairs two at a time and grabbed it. As she typed in her passcode, she realized the buzzing was gone.

She looked out of the window. Nothing. No machine, and no noise.

Hands shaking, she called Ben.

'Hi,' he said. 'You coming to breakfast? I can order for you, if you're feeling better.'

'I'm fine,' she said. 'But, Ben – there was – there was a thing here.'

'What do you mean?'

'There was a – some kind of machine. In the backyard. Like a helicopter.'

'Sarah,' Ben said. 'You're not making much sense. Are you sure you're OK? Do you want us to come home?'

'No,' Sarah said. 'I want to get out of here. I'll come to you. I'll explain then.'

*   *   *

142

She sat in the café and told him what had happened at the house.

'It sounds like a quadcopter,' Ben said.

A quadcopter. That made perfect sense: the four helicopter-like rotors. What didn't make sense was what the hell it was doing in her backyard.

What the hell it was doing looking at her through the glass panel of her back door.

He tapped on the screen of his phone then handed it to her.

'Was it like these?'

It was a page from Amazon showing a selection of quad-copters ranging in price from around thirty dollars up to a few thousand. Some had cameras, some did not.

'Yes,' she said. 'It was exactly like those.'

'Then it was a quadcopter,' Ben said. 'Probably with a camera which would have been sending a feed to a phone or tablet. Whoever's flying it can see whatever it sees. They have good resolution.'

Sarah's vision blurred, then started to swim, then narrowed. Her heart began to speed up and her throat constricted. She felt suddenly precarious, unbalanced, as though the wooden chair she was sitting on would collapse underneath her.

She gripped the edges of the table, squeezing hard in an attempt both to steady herself and to give some kind of focus to her attention. She forced herself to breathe deeply, but it felt like the air was not getting into her lungs.

I'm dying, she thought, her mind out of control. *I can't do this. I can't take it. This has to stop.*

She became aware of a pressure on her bicep and someone calling her name, and she looked up to see Ben, his face bending over hers, his expression a mixture of shock and worry.

'Sarah,' he said. 'Sarah! Can you hear me? Are you OK?'

She blinked, and tried to nod. 'Fresh air,' she muttered, each word an effort.

Ben called to Miles, who was playing with the toys the café provided.

'Miles,' he said. 'Keep an eye on the girls. I have to take Mum outside for a second.'

One of the baristas appeared next to him.

'I'll watch them,' she said. 'Is she OK?'

'I think so,' Ben said. 'She needs air.'

'Should I bring out a glass of water?' the barista said.

Ben nodded. 'That would be great. Thanks.' He looked at Sarah. 'You ready?'

She let him help her from her seat and guide her outside. She was aware of people watching but she didn't care. She needed to get outside with a primal urgency and her legs felt too weak to carry her there, so Ben's assistance was vital.

He led her to a chair at an unoccupied table, and she slumped into it. A few seconds later, the barista put a tall glass of water in front of her. Hands shaking, she lifted it to her lips and took a sip.

'I think the worst is over,' she said.

'One too many glasses of wine last night,' Ben said, in the tone of voice he used when he was feeling uncomfortable and so decided to try and undo the discomfort by cracking a joke. Sarah usually found it endearing.

But not now.

'Ben,' she said. 'Even for you, that's a crappy joke.'

'Sorry,' he said. 'Didn't know what else to say. Did you have a panic attack?'

She nodded.

'Damn,' he said. 'I know you said you'd had another but I was hoping those were over.'

'Sorry to disappoint you,' she replied.

'I'm not disappointed for me,' he said. 'I'm disappointed for you.' He put a hand on her shoulder. 'Feeling better?'

'Yes. A bit.' She was, in a way. At least the symptoms had gone. But there was a feeling lodged in her sternum, a feeling of trepidation and fear.

Because she knew this would not be the last time this happened, and that was the worst thing about it.

32

She is starting to understand, now, dimly. Starting to perceive that this is real. This is not an elaborate joke, not an Internet scam, not a mistake.

This is deliberate. Someone is doing this, and they are doing it for a reason.

It was written all over her smug, stupid face when she saw the camera, although the smugness did not remain for long. It vanished quickly enough, replaced by fear.

The stupidity remained, though.

Of course, she is not stupid by normal measures. She graduated from Middlebury College – obviously, since people like her lack the imagination and curiosity to go to college anywhere other than places like Middlebury – and then went to medical school. Both of those things require intelligence.

But she is still stupid, and in the most important way.

She knows lots about lots of things, but she does not know herself. She does not know what she truly is. She is unable to see it. Her fancy education was unable to enlighten her about that.

But she will find out. Her education will be completed.

And soon. Everything is in place. It is only a matter of time.

33

She called Ian Molyneux when they got home and told him about the quadcopter.

'It's getting worse,' she said. 'That's what worries me. It was in my backyard, with a camera.'

'The problem,' Ian said, 'is that no laws have been broken. People can fly those things more or less wherever they want.'

'On to someone's property?' Sarah said. 'Really?'

'Well, if someone flew one into your house there might be a problem. Or if they used it to take photos of your kids. But buzzing you? I'm not sure what I could charge them with. If I even knew who to charge. But we have no idea who it was. Same as all the other stuff.'

'Don't those things have a range?' Sarah asked. 'Whoever was flying it must have been close by, right?'

'Right,' Ian said. 'But they could have been in a car. I'll ask around. See if anyone saw someone who looked like they were controlling one of those things. I'm guessing whoever did it wasn't wandering about in plain sight, though.'

'OK,' Sarah said. 'Thanks. Let me know if you find anything out.'

She put the phone down and went into the kitchen. Ben was pouring hot water into the teapot.

'I'm going to stay off work next week,' she said. 'I don't want the kids in camp. I'm going to stay home with them.'

He looked up at her. 'Are you sure?'

'Yes. This is getting out of control, Ben.'

He nodded. 'It does seem like that.' He walked over to her and put his arms around her. 'Are you feeling better?'

'In a way I am. I'm not having a panic attack, which is a relief. But I'm scared, Ben. And you know what freaks me out the most? When I was talking to Ian Molyneux I asked if those things had a range—'

'They do,' Ben said. 'Some are quite a long way. The more expensive ones.'

'Right. But even the expensive ones don't have *that* big of a range. Not, say, a hundred miles.'

'No. Not that far.'

'Which means the person who was controlling it was nearby. They were *right there*. Maybe only a hundred yards from our house. From our kids.'

Ben stiffened. 'Right,' he said. 'Of course. Shit.'

'Someone is after us, Ben. They're after me, I think. And I don't know who, or why, or what they plan to do. I don't have a clue. And there's nothing I can do about it. Not a goddamn thing.' She sat on the couch. 'And it's sending me fucking nuts.'

'I don't get it,' Ben said. 'This has come out of nowhere. And there's no pattern. Someone impersonating you on Facebook is one thing, but then there's the books and the email to Marla and the quadcopter.' He shook his head. 'I can't for the life of me see what anybody gains from this.'

'Which is my point,' Sarah said. 'But they want something. And until this is over, I'm not letting the kids out of my sight.'

'I agree,' Ben said. 'This has gone too far. The other puzzle

148

is who could actually do all these things. Figure that out, and I think we have the answer.'

'No one could do it, though. No one has access to my photos or Amazon account. Unless it's some kind of hacker, but I don't know where to even start with that.'

'Money?' Ben said. 'Do you think it might be about money?'

'How?'

'Someone creates all this mess and then asks for money to stop it? A kind of digital blackmail?'

'It could be,' Sarah said. 'I hope it is. Because if all they want is some money they can have it. Which, right now, seems like the best outcome.'

Right now, she would have handed over everything she owned to stop this, but somehow she didn't think it would be that easy.

34

'I want to go to camp!' Miles was red-faced, his arms folded, his expression fierce. 'It's so boring here and all my friends are there! I don't see why I can't go!'

He had a point. It was only midday on Monday and Sarah had pretty much run out of stuff for the kids to do. Kim was fine; she was happy to follow Sarah around, but Miles and Faye were a different matter. They needed structure and lots of activities. Drawing, playing with Lego, watering the plants: all done, and all rejected as boring. She understood: they wanted to be with their friends.

But she could not take the risk.

'Miles,' she said. 'I'm sorry – I know you're frustrated, but camp is off for this week. Maybe you can go back next week, but—'

'A week is so long!' he said. 'I can't wait a week!'

Me too, Sarah thought. Even if he did go back to day camp the next week – which was not guaranteed – the next six days seemed awfully long.

It turned out they were not so bad, after all. On Tuesday she packed up a lunch and they went for a hike in the woods;

Wednesday they went to Splashland, a trip which filled the whole day, and Thursday Sarah took them on the ferry from Portland to Great Diamond Island, where they had an ice cream and a swim on the beach.

And the best thing was that nothing strange happened: no emails, no books delivered, no spying quadcopters.

Sarah was starting – no more than starting – to hope it might all be over.

They got back from Portland shortly after 4 p.m. Ben's car was in the driveway.

'Oh,' Sarah said. 'Dad's home early.' It was unusual, but good news: she didn't feel like cooking dinner, so maybe Ben would be up for going out to eat.

He was sitting at the kitchen table, his laptop on his knee. Sarah walked over and bent down to kiss him.

He turned his face away from hers. He looked at her, his expression serious. Stern, even. She felt her throat tighten.

'Ben?' she said. 'Is everything OK?'

'We need to talk,' he said. 'Now.'

Sarah settled the kids in front of the television and went to join Ben in the kitchen. She opened the refrigerator door and took out a bottle of white wine.

'Why don't you hold on before starting on the booze,' Ben said. He picked up his work bag from the floor and reached inside. He took out a large envelope. 'This came to the office today,' he said. 'Take a look.'

The tightness in Sarah's throat intensified. The hope she had been starting to entertain that whatever had been going on was over evaporated.

'What is it?' she said. 'What is it this time?'

He looked at her. His gaze was, she noticed, skeptical, which was not what she would have expected.

151

'I'm surprised you have to ask,' he said.

'What do you mean?'

'Like I said. Take a look.'

She picked up the envelope and opened the flap. It was heavy; a book.

'Before you take it out, look at the address,' he said.

She turned the envelope so she could read it. She could not understand what she saw.

'Ben,' she said. 'This is – this is—'

'Your handwriting,' he said. 'But there's more. Get the book out.'

She pulled it out and read the title:

Dealing with Bereavement: Coping with Parental Suicide.

She shook her head, then read it again.

'Ben,' she said. 'I don't know what's going on. I didn't send this. I promise.'

'Really?' he said. 'Open the book. Front page.'

'Why are you being like this?' she said. 'Why are you being so mean?'

'I'm not being anything,' Ben said. His expression softened. 'I just want to find out what's going on. Open the book. There's an inscription.'

She turned the cover. There, in her handwriting, was a message.

Ben, it began, *I'm sorry to have to do this by such an unusual method but it's the only way I can think of. I need help, Ben. I'm drowning. I'm sending you this book because this is what I am worried it may come to, and I don't want it to. I don't want the kids to grow up without a mom, and I don't want you to spend the rest of your life wondering whether you could have or should have done more to help me.*

So help me now, Ben. I love you, and I know you
love me, so help me.
    Sarah

'So,' Ben said. His expression now was pure concern.
'What's going on, Sarah?'

35

Sarah looked at Ben for a long time. There was a kind of resigned finality in his tone, a tone which said *OK, enough is enough. It's time to come clean.* She took a deep breath.

'I don't understand the question, Ben,' she said.

'It's pretty simple. I want to know what's been happening.'

'And how would I know?'

Ben massaged his temples; he closed his eyes, as though she was making him frustrated and impatient because of her irrational stubbornness.

'Sarah,' he said. 'This is *your* handwriting.'

'No it isn't,' she said. 'It might look like my handwriting, but it isn't my handwriting. I'd know, because I didn't write it.'

'Then who did?'

It was now Sarah's turn to feel frustrated and impatient.

'I don't know!' she said. 'That's the whole point! It's the same person who wrote the email and posted on Facebook and did all the other crazy shit, and if I knew who it was, we wouldn't be having this conversation.'

'So you're asking me to believe that somebody forged your handwriting to send me a book about coping with suicide and ask for my help, a few days after the same person sent you books on how to cope with depression, which came—'

'From my account, I know. I don't have the answers, Ben, but I'm asking you to believe me. I didn't send this book or write this message.'

'Sarah,' Ben said. 'I am your friend in all of this. I'm the person who can help you. And I will. But I have to know what's going on.'

'And I told you!' She was shouting, aware she was losing control both of the conversation and herself. 'Someone else is doing this!'

There was a strained patience in Ben's voice now. 'This is *your* handwriting,' he said. 'It really is.'

Sarah sat on the couch. She felt suddenly drained. 'So what's your explanation, Ben? What exactly *do* you want me to admit?'

'The truth.'

'Which I already told you. But you clearly have something else in mind. So go ahead. Tell me what you think's going on.'

Ben nodded. 'This is only a theory, OK? I'm not saying it's true. I'm asking you to *consider* it.'

'Don't soft-pedal me, Ben. Spit it out.'

'OK.' He sat on a bar stool, then stood up again. It was like, Sarah thought, he was in court. 'One possible explanation,' he began, then stopped. 'Well, let me take you through the logic, OK?'

'OK,' she said. 'Take me through the logic.'

'So, whoever did this had the ability to get access to a number of things: our house, your Amazon account, the contact details of your friends. They also were able to get close enough to take photos of me and you and your friends and our family without being noticed. And they can copy

155

your handwriting.' He gave a little shrug. 'One of those things would be tough enough, but all of them? Almost impossible.'

'But not impossible,' Sarah said. 'Obviously. Or it wouldn't have happened.'

'Unless it is impossible,' Ben said. 'Which would leave only one person who we know has the ability to do all of those things.'

'Who is?' Sarah said, already pretty sure where this was headed.

Ben could not look at her. 'You,' he said, softly. Even though she had been half-expecting him to say it, it was still a shock when he did. Sarah started to protest, but he raised his hand. 'Let me finish,' he said. 'Please.'

'OK,' she replied. 'Finish, and *then* I'll tell you what bullshit this is.'

'The other problem here is motive,' Ben said. 'Even if someone could do this, why would they?'

'And why would *I*?' Sarah said. 'Your little theory doesn't answer that, does it?'

'It does,' Ben said. 'And like I said, this is only a theory, OK? But let's say you were struggling in some way. With – I don't know – depression or anxiety or whatever. And it was worse than you wanted to admit, even to yourself—'

'This is bullshit, Ben,' Sarah said. He ignored her and carried on talking.

' —and so you devised a way to bring it to my attention—'

'Stop it, Ben. Stop it now. This is total rubbish.'

'—and that's what all this is about. It's a cry for help. I mean, it's written right there in—'

'I said stop it!' Sarah shouted. 'Fucking stop it right now, Ben! This is bullshit, OK! Bullshit!'

'Mom?' Miles had opened the living room door and was looking at them. 'Mom? Are you all right?'

Sarah looked back at him. She wasn't, she wasn't at all, but she nodded. 'Yes,' she said. 'I'm fine. We're having a discussion.'

'It sounds like you're fighting.'

She glanced at Ben, and held her arms out. He moved toward her and hugged her. It was awkward, but they had made a promise to each other on the day they brought Miles home from the hospital that they would try not to argue in front of him – and any future siblings – and if they did, they would immediately make up.

It had become part of how they operated and who they were, so Sarah took it for granted, but it had been Ben's idea. Holding a sleeping, tiny Miles he had looked at his wife and told her all he wanted for his son was for him to be happy.

And to be happy he needs to feel loved, and secure. Until he's older – much older – we're all he has, Ben said. *And I want him to know we're there for him.*

Sarah had agreed, then asked why he was thinking like that.

My parents used to argue, he said. *I don't know if it was more than other parents or not, but I used to hear it and lie in bed – I must have been about eight at the time – convinced they were going to divorce. And, not knowing anything about how those things worked, I thought I'd have to choose who I lived with. I agonized over it. Tortured myself. How could I choose? How could I let one of them down? So I don't want my kids to go through the same thing. If they see us argue, we have to make up right there and then, so they see there's nothing wrong.*

And they had, ever since. This time, Sarah looked at Miles and smiled.

'Don't worry,' she said. 'We're not fighting. Not in the way you think. We have some important stuff to work out, that's all.'

He looked at them for a while, then nodded. 'OK,' he said, and closed the door.

The hug – enforced by the arrival of Miles – had broken the spell. The argument had been building into a wall that forced them apart, put each of them into their own box, but it had fallen away when they came together physically.

Sarah relaxed; she would explain to Ben why this was a mistake and they would move on.

'Look,' she said. 'I know this is hard to believe – forged letters and weird books – but I didn't do it. I promise, Ben. If I had, and this was a cry for help, now is when I'd admit it, and we could face it together. But it isn't. And for future reference, if ever I am in desperate need, then I'll come right out and tell you.'

'But it's your handwriting, Sarah,' he said. 'It's so hard to believe someone forged it. I mean, I know your handwriting, and this is it.'

'So you don't trust me?' she said, anger and disbelief growing. 'You think I'm lying?'

'I don't know what to think,' Ben said, softly.

'Let me help you figure it out,' Sarah said. 'There's one thing your theory doesn't account for.'

'Which is?'

'The drone.'

'Quadcopter.'

'Right. Whatever. Quadcopter. But here's the thing – how could I have been flying it? All the rest of the stuff I could have done – although it's totally insane to think I did – but not that. I wouldn't even know where to start with one of those.' She kissed him on the mouth. 'And here's another thing. The most important thing: I'm telling you the truth. I'm your wife. I don't lie to you. I won't lie to you.'

158

He looked up at her. She was startled to see tears in his eyes.

'You promise?' he said. 'You promise you won't lie to me?'

'I promise,' she said.

36

On Friday night Sarah was flicking through the options on Netflix when Ben put his head around the door.

'I'm going to bed,' he said.

Sarah glanced up. 'It's only nine o'clock,' she said. 'You want to watch a mindless TV show?'

'No. I'm tired. I need an early night.'

It had been that way between them since the argument: polite, courteous, but cagey. Sarah wanted it to stop, wanted them to go back to their easy-going, intimate relationship. She wanted to hold her arms out and hug him and have him hug her back and then reassure her he loved her and for her to reply that she loved him and it was all going to be OK, and then maybe kiss and have urgent, frantic sex. But she didn't. Marriages – theirs, at any rate – didn't work like that. Walls went up, arguments lingered, noses were cut off to spite faces. For some reason it was easier to cling to your pride, even when you didn't really want to, than to let it go and be the one who initiated the make-up.

'Good night,' Sarah said. 'Sleep well.' She turned back to the television and listened to him pad up the stairs.

*　　*　　*

A few minutes after midnight she followed him. She'd stayed up late, binge-watching a ten-year-old family comedy show. Despite the lack of sleep in the last few days she felt wired and alert, and knew there was no way she would be able to switch off until she was totally exhausted.

When she got in bed, she realized Ben was still awake.

He pretended he wasn't, though.

It was pointless of him – she knew what his sleeping body looked like. She had lain beside it often enough. There was a stillness, a depth, that a waking person could not simulate. Doctors had a test to see whether someone was truly unconscious: they would lift an arm and drop it. Someone who was faking it – and people did, for all kinds of reasons – could not, however hard they tried, let an arm fall like it did when its owner was asleep. There was always some resistance, some muscular engagement.

But if he wanted to pretend, she'd let him.

She lay beside him, also not sleeping, listening to the creaks the house made and wondering if they were the footsteps of an intruder.

She'd never been a very relaxed person; she'd always had a heightened sense of the threats out there in the world. When they went camping in the woods she imagined bears behind every tree, even if they were in an established campsite with many other campers; if she went swimming in the ocean she spent most of the time wondering what was below, and she was never far from interpreting some shadow as a shark and setting off, arms whirling, for the safety of the beach.

She was the same at night. Often she awoke in the small hours, convinced she had heard a noise, terrified someone was there, creeping about, ax in hand. It could take hours for her to calm down and go back to sleep unless she went downstairs and checked every door and window. Ben did not suffer from the same fears. He slept soundly, swam fearlessly, camped with abandon.

She reached out a hand and placed it on his shoulder. He was hot to the touch.

'Ben?' she said.

After a pause he shifted and turned to her. He opened one eye.

'Yes?'

'You're still awake?'

He nodded. 'Couldn't nod off.'

'Everything OK?'

'So-so,' he said. 'But then you know that.'

'I don't think I'll be able to sleep,' she said. 'I can't relax. I can't get all this stuff out of my head.'

'Me too,' he said. 'I keep trying to think of what I – we – can do, but I come up blank.'

Sarah slid her hand lower until it rested on his hip. 'You know,' she said. 'There is some evidence that having sex produces a hormone which helps with relaxation and sleep.'

'Really? Or are you making that up so you can get in my pants?' Ben said.

'I'm a doctor,' Sarah said. 'That would be unethical.'

'How much evidence for the existence of this hormone?' Ben said.

'Some. Not enough.' She pressed herself up against him. 'I think we need to do an experiment.'

The next morning, Ben woke late. When he came downstairs, Sarah smiled at him.

'Miles and Faye have karate,' she said. 'But I'll take all three of them. You have a morning off.'

'You sure? I'm happy to stay with Kim.'

'It's fine. She can come. She'll have a good time.'

Miles and Faye went to karate lessons on Saturday mornings

at a local martial arts center, Riverland. It was the first session back after a two-week summer break.

The center was a few miles away, in a rural setting by a small river. Sarah watched as the instructors led the kids – dressed in black karate uniforms – over a series of obstacles and stations where they performed martial arts exercises. She had been skeptical at first, but the training was largely focused on drawing lessons from nature and on building physical strength and balance, not, as she had first thought, on learning how to fight.

When it was finished, Miles and Faye ran up to her.

'Have you got any snacks?' Miles said. He asked with an unusual intensity; Sarah recognized it as a sign he was running low on energy. At work a few weeks ago someone had described themselves as 'hangry', a new word which was a combination of 'hungry' and 'angry' and which was perfect for Miles when he did not eat.

And she had neglected to bring snacks.

'I don't,' she said, and saw the 'hanger' flash in his eyes. 'But why don't we go to the Little Cat Café and get a treat.'

'Yay!' Faye said. 'Can I get a blueberry muffin?'

'Sure,' Sarah said. 'You all can. Let's go.'

'Look,' Miles said, as they walked from the car to the Little Cat Café, 'Daddy's here.'

'Where?' Sarah said.

'Inside,' Miles replied. 'His bike's there.'

Ben had an old green (British Racing Green, he called it) Raleigh racing bike that he had bought when he was a student in London. It was scratched and beaten, but he refused to replace it, although for what he paid to maintain it – the parts were hard to find – he could have bought a decent new bike every few years.

'Oh,' Sarah said. 'Great! You can tell him about karate.'

She bent down to pick up Kim; she was a handful at the best of times, but having her running about while Sarah tried to order promised to be quite a pain. It was going to be useful to be able to hand her to Ben.

She saw him immediately, sitting on a stool at the bar along the rear wall. He was facing the other way, but she knew the back of his head as well as she did the front. After nearly ten years of marriage it was easy to pick out your husband or wife in a crowd – hair, gait, clothes: there was rarely a new perspective on your partner.

It took her a moment to realize he was not alone. He was talking to someone, nodding vigorously as he listened.

The someone was also familiar.

It was Rachel Little.

Sarah pulled a chair out from under a table. 'Sit here, Faye,' she said. 'Miles, you join her. Stay there until I get back.'

She set off across the café. It was busy, full of late break-fasters and early brunchers, and she had to push through the people lining up to place their orders.

And then she was no more than a few feet from Ben and Rachel. She was slightly behind Rachel, out of her eyeline, and Ben was too absorbed in their conversation to notice her.

'There is a thing,' Rachel said, 'called dissociative fugue—'

'I've heard of it,' Ben said. 'But go on. I'm not an expert.'

'When it happens, people can do all kinds of things – go on long trips, have detailed conversations, commit crimes – which they don't remember at all. They can have no memory of them. It's often,' she continued, 'linked to people taking a new identity.'

'In this case, it would be her *own* identity,' Ben said. 'Which—'

Before he could finish, Kim noticed who was speaking.

164

'Dada!' she shouted, and reached for him. 'Dada!'

Ben's head snapped round like he'd heard a pistol shot. He paled.

'Kim,' he said. 'Sarah.'

Sarah stared at him. She handed Kim to him. Without her daughter to hold she realized she was shaking.

He'd been talking about *her*. Asking for advice about *her*. Talking about dissociative fugue. She was a doctor – which was more than Rachel Little could say – and she knew what it was.

And what it meant. It meant he thought she was doing all of this while in some kind of fugue state. And he was sharing it with Rachel fucking Little.

She wasn't sure exactly how she felt: betrayal, shock, confusion were all mixed in, but there was no doubt about one thing.

She was angry.

'Your kids are sitting over there,' she said, straining to keep from shouting, her eyes locked on his. 'You can bring them home.'

'Sarah,' Rachel said. 'Let's—'

'Shut up!' Sarah said. A few heads turned to see what was going on. 'Not another word!'

She looked back at Ben and took the keys from her pocket. 'You'll need these,' she said, and threw them at him.

37

She is facing the end now. The walls are closing in.

The past is coming back to haunt her. Actions cannot be denied; consequences are real. Consequences are inevitable.

The price must be paid.

And her price is that everybody she knows will doubt her. Will turn away from her.

Until eventually she will start to doubt herself. After all, there is only one explanation for all this.

At least, that is what she – and others – will conclude.

And they will go on believing it, for the rest of their lives.

The only one who will find out the *real* reason is her. But it will not help her at all.

38

The bike had fallen over.

He'll be pissed at that, Sarah thought. Not the scratch – there are already plenty of those – but the fact someone knocked it over and didn't pick it up.

She lowered the seat and climbed on; it was unlocked. He never locked it; Barrow wasn't the kind of town where people stole bikes, according to Ben, and in any case, who'd want his? All they'd be getting was a constant repair bill.

She rode – it really was a very uncomfortable bike – along the river path. The river, once one of the most polluted in North America, victim of the tanneries and paper mills which used to line its banks, now shone under the summer sun. Cormorants bobbed on the surface, white pines and firs framed the shore.

Sarah saw none of it. All she saw was the image of Ben facing Rachel, listening intently, absorbed in what she was saying.

Absorbed in her bullshit theory about Sarah suffering from dissociative fugue, episodes in which she entered a different state, became, almost, a different person, a person who did things and thought things and said things Sarah had no memory of.

It was not Sarah's area of medical specialty, but it was a well-recognized phenomenon. It was the idea behind Robert Louis Stevenson's book *The Strange Case of Dr Jekyll and Mr Hyde,* and now it was Ben's explanation – prompted by that bitch Rachel Little – for the Fake Sarah Havenant.

Except in this case there was no Mr Hyde. This was The Strange Case of Sarah Havenant and Sarah Havenant.

The problem was, it was all rubbish. She was not having dissociative fugue, not doing all this stuff and then not remembering it. She would have doubted herself, she really would, but for one thing: she knew it wasn't true, because she had seen the quadcopter. She remembered it. If this was fugue, then she would have no memory of it, but she did. And that one fact allowed her to cling to her sanity. Whoever was behind this had made a mistake, so fuck them.

And fuck Ben and fuck Rachel Little.

She stopped and got off the bike.

She was so *angry* at him. She couldn't believe he had done it – arranged a secret meeting with Rachel Little to talk about her, about his own wife. What else was he lying about? Was he fucking Rachel?

Sarah doubted it, but she wasn't sure. If he could betray her like this, then why not like that?

The *bastard.*

She looked at the river. It flowed on below the bike path. It got very deep, very close to the banks, apparently.

Good. Then they would never find this.

She picked up Ben's bike and hurled it over the railings. She knew she shouldn't do this, it wasn't good for the river, but she felt the river gods would allow her this one small trespass on their territory.

There was a loud splash, and then the bike was gone.

When she got home the car was in the driveway. She heard Miles's voice coming from the backyard so she opened the gate and walked around the side of the house.

He was standing by a hole in the flowerbed, a small metal beach shovel in his hand. Next to him, Faye was holding a hose which was spraying water into the hole. Kim was on the other side of the hole in only her diaper.

'OK,' Miles said. 'Kim, you get in the swimming pool.'

Kim grinned as though someone had offered her a lifetime's supply of chocolate, and stepped into the watery hole, like a tiny and very cute hippopotamus wallowing in its mud.

'Erm,' Sarah said. 'Miles and Faye, are you sure that's a good idea?'

Kim glowered at her. 'Go away, Mommy,' she said.

So her baby didn't want rescuing after all. It was the lot of the third child; anything to get some attention.

'Fine,' she said. 'But make sure you wash off before you come in the house.'

Miles's eyes widened at the thought of a parentally sanctioned hosing down of his sisters. 'Cool, Mom,' he said. 'We will.'

Inside the kitchen, Ben was standing at the counter, looking at his phone. Sarah was pretty sure he wasn't really reading it. He was finding something to do while he waited for her.

He looked up, and put the phone in his pocket. Sarah stared at him. It was odd how the way you saw someone could change so quickly. Normally he appeared to her as a soft-edged, warm person; now he was different; harder, somehow and more real.

169

He didn't look, she noticed, apologetic.

'Hey,' he said. 'How did you get back? Did you take the bike?'

She nodded.

'Where is it?'

She felt her anger – already at a dangerously high level – mount further. 'You want to talk about your bike?' she said. 'Really?'

'No,' he said. 'Of course not. I'm sorry.'

'We can,' she said. 'It's in the river, since you're so concerned.'

'The river?' he said. 'What river?'

'The big wet one downtown.'

He blinked. She could see he was fighting hard not to react.

'Sarah,' he said. 'You threw my bike in the river?'

'Yes,' she said. 'I did.'

'Right.' He shook his head. 'We need to talk.'

'We certainly do,' Sarah said. 'Let me start. Are you sleeping with her? Or just betraying my secrets to her? Having some chit-chats about whether or not I'm crazy?'

'Let's get this part of the conversation out of the way,' Ben said. 'I went there for some fresh air and to read the paper. Rachel showed up and said hello and we got chatting. She asked after you, and I mentioned a few things and she asked some questions and – she's very easy to talk to. And it's been on my mind. It was nice to get it off my chest. I'm sorry.' He shrugged. 'But not too sorry.'

Sarah shook her head. She was finding it hard to believe he was so dismissive of the situation. 'Not too sorry? You go behind my back—'

He lifted his hand. In it he was holding a piece of paper.

'Don't talk to me about going behind people's backs,' he

said. There was a bitterness in his voice which she had never heard before.

'What do you mean?' she said. 'What's does that say?'

He held it out. His expression was cold and distant.

'Read it,' he said.

39

She took the paper and looked down. It was a letter, hand-written.

Handwritten in her handwriting.

'Ben,' she said. 'I don't under—'

'Read it,' he said. 'Before you say anything, read it.'

She started to read.

Dear Ben,

How are you my darling? Well, I hope, and I apologize in advance if this letter changes that, which, sadly, I think it will.

Ben, I love you. I have since I met you and I will, always. What I am about to tell you does not change or alter this in any way. Please keep this in mind as you read this.

I am not perfect, Ben. None of us are. We all make mistakes, and I want – need – to confess mine to you. It was a long time ago, three years, and I was hoping it could remain in the past, but sadly it cannot.

Sarah closed her eyes as she realized what this was. She lowered the paper to her side.

'Finish it,' Ben said. 'Then we can talk.'

The reason – and I hope you can take this into account – is my conscience. I cannot live with the guilt. I have no doubt you would never find out about this – you haven't so far – but I have to tell you for my peace of mind. At least, whatever other faults I have, I will be able to say I have been honest.

I had an affair, Ben. Brief, and meaningless, but an affair all the same. It was with Josh, my physical therapist. We had sex, but only once, and I regretted it immediately afterwards. During, in fact. And I never saw him again.

But now I need you to know. I'm sorry, more than you can understand. And I hope you can forgive me.

Your loving wife,
Sarah

'Well,' he said. 'I'm glad you regretted it while it was happening.' He gave a false, high-pitched laugh. 'It would be much worse if you said you'd enjoyed it!'

Sarah looked from Ben to the letter and back to Ben. She didn't know where to start. She could deny sending the letter, but that wouldn't help with what it contained. And, by denying it, she would be saying she had not been planning to come clean, which was the only saving grace in this mess.

But then by admitting it, she'd be admitting she had sent the book and all the rest of the stuff. She'd be admitting she was behind all of it.

And maybe she was. Because who else knew about the affair? No one.

Apart from Josh. But it couldn't be him. He was living in

Montana now, at least she thought he was. But maybe not. Maybe he was back, and he had a grudge against her, and he was the one doing all this.

She had no idea. But she would have to think about it later. For now, she had a bigger problem.

'You know,' Ben said. 'Since I got home from Little Cat and found this in the mail, I kept asking myself whether this is some kind of a joke. Whether this is all part of the weird shit that's been going on. But looking at your face I can see it's not. This really happened, didn't it?'

Sarah nodded. 'Yes,' she said. 'It did. But – it's complicated. And I didn't send the letter, Ben.'

He closed his eyes. 'This has to stop, Sarah. There's no one else it could be. You need to admit it's you, and, if you are doing it in some kind of fugue state, then you need to come to terms with it.'

'It isn't me,' she said. 'I'm not crazy.'

He stared at her. 'Maybe not,' he said. He gestured at the letter. 'But either way. Why? Why did you do it?'

'I'll tell you,' she said. 'It's not a great story, and it won't make you feel better, but I'll tell you, if you want me to.'

'Tell me,' he said.

40

'This is not an excuse,' Sarah said. 'I don't expect you to forgive me when you hear it. But it is the explanation. It's feeble and pathetic but it's what happened.'

'Go on.'

'It was when I was having the panic attacks, when they were at their worst,' she said. 'Before we had Kim. I felt so hollow. It was as though there was a gray curtain between me and the world. I couldn't engage with anything – you, Miles, work—'

'I remember,' he said. 'It was awful.'

'Then you'll remember how desperate I was,' she said. 'I lived in constant terror of another panic attack – they could happen at any time. Maybe that's why I couldn't engage with anything – because I had to withdraw to protect myself. And I didn't know how I could go on, how I could live the rest of my life in fear.' She looked into his eyes. 'I thought about killing myself, Ben. And then I met Josh and for some reason it made me feel better. He was a way out, maybe because he was so totally outside the rest of my life.'

'So he was a way out from your terrible, shitty life? Not

me? Not your husband? I couldn't make you feel better, but he could?' He shook his head. 'This isn't exactly helping, Sarah.'

'I'm not trying to help. I'm just telling you the truth. And it didn't last. We had sex, once. And as soon as we did, I snapped out of it. I realized he was not what I needed. What I needed was you and the kids and proper treatment. And then I ended it.'

'You said you wouldn't lie to me,' he said. 'The other day. I asked you if you would lie to me and you said you wouldn't. Yet all along that's exactly what you've been doing. How can I trust what you say now?'

'Because I'm telling the truth. I have no reason not to.'

Ben rubbed his eyes with his forefingers. He looked wretched. Pale, eyes sunken, the muscles in his face slack. This was, she saw, devastating for him. Their family was all he had, and it was now at risk.

'Is she mine?' he said. 'Kim?'

Sarah rubbed her temples. 'Yes,' she said, simply. 'Yes, she is. It was one time, Ben. We used a condom. She's your daughter. And if you need to take tests to have peace of mind, then you should go ahead.'

He nodded, slowly.

'Ben,' she said. 'I love you. And we'll get through this, I promise. We're going to keep our family together. You know that, right?'

'I don't know anything,' he said. 'I don't know whether I can trust you when you tell me about your affair, and I don't know whether I can trust you when you tell me you didn't send the letters and buy the books and all the rest of it. But it seems to me like you have a track record here, Sarah. You have the panic attacks and you have an affair. They start again, and all this happens. You can see why I might think it's *you* who's been doing it all?'

'I can. And I would agree. I'd accept it might be me, acting in some dissociative state, but for the quadcopter. I didn't do that, Ben. I saw it, and if I was having these fugues then I wouldn't have.'

'Unless you didn't see it.'

'Are you suggesting I was – what? – hallucinating?'

He shrugged. 'Maybe. It makes as much sense as anything.'

'Ben,' Sarah said. 'I'm not crazy.'

'Aren't you? Having affairs with younger men because you're not in control of yourself is normal? Sending letters and books and emails to yourself is run-of-the-mill, bog-standard? I don't think so.'

'I didn't do it, Ben.'

Ben gave a little snort, followed by a wry smile, as if saying, *Right, of course you didn't.*

'Either way,' he said. 'You had an affair, Sarah. What the hell do you expect me to do now?'

What he did was get drunk and sleep on the couch.

In the room above him, separated by a thin ceiling and a wall of resentment and doubt, Sarah lay in bed, curled up in a ball, eyes wide open but unseeing, heart thumping so hard it was physically painful, her chest tight, her breath shallow and labored.

If she hadn't known better, she would have thought she was having a heart attack.

She would have preferred it. At least it would end in death or treatment, but this, this was a curse she could not shake, lurking in the shadows of her life, ready to strike whenever it wanted.

She forced herself to breathe deeply and slowly. When she could, she got to her feet and padded, hunched over, to the medicine cabinet. She took out a yellow pill container and shook one, then another, pill into her hand. She jammed them into her mouth and swallowed, then stumbled back to her bed.

This had to stop.

This, and the emails and books and the rest of the shit. It was spiraling out of control: she had lost her grip on the present, on the past, on the future. She needed to repair her relationship with Ben, to figure out with him how they could move forward. And they could, she was sure of it. But not when the rest of this was going on. Not when he was meeting with Rachel Little to discuss if she was crazy or not – which was what they were discussing, whatever Ben said.

She closed her eyes.

Maybe she *was* crazy. She'd resisted the thought, until now. Once or twice it had forced its way into her mind, but she had ignored it. But perhaps now she had to accept it might be true. After all, it was the most obvious explanation. Maybe she was making all this up. Maybe she was ill and she was doing all this and forgetting it.

It was possible; as a doctor, she knew that. A tumor on the brain, or a mini-stroke, or a psychiatric illness of some kind.

And it accounted for everything. All the facts. All the facts except one.

She *knew* it wasn't her. She didn't know how she knew and she wouldn't have expected anyone else to believe her, but she knew.

There was another explanation. All she had to do was figure out what it was.

She was interrupted by her phone buzzing. She picked it up.

There was a text message from a number she did not recognize.

Girl, you really did it this time. Why are you doing this to yourself? To me, that is? You need to stop it, and come clean. It's the only way. Admit you are powerless and surrender to a higher being. OK, babe? Sarah H xxx

She cried out and threw her phone on to the rug, but then she smiled. She hadn't sent this text – she'd been sitting there, thinking. It was nothing to do with her.

So, whatever Ben or anyone else thought, she had proof she wasn't crazy.

She woke early; Ben was already up, sipping a coffee on the couch he had slept on.

'Sarah,' he said. 'I came to a decision last night.'

She startled and looked at him, her eyes wide.

'What?' she said. 'What decision?'

She felt as though she didn't need to ask. He was going to tell her their marriage was over.

'It's good news,' he said. 'I realized we need to get away.'

'What do you mean?'

'We need to leave Barrow. Take a break, so we can sort all this out. Re-establish ourselves.'

She nodded. 'What kind of a break?'

'A long one. Far away.'

'Like where?'

'London. I thought we could go home for a couple of weeks. Maybe travel around a bit. We could stay with my parents. I spoke to Mum and she said it was OK.'

'You spoke to your mom? About us?'

'I didn't give her any details. I told her we wanted to get away. That's all.'

Sarah stared at him. He'd spoken to his mom and they were going to stay with her, because Barrow was no longer the right place for them.

And if Barrow was no longer the right place, then Diana

179

Havenant would have her son and her grandchildren back where she wanted them. Where she'd always wanted them.

It was *her* behind all this. What was the Latin phrase Ben had used? *Cui bono?* Who benefits? Well, it was suddenly clear who benefited.

Diana Havenant. And her home was the *last* place Sarah wanted to be.

'I don't know,' she said. 'I'm not sure I want to.'

Ben looked at her through narrowed eyes. 'This is what we need to save our marriage,' he said. 'I can't believe you're saying no.'

Sarah was about to tell him she didn't care what he believed, she wasn't going to stay with Diana, but she caught the words on her lips.

That was *exactly* what Diana would have wanted her to say, because it would push her and Ben further apart. It was a clever plan: if she said no, she made things even worse with her husband. If she said yes, then she gave her mother-in-law what she wanted.

Except Diana didn't know that Sarah had figured out what she was up to. She made up her mind: she'd go there, and she'd deal with Diana when the time came.

'OK,' she said. 'I think it's a great idea.'

PART TWO

Ten Years Earlier

No body, no crime.

That was what the cops were saying, although everyone knew they suspected the father.

They thought it was Jack. Older, from out of town. A quiet man – some would say taciturn – who had kept himself to himself since he showed up in Barrow, which was not the Barrow way, not the way of someone who was saying to the world *I've got nothing to hide, come on over and stop by anytime you like.*

And now his girlfriend – he hadn't even married her, poor Karen, despite the two babies that had come along, which was another clue to his character – now his girlfriend and the mother of his children was gone.

Just like that.

So yes, they thought it was him. They brought him in for questioning. Laid out a scenario for him. Maybe she came home late and he accused her of . . . of the things younger folk might be accused of, and they got into an argument. Perhaps the argument got a little out of hand and he raised his fist to her and she fought back and the next thing you know – well, she could have slipped and hit her head.

It could have been an accident. Manslaughter, not murder. He'd be out in a few years; confess and tell them where the body was and this would all be over.

Unless it was more sinister. Unless he had meant to kill her.

But he should confess that, too, because they'd find out eventually, and when they did it would be much worse for his refusal to cooperate.

But he denied it. Said she'd never come home.

Which was impossible. Women didn't simply disappear on their way home in Barrow.

But he refused to budge an inch.

Told them he knew his rights and to charge him or let him go the hell free.

Which made them wonder why he knew those rights so well. Maybe he'd been in this position before, they asked him.

He replied that he'd watched a lot of cop shows on the TV and now could he go, please?

And they let him. They had no choice.

No body, no crime.

And until the body showed up, there was nothing they could do. She might have simply chosen to leave, after all, although why she would do so was a mystery as big as any other.

And the longer it went on, the lower the chances of finding her – or her body.

And so Jack – who no one looked at anymore – remained a free man.

Which was, in the eyes of the people of Barrow, a disgrace. But there wasn't a damn thing anyone could do about it.

1

It is laughable.

She thinks she can run away.

She thinks she can get away from this by a strategy as simple as *moving*. Thinks that because she is a long way away she is safe.

Which is exactly her problem. She does not understand what is going on. She thinks this is about some kind of threat 'out there'. Some physical challenge to her world which she can get rid of by going far away from it.

How stupid she is. That is not what is happening *at all*.

It makes no difference. It is irritating, yes. *Very* fucking irritating. But it will make no difference to the outcome.

For this is not about *distance*.

This goes much deeper. This is fundamental to her life. It cannot be ignored or run away from. A mind much greater than hers has planned this in every detail, for months and years.

This is happening whether she likes it or not.

2

In the seat to her left, Miles slept, his head on Ben's lap. Ben was sleeping too, his head wedged between his coat and an inflatable pillow, his knees pressed uncomfortably up against the seat back in front of him. Faye, to her right, had struggled through a movie, then closed her eyes and given in to tiredness.

Kim had shown more determination to resist. She had cried and screamed and fought to get out of her seat and run around the aisles. Before he went to sleep, Ben had tried creating a play space in the gap between their seats – they had the middle row of five – and the seats in front by blocking her exit with their bags, but she had clambered to freedom.

At first, Sarah got wry, sympathetic looks from the other passengers or comments about how cute she was, but after the meal had been served and people were trying to grab a few hours of rest, the looks turned to glares, especially from the people around them.

Eventually, Sarah took her to the galley and tried to rock her to sleep; after quarter of an hour of wriggling and shouting Kim finally consented to her mom's fervent wishes and gave in to the charms of slumber. Sarah returned to her seat and closed her eyes.

She didn't sleep; she never did on planes. She didn't like flying, had a fear of being so high above the world, a thin metal tube the only thing between her and her maker. She knew air travel was statistically one of the safest forms of travel, but it didn't help. It felt wrong. It *was* wrong; there was nothing natural about being in a metal cylinder thirty thousand feet above the surface of the earth. So she couldn't relax, and without relaxation there was no sleep.

Besides, it didn't really matter whether she slept or not. They had nothing to do when they arrived other than settle in at Ben's parents' house and take their time getting over their jet lag. They could nap, take walks, visit London, do whatever they wanted. There was no pressure on them to be anywhere or do anything, and Sarah intended to keep it that way.

This trip was their opportunity to get away from Barrow and all the goings on, to spend time as a family, to get perspective. It was a chance for her and Ben to put aside the recent past – and, given the letter he'd received about Josh, the more distant past – and reset their marriage.

She didn't think it would be easy. He had been very reserved since she had confessed to the affair, withdrawn and quiet, unmoved almost, although she knew him well enough to see he was deeply wounded. She would make it better, though. She would do whatever it took.

And she would deal with Diana. How had she done all this? How could she have known about the affair? Sarah didn't know, but all options were on the table at the moment. And at first she would play dumb with Diana. Pretend she did not suspect her, lure her into revealing herself, and then – well, she didn't know what she would do then. But she would find a way to stop this, once and for all.

Before they left she had called Jean.

We're going away, she said. *To England.*

How long for? Jean asked.

A couple of weeks. I can't take it anymore.

What happened now?

Ben thinks I'm doing it myself, but I don't remember it. It's called dissociative fugue.

Whatever it's called, it's bullshit, Jean said. *Why would you be doing this stuff?*

Because it's the only way I can get the help I need, Sarah said. *The books were about suicide and depression and the notes were me saying I needed help but wouldn't admit it. Ben's theory is that my subconscious is crying out for help but I'm too stubborn to admit it, so the only way it can get it is by doing all this stuff.*

Jean had laughed. *Sounds pretty far-fetched.*

Not for Rachel Little. It's her putting it in his mind.

I didn't know they were friends.

They're not. But she's wormed her way into his life.

You think she's behind it?

I did, Sarah said. *But then another note came. It was a confession.*

To what?

To an affair I had.

There was a long silence. *You had an affair,* Jean said, at last.

Yes. It wasn't much—

With who?

With a guy called Josh. He worked at the medical center for a while. The letter—

How long did it go on for? Did you – you know?

Once, Sarah said. *And Ben knows. The letter – supposedly from me – told him. And Rachel couldn't have known. He thinks I sent it myself so I could confess.*

Jesus, Jean said. *It doesn't make any sense.*

It *did* make sense, though. The theory that it was her – suffering, unknown to her conscious self, from anxiety, depression and thoughts of suicide – made a lot of sense. At least, it made more sense than any of the other theories: ex-boyfriends, Rachel Little, Ben himself. None of them would have been able to do most of the stuff, and none of them had any reason to.

The flaw was that she wasn't depressed or suicidal. Suffering from anxiety, yes. But not the others.

At least, she thought not, which only left Diana.

And this trip was a way to find out, once and for all, because Sarah was sure that, with Ben and her grandchildren where she wanted them, Diana would reveal herself. And if she and Ben both saw it, then they could tackle this together.

Diana was waiting outside the arrivals hall. She was wearing a dark skirt and expensive-looking silk blouse.

And a headscarf.

Sarah stared at her. She had a feeling that under the scarf her head was hairless.

Which meant only one thing.

'Hello,' Diana said. 'How lovely to see you all.' She held out a hand to Miles, then bent to kiss Faye. Kim was sitting on the luggage cart; she brushed her cheek with her forefinger and smiled.

'Aren't you pretty,' she said, then looked at Ben. 'Well,' she said. 'Don't you have a kiss for your mother?'

Ben looked at her, then glanced at Sarah, then stepped forward and gave her a kiss on the cheek.

'Mum,' he said, and gestured to her headscarf. 'Is – are you—'

Diana waved away the question. 'Not now,' she said. 'The answer's yes, but not now. When we're at home and small ears are otherwise occupied.'

Ben gave Sarah a hopeless look.

'OK,' he said. 'Later.'

*   *   *

She had about six months to live, although from what she said, Sarah wasn't sure she would make it that long. Her cancer was aggressive and widespread, and had been discovered late. She had put her back pain down to advancing age but it turned out to be something far more sinister.

She had, typically, a no-nonsense attitude to her illness.

'Why didn't you tell us?' Ben said.

'Because I didn't want you rushing over here when you've got other things to be getting on with.'

'Were you planning to tell us?' Ben said. 'Or was I going to get a surprise phone call one day?'

'Of course I was. But not for a while. And then you said you were coming anyway, so it all worked out.'

Roger – Ben's dad – coughed. 'I did try to change her mind,' he said. 'But you know how easy *that* is. And you're here now, which is the main thing.'

'Yes,' Diana said. She looked at them intently. 'And why *are* you here? It's very sudden. Ben mentioned you needed a break, but it's unlike you both to be so impetuous.'

'It's kind of a long story,' Ben said.

'Oh?' Diana got to her feet; it was clear from the wince she gave that it took some effort to do so. 'I'll put the kettle on, then.'

Ben stood up. 'Let me, Mum,' he said.

She waved him away. 'Do not,' she said, 'treat me like an invalid. I will *not* have it.'

After she brought the tea – china cups on china saucers, tea in a teapot – Ben told the story. Sarah – reluctantly – filled in the gaps. He did not mention the letter about the affair, or the idea that Sarah might have been doing it herself, but then he didn't need to.

If Sarah was right, Diana knew all about it anyway.

'So there you have it,' Ben said. 'That's the reason we

190

wanted to get away. Someone's messing with us and we don't know why.'

Diana looked across the table at them. She looked, unusually for her, troubled.

'Then stay,' she said, 'as long as you like.'

3

'I'm so sorry,' Sarah said. Ben was lying next to her in the bed in the guest room. It was hard, the mattress unforgiving. 'It was such a shock to see her at the airport.'

Ben shook his head. 'I can't believe she didn't tell me,' he said. 'Seems to be a pattern with the women in my life. A few days ago you tell me about your affair; today Mum tells me she's got six months to live. I don't know where to start.'

Sarah wished he would start with her, would turn and lay his head on her shoulder so she could hold him and provide comfort and support, but she knew he wouldn't. For the moment she was not a source of solace; rather she was a source of pain.

And he had plenty: not only her infidelity and his mom's cancer, but the situation they had run away from. From his point of view, his life was falling apart.

'She told Sam,' he said. 'I asked her. She told my brother, and she told him not to tell me.'

'We're seeing him tomorrow, right?'

'He's coming for lunch. We can have it out then.'

'Are you sure you want to? It might be better to put it aside and move on.'

He looked at her, his face sallow. 'You would say that. But it's not always possible to put things aside, Sarah. Some things have to be dealt with.'

And then, in what Sarah thought was a pretty convincing display of not dealing with things, he rolled on to his side and pretended to go to sleep.

She woke shortly after ten in the morning. The bed was empty. She got out and looked in the kids' room; their beds were empty too. She could hear them playing downstairs, along with the voices of some other children.

Sam and Callie – Ben's brother and sister-in-law – must have arrived with their two, Michael and Olivia. Sarah showered and dressed and went downstairs; Ben and Sam were sitting at the kitchen table, drinking tea.

'Hey,' Sam said. He stood up and hugged her. 'Good to see you.'

'You too.' She turned to Ben. 'Why didn't you wake me? I feel like a slob, getting up this late.'

'You looked so peaceful,' he said. 'I didn't have the heart.'

Sarah rolled her eyes. 'I'm sorry about Diana,' she said. 'It was quite a shock when we saw her.'

'I'll bet,' Sam said. 'Benny and I were just talking about it. She only told me a couple of weeks back. She said she wanted to tell you herself. I protested but—' he gave a little shrug, 'you know Mum.'

'Where's Callie? And the kids?'

'Outside. Go and say hi. She's looking forward to seeing you.'

Callie was sitting at the garden table with Diana and Roger. On the lawn – perfectly manicured, each blade seemingly a uniform size and shade of green – Miles, Faye and Kim were playing at a water table with their cousins.

Callie – tall, with curly blond hair and blue eyes – jumped up when she saw Sarah.

'Hi!' she said. 'I can't believe you're here!'

Sarah grinned; Callie was one of life's enthusiasts. There were cup half-full and cup half-empty people and then there was Callie: the cup was always overflowing. She had the rare ability to instinctively get the best out of any situation. She seemed to zero in on whatever positives were on offer, and then focus on them to the exclusion of anything else.

'I know,' Sarah said. 'It was a bit of a last-minute decision to come. You look well.'

'You too! And the kids are so cute! I *love* Kim.'

'You can have her. She was up a lot last night with jet lag. It's brutal.'

'I remember when we came back from visiting you,' Callie said. 'Olivia wouldn't sleep for days. It was kind of fun, though. We got to spend some time together. One night there was a meteor shower – at, like four a.m. – and we went outside and watched it. I don't think she remembers it, but it was magical.'

There it was: sleepless nights with a jet-lagged baby were magical. Only Callie.

'Morning,' Diana said. 'Did you sleep well?'

Sarah blushed. She was embarrassed about waking so late. Diana was not the type who succumbed to jet lag; when she'd visited Maine she had set her watch to US time as soon as she had landed and acted as though jet lag was an invention of the weak-minded.

'Yes,' she said. 'I didn't mean to sleep in so—'

Diana shrugged. 'Sleep as long as you like,' she said. 'You're on holiday.'

Callie looked at Sarah and raised an eyebrow. 'Grandma Dee took Olivia shopping last weekend,' she said. 'She came back with a lovely set of earrings. And pierced ears to put them in.'

194

'Well,' Diana said, a smile on her lips. 'Seven's old enough for pierced ears. And she said her mum had told her it was OK.'

'Which was not *exactly* the truth,' Callie said. 'But they are nice earrings. And it doesn't really matter, in the scheme of things. She was going to get them pierced sooner or later.'

'Exactly,' Diana said. 'What is it you Americans say? No harm, no foul?'

Sarah stared at her mother-in-law. 'We do,' she said. 'I didn't have you pegged as the no harm, no foul type, Diana.'

Ben's mom nodded. 'I don't suppose I ever was. But when you are in my current condition you work out how to put aside those things that are not important and how to focus on those that are. Spending time with Olivia – and all of you – is important. Worrying about earrings is not.'

Sarah found it hard to believe what she was hearing. Diana seemed like a different person, a much more pleasant person. A person who had changed because of some great event in their life.

The question was whether it was because of her illness.

Or because she thought she had won.

They had lunch in a pub; Ben drank pints of dark beer with his dad and brother, and showed Miles and Faye how to play darts. By the time they left, Faye had figured out how to get the darts to end up in the general vicinity of the board; Miles was still peppering the surrounding walls with little holes.

As they walked outside Ben yawned. 'Tired,' he said. 'Damn jet lag.'

'And the beer,' Sarah said. 'You're not used to lunchtime drinking. You rarely do it at home.'

'Ah,' Ben said. 'That's because there are no decent pubs. If we had decent pubs to go to – well, it'd be boozy lunches every weekend.'

'I'm glad you're having a good time,' Sarah said. 'It's nice to be here. Nice to see you in your home.'

'It's good to be here,' Ben said. 'But this is a holiday, Sarah. We have to go back, eventually. And I worry that when we do, we'll be back to square one.'

Sarah didn't reply. She didn't want to.

She didn't want to admit to sharing the exact same fear.

4

Sarah had been amazed by London's parks when she first visited; they were no less impressive now. If you knew what you were doing – which Ben did – you could walk long distances in the city without stepping for more than a few yards on a road.

On Tuesday evening they walked through Hyde Park – one of Sarah's favorites – on their way to dinner with Adrian Jameson, Ben's former boss. Sarah had never met him, but he and Ben went way back. They had been a year apart at university and Adrian had persuaded Ben to join the same law firm as him when he had graduated.

They walked into the restaurant, a modern, brightly lit room loud with the chatter of patrons. Adrian was sitting at a table in the corner; he stood up and gestured to them to join him.

'Ben,' he said. 'Great to see you. This must be Sarah.' He shook her hand. 'Delighted to meet you.'

'You too,' Sarah said. 'I've heard a lot about you.'

'Don't tell me what he said,' Adrian replied. 'I've changed since then.' He leaned forward. 'We were on the same rugby team,' he whispered. 'Enough said.'

'Oh, yes, he mentioned the rugby,' Sarah said. She had always found it hard to believe that Ben, with his slender build and relaxed, uncompetitive attitude, had played rugby, which to Americans looked like a huge, sprawling, eighty-minute fight.

'He was pretty good,' Adrian said. 'A bit of a demon out there.'

'Hardly,' Ben said. 'I spent most of my time on the wing where I couldn't do much harm.'

Adrian laughed. 'Fair enough,' he said. 'You said it though, Ben. Not me. Anyway, what brings you over here? Holidays?'

'Kind of,' Ben said. 'A few other things going on.'

'Anything serious?' Adrian said.

'Mum's ill. Cancer.'

'I'm sorry to hear it.'

'Although I only found out when we got here. She was keeping it to herself. Soldiering on. Stiff upper lip, etc. You know the drill.' Ben rolled his eyes.

'So you didn't find out until you arrived?' Adrian said. 'That wasn't the reason for the visit?'

'No,' Ben said. 'We needed to get away. Have a break. You know how it is.'

Adrian looked at him. Sarah could see his lawyer's mind whirring, sensing the mystery, wondering what was going on.

'Well,' he said. 'If you ever decide to move home, let me know. We'd take you back at the firm in a heartbeat.'

'Thanks,' Ben said. 'But I doubt it'll come to that. We're pretty settled over in Maine.'

After dinner they left Adrian and went outside.

'Cab it back?' Ben said.

Sarah shook her head. 'I'm full,' she said. 'Let's go for a walk.'

The offer of the job had set her thinking.

Why *not* move here? The more time she spent here, the less sure she was it was Diana who was behind the Facebook account and the emails and all the rest of it – it was hard to see how she could have been, in her condition. And even if she *was*, well, she wouldn't be around much longer.

And if it wasn't Diana, then they were better off here anyway. If it wasn't Diana, then she didn't want to be anywhere near whoever was doing it.

They set off into Hyde Park. For the first time in weeks she felt fully relaxed; the constant fear of what she'd find when she checked her phone or opened her mailbox had receded.

As they walked along, she took Ben's hand in hers. He didn't snatch it away.

'You know,' she said. 'Maybe we should move here. If he was serious about you having your old job back, it'd be easy. And I'd get a medical job, when the time was right. There'd probably be some accreditation I'd have to get, but it shouldn't be a problem.'

'I don't know,' Ben said. 'Our life's in Barrow. It would be a huge upheaval.'

Our life, she noted, with relief. *It's still our life.*

'The kids are young enough,' Sarah said. 'And *our* life wasn't exactly awesome. Which is why we're here. It'd be a fresh start.'

'We came for a break,' Ben said. 'Not forever. Once we're home, things'll get back to normal. I think moving permanently is a bit of a drastic step.'

Sarah didn't reply. He was right; it was probably an overreaction. But at that moment it felt like an answer to all their problems.

The rest of the week slipped by. They visited the Transport Museum, went to Kent to see Phil, a friend of Ben's who had become a cider maker, and spent a day at Churchill's former home, Chartwell.

At lunchtime on Saturday, Ben, Diana and Roger took the kids for lunch at the pub; Sarah stayed at the house.

She sat in the back garden in the sun, sipping a mug of coffee. She knew this was a holiday, and the reality would be different if they moved here, but she couldn't shake the thought that it would be a good idea. They should at least consider it.

Ben was in his element, the kids were happy, and she felt *great*. The feeling of tightness in her chest, of shortness of breath, of low-level anxiety that threatened at any moment to break out into full-blown panic, was gone. Vanished. Totally absent. She felt lighter, freer, able to give her best self to Ben and the kids. It was an intoxicating feeling, and she couldn't bear the thought of going home and losing it again.

She picked up her phone and checked her email. There'd been nothing odd all week. Maybe there were books about depression and suicide piling up at the house, but so what? It didn't matter, not when they were so far away.

Although it would be hard to leave. The kids had friends. Her roots were deep; Jean would miss her.

She opened FaceTime and selected Jean. After a few rings, her friend's face appeared. She was in her backyard.

'Hey,' she said. 'How's it going?'

'Great,' Sarah said. 'Really great. Lot's happening, though.'

'Fill me in,' Jean said. 'What's going on?'

'Ben's mom's sick,' Sarah replied. 'A few months left, at best.'

Jean looked startled. 'God,' she said. 'I'm so sorry. Tell Ben, would you?'

'I will. The weird thing is, she's so much more fun now. Relaxed and happy, in an odd way. We're having a lovely time.'

'I'd love to visit London,' Jean said. 'Maybe some day. What are you doing?'

'Hanging out, mainly. Although we're going to Madame Tussauds on Tuesday morning, then to Regent's Park. Maybe London Zoo.'

'Sounds fantastic.'

'It should be. And guess what? Ben was offered his old job back.'

There was a long pause. 'Is he going to take it?'

'I don't know. I don't think he necessarily wants to. But I think he should at least consider it.'

'And then you guys would live in different countries?' Jean said. 'Is this because of the affair? Are you breaking up?'

'No,' Sarah said. 'We wouldn't be breaking up.' She looked at her friend's face on the screen. 'We'd all move here.'

5

Jean blinked a few times. Even on the tiny screen she looked shocked, then disbelieving, then amused.

'It's a bit sudden, isn't it?'

'Maybe,' Sarah said. 'But all the stuff that was going on – it really got to me. I was having panic attacks, starting to doubt my own sanity. I'm not sure I want to go back to it.'

'Sarah,' Jean said. 'When you're away it always feels better. You don't have work and the stress of managing the kids. But you'll get jobs and it'll be the same over there.'

'Except there won't be someone pretending to be me sending emails to people, or writing letters to Ben in my handwriting.'

'Ben thought it was you, right?'

'Yes, but it wasn't me.'

'I know, but bear with me.' Jean paused. 'What if it *was* you, Sarah? What if all the stress – work, kids – as well as the guilt of hiding the affair, was getting to you?'

Sarah tensed. She could feel the panic fluttering around her for the first time since they'd arrived in England.

'But it wasn't, Jean. I explained it to you. The quadcopter—'

'I know. I'm only saying, what if it was? Then you would

202

only be bringing it to a new place. When the stress started – it could all start again.'

Sarah felt tears in her eyes. She couldn't believe Jean doubted her. Jean, of all people. God, even five minutes talking to someone from Barrow had destroyed her peace of mind. It made her never want to go back. She was going to talk to Ben as soon as he got home.

'I have to go,' she said. 'Speak later.'

When Ben came home she steered him into the back garden. They stood on the edge of the lawn and Sarah told him about her conversation with Jean and her decision to ask him if they could stay for good.

Ben didn't answer for a few moments.

'I don't think it's the right time to make such a big decision,' he said. 'I don't think it's necessary.'

'It's the perfect time,' Sarah replied. 'Don't you see?'

'No,' Ben said. 'I see it as the worst possible time.' He looked at a hedge to avoid looking at her. 'We just went through a very difficult few weeks,' he said. 'And then you told me you'd had an affair.'

'Right,' Sarah said. 'Exactly. And you said it yourself the other day. Things are better here, and you're worried if we go home we'll be back to square one. Well, I am too. So let's stay. We need to put this behind us, and moving here is a fresh start.'

'And I don't want a fresh start,' Ben said. 'I'm not even sure yet what the future holds for us, never mind making a massive decision to uproot our family.'

Sarah stared at him. 'What do you mean, you're not sure what the future holds for us? Are you saying you want to break up?'

'No, not exactly.'

'Then are you saying you think we might break up?' Sarah said. 'Because I didn't think that was even on the table.'

203

Ben gave an incredulous laugh. 'You had an affair, Sarah. You have your excuses – how you felt at the time, whatever other bullshit – but the fact is you had sex with another man, and I only found out because someone sent me a note. Someone who claims to be you – a claim you deny.'

'Because it's not true.'

'But don't you see, that makes it worse?' He shook his head. 'That means you had no intention of ever telling me. But you got busted, so you did. Or, you did send the letter, which means you did all the rest of the stuff, and in that case you're lying, too.'

'Or I'm crazy. Dr Jekyll and Mrs Hyde.' She laughed. 'I really can't win, can I?'

'No,' he said. 'You can't. And so, to answer your earlier question – yes, it is on the table. For now, anyway.'

She didn't reply. After a long pause, he spoke again.

'But only on the table, Sarah. It's not what I want. So let's let things settle down. One step at a time, OK?'

Sarah nodded. She had no choice.

6

From her visit years ago she remembered Madame Tussauds as a bit dark and tawdry, a city-center version of a fairground attraction, but in its current incarnation it was fabulous. There was a magical sheen to the wax figures; even though you knew they were not real your mind was tricked by how closely they resembled their subjects, and when you stood near them there was a small surge of adrenaline, as though you were somehow closer to the actual person.

And for the kids it was a massive thrill: they posed with Kim Kardashian and Kanye, sat with the members of some boyband Sarah didn't remember the name of, copied Usain Bolt's lightning-bolt pose. Ben played air guitar beside Freddie Mercury – she could see he almost believed it was real, too – and she took her place beside Sherlock Holmes – the Benedict Cumberbatch version.

Afterwards they walked through Regent's Park, where they stopped to admire the black swans.

'Don't seem all that rare,' Ben said. 'At least not here.'

'Where do they go in winter?' Miles asked.

'To Africa,' Faye replied. 'Birds go to Africa, where it's warm.'

Miles smiled at his sister. After a week and a half away they were closer, friends as well as siblings. They all needed this as a family, needed this time to deepen the bonds between them. And, whether Ben was prepared to admit it or not, it was good for him too. He was relaxed, more himself. This was the right place for them; the longer they spent here, the clearer it became to Sarah.

'I'm not sure swans go to Africa,' Ben said. 'It's probably a bit far for them to fly.'

'They do,' Faye said. 'I *know* they do.'

'Maybe you're right,' Ben said. 'What do you think, Sarah? Do swans fly to Africa in the winter?'

Sarah looked at the swans, paddling over the surface of the pond. They were beautiful, strong and regal, but she didn't think they went to Africa in the winter. She couldn't imagine them, flying south in a V-formation.

But geese did. Maybe swans did too. She realized she didn't really know.

'You know,' she said. 'I'm not sure. We can ask someone and find out.'

'Google it,' Miles said. 'Give me your phone and I'll Google it.'

Sarah took her phone from her bag and handed it to him. 'There you go,' she said.

'Mom,' Faye said. 'Where's Kimmy?'

Those two words – when spoken about a two-year-old in a public park near water – explode in your mind like a bomb. Sarah spun round, looking for her daughter.

She was not there. Not in their immediate vicinity. She looked up and scanned the rest of the park.

'Ben,' she said. 'Kim. She's gone.'

'I know,' Ben said, his voice tense. 'I'm going to look for her. Stay with the kids.'

He began to run along the path, calling Kim's name. Sarah

felt the edges of her world close in. This couldn't be happening, not now, not here, not when things had been going so well.

'Mom,' Miles said. He pointed to the other side of the pond. 'She's over there. Next to the trash can.'

Sarah followed the line of his finger. Half-hidden by a tall black trash can was the figure of a toddler.

It was Kim. In the water in front of her there was a large group of ducks; she was holding a plastic bag in one hand and with the other she was taking out chunks of bread and throwing them to the ducks.

'Stay here.' Sarah sprinted around the pond. 'Ben,' she called, as she ran. 'Ben, she's here.'

Ben – fifty yards away now – stopped and turned.

Sarah reached Kim and scooped her into her arms.

'My God,' she said. 'Don't do that, Kim. Don't ever run away again. Mommy was scared.'

'Feeding ducks,' Kim said.

Sarah looked at the bag in her hand.

'Where did you get that?' she said.

'The woman gave it to me,' Kim replied. 'She was nice.'

'What woman?' Ben said. He was out of breath; he pressed his face to Kim's cheek and she pulled away. 'Is she nearby? Can you point to her?'

Kim looked around. She shook her head. 'She's gone.'

'Was she old? Young?' Sarah said. 'What did she look like?'

Kim frowned and touched her head. 'Hat,' she said.

Sarah looked for any hat-wearing woman in the vicinity; there were a few baseball caps, but nothing else. It was pointless; she could hardly accost every woman in a hat and ask if they had – done what, exactly? Given a toddler a bag of breadcrumbs to feed the ducks? They hadn't harmed her, or taken her. It was, at worst, an inappropriate thing to do without consulting the parents, but it wasn't exactly a crime.

Although Sarah thought it should have been.

She was being over-sensitive because of what had been happening back in Barrow. This was nothing; she knew that.

But even so, Sarah could not shake the uneasy feeling there was more to this than she could see.

7

So, she comes to the final scene.

She thought she was safe on her vacation, the poor fool, but she is having doubts now, because of the woman in the park.

Really, she should have known. Did she think this is like a schoolyard bully? A clingy ex-boyfriend? An awkward situation at a party?

It is almost an insult. She should have figured out this is not some simple stalker or ill-wisher messing with her life.

This cannot be run away from or ignored or wished away.

This can no more be run away from than cancer. A change of location makes no difference whatsoever.

The only thing she could do would be to excise it. Cut it out. Cleanse the system of its poison. But she will not. She cannot. She would not know where to even start looking.

So instead she runs away. Pathetic, really. Feeble. And irritating.

And this was her best effort. This is all she had. Never mind; her best effort will soon be over.

She is a fish on a hook and the hook is stuck. The more she struggles the deeper it goes.

And now it is deep enough. It is time for this to come to its inevitable conclusion.

8

'What about Hampton Court?' Diana said. 'I thought you were going there today?'

Sarah shook her head. She sipped the tea her mother-in-law made every morning for breakfast. 'Slight change of plan. We decided to stay local. Have a low-key day.'

'Oh.' Diana raised her eyebrows. 'Well, it'll be nice to have you around. But I hope it isn't too boring for the children.'

'They'll be OK. They're tired after yesterday. They might even have a nap.'

Which would be a bonus, but it wasn't the reason they'd decided to stay home. The real reason was that Sarah felt safer there. Yesterday's duck-feeding episode was probably nothing, but she couldn't shake the unsettled feeling it had left her with. And so a day at home was fine by her.

And she couldn't fully shake the suspicion it could have been Diana. A woman in a hat – it fitted. Diana was wearing hats and scarves these days. And, with sunglasses and a disguised voice, Kim wouldn't have recognized her. She didn't see much of her grandmother, after all.

'Diana,' Sarah said, forcing a nonchalant tone into her

voice and immediately regretting the obviousness of her effort, 'where were you yesterday?'

'At a medical appointment,' Diana said. 'As usual.'

'Oh? What did they say?'

'What they've been saying for a while.' Diana looked at her. 'Is this professional interest?'

She seemed defensive, which *could* be because she had been at the park. It could also be because she was a private person.

And then, why would she be at the park? If she had created all this to scare Sarah and Ben into leaving Barrow, why upset them now they were here?

'No,' Sarah said. 'I was just asking.'

Before Diana could reply, there was a slap as the letterbox flapped shut. Diana stood up. 'I'll go.'

When she came back into the kitchen Diana was holding a postcard in her hand. She had an odd expression on her face: part confusion, part concern.

Sarah recognized the expression. It was how Ben had looked when the books and letters started to show up at their house.

'What is it?' she said.

Diana held it out to her. 'I don't know,' she said. 'It's a bit strange. Take a look.'

The postcard was of the swans in Regent's Park. Sarah didn't need to turn it over to know what she would find on the other side.

It was her handwriting.

Dear Ben, Miles, Faye and Kim

I hope you are having a wonderful holiday. Both of me are! I AM! says one of me. ME TOO! says the other.

All the best! Sarah / Mom (or 'Mum', as they say here!)

Diana poured a glass of water. 'It looks like your hand-writing,' she said. 'Did you send it?'

Sarah shook her head. 'No. I didn't.'

Diana nodded. 'OK,' she said. 'But then who *did* send it?'

'I don't know,' Sarah said. She could hardly get the words out; her chest was constricted, her breathing shallow. She fought a growing dizziness. She inhaled deeply, then slowly let the breath out.

'Sarah? Are you OK? You look like you're having a heart attack.'

She took another deep breath. 'It feels like it,' she gasped. She swayed in her seat. 'It feels like a fucking heart attack.' She looked up at her mother-in-law. 'All this stuff at home,' she said. 'I thought it couldn't touch us here, but I was wrong.'

The door opened and Ben came in. There was a long, uncomfortable silence.

'Wrong about what?' he said.

Sarah slid the postcard across the table to him. 'This came.'

He read the card and paled. 'Shit. I thought this was over.'

'I hoped we'd be safe here,' Sarah said. 'I was enjoying feeling free again.'

'No,' Diana said. 'Whoever's doing this wouldn't be stopped by geography.' She folded her arms. 'Whoever it is, they are not sane, Sarah. These are not the actions of a rational human being. I'm at a loss, though, as to who it would be. Or why.' She looked at Ben. 'This could be dangerous person. You have considered that, I hope?'

Ben nodded. 'We have. Can I talk to Sarah? Alone?'

'I'll go upstairs,' Diana replied.

'It's OK,' Ben said. 'Would you mind keeping an eye on the children? We'll go for a walk.'

* * *

They set off along the street. There was a Lebanese café on the corner; Ben sat at a table outside. The waitress came and he ordered a coffee; Sarah didn't want anything.

'So,' he said, and put the postcard on the table. 'Regent's Park. Sent yesterday. We were there yesterday.'

'I know.'

'Your handwriting.'

'I know that too.'

'Then you also know how this looks.'

Sarah gave a wry smile; she knew what was coming, but he might as well say it.

'How *does* it look?'

'It looks like you sent it.'

'I didn't. And when would I have done? We were together all day.'

He shrugged. 'Trip to the bathroom? It wouldn't have taken long to write it, and then you could have slipped it in a postbox. Christ, we almost mislaid our daughter. A surreptitious posting of a postcard is hardly beyond the realms of the imagination.'

'I'm telling you I didn't.'

'Then let me ask you a question. I'll give you some facts, and then two explanations. You tell me which of them is more likely. OK?'

She nodded. 'OK.'

'The facts: there is a person who is able to impersonate your handwriting, has access to your Amazon account, has been in our house and has been near our kids and friends for months. This person has been taking photos of you and your kids in places you have been. They send you books about depression and letters – purporting to be from you – telling you to seek help. They know your secrets, about your affair. And now, they are in London at the same time as you and in the same park. And they have written a postcard to

214

your family which suggests you have a split personality of some type. Those are the facts, right?'

'More or less. And you don't have to be so lawyerly.'

'Sorry,' Ben said. 'But bear with me, if you would. So, on to the explanations. One, there's someone with a grudge against you who somehow is able to do all these things. They've stalked you online and in person for months, but they've never actually approached you in any way. And now, they've come to London.'

He sipped his coffee.

'Explanation two: it's you who's doing this. You're suffering from a psychiatric illness in which you do things you don't recall. Almost like there are two separate people. As a doctor, the other you knows you need help, so she's trying to find a way to communicate with you. Letters, books, whatever. And you said you've been through this before. The suicidal thoughts, when you were having the panic attacks.'

'Ben,' Sarah said. 'I can't believe you're using that against me!'

'I'm not using anything against anyone, Sarah. I'm merely laying out the facts. Considering the alternatives. And, if you were me, which would you think is more likely?'

'The second,' Sarah said. She was suddenly deeply sad. There was a rift between them, and she didn't know how to cross it, let alone close it. 'I would think the second is more likely.'

'Exactly!' he said. 'Think about it: a couple of days after talking to Jean and getting upset again, this happens. You see what I'm saying?'

'I do.'

'Then you see it explains *everything*, Sarah.'

'I do see,' she replied. She realized she had started crying and wiped a tear from her cheek. 'I agree with everything you said, Ben. Everything except for one thing. I know it wasn't me.'

His face fell. She felt sorry for him. He had an explanation, had found the cause of the problem; all that was left was to fix it. But she was telling him no, his explanation was not right, the cause he had identified was the wrong one, there was no fixing this problem, not yet. This problem was not going away. It was not going to be fixed.

'How?' he said. 'How do you know?'

'I can't explain,' she said, quietly. 'But I do.'

She reached out and put her hands over his. She didn't have the answer, not yet, but now Diana was no longer a suspect she knew what she had to do.

She had to face this, once and for all.

'Ben,' she said. 'It's time to go home.'

9

Barrow was – well, Barrow was Barrow. Unchanged, but hot. Late summer hot. Not the clean heat of July but the muggy, unyielding heat of the dog days of summer.

It's been like this for a few days, Jean said, when she came over to welcome them home with fresh milk and a loaf of bread, *and it looks like it'll last a few days more*.

They had stayed to the end of the week; Sarah had suggested they leave immediately, but Ben had been reluctant.

So now you want to go back to Barrow, he said. *Not long ago you wanted to move to England for good.*

I know, but things changed. The postcard came.

Well, he said. *It's probably a good thing. At least you're accepting you'll have to face this.*

She knew what he meant: he thought she was conceding her guilt, that she couldn't run away because wherever she went she brought it with her. She knew he was wrong, but she was prepared – for now – not to argue. There wasn't much she could say in any case: the evidence suggested she was, at the very least, a strong candidate, so she couldn't blame Ben for reaching that conclusion. She would have to prove otherwise, which would entail getting to the truth.

217

And so now they were back. Home. With friends, and family, and the old familiar places and faces.

And another thing. An unknown thing, lurking, hidden in the shadows.

A thing only Sarah believed was there.

A thing Sarah would have to face on her own.

They all woke early. Kim was first, at 3 a.m. Wide awake and ready to party. The thunder of her footsteps – for a toddler she had an incredibly loud footfall – woke Faye, and the sound of their playing woke Miles.

At four, Ben gave up and got out of bed.

'I'll make some breakfast,' he said. 'Then head into the office. I might as well get started early. It'll stop me having to stay too late, catching up on everything.'

Sarah lay in bed, listening to the sounds of her family starting the day: the coffee machine gurgling, pots and pans clanking, the TV playing some kids' show. It was dark out; dawn was an hour away, at least, but she was fully alert. It was 9 a.m. in England, and, although they had crossed the Atlantic, their body clocks were still in London, ticking along to the rhythm of life in Diana and Roger's house.

Diana, who could be dead shortly. She wondered how Ben would take it; he was not close to his parents, but you never knew how losing them would affect you. Would he feel guilty about moving away? Regret that he had not seen much of them in the last few years? Sadness it had taken his mother's death to make him realize he could – should – have done more?

It was hard to say. But they were going to find out soon enough.

'So,' Jean said. 'You came home after all?'

Sarah reached into the brown paper bag and took out two

bagels. She handed one to Jean; she'd picked them up earlier, desperate to get out of the house with the kids.

'A postcard came,' she said. 'Same as the other stuff.' She shook her head. 'Addressed to Ben and the kids, my handwriting, from the place we'd been the day before.'

Jean made a pained face. 'That's—' she looked around to make sure no kids were in earshot – 'that's fucking freaky. I mean, someone was there, Sarah. In London.'

'I know. I thought we'd got away from it, but' – she shrugged – 'we hadn't. So we came back.'

'What are you going to do?'

'I'm not sure. I have a few ideas.'

'Like what?' Jean said. 'Call the cops?'

'Again? They'll ask me what crime has been committed. Letters, postcards? And what would they do?' She shook her head and leaned forward. She lowered her voice. 'No, I have to deal with this myself. And the first step is proving to Ben it wasn't me who sent this stuff.'

'But how can you? There's nothing to prove it wasn't you.' She held up her hands. 'I believe you, by the way.'

Sarah wasn't convinced she did, but she let it pass.

'There is,' Sarah said. 'I *know* it wasn't me, so the handwriting isn't mine. Someone else wrote it. So even if an untrained eye can't see it, there will be differences, however slight.'

'And?' Jean said.

'Think about it. If this was a court case, they would bring in a handwriting expert who would testify whether the documents were written by the same person. So I'll find a handwriting expert. And when they tell me I didn't write this stuff, I'll have my proof.'

Jean nodded her head slowly. 'Great idea,' she said. 'That is a *great* idea.'

10

Sarah was not exactly sure what to expect a handwriting expert to look like. In the back of her mind she had an idea they were a bit like fortune tellers or tarot card readers. She knew graphology was more scientific than telling fortunes, nevertheless she couldn't shake the impression. She had scheduled an appointment with one based in Portland – *Donna Martin, Graphology Expert, Used by Law Enforcement Agencies and Attorneys* – who had agreed to come to Barrow to meet her.

Can you tell a forgery from the real thing? Sarah had asked on the phone. *Accurately?*

Dr Havenant, Donna Martin replied, *what to you might look like identical scripts bear, to me, almost no relation to each other. It's like a mother with identical twins. The rest of the world cannot tell them apart, but to her they are instantly recognizable.*

Sarah didn't mention that there were plenty of examples of parents having to make sure they could tell twins apart by putting a bracelet on one and not the other; she got Ms Martin's point. She only hoped it was accurate.

At two minutes to two there was a knock on the door.

Graphology experts, it turned out, drove Ford Mustangs and wore red lipstick, or, at least, this one did.

'Donna Martin,' she said, and held out her hand. 'Pleased to meet you.'

'Sarah Havenant. Come in.'

Miles came out of the living room. He looked out of the window. 'Is that your car?' he said.

Donna Martin nodded. 'Ford Mustang GT,' she said. 'Five-liter V8 engine delivering a few hundred of the finest Detroit ponies.'

'Cool,' Miles said. 'I like it.'

'Work hard in school,' Donna said, 'and you can get one too.'

Miles nodded. 'I think I will,' he said.

Sarah smiled. She hadn't tried the carrot of a V8 Mustang to motivate him to work hard, but it seemed it was an effective way to do it; he looked very serious, although whether his new commitment would last remained to be seen.

'Come through to the kitchen,' she said. 'I'll show you the handwriting.'

She had laid out the book and postcard on the table, along with three other samples of her actual handwriting.

Donna Martin looked at them in turn.

'Well,' she said. 'One thing's for certain. You're a doctor. I don't know how you lot get through all those years of education without being able to write better than a fifth-grader.'

'We do it deliberately,' Sarah said. 'It's the final test at med school: you have to develop unintelligible handwriting.'

'That explains it,' Donna said. She stared at the samples, looking at them one by one.

'Well,' she said, after a while. 'If they are forgeries, they're good ones.'

What happened to telling them apart like a mother with

her twins? Sarah thought, but she held her tongue. She had a sinking feeling.

'You don't think they're forgeries?' she said.

'Oh, I'm not going that far,' Donna said. 'But they're not obvious forgeries. I'll have to take them for more analysis.'

Of course you will. More analysis, and more fees.

'OK,' Sarah said. 'Any idea when you might be ready?'

'I should have them back to you by Friday,' Donna said. 'I need to measure the letters. Look at the tails on the "g"s and "y"s – that sort of thing.'

'And will it be conclusive? When you've done the analysis?'

'Oh yes,' Donna said. 'I'll tell you one way or another whether these were all written by the same person or not.'

'I hope so,' Sarah said. *Because then*, she thought, *this will be one step closer to being finished.*

After Donna Martin left, Sarah called Jean.

'What did she say?' Jean asked, her voice tense. 'Are they fakes?'

'She wasn't sure,' Sarah said. 'But she's going to do some more analysis. She'll know in a few days. She'll have her answer by Friday.'

'Great,' Jean said. 'And then you can show Ben this wasn't you after all.'

11

Sarah sat on an old wooden bench at the back of Jean's yard. It had been there since she and her husband bought the house. He had planned to restore it; Jean wanted to throw it out. But after he died she had kept it, and it still did its job.

She and the kids had stopped in after breakfast; all five children were playing in a sandpit beside the house. It was amazing how they managed to find a way to play together, despite the range in ages. Miles could play sophisticated games with older kids, but he was also happy to push a dump truck in the sand with Kim.

Jean came out of the back door. She was holding a tray with three mugs of coffee on it.

Sarah gestured at the tray. 'Three?' she said. 'Who else is coming?'

'Rachel,' Jean said. 'She texted me a few minutes ago asking if I wanted to get together. I told her to come over.'

Sarah tensed. She hadn't seen Rachel since the episode with Ben at the Little Cat Café, and she didn't want to. If she'd known Rachel was going to be here, she wouldn't have come, but it might work to her advantage.

'Would you do me a favor?' Sarah said.

'Depends what it is,' Jean said.

'I need you to get a sample of Rachel's handwriting for me.'

'Handwriting?' she said.

'Yes. Then I can show it to the graphologist. See if it *is* Rachel.'

Jean frowned. 'OK,' she said. 'I'll try.'

'Then I'm going to leave,' Sarah said. 'Call me later and let me know how it went.'

Sarah, Miles, Fay and Kim were riding bikes in the quad of Hardy College when Jean texted.

> Handwriting sample in your mailbox. I asked Rachel about yoga classes I could attend. She wrote some down for me.

Later, Sarah emailed a scanned copy of the list of yoga classes to Donna Martin; the graphologist said it would be enough to go on. The answer would be with her Friday, the same as the original request.

I have to say, Donna Martin replied, this is intriguing. *Bit of a change from my normal work.*

Sarah wasn't sure how she felt about being intriguing to a graphologist who specialized in criminal cases, but then she didn't really care. She pictured herself receiving the call from Donna, listening as she told her there was no way Sarah had written the message in the book or the postcard, and that it was incontrovertible it was the person whose handwriting sample Sarah had sent over – Rachel Little – who had written them.

Then, when she put down the phone, Sarah would let out a loud YES! and Ben would look up from his post-work beer and ask what had happened and she would tell him.

It was all Rachel Little, she'd say. *I have proof.*

And then she'd call Ian Molyneux and tell him and he'd arrest Rachel and slap her with a restraining order or maybe a prison sentence or whatever they did to crazy bitches like her who stalked people.

But that was Friday. Until then, she'd have to wait.

12

She is happy again.

She thinks she has found a way out of this. She thinks she knows what is going on and how to stop it. She thinks she can prove it is not her who is crazy, not at all, and then everything will be back to normal.

She will see to her patients and go to the gym. Her husband will kiss her and the kids when he comes home from work. On Friday nights they will drink a little too much and have sex, both of them wishing the other one would be a bit more adventurous between the sheets. Change the routine; maybe try something different. Or maybe not. Maybe they will carry on doing it the same old way after all. Maybe it was only a nice thought to pass the time until it is over.

As if it is so simple.

As if this can all be undone.

She is mistaken, as usual, because she thinks if she applies her logic, her rational thinking, then she can figure this out.

But this is not a crossword puzzle. It is a not a disease with symptoms which can be diagnosed and treated. No: it is a hook. A hook that has caught its fish.

And a hook is not rational. It is not worming its way deeper into her flesh because it wants to. It is doing it because this is what a hook does. It cannot be persuaded to stop any more than it can be persuaded not to be a hook.

And this will only get worse. Soon she will be wishing for things to go back to the way they are now. She will remember these as the golden days.

And they are, in a way. From now on in, this is as good as it gets for Sarah Havenant.

13

'You're in a good mood,' Ben said. It was quarter after six and he had only been home a few minutes – often on a Wednesday there was a partner meeting at the office until late – and Sarah was humming along to a pop song – something about 'Cake by the Ocean' – as she unstacked the dishwasher.

'We had a good day,' she said. 'We went to the beach. Getting over the jet lag finally.'

On the table her phone rang. Ben glanced at it.

'It's your office,' he said. 'They don't normally call so late, do they?'

Sarah shook her head and picked it up.

'Hello?' she said.

'Dr Havenant, this is Denise. Do you have a minute?'

'Sure,' Sarah said. Denise worked in the administrative office as the general manager. It was rare for her to call at all, never mind at this time. 'How can I help?'

'I know you're still on vacation, Dr Havenant, but we have a bit of a crisis in the practice.'

'Oh? What's happening?'

'Well, Dr Deck and Dr Audett fell ill today – there's a norovirus doing the rounds. It's pretty nasty, and they won't be in work until next week. I found cover for tomorrow, but I can't arrange any for Friday. I was wondering whether there is any chance you could come in? I'm sorry to ask, but I've tried every other avenue.'

Sarah didn't want to go in, but at least work would help pass the time until she got the graphology report, and besides, she'd been off work for nearly three weeks now, and she was feeling a little guilty. 'I'll be there,' she said. 'Eight a.m.?'

'Thank you, Dr Havenant,' Denise said. 'We'll see you on Friday.'

'Work?' Ben said.

'I have to go in on Friday. The other doctors are dropping like flies. A norovirus. Is there any chance you could stay home with the kids?'

'None,' Ben said. 'I'm still behind after the UK trip. We'll have to find a babysitter.'

'We need someone we can trust. I'll ask Jean. She might be able to help.'

'Are you sure you're OK to watch them on Friday?'

In the passenger seat, Jean nodded. They were on their way to the beach – if everything went to plan it might be the last midweek beach trip of the summer as, once Rachel Little was off the scene, Sarah would be able to go back to work full-time.

'I'll be fine,' Jean said. 'It's only one day. And it'll be good for you to be back in work.'

'Call me if anything comes up, OK?'

'Of course,' Jean said. 'But nothing will come up.'

They pulled up in front of the sand dunes that separated the parking lot from the beach and unloaded the kids. Miles and Faye sprinted up the dunes, Kim waddling behind them.

'Miles! Faye!' Sarah shouted. 'Come back and help carry the beach gear.' She looked at Daniel and Paul; they were loading up with towels and shovels and bags.

229

'Your kids are so well behaved,' Sarah said. 'I don't know what I'm doing wrong.' She looked back for Miles and Faye. They were nowhere to be seen, their beach toys still by the car. Kim was sitting by some kind of scrubby bush, putting something in her mouth.

'Kim!' Sarah shouted. 'Stop it! Don't eat things from bushes!'

Jean laughed. She picked up Sarah's tote bag. 'Here,' she said. 'Let me give you a hand.'

Perhaps it was the time of the year – the late summer – or perhaps it was the hot weather or perhaps it was purely random, but the shallow water of the beach was crawling with crabs. Most were no more than an inch or two in diameter, but there were a few which were much bigger.

Sarah stood in the water and watched them.

'Can you eat them?' she said.

Jean nodded. 'Sure. There's not much in the little ones, but the bigger ones would be fine.'

'You don't need a permit to fish them?'

'No,' Jean said. 'I don't think so. But anyway, who's going to know?'

Sarah shrugged. 'All right,' she said. 'Then let's get a bucket.'

They ended up with six or seven good-sized crabs. Sarah put them in a bucket at Jean's feet for the trip home.

'You want some?' she said.

Jean shook her head. 'No thanks. My kids won't eat them and they're a hassle to prepare. It's not worth it. You share with Ben.'

'You can come over, if you like? We can all eat together.'

'It's OK. By the time we get showered the kids will be ready for bed. But thanks.'

The beach was out of cell phone range – it was one of the

things Sarah liked about it – and as they turned on to the main road her phone buzzed. She had a missed call and voicemail from Ian Molyneux.

She put her phone to her ear.

'Sarah, this is Ian Molyneux. If you could call me when you get a chance, please do.'

There was an official tone in his voice which made her think this was not a social call. Her throat tightened, and she called him back.

He answered on the second ring.

'Sarah,' he said. 'Thanks for calling back. Are you at home?'

'No. On the way back from Small Point.'

'So you'll be back in around half an hour,' he said. 'I'd like to talk to you, if that's OK.'

'Can you talk to me now?'

'No. It'd be better at your house.'

'Ian,' Sarah said. 'What's going on?'

'I'll tell you when you get home.'

14

Sarah pulled up outside the house. Ian Molyneux was sitting in a squad car, waiting for her.

Jean put a hand on her arm. 'I'll take the kids and feed them. You can come and pick them up when you're ready.'

'Thank you,' Sarah replied. 'I hope it doesn't take too long.'

'Take whatever time you need. We'll be fine.' Jean smiled. 'Good luck.'

They sat in the kitchen, Ian on a stool, Sarah at the table. He had not accepted her offer of a drink.

'So,' she said. 'What's going on? I've been on edge all the way home.'

'We've had a complaint,' Ian said. 'Well, less of a complaint. It's more the raising of a concern.'

'What about?'

'About you.'

Sarah blinked. She felt the panic clawing at her and she closed her eyes. After a few seconds she looked at Ian.

'What kind of a complaint? Or concern?'

'This is' – Ian hesitated – 'this is a delicate topic. It's not really a police matter, but I thought you should know about it.'

'About what?'

He pulled his phone from his vest pocket and tapped on the screen.

'Are you familiar with Craigslist?'

'Of course,' Sarah said. 'Why?'

'The complaint was about this.'

He handed her the phone. As she read the screen her throat tightened.

'Ian,' she said. 'I've never seen this before. I promise.'

I'm married but bored. Looking for NSA fun with like-minded. Clean, discreet, healthy (I'm a doctor!).

I can't host but can travel. During the day better than evenings but I can be flexible.

And then there was a photo.

A photo of her, on the beach, in her red bikini. It was taken from behind; she was looking to the side, in a pose that suggested she was unaware of the photographer.

Which she had been.

'Ian,' she said, 'I did *not* post this. I didn't even know people used Craigslist for this kind of thing.'

'A woman called it in,' Molyneux said. 'She said she didn't think her doctor should be engaging in this kind of activity.'

'Who was it?' Sarah said.

'She didn't give her name.'

It was Rachel, she was sure of it.

'Did you speak to her? What did she sound like?'

'I didn't take the call. And even if I did, I couldn't tell you anything.'

'Fine,' Sarah said. 'But I'm not engaging in any kind of activity. This is bullshit.'

'Even if you are, there's no crime, which is what we told

233

her. And I would have left it at that, but given what's been going on I thought you should know.'

There was a noise from the kitchen door. They both looked up.

'Know what?' Ben said.

Neither of them replied.

'She should know what?' he said. 'Even though there's not been a crime committed?'

Ian stood up, stiffly. 'I'll leave you two to sort this out,' he said. He tapped on his phone. 'I've sent you the link. Let me know if you need anything.'

15

Sarah stared at her husband. This was not going to be easy to explain. Stupidly, she felt guilty, even though she knew she had done nothing wrong.

'So?' he said. His expression was grim; he was used to this stuff now.

'Ben,' Sarah said. 'Before I show you this, you need to know I had nothing to do with it.'

'Like you had nothing to do with the rest of the stuff,' he said. 'Honestly, as an excuse it's getting a little thin. But never mind. What is it this time?'

'It's not an excuse.' She opened her email and clicked on the link Molyneux had sent. 'The police had an anonymous complaint about this being inappropriate for a local doctor. Here it is.'

'Inappropriate for a local doctor? What the hell is it?'
'Read it.'

He read it slowly. When he looked up, his expression was hollow. 'I don't believe this. What have you been doing?'

'Nothing. I didn't post this. It's a fabrication.'
'By who, Sarah?'

Sarah took a deep breath. 'I don't know. But if I had to guess I'd say it was Rachel.'

Ben closed his eyes. 'Jesus,' he said. 'You think Rachel did this?'

Suddenly it was all clear to her, and the words came tumbling out.

'I *know* she did. She did it all. The Facebook page, the emails, the books. Everything.'

'She moved here a few weeks ago. The Facebook page is months old.'

'She could have done it from anywhere,' Sarah said.

'OK,' Ben said. 'Then why?'

'Because she wants to drive a wedge between me and you. She wants to steal you from me.'

Ben looked away. When he turned back to her he had tears on his cheeks. 'Sarah,' he said. 'You need help. Listen to yourself. You think Rachel did this because she wants to steal me from you? This started six months ago, before she'd even met me.'

'It's all linked to this guy at high school. He was into me and I think it got to her. So she married my ex, and now she's after you.'

'Sarah. You sound—'

'I sound what?'

'You sound a little unhinged. This is paranoia.'

'No, it isn't. Paranoia is irrational. This is real.'

'That's what every paranoid person says.' Ben shook his head. 'I'm not angry, Sarah. I know this is not your fault, and I want to help you get better. But you're going to have to start by admitting it.'

'There's nothing to admit!' Sarah shouted. 'More to the point, why don't you believe me?'

'Because what I see are the classic symptoms of bipolar disorder,' Ben said. 'Highs – often characterized by grand, implausible plans like moving suddenly to another country, or by promiscuity – and lows, filled with anxiety and paranoia. I've been reading about—'

'Reading?' Sarah said. 'Or talking to Rachel Little?'

'Reading,' Ben said. 'And your question only proves what I'm saying. You're convinced Rachel is out to get you – or me – but she isn't.'

'Really?' Sarah said. 'Well, I can prove she is.'

'You can?' Ben said. 'Then go ahead.'

'Wait there.'

Sarah went to collect the samples of handwriting she had sent to Donna Martin: her real handwriting, the forgeries in the book and postcard and the list of yoga classes Rachel had written. She brought them into the kitchen and laid them on the table.

'I've sent these to an expert graphologist,' she said. 'One who testifies in court. The first thing she's going to do is show my real handwriting and the stuff that was sent to us, purporting to be from me, aren't the same.'

Ben looked at the samples. 'They look pretty similar,' he said.

'Maybe. But she will be able to see the subtle differences,' Sarah replied. 'And when she's done *that*, she's going to prove the fakes are by the same person who wrote this list of yoga classes. Which was Rachel Little.'

Ben looked again. He bit his lip.

'They look nothing alike,' he said. 'Nothing at all.'

On the surface, Sarah could see he was right, but he needed to look deeper. He needed to have faith.

'She will find the similarities,' she said. 'She's an expert.'

'And if she doesn't?' Ben said. 'Or more likely, when she doesn't? Will you admit this was you all along?'

'It won't happen.'

'If it does?'

Sarah didn't answer. Ben sighed.

'This is the problem,' he said. 'You aren't prepared to listen to reason.' He tidied up the papers and handed them to her. 'It's pointless me trying to convince you,' he said. 'This graphologist is going to give you an answer you don't like, and you'll ignore it. You'll move on to the next crazy theory, when what you should do is admit you need help. But until you do, I'm powerless.'

'Wait,' Sarah said. 'You'll see, tomorrow. And then we can resolve this.'

'OK,' Ben said. 'I hope you're right.'

16

In Jean's kitchen Sarah kissed Miles, Faye and Kim goodbye, then hugged Jean. It felt good to be in her work clothes. It felt almost normal and for a time she'd forgotten what normal was.

'Thank you,' she said. 'I can't tell you how much I appreciate this.'

'No problems,' Jean replied. 'Is everything OK? Your eyes are a little bloodshot.'

'I didn't get much sleep,' Sarah said. The truth was she had barely slept at all. Ben had gone to bed at nine in the spare room, after a tense hour downstairs during which they hardly spoke to each other. Normally she would have tried to talk it through with him to avoid going to bed on an argument – that was their agreement – but there was little point. There wasn't much she could say, and besides, she might as well wait for Friday, when she would have proof she was not paranoid or bipolar or making all this up.

'Are you sure you want to go to work?' Jean said.

'I have to. They have no other cover. And anyway, I need to keep my mind occupied. I want this day to be over as soon as possible.'

* * *

It was odd to be back at the office. Nothing much had changed; there was an outbreak of mono among Barrow's teenagers, so she saw a host of guttural fifteen-year-olds. One guy, a contractor in his fifties, hobbled in with a swollen foot – *Maybe an infection*, he said, *nothing serious* – which turned out to be a broken ankle, and there was a woman in her forties suffering from bouts of nausea. She – to her surprise and joy – was pregnant.

And then she looked at her schedule and felt a wave of dizziness and nausea.

Derek Davies was her next patient.

She walked over to the receptionist.

'Denise,' she said. 'When did Mr Davies make his appointment?'

'He called yesterday,' Denise replied.

'Thank you,' Sarah said. She looked past the receptionist into the waiting room. Derek Davies was sitting in the corner, reading *People* magazine.

She stared at him. How had he known she was back today, for this day only? *Had* he known? Or was this another coincidence?

'Denise,' she said. 'Is there any way you can find a slot for him with one of the other doctors? I'm very busy.'

Denise tapped on the keyboard. 'I think Dr Bisson could fit him in. Is everything OK?'

'Yes, thank you,' Sarah said. 'Everything's fine.'

As she headed into a post-lunch appointment with someone complaining of swellings in their neck, Denise came over to her.

'Dr Havenant,' she said. 'Sorry to interrupt. I have a message from Jean.'

'Oh,' Sarah said, the hairs on her neck prickling. 'What is it?'

'She called about her son, Daniel. He fell and she thinks

he may have broken his arm. She's taken him to the Emergency Room, along with your children. She wants to know whether you can come for them.'

'I can't,' Sarah said. 'I might be able to get away by four, but that's a couple of hours.'

Denise nodded. 'What about your husband?'

'I'll try him, but he doesn't always answer his phone during the day.'

'Could you try? I'll let your patient know you'll be another couple of minutes.'

Sarah nodded. 'Thanks, Denise.'

Ben – for a change – answered immediately. He sounded guarded, reluctant to talk.

'Ben,' Sarah said. 'Are you free?'

'No,' he replied. 'I'm at work.'

'I mean, can you get free? It's important. I got a message from Jean. I called but it went to voicemail. She needs someone to come and get the kids.'

'For fuck's sake,' Ben said. 'What now?'

'Daniel broke his arm, so Jean had to take all the kids to the ER. Is there any way you can pick them up?'

It was a few seconds before Ben replied.

'Fine,' he said. 'I'll be there in half an hour.'

'Thanks, Ben,' Sarah said. 'Go straight there. I'll see you at home later.'

She broke the connection then checked her email.

Nothing from Donna Martin yet. But it'd be there by the end of the day and she'd be able to walk into the house and show it to her husband.

It couldn't come soon enough.

241

17

Her phone rang as she was collecting her bag and getting ready to leave work. It had been in there all afternoon; she had run from appointment to appointment and had no time to check it.

It was Donna Martin. She glanced around, then lifted it to her ear. As she did, she noticed she had two missed calls from Ben, both a couple of hours ago.

She'd see him in a few minutes at home. She needed to talk to the graphologist. She answered the call.

'Donna,' she said. 'Thanks for getting back to me.'

She felt the kind of nervous expectation she had not felt since the end of medical school when she was waiting to find out her results. She'd been pretty sure she had got the grades she needed, but so much was riding on the outcome that even the slender possibility she hadn't was enough to cause a high level of anxiety.

This was the same. This was the moment when her life got back on track.

If, that was, Donna Martin told her what she was hoping she'd tell her.

'No problem,' Donna said. 'I completed my analysis this afternoon. It's conclusive, actually.'

'And?' Sarah said. 'What did you find out?'

'Well, there were two questions. The first was whether your handwriting matches the handwriting in the other samples you gave me. And it doesn't. You did not write the postcard and the message in the book. I'll send you the details in my report next week, but, as I said, it's conclusive. There's no doubt.'

The sense of relief that flooded through Sarah left her feeling weak. This was the proof she needed to convince Ben she was not doing this herself. Which was wonderful, amazing, uplifting. It did, though, leave another question unanswered.

'The other handwriting I sent you,' she said. 'The list of yoga classes. You were going to compare it to the forgeries to see if the same person wrote them both?' *And confirm that Rachel Little is behind this*, Sarah thought.

'I did,' Donna Martin said. 'It didn't take long, to be honest. It was fairly obvious.'

Sarah was aware that a smile was spreading over her face. *It was fairly obvious* could only mean one thing: there were lots of clear similarities.

'I haven't written a detailed report,' Donna went on. 'I can, if you'd like, but there's not much point. There's no way the same person wrote those two things. No way at all. I've rarely seen two samples of handwriting as different as those two.'

Sarah's smile faded. 'Sorry,' she said. 'You're saying it's not the same person?'

'I'm saying there's no way in hell it's the same person.'

Her smile faded. Sarah closed her eyes and rubbed her temples.

'Thank you,' she said. 'This is very helpful.'

*   *   *

243

Which it was. More than helpful: it was wonderful. If she was honest, there had been moments when Sarah had started to wonder whether it *was* her doing this. She knew it was possible for someone to enter a fugue state and do all kinds of things without having any memory of them. There was a famous case of a man who had two families in two different cities. They knew him by different names and he went between them, telling them he was traveling for work when he was away; the odd thing was that when he was caught by one of his wives, he denied everything. She had incontrovertible proof; it didn't matter. He denied it all, and he wasn't lying.

It turned out that when he switched between names, he became the new person and lost all memories related to his alter ego.

So she could have been doing the same, and it was a relief to know she wasn't.

But it was also a problem. Because it meant someone else was doing it, which meant she and her family were not safe.

And she had been sure it was Rachel Little. But she was wrong. The handwriting was totally different.

Unless. Unless that was the very thing which proved it was Rachel, after all.

She replayed Donna Martin's words: *I've rarely seen two samples of handwriting as different as those two.*

Which was the clue that pointed to Rachel. In order to forge Sarah's handwriting so successfully, Rachel would have to have a detailed knowledge of graphology – which was exactly the kind of weird, hippy-ish bullshit she specialized in – and if she had, she would have made sure any handwriting she gave to Sarah – or Jean – was totally different to the forgeries.

She would have made it so someone such as Donna Martin would conclude she had *rarely seen two samples of handwriting as different as those two.*

So it was her, Sarah was sure of it. All she needed was another way to get the proof.

But that could wait. For now, she was going to go home and give her husband the good news.

She turned into her street. Ben's car was not parked outside the house. It was odd; he'd picked up the kids from the Emergency Room – she must call Jean and see how Daniel was doing – a few hours ago, so he should have been there. Perhaps he'd gone out to eat with them, but he would normally have texted her to let her know.

She parked and got out of her car. There was no one home. Which was odd.

It's fine, she told herself. *They're out running an errand.*

She unlocked the front door and went inside.

The house was silent. At the bottom of the stairs was a small, purple stuffed dog. It was Kim's comfort toy, the thing she slept with every night. They kept it in her bed; on a couple of occasions she had left it at a store or at someone's house and she had screamed the place down, so to avoid a repeat they made a rule that it stayed in her cot.

Unless they were going away for the night.

She pictured them leaving in a hurry, Kim dropping the dog in the confusion, Ben failing to notice it, She shook her head. It hadn't got here that way. There was some other reason.

She picked it up and walked into the kitchen. It was clean. No dirty plates in the sink, no pots and pans on the stove top. Wherever Ben and the kids were, they hadn't had dinner. She put Kim's dog on the counter, and saw it.

A piece of letter paper. Two messages written on it.

The one at the top in her handwriting.

The one underneath in Ben's.

18

She thinks she has found a way out. She thinks she can get *evidence*, find *proof*, use it to bring this to an end.

What a fool she is.

She has always been a fool. Not stupid, of course – no doctor is stupid – but a fool all the same. If she was not, she would have seen this coming long ago, when she could have – maybe – taken steps to stop it. But she did not because she could not. She had no idea what was being built around her, did not notice the threads being drawn through every facet of her life, ready to be pulled together into the web that will finally trap her.

And the web is now complete. She will wake up tomorrow to the knowledge she is trapped. Powerless. No longer captain of her own ship.

A fish on a hook.

A fly in a web.

A dog on a leash.

And tomorrow it is over. No more letters. No more emails. No more books.

No more Sarah.

19

Dear Ben, the note read,

I'm sorry for the wild-goose chase with the kids. I needed to know you were not going to show up at the house this afternoon. When you found that the kids weren't at the hospital I could say it was another weird thing happening.

I was planning to meet a man here, Ben. I had it all lined up. He contacted me after the post on Craigslist and we arranged to hook up. He pulled out at the last minute.

And I saw myself clearly. Saw how erratic and crazy my behavior has become. I realized that I don't – can't –– trust myself anymore. Some nights I lie in bed and I can't believe the thoughts I have. I don't know WHAT I might do – to you, the kids – and it terrifies me.

I can't go on like this. Living a lie. Hiding in plain sight.

I need a break. I need some time to figure out what I want to do. What I want US to do. Maybe we can make this work, maybe we can't: but I need some space to think.

I'm sorry, Ben. I love you, I truly do. It's a cliché, but this is about me, not you.

So go. Take our children away somewhere for the weekend. Tell them Mom's working. Don't call me. Don't answer my calls. And when you get back, let's talk.

S xxx

And then, underneath, hastily scrawled.

Sarah – I don't know what's going on but I'll do as you say. We'll be back Sunday afternoon. You know this is very fucked up, right? And we have to resolve it, one way or another. Right now, I don't much care which way, but like you say – I can't go on like this.

Sarah put the note on the countertop; the paper shook noisily, her hand unsteady. She looked at Kim's purple dog. She'd miss it tonight. Ben would have difficulty getting her to go to sleep.

She sat heavily on a stool, and leaned her forearms on the counter. She was dizzy, her legs weak.

She picked up her phone and called Ben. He needed to know right away that she wanted him back.

It went straight to voicemail, which meant it was switched off. If he was on another call it would have rung, giving him the option to hang up his call and accept hers.

'Ben,' she said. 'This is all a huge mistake. Come home. And call me as soon as you get this. I can explain.'

She hung up the call and then it hit her.

Rachel Little had been in her house.

She had been in here, left the note, and gone.

The timing was not a mistake. Rachel knew she had the proof she was innocent and so she had taken this step, written this note, before Sarah could tell Ben what Donna Martin had concluded. She wanted Ben gone.

She wanted Sarah alone, and vulnerable.

Suddenly Sarah saw how foolish she had been. She had been convinced that what Rachel wanted was to drive her and Ben apart so she could move in on Ben, and as a result she had become fixated on proving it wasn't her doing it so she and Ben would not be driven apart in the first place.

But Ben wasn't the target.

She was the target.

She didn't know why. She didn't know what she had done to Rachel Little to provoke this, but it didn't matter.

And now, at least, she knew what she was up against. And, in a way, it was a good thing Ben was gone.

It left her free to do whatever she needed to stop it.

20

She made some coffee and then moved to the couch. She had a numb feeling – the beginnings of shock, maybe – and she could tell she was losing her grip on reality. She forced herself to think through what had happened.

Ben had gone to get the kids from the Emergency Room, but, presumably, they had not been there. He had called her – twice, it seemed, if the missed calls were anything to go by, then come home to find this letter.

In which she confessed to having wanted him out of the house so she could have a random assignation with someone she had met on Craigslist, then confessed to erratic feelings which made her fear for her own predictability and the safety of her children, and then asked him to leave with the kids.

Which he had done.

And the kids had been with Jean, so he must have gone to get them there. She picked up her phone and called her friend.

'Hey,' Jean said. 'How's it going?'

'Not great,' Sarah said. 'Did Ben come for the kids?'

'Yes. A few minutes before three. I was surprised he was so early, but I guess it's Friday, so maybe he got done at work.'

250

'That's not what happened.'

'What do you mean? What *did* happen? Is everything OK?'

'Before I tell you, I need to ask a question.' Sarah paused. 'Did Daniel break his arm today?'

'No,' Jean said. 'Of course not.'

'And you didn't leave me a message at the office asking me to collect the kids from the ER?'

'Sarah,' Jean said. 'What's going on?'

'Someone – saying they were you – called the office and gave them a message for me, saying Daniel had broken his arm and you were taking him and all the other kids to the ER. As a result, you needed me or Ben to pick them up. I couldn't, so I called Ben.'

'Who called?'

'Someone who knew I was back at work and that I would have to ask Ben to go to the ER, which he did, only to find no kids. So he came home, and there was a letter from me.'

There was a sharp intake of breath. 'What was in the letter?'

Sarah told her. There was a long silence on the line.

'Holy shit,' Jean said, eventually. 'That's crazy.'

'Right. And now Ben's gone. Did he say anything when he came to get them?'

'No,' Jean said. 'Other than thanking me for helping out.'

'Did he seem OK?'

'Yes. You know Ben. Doesn't give much away. Have you called him?'

'Yes,' Sarah said. 'His phone is switched off. I'll keep trying. But God knows what I'll tell him.'

'You think it was Rachel?' Jean said.

'I know so,' Sarah replied. 'And I'm going to sort this out. Tonight.'

*　　*　　*

Rachel was renting an apartment in a building near to the college. She had the top floor; the bottom was occupied, according to the label under the bell, by Gerard Makinson.

There was a shared entrance. Sarah stood outside it and rang Rachel's bell. She heard it chime in the interior and listened for the sound of footsteps.

Nothing. No doubt Rachel had peeped out a window and seen her standing there and did not want the confrontation.

She rang the bell again. Rachel needed to know Sarah wasn't going anywhere.

Still no response. This time she hammered on the wooden door.

'Rachel,' she shouted. 'Open up! I want to talk to you!'

Still nothing. She felt her anger mount. After what Rachel had put her through the absolute least she could do was talk to her.

She banged on the door again and called Rachel's name.

To her left, a window opened. A man's head appeared in the gap. He was in his fifties and had bleary eyes.

'Keep it down, miss,' he said. 'I was having a nap.'

'I'm sorry,' Sarah said. 'But this is important. I need to see Rachel as soon as possible. She's the woman who lives here.'

'I know who she is,' the man – presumably Gerard Makinson – said. 'And you can need to see her all you like. She ain't here.'

'What do you mean?'

'I mean this here is a building where sometimes people are and sometimes people aren't. And she's one of the ones who aren't. Not right now, anyway.'

Sarah hesitated. 'Then where is she?'

'About now she's probably thirty thousand feet up in the air,' Gerard said. 'Flying to Texas. Least, that's what she told me when I dropped her off at Portland Bus Station at midday.'

'You dropped her off at the bus station at midday?'

'Yup. I was headed to Portland to meet an old veteran buddy of mine and when I was on my way out I seen her lugging her bag to the bus station here in Barrow. I asked if she was headed to Portland and she hopped right in.'

Sarah thought it through: the timings worked out. The message – supposedly from Jean – had come around lunch-time. Rachel could have put the letter in the house after calling the office, and then headed to Portland.

Commit the crime, then flee the scene. It all added up. Never mind the handwriting analysis: there was no doubt now that it was Rachel.

'Are you sure she got on the bus?' Sarah said. 'She didn't come back here?'

'If she did, I haven't seen her,' Gerard said. 'You want me to pass on a message?'

Sarah shook her head.

'It's OK,' she said. 'When I see her I'll tell her myself.'

21

So had she skipped town? Or was she still around? Sarah tried to think what she would have done.

She couldn't. Since she was not a crazy, vengeful, psychopathic bitch she could not see which of those options a crazy, vengeful, psychopathic bitch might choose.

She called Ben again. Left him another voicemail. Then she called Jean.

'She's not here,' she said.

'Who's not where?' Jean replied.

'Rachel. She's not at her apartment.'

'You went to her apartment? Are you nuts?'

'I wanted to confront her,' Sarah said. 'I've had enough. I wanted to tell her I know what she's doing and she needs to stop it. And then claw her fucking eyes out if she didn't promise to cease and desist right then and there.'

'Are you sure that was a good idea? You don't know for certain it's her.'

'I do. But it makes no difference now. She wasn't there anyway.'

'Where is she?'

'Texas. Bit of a coincidence she happened to leave today.'

'Jesus, it *is* her,' Jean said. 'So what next?'

'I go home,' Sarah replied. 'Try to call Ben. And work out my next steps.'

She also called Ian Molyneux and told him what had happened.

'I need a favor,' she said. 'I need you to help me find Ben. Check hotels. My guess is he's in Boston.'

'I can't really do that,' Ian replied. 'He's not done anything wrong. I can hardly ask the BPD to search the city for a guy who's not committed any kind of a crime.'

'What if you tell them he's kidnapped his own kids?'

'Maybe I could. But the problem is he hasn't,' Ian said. 'And when they found him and discovered he'd had a domestic argument and his wife had wanted the cops to find him so they could work it out and then maybe have some frantic make-up sex before their next argument, they'd flip out. I'd probably lose my job.'

'So there's nothing you can do?' Sarah said.

'Nothing. At least not about Ben. But you can call me anytime if you need help.'

'Thanks, Ian. I appreciate it.' Although it wasn't what she had called for, it *was* comforting to know she had his support if she needed it.

She only hoped she didn't.

22

'Want some company?' Jean said.

Sarah held the phone between her ear and shoulder and fished in her bag for her bank card. There was a bottle of Marlborough Sauvignon Blanc and a box of pizza on the counter of Bingham's, her local market.

'I thought you had a date?' she said.

'I did. I can cancel. I figure you might not want to be alone.'

'Jean,' Sarah said. 'You don't have to do that. Your date's more important.'

Although it would be nice not to be alone, Sarah thought. *But I don't want to tell her.*

'I don't mind,' Jean said. 'I'll come over.'

'I feel bad,' Sarah said. 'I don't want you to change your plans for me, although I appreciate the thought – it's true I'm not looking forward to a night – let alone a weekend – alone. But I don't want to ruin your evening. Really, I don't.'

'It's fine,' Jean said. 'Here's a compromise: I'll go out with Carl for a drink, and then I'll come to see you.'

'You don't have to do this,' she said. 'But thanks, Jean. I really appreciate it.'

She picked up another bottle of wine. If she was going to have company, she could use it.

At home she poured a glass of wine and called Ben. It went to voicemail.

She felt a rising anger toward him. Even if she had written the note, he still shouldn't be ignoring her calls.

But then look at it from his point of view: she'd had an affair, he had reasonable grounds to suspect she was suffering from a severe psychiatric disorder – because if it was her doing all these things, but being unaware of it, then that would be classified as pretty damn severe – and he had been sent, by her – because it was her who had called him – to the ER to pick up his kids, only to find they weren't there.

And then he had come home to a letter from his wife telling him she didn't trust herself around their kids, and she wanted him to leave her for a while. Oh, and she'd been planning a random hookup with someone from Craigslist.

So it was no wonder he was angry and didn't feel like talking to her.

She had never realized how vulnerable she – everyone – was. Between Facebook, Twitter, Craigslist, emails, online accounts with hackable passwords and all the rest of our digital footprints, we were putting ourselves in full public view in a way which would have been considered foolhardy, even irresponsible, a decade ago.

Back then, who would have announced to the world the dates of their holiday? Or their children's birthdays? Their wedding anniversary? Their maiden and middle names? Imagine somebody putting up a pinboard outside their house and tacking all that information to it, along with a daily update on their activities and whereabouts. Nobody would have done it.

Yet that was what exactly we did with Facebook. In fact

we did worse: a board outside your house was only visible to those who happened to pass by. Social media was available to the whole world.

Yes, there were security settings, but a lot of people didn't use them or missed an update which changed them or didn't think about them at all. And then even if you did, all someone needed to do was to become a friend of a friend, or impersonate someone you knew, or find some other way to get into your personal data and with it, into your digital life.

And all you could do was wait for them to go away, and hope it wouldn't spill over into your real life.

Which for her it already had.

It was gone eight thirty when there was a knock on the door. She checked from behind the curtains – to make sure it was Jean – before she let her in. She was holding an open, three-quarter-full bottle of red wine.

'How was Carl?' Sarah asked.

'Good. He's a nice guy.'

'I hope he wasn't too disappointed.'

Jean shrugged. 'I told him my babysitter had to leave early. He suggested he could come to my place, but I told him it's a bit too soon.'

'Where did you go?'

'The new Spanish place downtown. We had some tapas and a drink. It was fun.'

'I'm sorry,' Sarah said. 'I wish your date wasn't ruined.'

'It's OK. This is more important. And there'll be plenty of time for Carl when this is all over.' She held up the bottle. 'Drink?'

'I've got a glass of white. You want one?'

'Try this,' Jean said. 'It's the good stuff. Some kind of Italian wine called Amarone. Carl gave it to me. He told me about it; it's pretty strong. I think he was hoping we'd drink it together. On the couch. All cuddled up.' She laughed. 'But he'll get a chance, soon.'

Sarah looked at the bottle. 'Did you drink it at the tapas place?'

Jean shook her head. 'No. It's not BYO.'

'It's open,' Sarah said. 'I thought Carl just gave it to you?'

'Oh,' Jean said. 'Right. I had a glass before I came here. It's really good.'

'OK,' Sarah said. 'I'll have some later. Sounds delicious.'

They sat on the couch. Jean had a glass of water – *I need a soft drink before I have another glass of wine*, she'd said – and Sarah took a few bites of pizza. She wasn't really hungry.

'So Rachel was gone?' Jean said. 'It is kind of a weird coincidence.'

'It's not a coincidence,' Sarah said. 'It's her. I know it. And I'm going to prove it.'

'I think you're probably right,' Jean said. 'It's hard to be sure, but it does seem like she's the most likely person.'

'I think it goes back to Jeremy,' Sarah said. 'Although how, I don't know.'

'Jeremy from high school?'

'Yes. I mean, it's fucking crazy but I think she has a grudge against me because of him, which is why she married my college boyfriend, and why she's after Ben now.'

'But that would mean she's been doing this for years,' Jean said.

'I know,' Sarah replied. 'And it terrifies me.'

Jean put her glass down. 'I'm going to the bathroom,' she said. 'You want a drink while I'm up?'

'Sure,' Sarah said.

'I put the red wine on the countertop in the kitchen. Let's

259

try it. Otherwise it'll go off in the week. I won't drink it on my own. I'll grab it on my way back.'

While Jean was gone, Sarah tried calling Ben; again it went to voicemail. She heard the toilet flush, and then Jean came in holding the bottle and two glasses.

Jean poured a glass – nearly to the brim – and handed it to her. As she took it Sarah hesitated. Was this what Jean thought she wanted? A huge glass of wine? Was she the kind of person who people saw as a big drinker?

'You going to try it?' Jean said.

Sarah nodded slowly. 'Sure,' she said. Ben had mentioned her drinking; she didn't think she had a problem, but suddenly she didn't think she wanted a drink after all. She didn't need an alcohol issue to go with everything else.

But she wouldn't tell Jean. Not right now. Jean was proud of her wine and she didn't want to disappoint her.

She sipped the wine. No doubt on another evening she would have found it delicious, but it tasted bitter; it was hard to enjoy anything.

'Wow,' she said. 'It's lovely. Perfect.'

Jean smiled. 'Yes,' she said. 'It is.'

23

They sat on the couch.

'Did I ever show you the postcard?' Sarah said. 'I think I should. I'll grab it from the office.'

She stood up and left the room, bringing her wine with her. She put it on the desk she and Ben shared and noisily opened a drawer. The postcard wasn't in there; it was in a file on top of the desk, but she wanted Jean to hear her searching.

When the drawer was shut she listened for the sound of footsteps. Satisfied there was nothing, she emptied three-quarters of the wine into an empty mug on the desk. She could clean it up later. Then she grabbed the postcard and went back into the living room.

Jean glanced at the wineglass – now nearly empty – as she handed her the postcard.

After a few moments, Jean looked up.

'You know,' she said. 'I think it's a man who wrote it.'

'Why?' Sarah said.

'The tone. It feels like a man. And it's more likely a stalker would be a man.'

'It's Rachel,' Sarah said. 'I'm sure of it.'

She picked up the nearly empty wineglass and took a small sip.

'Did you like it?' Jean said.

'I did,' Sarah said. 'It's lovely. Carl is a good judge of wine.'

'You want some more? I'll get it?'

Sarah shook her head. 'That was plenty for me, but thanks. I'm already feeling it.'

'OK,' Jean said. 'Well, I need to go. The kids'll be up early, as usual.'

Sarah walked her to the door and locked it behind her. She called Ben again and left another message on his voice-mail.

Ben, she said. *I think I know what's going on now. It's all going to be fine. Please come home so I can explain. I love you and I think you love me. It's time to put this behind us. I know you're mad at me, but trust me, OK?*

She took her wineglass to the kitchen and emptied it into the sink. She picked up the bottle of wine Jean had brought and read the label. AMARONE DI VALPOLLICELLA. It looked expensive. It was a shame for Carl that he wouldn't get to taste it.

She jammed the cork in and put the bottle in a cupboard. She'd give it to Jean tomorrow.

It was strange to go to bed in the house alone. Normally, even when Ben and the kids were fast asleep, the house felt full. In winter there were the clicks and ticks of the heating system; in summer, Ben kicked the covers off, snorting in his sleep. In the kids' rooms fans whirred. From time to time one of them coughed or laughed or cried out, in the grip of a nightmare.

Zombies were chasing me last night in my dream, Mom, Miles said once. *But in my room there was a magic blanket which I threw on them and they disappeared.*

She wished she had a magic blanket she could use to make her troubles disappear. But magic blankets were the stuff of children's dreams, and were only of use against the zombies that populated them. The problems in adults' lives were harder to solve.

And they seemed even harder, lying alone in a quiet, still house, listening to it creak as the heat of the day dissipated and the house settled into its sleeping state.

She'd have thought the silence would help her to sleep; there had been plenty of times in the last few years when she had wished for a night without interruptions from her family, a night when she could fall asleep knowing no one would wake up or be sick or pee in the bed. Now, though, she wanted nothing more than to hear a cry of M*om!* from Kim's room and to go in and see her daughter standing in her crib, arms outstretched, in need of some maternal comfort.

Soon, she thought. *Soon. And then I'll never complain about anything again.*

Eventually she fell into a fitful, shallow sleep. Her mind was stuck on a loop in which she tried to explain to Ben but he kept interrupting, wouldn't let her get her explanation out. She'd become more and more annoyed until she'd shout at him and wake herself up, before slipping gradually into the same unpleasant dream.

It was almost a relief when the noise of a stair creaking woke her up fully.

For a second she thought it was the creak of the house settling, but it was louder than she would have expected.

It sounded like someone on the stairs.

But it couldn't be. It was one of the noises houses made at night. She breathed in slowly, and listened.

And then she heard it again.

She lay in bed totally still, eyes wide open. In the light

263

from the moon she could see – just – the shape of the door, light against the darker walls.

A few seconds passed. Nothing.

She started to relax, her heart thudding in her chest as it slowed. She was hearing things. It wasn't a surprise, with what had been happening. Wide awake, she levered herself up on her elbows.

There was no hope of sleep now. She was alert. She might as well go downstairs and find some activity until she calmed down. Better to watch a crappy movie and nod off on the couch.

She was about to push the covers back when she heard it again.

This time there was no mistaking it. The long, slow creak of someone stepping on a floorboard.

And it was right outside her room.

Shit. She needed to call Ian Molyneux and tell him there was an intruder. He'd be here in minutes.

Unless it was Ben.

No. Ben would not be moving so stealthily. This was his home.

She looked for her phone on the nightstand. But it wasn't there. It was still downstairs, charging on the kitchen counter.

Shit.

Her hands bunched into fists as her mind scrambled to think of anything in the room she could use as a weapon.

A belt? A coathanger? The scissors in the bathroom?

There was another creak and then the door began to open.

She lowered herself back on to the bed, her instinct to pretend she was asleep. She pictured herself springing on the intruder, knocking them to the floor and then sprinting into the street, shouting for help.

And then the panic took over.

24

For a time, back in medical school, Sarah had considered joining the Medical Corps of the Army. Her grandfather, Stan, had served as a medic in the Second World War, and she asked him for his opinion.

Well, he said, *the question you have to ask yourself is how you would react when you're terrified, when bullets are flying and bombs are falling. When your life is under threat. For some people the fear brings focus. They think clearly and act quickly. That wasn't me. I felt paralyzed. There were medics there with half my training but twice the ability to think in those situations and they were a lot more effective than I was. I wanted to run away. So that's the question you have to ask yourself. And the thing is, you never really find out until it happens.*

She'd decided not to sign up. It had been a vague idea in the first place, and so she'd never found out how she would react when she was terrified.

Well, now she knew. She would have been a *terrible* army medic.

As the door opened, she stared at it, eyes wide, totally frozen in mind and body. Any thoughts she'd had of finding a weapon or escaping through the window were long gone.

She could think nothing other than *oh shit, oh shit, oh shit*.

When the door was half-open it stopped moving.

Someone stepped through the gap and into the room.

They stood for a moment, silhouetted against the lighter walls. On their head was a baseball cap; in one hand was a bag.

It's Derek Davies, she thought. *Why oh why did I not tell someone about him when he showed up at work?*

And then the intruder spoke.

'Sarah?' a woman's voice whispered. 'Sarah. Are you awake?'

It took Sarah a second to recognize the voice, and when she did it took another second to accept who it was.

It was Jean.

Sarah was about to reply; the fear had subsided now she knew it was not some masked intruder hell-bent on killing her, and she assumed her friend was coming to check on her, which, although Sarah appreciated the gesture, could have been done in a less terrifying way, but what Jean did next stopped her.

She walked over to Sarah's bureau, and laid the bag on it. Then she took something out; there was the ping of a strap and a light came on.

She was wearing a headlamp. Sarah watched – her eyes now slitted, so if Jean looked at her she would appear asleep – as Jean took out a pad of paper and a pen and began to write.

Was it a note to Sarah to say she'd been here to check on her? If so, it was a long one. Her hand was moving over the paper, the only sound in the room the scratching of the pen. It reminded Sarah of college, of lying in her bed at night while her roommates – Toni and Anne – took notes on some book they'd left it to the last minute to read.

This was ridiculous; Sarah's fear was quickly being replaced by irritation. What the hell did Jean think she was doing, coming into her house like this? It wasn't breaking and entering, as such – she'd given Jean a key a few years back in case Sarah lost hers and was locked out, but she was beginning to wish she hadn't.

She'd had enough.

'Jean,' she said. 'What the fuck are you doing?'

25

Jean spun around, banging her hip loudly against the bureau. Sarah almost laughed; all she could see was the headlamp. Jean could have been a miner approaching from a long, dark tunnel.

'You're dazzling me,' Sarah said. 'Turn the headlamp off.' She reached out and switched on her bedside lamp.

'You're awake,' Jean said. 'How?'

'Because you're in my house in the middle of the night,' Sarah said. 'What's going on?'

Jean smiled. It looked forced, and the light from the headlamp distorted it into a grimace, her teeth looming large like a fairground clown.

'I shouldn't have crept in here,' she said. 'I was just checking on you. But I didn't want to wake you. Not after what you've been through.'

'What were you writing?' Sarah said.

Jean gestured to the piece of paper. 'I was leaving you a note to say I'd been. That's all. Come and see.'

Sarah nodded. It made sense, kind of. But there was something not quite right about what Jean had said nagging at her. It would come to her. She swung her feet on to the carpet and stood up. She walked toward Jean, then held her hand out. 'Pass it over.'

Jean slid the paper off the bureau and held it out.

Sarah reached for it. When her hand was halfway to the paper she stopped and stared at it. Even before she had it in her hand, Sarah could see the most important thing about it. The shock hit her with a physical force; it felt like she had been hit in the stomach.

It was her handwriting.

Her hand fell to her side.

'Take it,' Jean said. The grin was wider now, made even more sinister by the headlamp. 'Read it.'

Sarah stared at her, blinking. Jean was in her house writing a letter in Sarah's handwriting.

Which answered a lot of questions. It answered the question of who had written the postcard, who had written in the book, who had sent the emails, who had set up the fake account.

It was Jean who had done everything.

'Was it you?' Sarah said, her voice a whisper. 'Did you do all this?'

Jean nodded, the paper still in her outstretched hand.

'Why?' Sarah said. 'Why, Jean?'

'Read it,' Jean said. She reached up and switched off the headlamp. 'Then you'll know.'

Sarah took the paper and started to read.

Ben

This has been the hardest decision of my life. I needed space to work it out, which is why I needed you to leave the house with the kids. It's selfish, I know, but it's what I had to do. And it's bad for me, too, because it means I won't get a chance to say goodbye to you, Miles, Faye and Kim.

269

I love you all, Ben. Make sure the kids know that, as they grow up. Make sure they know their mom loved them every minute of every day. Make sure they know I would have stuck around, if there was any way I could have done.

But there isn't. I'm tired, and sad, and I've had enough. It's such a struggle, Ben. Everything. Even waking up and getting dressed is a monumental effort. And it's not getting easier.

I'm sorry, but I'm not strong enough to carry on. After writing this I'm going to take sleeping pills – strong ones – and then I'm going to sleep. Forever. It's

That was as far as Jean had got. Sarah lowered the paper – the *suicide note* – and looked up at Jean.

But Jean had moved.

26

Sarah heard a shuffling noise behind her – feet on carpet, she thought, then wondered why she was noticing that and not the important stuff, like why was Jean behind her in the first place, a question which was answered when, before she could turn around, Jean clamped an arm around her neck, the hard bone of her forearm pressing painfully against Sarah's throat.

The pressure grew and she gasped for breath; it felt like the air was not able to get past her neck. She tried again, but Jean was tightening her grip and all she could take was the shallowest of breaths.

She knew what was happening, could picture her trachea being compressed, understood limited air was making it to her lungs so they could transfer the oxygen it contained to her blood, blood which would flow to her brain where it would unload its precious cargo, a cargo which was necessary for life.

She knew it would not take long to extinguish that life if it was denied the oxygen it needed.

She knew all those things. It was basic medical knowledge.

What she didn't know was what she could do about it.

'Jean,' she said, but all that came out was a croak. Jean didn't reply; she increased the pressure. Sarah's vision was starting to blur; she lowered her chin, digging it into the muscle in Jean's forearm in an attempt to relieve the pressure.

It worked, a little. By tilting her head down she had pulled her neck back from the pressure of Jean's forearm, leaving a small gap. She raised her hands and tried to work her fingers into it.

The pressure lessened, slightly. Sarah breathed in; she could feel the air flow into her lungs. She pulled again, and then dug her fingernails into Jean's skin.

Jean grunted, then lifted her free hand to Sarah's face, and pushed the hard bone at the side of her wrist into the angle where the base of her nose met the top of her lip.

The pain shot through Sarah's nose and jaw. It was incredibly intense and Sarah remembered one of the professors at medical school telling the class the base of the nose was a pressure point; he had been a cop and explained how, if you could get to it, you could force anyone to submit. No one could stand the pain.

Sarah pulled her head back to try and escape it, but in doing so she pushed her throat into Jean's forearm. Sarah tried to lower her chin, but that meant pushing her nose into Jean's wrist, which was an agony she could not bear.

As the pressure grew, her breaths became shallower and her vision started to dim. As it did questions swirled in her mind.

Where had Jean learned to do this? And the forgery? Where has she learned that? And why the fuck was she doing all this in the first place?

Her last thought, though, was none of these. Her last thought was the realization she would never find out.

And then, only darkness.

PART THREE

Ten Years Earlier

The body never showed up.

They looked for it, at length, after they found out what Karen had done, but they didn't find it.

It wasn't a surprise; the ocean rarely gave up its secrets and there was no reason why it should be different this time. She had left a note tucked into one of her New Balance sneakers about how she didn't think she could carry on, about the deep depression and crippling anxiety she had been struggling with for months. She had tried to cope with it but couldn't, simply couldn't, and she had nowhere to turn, and she was sorry, so sorry, for Jack, but even more for Daniel and Paul, her two boys who she loved with all her heart, she really, truly did, but love wasn't enough.

And so she had committed herself to the ocean. Drunk a bottle of vodka – pretty much enough to kill her on its own – and gone for a night swim on an outgoing tide.

The coastguard, local lobstermen, owners of pleasure boats: all kept an eye out for her body, but nothing showed up. She could have been carried miles offshore by the tide, left hundreds of feet deep, food for the lobsters and crabs which adorned the plates of Maine's myriad vacationers.

Some still suspected her boyfriend, Jack. It was too neat: two weeks after her disappearance, a suicide note was found with her clothes. They were in a remote spot, but people still wondered why it had taken so long to find them. It was very convenient for Jack, and he could easily have planted them there.

But with no body, what could the cops do? No body, no crime.

There was hope a body might show up. They sometimes did, weeks or months after a fisherman fell overboard.

But what nobody knew was that this would never happen.

Because the body was not in the ocean. It never had been.

It was somewhere else entirely. Somewhere no one could ever have imagined.

1

Ben knew it was early when he woke up; the curtains in the hotel room were only partially drawn – they were on the fifteenth floor of a hotel in downtown Boston, and the night before Miles and Faye had been fascinated by the lights of the city far below – and it was still dark outside.

He lifted his head from the pillow and looked at the red digits of the alarm clock: 4.50 a.m.

Next to him, Kim slept. Miles and Faye had fallen asleep on the sofa bed but Kim had refused to be put down and so he had eventually let her fall asleep on his chest.

There had been a lot of questions about where Mom was. He had avoided answering directly – what could he say? – contenting himself with a vague muttering that she was working this weekend and they would see her in a day or two. The kids seemed to accept it, but he knew at some point he was going to have to come clean.

Mum's struggling, he'd say. *She needs some space. We're going to live without her for a while.*

Which may or may not be true. This whole situation was ridiculous; he had no idea what was going on but he knew she needed help. Whatever was happening, the idea that someone was doing all of this to her was becoming harder and harder to swallow. There was simply no evidence for it, whereas there was plenty to support the idea she was doing it in a fugue state to call attention to her problems.

But Sarah wouldn't accept it.

Or, at least, she hadn't, until now.

The note she had left him suggested she was coming to terms with it, gave him hope she had accepted the fact she needed help and was getting ready to seek it. Of course, if he asked her outright she might deny having written it, which was part of the reason he had not called her or answered the messages she'd sent him. He didn't want to hear her say it wasn't her; he wanted to cling to the hope she might finally be on the road to some kind of recovery.

Part of the reason.

The other part was that he was so fucking *angry* at her.

First there was the affair with the guy from the practice. The fact she'd done it was bad enough; that she'd only come clean because she'd been forced to was worse; but worst of all was how it made him think of her: as some desperate housewife unable to resist the advances of a younger man. It was pathetic; *she* was pathetic. It was like a rich, older man marrying a much younger woman and convincing himself it was because she loved him. What did Sarah think? This younger guy found her irresistible? No – he wanted a cheap screw, and she'd given it to him.

He might forgive her, but he wasn't sure he'd ever respect her again.

Then there was the rest of it. He didn't blame her, as such. She was clearly mentally ill, so it was hardly her fault, but Jesus, it was hard to take. Emails and letters and books were one thing; the Craigslist stuff, the random hook-ups were another entirely.

280

They were humiliating, for him and her, and, for that matter, the kids.

So no, he hadn't wanted to speak to her. He'd fumed his way through the evening and eventually fallen asleep.

I'll deal with this in the morning, he told himself.

Well, it was morning now, and his anger had faded, a little. He picked up his phone and listened to the voicemail Sarah had left.

Ben. I think I know what's going on now. It's all going to be fine. Please come home so I can explain. I love you and I think you love me. It's time to put this behind us. I know you're mad at me, but trust me, OK?

There was a more upbeat tone in her voice than he had heard for a while – not exactly happy and relaxed, but an improvement – but it didn't fill him with joy. It had the opposite effect: he was pretty sure when she said she knew what was going on it she meant that she had some new theory about how this was all Rachel Little. He doubted she had accepted she needed professional help.

Which was ridiculous. Of course she needed help. And how could it be Rachel? It made no sense. The idea that it all went back to some high-school thing was all the proof he needed that Sarah was paranoid.

Either way, though, he needed to go home. She'd told him to stay away, but there was no point. It was only putting off the inevitable. It was time for a final reckoning between them.

He got out of bed and went to the bathroom to get a glass of water. It was warm; he swilled his mouth out with it then spat it out. There was a phone by the sink; he called reception.

'Is it too early for coffee?' he said.

'No, sir,' the receptionist replied. 'We can send up some breakfast, if you'd like? Cheese Danish, maybe?'

Cheese Danish. He had no idea what a cheese Danish was.

He'd lived here for a decade but there were still things he didn't understand.

Whatever. It was never too late to learn something new.

'Sure,' he said. 'Sounds lovely. Thank you.'

'Thank *you*. They'll be right up.'

He should let Sarah know he was coming. He picked up his cell phone and dialed her number.

It rang through to her voicemail; she was probably asleep. A small smile played on his lips at the irony it was now him who could not get in touch with her.

'Hey,' he said. 'I'm coming home. I'll be back mid-morning. See you then.'

So, the die was cast. Coffee. A first-ever Cheese Danish. And then, once the kids were up, back to Barrow to see his wife and figure out what to do with what was left of his marriage.

2

At first, all she knew was that she had woken up.

There were no physical sensations, not yet. Her eyes were still closed, and her body was still numb. But her mind was active.

It was like waking up after a night when you had drunk far too much: a slow climb from a deep pit, a climb that started with nothing other than the dim, groggy awareness of your mind switching back on, of a cursor blinking on an otherwise black screen.

And then there was the beginning of pain. The rasp of each breath. The tenderness of the muscles in her neck. The ache in her left shoulder where it lay on a hard floor.

A hard, cold floor.

She placed her hand on it. It was dry and dusty and rough.

And then the memories came.

The middle of the night.

Jean in her bedroom, with a headlight, comical and demonic at the same time.

The suicide letter.

Jean – no longer comical – choking her out.

The *suicide* letter.

Jesus. Where the *fuck* was she?

She opened her eyes.

Nothing. Total, pitch-black darkness. No lights, no windows, no patches of shadow.

Just her, lying on her side on a hard floor, her head throbbing, her throat raw.

She pushed herself up into a sitting position. The ache in her shoulder subsided and she felt around herself for a wall. There was nothing; she had no idea of the size of the place she was in. She would need to walk around to figure it out.

She stood up, and yelped in pain.

3

She is awake.

From the sound of her cry, she has hurt herself.

No matter. It won't be the last time. And, as she will soon learn, a little pain is the least of her worries.

A *lot* of pain is the least of her worries.

Because her worries are many. They extend well beyond pain and fear and panic. She will come to understand this.

She will also come to understand that they extend beyond anything she can imagine.

The worst she can imagine is a slow, painful, drawn-out death in her dark cell.

Which is only the start.

The legacy of this will extend to her children and her children's children and – hopefully – to her children's children's children.

But more of that later.

Right now she will be wondering where she is. Right now she will be filled with panic.

Panic. Let's consider panic for a moment.

It is a word with which she is familiar. She has *panic* attacks, the poor little flower. Despite not having a fucking care in the world, she has *panic* attacks. She suffers from *anxiety*.

Pathetic. But at least now she has a reason to panic. Her heart will be fluttering away as she waves her arms around, feeling for the walls of her cage.

She will not find them. Not yet.

She will start to ask questions: Where am I? What is happening? What is Jean – for she knows it is me now – thinking?

She will not get answers.

Not yet.

4

The pain.

Sarah slumped to the floor, clutching her throat.

When she'd tried to stand up it felt like someone had grabbed her by the neck and yanked her back down. There was a sharp pain, like a muscle tearing.

She raised her hands to her neck. There was a metal collar around it. She ran her fingers along the collar to the back, where there was a chain, cold and hard and about the thickness of her finger. She followed it until it reached a wall. The wall was rough – concrete, she thought – and the chain was attached to a link which was embedded in it. She grabbed it and tried to move it.

It was stuck fast.

She ran her hands over her sides and hips and down to her ankles, feeling for any other restraints. There were none. Only the collar around her neck.

She started to shake, her eyes blinking. Panic took over her; she wanted to attack the chain, tear it from the wall, beat her fists against the floor and scream for help.

She sat still and took a deep breath. She closed her eyes –

although it made no difference – and exhaled slowly, concentrating on the air passing her lips.

Inhale. Exhale. Inhale. Exhale.

Her heart slowed, and the feeling of panic subsided enough for her to think.

This was a basement, she was sure of it. It had the dank, musty smell of a basement, of a room under the level of the earth.

But whose basement? Jean's presumably, but she had been in Jean's basement many times and never seen a chain embedded in a wall.

But if not Jean's then whose was it? It was Jean who had attacked her, but perhaps she was not doing this alone. That would make sense.

But she was left with the same question. Who else was involved? And what the hell was going on?

The panic started to rise. Heart, stomach, head: all malfunctioning. But this was not an anxiety attack, this was not her body fight-or-flight mechanism responding disproportionately to an imagined threat.

This was the real thing.

She breathed in and out, deeply and slowly. Gradually she got control of her thoughts. When she did she tried to lay out all the pieces of the puzzle.

None of it made sense. She could see – dimly – what Jean was trying to do, but she had no idea to what end. Had she not been chained to a wall in a dark basement with a throbbing head – which must be from some kind of drug – and a crushed throat she would not have believed it was Jean who was behind all of this. Even so, it was a struggle.

She took another deep breath, then she started to shout.

'Jean!' she called. 'Jean! Where are you? Jean! We need to talk!'

There was silence.

She tried again. Again, nothing.

Sarah leaned back against the wall.

And then she heard the click of a lock.

A door opened directly opposite her. A dim light came from it – she could tell there was no light source close to the door, which made her think it was at the end of a tunnel or corridor. Either way, the light was enough for her to see that the room she was in was a concrete box, about eight feet from side to side and from top to bottom.

She looked around. There was a hatch high in the corner. It was secured with a heavy padlock.

Below it a chain was fixed to a metal plate in the wall. It had a collar on one end, a collar that was clearly a companion to the one around Sarah's neck.

What – and where – was this place?

Jean walked into the room. She stood, motionless, silhouetted against the light coming from the open door. Eventually, she bent down and reached for something on the floor. She picked up a small plastic device – a baby monitor, it looked like – and a packet of Chesterfield cigarettes. She opened it and took out a cigarette and a lighter. She struck a flame and lit the cigarette.

Seeing her friend – former friend – smoke was almost the most shocking thing about the whole situation. They had all experimented with smoking – cigarettes and dope – in their teen years but Sarah had assumed it was long behind them now. She didn't know anyone who smoked anymore, but then, it seemed, she knew less than she had thought about her friends.

Jean turned a dial on the baby monitor.

'Don't need this on anymore,' she said. 'I only wanted to know when you woke up.' She tucked it into the back pocket of her jeans. 'Been very handy over the years,' she said. 'I doubt Jack thought it would have so many uses when he bought it. He was surprised, actually, when he found out I was using it. He assumed Karen had thrown it out, but she hadn't. Like most moms she was sentimental about her kids' stuff. Wanted to preserve the memories. Waste of fucking time, if you ask me. Didn't do her much good, in any case. But useful for me.'

Useful? Sarah thought. *How were baby monitors useful when you didn't have babies?*

'What do you mean, useful?' Sarah said.

Jean stepped forward and her face came out of the shadow. Her expression was impassive, distracted almost.

'Oh,' she said. She took a drag on her cigarette then exhaled, long and slow. 'You'll find out. But for now we have other things to talk about.'

'Where are we, Jean?' Sarah said. 'Where the hell is this place?'

'My house,' Jean said.

Sarah shook her head. She'd been in Jean's house thousands of times. She knew every inch of it. There was no way she would have missed an entire room.

'It can't be,' she said.

'But it is. You're so *certain*, Sarah. So *rational*. So sure that what you see is all there is. You think because you haven't seen it, it can't be there. Well, it is, like I am. You didn't see me coming, either. Did you?'

'So what is this?'

'A former owner built this as a bomb shelter during the Cold War. Everyone was building them back then. None of them were ever needed, of course, so it was all a waste of money. But it turned out well for me. The door' – she pointed behind her – 'opens on to some steps which go up to a bulkhead in the corner of my basement. I keep a box of old clothes on top of it.' She leaned forward, pointing the cigarette at Sarah. 'Stop prying eyes from seeing things they shouldn't.'

So, it was a fallout shelter. Built in the fifties, at the height of the Cold War, when nuclear annihilation was the thing keeping people up at night. Now it was extreme weather or water security or terrorism; there was always some source of impending doom. People were programmed to worry, to constantly be alert for threats. It was a useful survival mechanism; it kept you on your toes, made sure that if anything was going to go wrong you got ahead of it as soon as possible.

It hadn't helped her. She hadn't seen this coming. Should she have? *Could* she have figured out it was Jean?

Probably not. Jean was right: she trusted what she saw. She found it hard to believe – even now when she knew it was actually happening, when she was a captive in a Cold War era fallout shelter she never knew existed, she found it hard to believe Jean was doing this.

Which was exactly the reason Jean had been able to do it.

There used to be a lot of these shelters. She'd seen one, years back, at the house of one of her dad's colleagues. It was at the end of his backyard, a low, grass-covered hump under a large oak tree. He'd opened the metal door.

Want to go down? he said.

The air coming out was cold and smelled stale. Sarah shook her head.

What if the bomb fell and something landed on the door? she said.

He smiled. *They thought of that. There's a back door. Opens into a tunnel leading to another entrance a few yards away.*

Which meant there was another door here. She glanced at the hatch in the corner. The padlock was large, and rusted.

'Don't get any ideas,' Jean said. 'Even if you could open

it, there's no way through. It used to lead to another exit, but we built the garage over it.' She chuckled. It was a cold, mirthless laugh. 'You're going nowhere, Sarah,' she said. 'This is the perfect place for you. Soundproof, too.' She held up the baby monitor. 'Which is why I need this.'

'What the fuck is going on, Jean?' Sarah said. 'What are you doing?'

Jean ignored the question. 'It's lucky I have this little set-up down here,' she said. 'Or I might have had a problem. I had *not* planned to have you down here.'

Sarah had not, until that point, wondered why Jean had chains in her basement, although she was starting to get a horrible feeling she might be able to guess. There were more pressing concerns, however.

'What *did* you have planned?' she said.

'Not this.' Jean said. She took a step toward Sarah. 'I might tell you later. But since you only believe what you see for yourself, I want to show you something. Put your hand on the floor.'

'What are you going to show me?'

'Put your hand on the floor.'

'No,' Sarah said. 'No, I won't.'

Jean sighed. 'Don't make this more difficult than it needs to be,' she said. 'It's not worth it.'

'I don't care. I'm not doing it.'

'OK.' She sounded totally matter of fact, as though they were having coffee and Sarah had said she was going to the ladies' room. 'Don't blame me. I told you not to do this.'

Without any warning, she stepped forward and swung her foot in an arc. It connected with Sarah's right temple and sent her sprawling to the ground; as she hit the floor, the chain snapped her back and she scraped the side of her face on the rough concrete. She held her hands up to protect herself. Jean moved toward her, but did not kick her again.

She did not touch her at all. Instead she bent down and grabbed the chain in both her hands then yanked it upward. Sarah jerked into the air, her cry stifled by the metal collar crushing her throat.

It took a few seconds for the pain to register, and then it was all she could think of.

'OK,' Jean said, slowly, the cigarette dangling from her lips. She was breathing heavily. 'Put your motherfucking hand on the floor. Palm down.'

Sarah stared at her, her cheek against the rough concrete. Before she could speak, Jean kicked her again, this time in the ribs.

'Palm *down*,' she said, frustration mounting in her voice.

Sarah put her hand on the floor. It was level with her nose.

'What were you going to show me?' she said, hoping to distract Jean.

'I was going to show you,' Jean said, 'exactly what the situation here is.' Jean placed her foot on Sarah's wrist and pressed down hard, then she took the cigarette from her mouth, leaned down and ground it into the back of Sarah's hand.

The pain was searing, a hot, stinging burst of agony. Sarah screamed, the smell of burning flesh filling her nostrils. Jean pressed it harder into her, then, suddenly, let go of it. It stuck upright in the melted skin.

'There,' Jean said. 'Get it? Did my demonstration work? I'm going now. But I'll be back.' She nodded at the cigarette. 'That'll help you remember me while I'm away.'

And then she was gone, and the room was only darkness and pain.

5

Sarah lay still, making a mental inventory of the areas of her body that were in pain. Her right temple throbbed; her left cheek felt raw where it had scraped on the rough concrete floor. Her neck was a mess of pain; she tried to swallow; the constriction of the muscles in her throat made her shudder.

And then there was her hand. Bizarrely, it felt huge, as though it had needed to swell in order to produce so much pain.

Sarah reached out and plucked the cigarette butt off her hand, then threw it across the room. In the darkness she pictured the wound: an angry red welt, raised and bubbled, dark ash embedded in the burnt flesh. Normally she would have swabbed it with rubbing alcohol then dressed the damaged area but there was no chance of doing that. At least it was unlikely to be infected – yet – as the heat would have killed any pathogens.

But fuck, it hurt.

The pain, though, was secondary. She was starting to realize Jean was only tangentially interested in causing her pain. Whatever she was doing was much worse. Once again, the panic rose up; this time the deep breaths she took had no effect.

She started to scream. Over and over and over. She lifted her hands to the chain and tried to rip it from around her neck, yanking her head from side to side as she did. The chain held fast, and in fear and frustration she slammed her fists on the floor, scraping at the concrete as though she could dig through it with her bare hands. When her nails split and tore and the pain became too much she fell to the ground and sobbed.

Eventually she calmed down. She took a deep breath, then sat up, her legs crossed, her injured hand cradled in her lap.

She had to think, to try and understand what was going on. She needed to lay out all the pieces and see what she could glean from the picture they made.

She was trapped – chained – in a secret basement in her oldest friend's house. Whatever the reason, and whatever Jean's plans, this was the latest installment in a scheme which went back at least six months.

Six months in which Jean had stalked her online, sent messages purporting to be from her, forged letters to her husband, and all, it seemed with one goal in mind.

To make her look like she was insane and suicidal, and then kill her.

It was all there in the suicide note Jean had been writing.

Sarah let out a cry, in part shock, in part anguish. She had been planning to kill her, and make it look like suicide. That was what all of this had been aimed at. Jean wanted people to think she was unstable, so they would believe she had taken her own life.

But then Sarah had woken up, and so Jean – as she had said – had been forced to change her plan. The choke-hold she'd used on Sarah would have left bruises if she actually killed her, and that would have put an end to the suicide theory.

So here she was. But what did Jean intend to do now? Kill her? Then why not do it right away? Sarah didn't know, but she did know one thing. One ugly, important fact was staring her in the face.

No one knew where she was. So Jean was free to write whatever suicide note she wanted for Ben to find, and she, Sarah, could do nothing to stop her. It would be about her disappearing, and when he read it, Ben would believe it. The cops would ask him how Sarah had been these last few months and he would tell them she'd been finding it hard. She had ordered books on depression and coping with parents with bipolar. All kinds of inexplicable things had been happening – the letters, emails, photos on Facebook – and one explanation was that Sarah had been doing them herself.

An explanation that looked all the more likely, now – according to the note – she had been driven to take her own life.

She closed her eyes. So now what? What could she do?

Her scream was almost involuntary, and once she started she couldn't stop. When her throat was raw – more raw – she looked up into only darkness.

'Jean!' she shouted. 'Jean! Come back! Please, Jean! Help me!'

But the words went unanswered. Only silence followed.

Sarah lay on her side, curled up like a fetus, and quietly cried.

She was woken – it was amazing she had fallen asleep – by a pressure in her bladder and – worse – in her bowels.

She guessed it was morning. It was around 2 a.m. when Jean had come into her house, and, although she had no way of knowing, she assumed, after Jean strangled her, she had not been out for very long. To cut off the oxygen to someone's brain for long enough to leave them unconscious for hours would probably have left some permanent damage, if it hadn't killed them outright. Add to that the conversation with Jean and the short sleep – it felt short – and it was a reasonable guess that outside it was dawn.

And then there was her need to go to the toilet. Most mornings were the same; wake up, drink coffee, move bowels, then get ready for work.

So the fact she was feeling the need to go now was a pretty reliable clue it was the beginning of the day.

Except there was nowhere to do it. Only the floor. Which she was not going to do.

The pressure in her bladder grew. She blocked it out. Maybe Jean would be back soon and she could ask her for – for what? A bucket? An opportunity to go upstairs and use her bathroom?

It didn't matter. She'd tell Jean she needed some kind of bathroom facilities. She wasn't going to go on the floor. No way.

She sat and waited.

At first, in an attempt to keep track of time, she counted the seconds.

One thousand, Two thousand, three thousand.

When she got to five hundred thousand – a mere five hundred seconds – she stopped. It was harder than she had expected – her mind kept drifting – plus it was boring. She was already losing track and she'd only got to five hundred seconds, which was not even ten minutes. What if she was in here for hours? Days? There was no way she could keep it up.

She planned what she would say to Jean when she came back.

Look, she'd say. *I don't know what this is about, but whatever it is we can fix it. Let me out and I'll forget this ever happened. We'll draw a line under it and move on. You can have money, whatever you want. I won't tell the cops. I just want out.*

But Jean didn't come.

And the need to go to the bathroom grew.

She had to go. She had no choice. It was becoming painful, and the more she thought about it, the worse it became.

But only a piss. The other could wait. She was not ready to do that yet.

She moved as far as the chain would let her and squatted, then pulled her pants – loose fitting pajamas – down. The stream of urine jetted on to the concrete; she was glad it was dark so she couldn't see it spread. When she was done she pulled her pants back up and moved as far away in the other direction as she could.

She shivered. It was cold.

She waited.

As she waited, she heard a click from the door.

6

The handle creaked as it turned. The door opened.

Jean stepped into the room. She looked at Sarah, her arms folded, then reached down to pick up the packet of cigarettes. Evidently she kept them down here so no one found them in the house.

'Well,' she said, nodding at the pool of urine. 'I see you found the bathroom facilities.' Her voice went up in tone at the end of the sentence, as though she was making an amusing observation.

Sarah didn't see anything funny about the situation. 'I need the bathroom,' she said. 'You can't treat me like this.'

'Looks like you already went.'

'I mean for a' – she paused – 'for a number two.'

Jean laughed.

'A number two? How prim! I can see how you'd think I couldn't be so awful as to make you do a number two on the floor when you don't even want to say the word "shit". But here's the thing: I can treat you like this. I can do whatever I want to you. And this is your bathroom. So fucking get used to it.'

'No,' Sarah said. 'I won't do it here.'

Jean laughed again.

'Fine. But it'll happen eventually. You know that; you're a doctor.'

She took a headlamp from her pocket and put it on her head. It was the same one she'd been wearing the night she came to Sarah's house, and now Sarah remembered where she'd got it from, remembered the day Ben had given it to her in the kind of brotherly gesture he often made toward Jean. He'd upgraded his to some new ultra-low-energy and high-output one, a headlamp he didn't need and rarely used but which some sales associate at LL Bean had persuaded him was worth the extra fifty bucks he'd paid, which was typical of his naïve enthusiasm and one of the things she loved about him. And now Jean was pointing his old one at her in a secret fallout shelter.

Jean switched on the headlamp and closed the door.

'Don't want the smell to get in the house,' she said. She lit a cigarette. She put the lighter back in the box and placed it on the floor behind her. 'Some always gets out though, but only into the basement.' She looked up. 'There's a gap somewhere.' She shrugged. 'But no one will know. Only I go into the basement. The kids hate it.'

The beam of light blinded Sarah; she could not see Jean at all.

'Can you point that to the side?' she said. 'It's dazzling me.'

'Sure,' Jean said. She turned the beam so it faced the wall to Sarah's left. It was studded with two by fours, as though someone had planned to convert the room into a finished space and then given up. Sarah stared at them. They weren't much to look at, but she'd been in darkness for God knew how long, and they were the only thing in the room that wasn't rough concrete.

Sarah shook her head. This was ridiculous. 'Jean,' she said. 'What's going on? What the hell are you doing?'

'First I have a question for you,' Jean said.

'I'll answer if you let me go to the bathroom.'

Jean frowned. 'You mean upstairs?' She laughed. 'Fucking hell, Sarah. You really don't get it, do you?'

'Get what?'

Jean swept her hand around. 'This is for real. You're not down here for laughs. Your world has changed, Sarah. You don't get to negotiate. You don't have rights. OK? So, my question.' She folded her arms. 'How come you woke up when I came to your house?'

'Because there was an intruder in the middle of the night.' Sarah held her palms upward in a gesture that said *Why are you asking such an obvious question*. 'It would be more of a surprise if I hadn't woken up, Jean.'

'You didn't drink the wine?'

'No,' Sarah said.

'Your glass was empty.'

'I poured it away. I've been drinking too much.'

'Why did you tell me you drank it?'

'Because it seemed to be important to you. You wanted me to taste your special—' Sarah froze. 'My God,' she said. 'It *was* important to you, but not because Carl had given it to you. It was because it was *drugged*.'

'Yes,' Jean said. 'It was. That was my plan. You take some sleeping pills, drink some wine. Write a suicide note explaining it all to your family – you love them, but you can't go on. You read it; you know.'

'But how? Crushing a few pills in some wine wouldn't kill me,' Sarah said. 'I'd wake up with a very bad headache, but not much more.'

'I know, Sarah,' Jean said. 'You think I'm stupid, don't you? You always have.' She shook her head. 'No. The pills were to make sure you were asleep. Then I was going to put you in your car in the garage and turn on the engine. Painless way to go. A coward's way. Perfect for you.'

Sarah looked at her hands – the burn from the cigarette was a real mess – trying to let Jean's words sink in.

'It wouldn't have worked,' she said flatly. 'Ben wouldn't have believed it.'

'Oh?' Jean said. 'You think?'

'Yes. He knows me. He knows I wouldn't leave him, or the kids.'

'He knows desperate people do desperate things. And, after all the things that have been going on, he thinks you're desperate.' She smiled. 'Not true, of course. But what else would he think? And what he thinks is what matters.'

Sarah shook her head. It was all so clear now, in hindsight. 'The police would look into it,' she said. 'They'd find your DNA on me, if you carried me downstairs to the car.'

'I was planning for it to be *me* who found you,' Jean said. 'In my grief, I'd drag you from the car and out of the garage. My DNA would have every right to be there. And on the suicide note, which I would find.'

'And they'd check the handwriting,' Sarah said. 'They'd find out it was forged.'

'You're clutching at straws,' Jean said. 'They'd only do that if they were suspicious, which they wouldn't be. They'd hear from me, and Ben, about your recent history of paranoia, depression and – possibly – dissociative fugue. Ben would explain how you'd asked him to leave – presumably so you could kill yourself – and they would close the book. They'd move on. Nice and neat. That's what they do,' she said. 'I know from my own experience. It's a tried-and-trusted method, Sarah. It worked last time.'

'What do you mean last time?' Sarah said. 'You've done this before?'

7

'Oh, yes,' Jean said. 'You remember Karen, of course'

Sarah nodded. Karen, Daniel and Paul's mum. Karen, who'd disappeared. Karen, who'd left her shoes and coat out by the ocean, with a suicide note.

A note explaining how she couldn't take it anymore and she had no options left other than to take her own life. A note like the one Jean had been writing for Sarah.

And then Jean had married Jack.

She looked at Jean. 'Holy shit,' she said. 'You did the same to her? You killed her?'

Jean nodded.

'Oh my God.' She stared at her friend. 'How? How did you get her out to the ocean?'

Jean laughed. It was an odd, girlish giggle that seemed totally incongruous with the situation.

'I didn't,' she said. 'I put her clothes out there with the suicide note. I actually killed her well before. The night she disappeared, in fact. I left the gap between the disappearance and the note to build suspense.' She giggled again, then sucked on the cigarette. 'It was a mistake, though, I killed her too soon. I wish I'd enjoyed her punishment – her *suffering* –

more. It was a missed opportunity. I won't make the same mistake with you. I'm going to enjoy having you down here before I finally let you die.'

The words hung in between them, then Jean carried on.

'You want to know how I killed Karen? It was very clever.'

Sarah was about to say no, she didn't, but Jean didn't give her the chance.

'We all went out the night you came home to Barrow,' she said. Her voice had changed, the tone lowered and bitter. 'Remember? Anyway, I left early. I had the Farmer's Market the next day. I was working at the organic farm in Topsham at the time. I needed all the work I could get. I wasn't a doctor like you, Sarah. I never made it to college. You remember the reason why, don't you? I hope so.'

Sarah started to reply but Jean silenced her with a wave.

'We'll be talking about that later,' she said. 'Karen, first. You'll want to hear this story, Sarah. I liked the farm job. Plenty of fresh air. And the farmer – Ethan – had a fantastic body and used to shower outside. He collected rainwater in a barrel. It was all part of his low-impact lifestyle. Anyway, by climbing on the roof of the barn you could watch him. A perk I enjoyed. And he paid well, too. Plus he gave me food. Eggs, milk, meat. He made sausages. You probably don't remember, but he was famous for his sausages. I could have as many as I wanted.' She laughed. 'I didn't eat any of the ones around the time Karen disappeared, though.'

She crouched down and leaned forward, then blew smoke into Sarah's face. 'You want to know why I avoided them? Because that was how I got rid of her body.'

Sarah twisted out of the way. She didn't want to hear this, didn't want to have to think about what Jean had done.

'I picked her up when she left the bar,' Jean said. 'Just happened to be passing, although really I'd been watching to see when she left. I was lucky she was alone; but if she hadn't been it wouldn't have mattered. I'd have got her eventually. I'm very good at waiting, Sarah, as you're finding out now. I don't care how *long* it takes for me to get what I want, so long as I get it. Anyway, I picked her up, told her I had to stop by the farm, and then I killed her.' Jean laughed.

'You're sick,' Sarah whispered. 'I didn't realize until now, but there's something very wrong with you. You're not well, Jean.'

'Really?' Jean said. 'It seems to me like you're the one in my basement. You might want to think about that when you decide who's not well. Anyway, I was telling you a story. Let me get back to it; it's a good one.'

Jean stood up. She inhaled a lungful of smoke.

'There was another advantage to working at the farm,' Jean said. 'If there's no body, there's no crime. Just a woman who disappeared. Maybe ran away for good, maybe she needed some time.' She flicked the cigarette butt at Sarah. It hit her cheek – there was a little sting – and landed on the ground in front of her. 'But if you kill someone, the corpse can always turn up. A grave can be dug up, a body can wash up on shore. The trick is to really get rid of the body. And the farm was a good place to get rid of a body.'

'Wherever you hid it, it could still be found,' Sarah said. 'You're not as smart as you think.'

'Oh, but I am,' Jean said. 'Karen's body will *never* be found.'

'You can't be sure.'

'Really? Let me tell you what I did with it, then you can decide for yourself.' She folded her arms. 'The night I killed her – strangled, by the way – Ethan was in Boston visiting his brother. The farm was empty; he'd asked me to grind up some pork for sausages.' She stared at Sarah. 'So I threw her in with them. And then, on the next few Saturdays, the good people of Barrow went to the farmers' market and picked up a couple of Ethan's famous organic sausages and disposed of the body for me. 'As for the bones,' she continued. 'They went into the organic bonemeal he sold to the gardeners of Barrow. She became fertilizer, which is somehow poetic, don't you think? She lives on in the trees and flowers. So no, I don't think her body will be turning up anytime soon.'

Sarah looked away. A wave of nausea washed over her. She knew Ethan, had bought meat – and sausages – from him. She may have eaten the ones Jean had made the night she killed Karen.

She retched, then pushed the thought away. It was the least of her worries right now. Right now she was trapped in the basement of her friend. A friend who happened to be totally crazy.

'And then,' Jean said, 'I waited a couple weeks before I took her clothes out to the ocean and left them with a suicide note. As you've found out, I have a talent for forgery.'

'But why?' Sarah said. 'What had she done to you?'

Jean's face darkened. 'She was making him marry her! Can you believe it? She wanted to get married to Jack and she was forcing him to do it.'

'They had children, Jean. Why wouldn't they get married?'

'He didn't want to,' Jean said. 'He told me he didn't want to, but she was threatening to stop him seeing the kids if he didn't marry her.'

Sarah raised an eyebrow. 'Why was he talking to you about that? Were you having an affair with him?'

'Yes!' Jean said. 'He loved me. But then he told me it was over. He loved me but we had to end it because of *her*. And he couldn't get rid of her because she would have taken his kids. He had no choice. At least, he thought he didn't.'

'So you killed her?'

'I had to. He wanted me to.'

306

Sarah doubted it. She was pretty sure Jack had gotten involved with Jean on the side and decided to end it, but to make it easier on Jean had told her he didn't want to, but what else could he do? He loved his kids, and didn't want to leave them. It was an old story. He just hadn't counted on Jean being insane.

'Did you tell him you'd killed her?' Sarah said.

Jean shook her head. 'I wanted him to think it was suicide. So he would hate her. I didn't want him feeling sympathy for her.'

'And you got him, in the end,' Sarah said. 'You got what you wanted. But then he died in a car accident, so you were back to square one.'

'Accident?' Jean said. 'There wasn't any accident. He had to go.'

Sarah felt the world narrow around her. 'You killed him, too?'

'I had to.' Jean gestured to the chains. 'He found those.'

Sarah didn't understand. But then, there was a lot she didn't understand about this situation. 'You killed him for that?' she said. 'For finding some chains?'

Jean chuckled. 'It wasn't the chains,' she said. 'It was the kids. They were in them. It's how I discipline the little shits.'

'You put your – *his* – kids in these chains?'

'Yes,' Jean said. She held her hands up in a gesture of surprise. 'It's called discipline, Sarah. You need a sanction if kids are going to do what you say. You always tell me my kids are well behaved. Well, this is the reason why. If *you* did this, then yours might not be such fucking savages.'

'No,' Sarah said. 'No. This is not the way.'

'It is the way,' Jean said. 'But Jack agreed with you – he was a fucking pussy – and he was going to call the cops. So he had to go.'

'But he was killed in a car accident,' Sarah said. 'How did you—'

'It took some arranging,' Jean said. 'But look at your situation, Sarah. I'm *good* at arranging things. I'm not as stupid as you think.'

So *that* was it? Jean was in love – if love was the right word – with Ben, and she was going to kill Sarah to get him, like she had done with Karen? Was she having an affair with Ben? Sarah doubted it, but maybe he had been friendly to her – like giving her the headlamp – and she had interpreted that as something more than it was.

Either way, Sarah knew what she had to do: she had to convince Jean she could have Ben without killing her. She would say whatever it took – maybe tell her he had told Sarah he loved Jean, or wanted to leave Sarah for her, confess to stopping him – in the same way Karen had to Jack – but now she knew how much he meant to Jean she would let him go. She would agree that he could leave with full access to the kids; she would put no obstacles in his path.

For the first time since she had been in the basement she felt a flicker of optimism.

'Jean,' she said, slowly. 'Is this is all about Ben? You have a new obsession? A new man you want?'

Jean frowned. 'Oh no,' she said. 'Ben's merely a side benefit. This is all about *you*.'

8

You can turn off the ringer on a cell phone. Or you can leave it in a different room or your car or work bag, or do some other thing so you don't hear it when it rings.

You can't do those things with a landline. You *might* be able to turn off the ringer, but if you could then Ben didn't know how to do it on their phone, and he doubted Sarah did either.

He was pretty sure Sarah would not have silenced the ringer, so either she was ignoring Ben's calls – odd, since she wanted to speak to him – or she was out. But there were not many places she would be at seven in the morning.

And the places she *might* be were not places that filled Ben with optimism for the future of his marriage, since most of them involved her sleeping in someone else's house, in which case it was understandable she would not answer her cell phone.

Presumably she would not want to embarrass or inconvenience whoever she was spending the night with.

It was a measure of how far things had deteriorated that Ben wasn't surprised she might at this very moment be having morning sex with someone she'd met on Craigslist. Disturbed, yes; upset, most definitely; but surprised? No, not any more. A year ago – a *month* ago – he would have found the merest suggestion of such a thing to be totally absurd, out of the bounds of possibility, but he had learned since then that the bounds of possibility were set pretty wide.

Much wider than he had thought.

He tried again; still no answer. He put his phone down on the nightstand and held his head in his hands.

'Hey, Dad. Morning.' Miles sat up in bed. 'What are we doing today?'

Ben smiled at his son.

'Going home,' he said.

'Is everything OK, sir?'

The clerk wore a concerned expression. Evidently Ben's desire to check out a day early and immediately after breakfast was a red flag indicating some kind of customer dissatisfaction. He looked Ben directly in the eye.

'Was there a problem with the room?'

Ben shook his head. 'No,' he said. 'Something came up. A personal matter.'

'Are you sure, sir?'

Kim wriggled in his arms.

'Put me down,' she said.

Ben didn't want to; he knew that as soon as her feet touched the floor she'd disappear. 'In a minute,' he said.

'Now, Daddy. Put me down.'

Ben looked at the clerk. 'Really, everything was fine,' he said. 'I'll pay and then we can go.' He reached for his wallet; as he did, Kim took advantage of the loosening of his grip to twist and dive at the floor. He grabbed her.

'Stop it,' he said. 'Be still for a second.'

'It's OK,' the clerk said. 'We have your card on file. I can use it to check out?'

'Yes,' Ben nodded. 'Yes, please.'

In the car, Faye refused to buckle up.

'I want to go to the aquarium,' she said. 'You promised we could go there.'

'I know,' Ben said. 'And we will, soon. But today we have to go home.'

'Why?' Miles said. 'Why did we come all this way just to go back first thing in the morning?'

'Because we did,' Ben said. 'OK?'

Before he had become a parent Ben had promised himself he would not fob off his kids' questions with answers like *Because I say so* or *Life's not fair, get used to it* or *Because we did*. His parents had done it to him, and so he'd decided to be the kind of parent who explained the reasons why patiently; by doing so he'd end up with reasonable kids who asked thoughtful questions and accepted his thoughtful responses.

Which was not how it turned out. He had not accounted for the fact that kids did not ask questions because they wanted an answer, they asked them because they wanted a thing – candy, video games, trips to the aquarium – and when you told them they couldn't have it, however thoughtful the reasons, they would simply ask why over and over until you gave in or said *Because I said so*. And then after a while, you stopped bothering with the thoughtful explanations and went straight to *Because I said so*.

He had not wanted to end up there, but there he was. Exactly like his own mum and dad.

His mum who was dying.

Which made this all the harder. He needed to be able to spend time back home, but how could he, when his wife was falling apart in front of his eyes? How could he leave the kids with her? It was the worst possible timing, and in his darker moments he wondered whether it was deliberate on Sarah's part.

He hoped not. That really would be the final nail in the coffin of their relationship.

And the coffin was already pretty full of nails.

'Right,' he said. 'Who wants ice cream when we get home? And pizza for lunch?'

'Me!' Faye said, a response which was echoed by Miles and Kim.

'Then buckle up and be quiet,' he said. 'Or it's broccoli and dry toast. OK?'

9

This is all about you.

Sarah had straightened up, sat upright, as the hope she had figured a way out of this grew.

Now she slumped. The hope was gone.

'What do you mean?' she said. 'How is this about me?'

Jean looked at her, eyes narrow, lips pressed thin. 'The very fact you have to ask,' she said, each word spoken slowly, hard and precise, 'is exactly why this is about you.'

It was obvious from both what Jean was saying and her expression – a mixture of anger, disdain and sheer hatred – that, as far as she was concerned, Sarah deserved this extreme form of punishment.

The problem for Sarah was in working out what it could have been. They were friends. They'd had the odd argument over the years, but nothing big enough to warrant this. It would have to be huge, yet Sarah had no idea what it could have been.

'Look at you,' Jean said. 'You're blind. Blind to who you are and what you've done. You can't imagine why anyone would hate you enough to want to destroy you.'

'No,' Sarah said. 'I can't. And even if I could, nothing would justify what you're doing.'

'What about an eye for an eye, Sarah? What about that?'

'What about it?' Sarah said. 'Are you talking about revenge? I don't think it's ever helped anyone, ever. There's a saying, Jean: "Before you embark on a journey of revenge, dig two graves." No one wins.'

'Only one grave needed on this journey,' Jean said. 'And I prefer the saying "Revenge is a dish better tasted cold."'

'Very fucking cold,' Sarah said. She leaned her back against the wall. 'What's the revenge for, Jean? What have I done to you?'

'Everything,' Jean said. 'Everything that ever went wrong for me is your fault.'

Despite the situation, Sarah laughed. It was ludicrous: she had no idea what Jean was talking about, yet she was holding her responsible for all the things wrong in her life.

'Don't laugh,' Jean said. Her voice rose to a shout. 'Don't you dare fucking laugh at me!'

'I'm sorry,' Sarah said. 'It's just – I don't know what else to do.' She started to laugh again, but the laughter turned into a cry as Jean lurched toward her and yanked on the chain.

She pulled it hard, again and again until Sarah thought her neck would snap. When she finally stopped, Sarah slumped into the fetal position, her temple on the floor. She lifted her hand to her throat and pressed it, feeling for damage.

'All curled up,' Jean said. 'Like the baby you killed.'

Sarah opened an eye and looked at her.

'*What?*' she said. 'What baby?'

'My baby,' Jean said. She stood up and lit another cigarette. '*My* baby, the one *you* killed.'

'Jean,' Sarah said. 'Are you talking about the time you were pregnant? When we were eighteen?'

Jean crouched next to her. 'Now you get it,' she said softly. 'Now you start to see.'

314

'I don't see how you think I did anything to you. You did it all yourself.'

Jean shook her head. Her lips curled up in a look which was part-hatred and part-fury.

'No,' she said. 'You took it all from me. I wasn't sure about doing it. You remember? I was considering having the baby. I was *going* to have it. But you persuaded me not to. You told me it was for the best. Took me to the clinic. Held my hand.'

Sarah bit her lip. She remembered the summer it had happened, remembered the excitement of college on the horizon, the sense of the world opening up, of new beginnings. And, along with it, hours of tears and long conversations with Jean about what to do about the baby growing inside her.

To Sarah it was obvious; it was a mistake and it needed to be corrected. She'd seen Jean's reluctance as nothing more than the result of confusion and worry.

'It wasn't like that,' she said. 'We were friends. I was there for you.'

'You were there to lead me astray!' Jean said. 'I would never have done it if it wasn't for you!'

'Jean,' Sarah said. 'I supported your decision, I didn't—'

'You persuaded me to do it!' Jean said. 'You told me it was normal and it would be OK and lots of people did it – and I trusted you! I trusted you and you abused my trust to persuade me to do it. And I know why you did it. You did it because you *liked* it. You like seeing babies die.' She shrugged. 'I mean, what other explanation is there? Who could want to make me do such a thing unless they liked it?'

'Jean,' she said. 'It's not true. I thought it was for the best.'

'But it wasn't, was it? There were *complications*. Something *no one could have predicted*. And the result was I didn't just lose my baby. I lost any chance to ever have a baby again.'

She stared at Sarah, and shook her head. 'Complications. Thanks to you.'

'I didn't make you do anything!' Sarah said. 'It's absurd to say I did!'

'No,' Jean replied. 'It isn't. If it wasn't for you I would not have done it. You remember at the clinic when I tried to pull out? You *pushed* me, you physically *pushed* me into the room.'

Sarah remembered the scene well; on their way into the medical room Jean had turned to the nurse.

Stop, she said. *Wait.*

She looked at Sarah. She spoke in a low voice.

I don't think I want to do this.

You do, Sarah had said. *It's hard, but you know you need to do it.*

And then she'd put her arm around her friend and guided her into the room.

Guided.

Not pushed.

But it seemed Jean didn't see it the same way.

'And that was it,' Jean said. 'My baby was gone. *You* killed her. You pushed me in there. I didn't want to go in, but you made me. I was too weak, too confused to stop you, and you saw it and took advantage of it. You may as well have done the operation yourself.'

'Jean, this is sick,' Sarah said. 'You're—'

'DON'T CALL ME SICK!' Jean shouted. 'How can *you* call *me* sick? How can *you* call *me* – anyone – sick? You *murdered* my baby, Sarah. You're disgusting.'

Sarah held her hands up. 'I didn't murder any baby, Jean.'

'You took my baby from me and it ruined my life.' She started to pace the basement. 'I had a place at college, up in Vermont, but I didn't go. You remember? I deferred a year but I never took it up. It would have been pointless; I was

316

trapped in my own head. All I ever thought about was my daughter. The one you killed. Every night, she was the last thing I thought of; every morning she was the first. All I wanted was to have her back. It was torture, Sarah.'

'You don't know it was a daughter, Jean. You can't know.'

'She was a daughter! I know she was. A mother knows these things, Sarah.'

'I'm sorry, Jean. I really am. I know how you felt. I've seen other—'

'You have no idea how I felt! And don't tell me you've seen it in other patients. And then you all went off and got degrees and jobs and I was stuck here. And Jack was my way out but that didn't work either, because he was too weak and stupid to see the kids needed some discipline. And so here I am. And you did it to me. Like you've kept on doing, ever since.'

'Jean,' Sarah said. 'I'm your friend. I've *always* been your friend.'

'You've never been my friend!' Jean screamed. 'You've looked down on me and patronized me and made me look stupid ever since we met. Like Sean. He turns up and you decide he needs a girlfriend, which is *typical* of you, by the way, interfering in everybody's lives, a fucking neighborhood busy-body, and so you set him up with Becky, your little friend with the good job.' She folded her arms. 'You never *thought* of me. I didn't deserve to be considered. You didn't even mention it to me.'

'Jean. This is a bit of an over-reaction to a date I set up for someone else. I thought they were a good fit, that's—'

'Bullcrap!' Jean shouted. 'And it's *not* a reaction to that. The fact you would even say such a thing proves my point! This goes back to the very beginning. I'm nothing to you, Sarah. I never have been. And you've never even noticed how I feel about you. You've never even bothered paying attention

317

enough to notice the single most important feeling I have about you.' She spat and a gobbet of phlegm landed on Sarah's cheek. 'Hatred.'

'Jean,' Sarah said. 'I'm sorry—'

'Don't even bother,' Jean said, the emotion drained from her voice. 'Like I said, this goes back a long, long way. But it was when you set up the doctor with your smug bitch friend that I decided it was finally time for you to pay. Time for me to get my revenge. So I set all this in motion. The Facebook account. All of it.'

Sarah didn't reply. There was no point; Jean was not asking for her opinion – she had her own facts, and they had taken root inside and been fed by her bitterness until they had hardened into part of who she was.

And there was nothing Sarah could do about it.

'So,' Sarah said. 'What's next?'

Jean stopped pacing and turned to look at her.

'I'm glad you asked,' she said. 'I'm going to enjoy telling you.'

10

'What I *was* intending,' Jean said, 'was to kill you and make it look like the suicide of a desperate woman who had been struggling for a few months. Ben wasn't really part of the picture.'

She began to pace the room again. Sarah felt a coldness chill her from the inside. Jean was not reachable, not a person she could reason with. She had formed her conclusions; any evidence would simply reinforce them, whatever it was. She couldn't even get started; if she confessed, then she was guilty and deserved punishment, if she denied it, she was demonstrating how callous she was. It was like the Oedipus Syndrome: display it and you proved it was correct. Show no sign of it, and you were suppressing it, which was merely more evidence it existed.

'And then,' Jean said, turning to look at her with the attitude of a teacher, 'you didn't drink the wine.' She sighed. 'At first I was annoyed, but the more I thought about it, the more I saw it was a good thing. If it hadn't happened, you'd be dead now. I'd be satisfied, but all this would be over. And it's been fun, watching you suffer. I want to watch it some more. I'm glad it turned out this way. I wish I'd thought of it myself.'

'So you're going to keep me down here and starve me? Stub cigarettes out on my hands? Drag me around by the chains?' Sarah closed her eyes. 'Is that really what you want to do? You're a torturer now? It doesn't exactly fit with your boasts about being such a great arranger.'

'Oh,' Jean said. 'It's much worse. I'm going to make you choose how you die.' She smiled. 'When the time comes, you will be given three options. They are variations on the same theme – the removal of one of the essentials of life – but they differ in the length of time they take. You can choose the removal of food. You can choose the removal of water. You can choose the removal of oxygen.'

She did a little hop.

'Neat, no? Starvation, dehydration, suffocation. You choose. But first I plan to make you truly suffer. So for now, you'll get food and water.' She smiled. 'Although no bathroom visits.' She pointed to the corner. 'You can do your business there, like an animal.'

'Why not kill me now?' Sarah said. 'Why wait? Suffocate me. Go on.'

'Not yet,' Jean said. 'Because, now I think about it, Ben *is* part of the picture.' She lowered her voice. 'Along with Miles and Faye and Kim. You see, Sarah, not only am I going to kill you. I'm going to take your family. Like I did with Jack. And – even better – you're going to watch me do it.' She glanced at the unoccupied chain. 'And when you're gone, I'm going to need a few more of those. Your kids are going to learn discipline, Sarah. And about fucking time too.'

'No,' Sarah said. 'No, Jean. Please. You can do what you want with me, but leave Ben and the kids alone. They haven't done anything to you. They haven't killed any babies.' *And neither have I*, she wanted to add, but didn't: she didn't want to start that discussion again. 'Please don't hurt them. Please.'

The thought of the three of them down here, chained in the darkness, was physically painful; she pushed the image from her mind. It made her want to tear the walls down to get out, rip the chain apart link by link, whatever it took. And in her anger she believed, for a moment, she could.

For a moment.

A moment that passed. And then she noticed Jean was looking at her with a puzzled expression.

'Hurt them?' she said. 'Why would I hurt them? Like you say, they've done nothing to me. I'm going to *help* them, Sarah. I'm going to teach them to be good people.'

'What?' Sarah said. 'What are you saying?'

'I'm saying they'll be better off with me. And they're going to need a mom, the poor little things. Think about how they'll feel when they learn Mommy killed herself, that she didn't love them enough to stick around for them. They'll be *devastated*. It'll take years for them to get over it, if they ever do. They are going to need a female role model in their lives.' Jean reached for another cigarette and lit it. 'Which will be me.'

'You're the last thing they need,' Sarah said. 'They need someone sane, for a start.'

'You mean like you?' Jean said, her tone syrupy. 'So they can grow up knowing their mom killed her friend's baby and got a bit sad so she fucked a man who wasn't her husband? You think you're a good role model?' She shook her head. 'No. They'll be better off with me.'

Sarah opened her mouth to speak but Jean raised her hand to silence her. 'Just think,' she said. 'With all they'll have been through, they'll probably have some behavioral issues. Which is where the basement will come in. Especially

Miles. He's going to need a *very* firm hand. See? I've got it all figured out.'

Miles. Her firstborn. The baby boy she'd cradled against her chest in the minutes after he came into the world. She remembered it all: the sleepless nights which were long but which she missed, now, because they had been full of wonder at the life she and Ben had created, the first time he'd crawled, the first word he'd spoken. The terror when he had been taken to the hospital because he had a serious sinus infection and they had watched him be taken into a room and given antibiotics intravenously. The pride on his first day of school; the tears on his first day of school.

And now Jean was going to chain him, her little boy, in a basement. Like she had Daniel and Paul. No wonder they did what their mom – their stepmom – told them. They were terrified of her.

'Please, Jean,' she said. 'Please.'

'Please what? Please *don't* help them? I don't understand you, Sarah. Why would I not do this? And Ben? Don't you want him to be happy? He deserves to love again, after his wife killed herself.'

There was no point explaining it; Jean was beyond expla-nation. But there was one thing which would put a stop to all this, one thing Jean could not control.

'Ben will never go along with this,' Sarah said. 'He's not interested in you.'

'You think?' Jean said. 'He's always been very good to me, Sarah. He admires me. You told me so.'

'He admires you because he thinks you've kept it together despite what you've been through.' *Like the loss of a husband,* she thought, *which, it turns out, was less of a tragedy inflicted upon her than it seemed at the time, given that she killed him.* 'But he'll never love you, Jean.'

'We'll find out,' Jean said. 'But admiration is a start. And

322

it's not a long way from admiration to whatever else I want it to be.' She took a drag on the cigarette. 'And I can be very persuasive, Sarah. I'm guessing you two haven't been having too much sex lately, what with all the goings on. And he's kind of upset with you. I'll be there to comfort him, pour him a drink. Give him a back rub. He won't need to feel guilty if one thing leads to another. It'll be a way to escape, at first. You of all people understand that, don't you? But it'll grow into more.'

'No,' Sarah said. 'No. It won't happen. He isn't interested in you. He isn't.'

'In my experience,' Jean said, in a low voice. 'When you put your hand in a man's pants and start to suck him off, he'll let you. Especially if his wife is no longer in the picture.'

'You're disgusting,' Sarah said. 'You're sick and disgusting.'

Jean ignored her. 'I'll make it irresistible to him, Sarah. Give him all the sex he wants, however he wants it. Tell him I *love* it. Beg him to do it to me. And he will go *crazy* for it. Men do, Sarah. And it can get addictive for them. So yes, at first I'll just be a distraction from the mess in his life, but it won't be long before he sees it's more than that. He needs me to help with the kids; it makes sense for us to live together, to create a happy, stable family environment for them. And if he gets filthy sex whenever he wants it, so much the better.'

'He won't,' Sarah said. 'I know Ben. He won't.'

'You keep telling yourself that. And in the meantime I'm going to enjoy telling you about it,' Jean said. 'I'm going to keep you down here, in the dark and quiet, and whenever I need a little pick-me-up I'll pop down here and fill you in on the latest. Maybe tell you about the meal Ben and I shared before I blew him on the couch in your house. You can give me some tips; tell me what he likes.'

323

Sarah looked at the door; it was closed. The room was soundproof, according to Jean.

But not when she was coming in or out. Then the sound could travel.

'Get out,' she said. 'Leave me alone.'

'You want me to bring you some food? Drink?'

Sarah shook her head. 'I don't want anything from you.'

Jean shrugged. 'You'll change your mind,' she said. 'One way or another. Or maybe not. But it'll be a painful way to go.'

She turned to the door and opened it and Sarah started to scream. It was a raw, hoarse sound and it hurt her bruised throat but it was all she had and she gave it everything. Anyone in the house – anyone near it – must have heard.

Jean slammed the door shut.

'You stupid fucking bitch,' she said. 'You think anyone can hear you?'

Her tone was sneering, but Sarah could see she was uncertain.

'Maybe,' she said. 'And so maybe this is all over.'

Jean laughed, but it was not a confident laugh. She pointed at Sarah, her index finger shaking.

'If it is, I'll still make sure you die,' she said. 'I'll come down here with an ax and hack you to death before anyone can stop me. So if I was you I'd be careful what I fucking hope for.'

Her anger was proof she was shaken; Sarah enjoyed seeing it. It was – however small – a change in the balance of power in her favor.

'Go on,' she said. 'Leave me.'

Jean studied her. 'I open the door and you'll scream,' she said. 'The chances are slim, but someone might hear. Anyone. I see your plan. It's smart.' She reached into her back pocket and pulled out a Buck knife. 'But not *so* smart. Did you think I'd come down here unarmed?' She shook her head. 'Tut, tut. Now, tell me Dr Havenant, can a person scream without a tongue?'

11

Yes, Sarah almost said, *yes, they could*. At least, they could make a noise. Words would be beyond them, but they would be able to make sounds.

But she kept silent. It was obvious Jean wasn't seeking her medical opinion.

'So can they?' Jean said. 'I suppose *you* already know, but *I* don't. I could find out, couldn't I? I have the perfect opportunity to do a little experiment. I mean, you'll be *trying* to scream for sure, so I'll definitely get my answer, one way or another.'

She put a finger to her lips in a theatrical display of thoughtfulness.

'Or maybe you'll bleed to death. Or choke on the blood. Or on bits of your tongue. It's not like I'm a skilled surgeon. I've never done this before.' She looked at the knife, and then lifted her gaze to Sarah. The thoughtful expression was gone, replaced by a look of barely controlled fury.

'But I *will* do it, Sarah. Trust me. I will hold your mouth open and slice your tongue out piece by piece. And I'll *enjoy* it. So here's what's going to happen. I'm going to open the door and leave, and you're going to be silent. If you so much

326

as squeak, you lose your tongue.' She smiled. It was a wide, flat, innocent smile, almost childlike. 'Do you understand?'

Sarah nodded. Her instructions were pretty clear. Insane, but clear.

'Excellent. Then I'll say goodbye. For now.'

'Jean,' Sarah said. 'We can still stop this. It's not too late. Let me go and it'll all be forgotten.'

Jean looked at her, an amused smile on her lips.

'Why would I do that?' she said.

'Because we're friends, Jean. We've known each other for thirty years. We were in *kindergarten* together, for God's sake. Whatever you think I've done to you, doesn't that count? For anything?'

Jean thought for a second, then shook her head. 'Not a thing,' she said, and turned away.

Sarah sat in the darkness. This was her world, she realized, and it was not going to change anytime soon. Jean was not going to relent.

This was it, for now, and for as long as Jean wanted it to be, which could be what? Days? Weeks? Months?

Years?

Her breathing became shallower and her chest constricted. Days she could take; weeks even. But longer? It was unthinkable. She'd lose her mind.

She'd read studies about the effects of sensory deprivation, about how effective a method of torture it was. Without sensory input the mind loses its bearings, becomes unmoored, floats out of itself.

Time, space, distance, direction: all of them were constants in a normal life, the points of the compass people organized themselves around. I have to be here, at this time. I have one hour to do this job. I am looking left, because I heard the sound of a car coming from that direction.

I exist, because all these things around me exist too. They were all gone. There was nothing, and if there was nothing, then how did she know she was still there, still alive?

She pictured Ben and the kids coming home. Finding the note. Ben shocked and lost and unsure what to do. Tell the kids? How? When? He'd need support and guidance, from wherever he could get it.

From Jean, if she offered.

Involuntarily, she scratched the floor with her torn finger-nails, hard, until she felt one come free and she yelped in pain.

She did it again; she was glad of the pain; it centered her, brought her back to herself, to her situation.

Which was grim. Hopeless. She was – and this was the worst of it – powerless. Jean had created another Sarah, a Sarah whom people believed was capable of killing herself. When they heard about her suicide note, a note in which she told Ben she couldn't carry on, that she was leaving him and the kids and the world, they would nod their heads and think, *Yes, tragic – but you could see it coming.*

As would Ben.

And he would be angry at her and alone, and in need of help and support. And if Jean offered it, why wouldn't he take it? And if she offered more, then why not take that, too? He'd be vulnerable, and Jean had already showed she was someone who knew exactly how to get what she wanted.

And all Sarah could do was sit here, in the darkness, slowly going insane.

12

At least she's here, Ben thought, as he pulled into the
driveway. Her car was parked in front of the garage door
– he noticed that the paint was peeling at the bottom;
he'd have to paint it again, which was annoying, as he'd
done it two summers ago. He got out and opened the
back door so Miles and Faye could climb out. Kim was
sleeping; he picked her out of her car seat and walked into
the house.

'Sarah,' he said, in a low voice. 'Sarah. We're back.'

There was no reply. He frowned, and listened for any noise
in the house.

Nothing.

She was probably out for a walk. Or maybe in the kitchen,
out of earshot of the front door.

Miles and Faye pushed past him and ran into the house.
'Mom,' Miles shouted – did he not see Kim asleep in Ben's
arms? – 'Mom. We're home.' He walked into the kitchen.
'Mom? Are you there?'

There was nothing. Not only no reply, but no footsteps,
no door opening upstairs, no flushing toilet.

'Dad,' Miles called, from the kitchen. His voice was high,

almost worried. 'Come and check this out. There's a note from Mom. It's kind of weird.'

Ben hurried into the kitchen. He'd been planning to put Kim in her bed before doing anything else, but he didn't want Miles reading any more of the note than he had already read. He grabbed it – a sheet of letter paper – from the counter and held it away from his son's reach.

'Hey,' Miles said. 'I was reading that.'

'It's not for you,' Ben said brusquely. 'Go and unpack. Or watch TV. OK?'

Miles rolled his eyes. 'Who made you the boss?' he said.

Ben didn't hear him. The world had narrowed to the words on the page in front of him.

And he couldn't believe what he was reading.

His legs felt unsteady, so he sat down, Kim cradled against his chest, and read what Sarah had written.

Dear Ben,

This is the hardest letter I have ever had to write, but it is nothing compared to how hard it was to make the decision that I am about to share with you.

I needed space to work it out, which is why I needed you to leave the house with the kids. It's selfish, I know, but it's what I had to do. And it's bad for me, too, because it means I won't get a chance to say goodbye to you, Miles, Faye and Kim.

I want you to know I love you. I love you, Miles, Faye and Kim with all my heart, and you need to remember that in the weeks and months and years to come. I am doing what I am doing not because of anything you and the kids have done. It is all about me.

I cannot carry on, Ben. I think you have some idea

of what I have been going through, but you cannot understand it all. You cannot understand the depths of my pain. Every day is a struggle, a constant fight not to give in to the voices in my head telling me it's not worth it and I'm not worth it and I can't carry on and I should curl up in a ball and die. There is no joy, Ben. No color. Just endless misery.

And it is beyond me to fight any longer. I have no strength left. I'm tired. And so, I'm going to say goodbye to you and Miles and Faye and Kim. Goodbye forever, Ben. I have sleeping pills and vodka and I'm going to go somewhere on the coast – I won't say where – and when the tide is going out I'm going to swallow the pills and drink the vodka and float out on the tide into oblivion.

I'm sorry, Ben. Truly, I am. And if there was any other way I would take it.

Lastly, and most importantly – don't feel guilty. There is nothing you could have done. If it wasn't for you this would have happened a long time ago. You gave me more years than I would have had with anyone else. You were the best man I could have married. But I could not go on. I'm sorry. Please tell the kids good things about me. I know you will.

All my love,
Sarah

'Dad?' Miles said. 'Dad? Are you OK?'

Ben looked at his son, then at the note, then back at Miles.

'Yes,' he said, slowly, unsure of what else he *could* say, not just then, but ever. 'I am.'

'Is Mom OK?'

Ben paused, blinking, but before he could answer there was a knock on the front door, and then the scrape as it opened, and a voice called into the house.

'Hello? Ben? Are you back? It's Jean. I saw the car.'

Ben nodded at Miles. 'Tell her we're in here,' he said. 'And Kim's sleeping.'

Miles walked to the front door; Ben heard him talking to Jean. A few moments later she came into the kitchen.

'Hi,' she said, then frowned. 'What's going on?'

Ben shook his head. 'I don't know. Have you seen Sarah this weekend?'

'We had a drink last night,' Jean said. 'She seemed in a bad way. I wanted to check in with you.'

Ben handed her the note.

'Read this,' he said. He was surprised at how calm he was, although he was pretty sure he was in shock. It wouldn't last; he could feel the anguish building up behind it. 'Read this. Tell me I'm wrong, Jean. Tell me I'm misreading it.'

13

The lock on the shelter door clicked.

There was no warning that Jean was approaching. No footsteps. No sounds from the house. The bomb shelter had been well built; it was well and truly sealed off.

Jean came in and shut the door behind her. She switched on the headlamp. The glare stung Sarah's eyes.

'Well,' Jean said. 'I saw Ben. He's home. He found your note.'

'No,' Sarah said. 'Please, Jean. Don't do this anymore.'

'He got back from Boston two hours ago and there it was. I went over as soon as he was back to check everything was OK. It wasn't, of course. He was sitting on the couch, reading the letter. By the way, it's a different one to the one you read. I had to adjust it now the plan has changed. It told him how you planned to take a bunch of sleeping pills and vodka and swim away on an outgoing tide last night.'

Sarah pictured him sitting there, reading the letter, his face gray and slack with grief, then calling Miles and Faye and Kim to him, folding them into his arms and whispering that Mummy was gone. She heard their wails, felt the rawness of their loss.

'What about the children?' she said.

'He didn't tell them. Kim was asleep and he put Miles and Faye in front of a movie. I guess he'll do it tomorrow.' She smiled. 'I'll let you know how it goes.'

She leaned down and picked up the packet of cigarettes. She put one in her mouth and lit it; the smell of smoke filled the basement.

'He was devastated,' she said. 'Kept saying he couldn't believe it. I stayed with him for two hours. He drank quite a lot of whiskey, but he didn't get drunk.' She shrugged. 'Maybe there are circumstances when even the demon drink can't numb you.'

Sarah stared at the floor. She had nothing to say. She didn't want to ask any questions, didn't want to hear any more from Jean. Didn't even want to look at her.

'I told him I'd be there for him,' Jean said. 'I'd help with the kids, help with meals. Whatever he needs. You know what he said?'

She paused, waiting for Sarah to answer.

'You know what he said, Sarah?' Jean repeated, a note of glee in her voice. 'Go on, ask me what he said.'

Sarah didn't reply.

'Sarah,' Jean said, speaking slowly and deliberately now, in the way Sarah had heard her speak to Daniel and Paul. 'Ask me what he said.'

'What did he say?' Sarah whispered. 'What did he say, Jean?'

'He said he would be grateful for any practical help I could give, but the main thing he needed was someone to talk to. You know me, he said. I'm going to have to process this somehow, but I don't want to talk to some stranger. I'm British. I couldn't think of anything worse. It needs to be someone I know, someone who knew Sarah, who can understand what I'm going through.'

334

Jean chuckled.

'It was *exactly* what I wanted to hear. It couldn't have been any more perfect. I lost Jack, so I understand how he's feeling. And we share our grief at your loss, Sarah,' Jean said. 'And that's what brings people together, isn't it? When they share things. And the kids had to go through losing their father, so I have experience with kids in this situation too.'

'What about Carl?' Sarah said. 'Isn't he going to miss you?'

'Carl?' Jean said. She laughed. 'Carl never existed. I made him up. I needed a reason why I was out in the evenings when I was preparing all of this stuff.' She shook her head. 'You know, this was so much easier than I'd expected. You fell for the whole thing. Next time you'll know what to look out for. But of course' – she dropped the cigarette butt to the floor then ground it out and turned to the door – 'there won't be a next time. You'll be in here for——' she paused, as though considering it for the first time – 'for a while longer. Then you get your choice. Your final choice.'

'Jean,' Sarah said. 'How did you do it? The letters? The photos? The books from Amazon?'

'It was easy,' Jean said. 'I know your Amazon password. I watched you type it in one day. Red front door, all one word, R, F, D capitals. I remembered it and stored it away for when I needed it.'

'And the photos on Facebook?'

'I took them from your phone. Let's say we were on the beach and you went for a swim: I grabbed your phone, emailed myself the photo I wanted and then deleted it from your sent items. I didn't need many; just enough to create my fake Facebook Sarah. And you never noticed, but then why would you? You didn't even look.'

'And how did you know when I'd found it?' Sarah said. 'You – Fake Sarah – sent me a friend request the same day.'

'That was a bit of luck,' Jean said. 'Originally I figured

you'd find it on your own and then mention it to me, your trusted friend. But then Rachel Little got in touch to tell me she was coming back to Barrow. She said she planned to contact you, but didn't know which was your real profile. I told her to ask you, which she did. I knew, because she sent the same message to the fake Sarah Havenant as well, which, since it was my account, I saw.'

'And the handwriting?'

'A skill I have. Took a lot of perfecting, but it's been *very* useful over the years. It was when I knew you'd seen the graphologist that I had to act, and so I set up the whole fake ER visit. Brilliant, no?'

Sarah shook her head. It was something, for sure, but brilliant wasn't the word. What Jean had done was find a way to inhabit every corner of her life, even the ones she had thought were secret.

'What about Josh?' she said. 'The guy I had an affair with? How did you know about him?'

'He told me,' Jean said. 'You weren't the only person he was enjoying himself with. He had a thing for older women, it seems.' She laughed. 'He told me you dumped him. You were all apologetic – it's me, not you, that kind of thing – as though you were worried he'd be heartbroken. The reality was, you were the only one who thought it was a relationship. He found it very funny. You think you're so clever, Sarah, but you're fucking clueless.'

This whole situation was crazy, but perhaps the most insane thing about it was that it had been building for years. Jean had been constructing this edifice around her for God knew how long and Sarah had not had a clue. No idea whatsoever.

'One more thing,' she said. 'How did you send the postcard to Ben's parents' house?'

'It was a *major* pain,' Jean said. 'When you told me you

were thinking of staying in London I had to find a way to make you see that nowhere was safe. So I got on a plane and came to see you.'

Sarah stared at her, blinking in disbelief. 'You flew to *England*?'

'What choice did I have? You needed to know your stalker was there too, so you'd come home. It had the added benefit of finally convincing Ben it was all in your head, so when you got back to Barrow it was all set up for the ending. For *this*.'

'Was it you? In the park?'

'Yes,' Jean said. 'It was. I had to keep my face hidden from Faye, but it wasn't too hard. And I enjoyed watching you, knowing your hopes of a new start were about to be destroyed.'

'What about Daniel and Paul?'

Jean nodded at the chains.

'Left them in here,' she said. 'I gave them food and water.' She tapped the headlamp. 'And Daniel had this. I'm not a *monster*, Sarah. It was only a couple of nights.'

And then she seemed to lose interest. She stubbed out her cigarette, closed the door behind her and was gone.

Sarah stared at the patch of black where, a second ago, the door had been. Now it was indistinguishable from any other part of the bomb shelter.

The bomb shelter where she might be staying for a long time. The reality was starting to sink in. At first she hadn't known what to think – it was a blur, finding out it was Jean who had started all this, had impersonated her on Facebook, sent emails, books, postcards. And then finding out why: because Sarah had, in her mind, forced her into having an abortion that had left her infertile and struggling with depression, which had led to her missing out on college and all the things Sarah had: career, husband, family.

337

And then the matchmaking, which had pushed her over the edge. Pushed her to do all this. Sarah shook her head; the resentment, the *hatred*, must have gone so deep, and yet she had never noticed it. She wondered whether other people had friends like this, or husband, wives, brothers, sisters. People who they thought were their friends, but who, secretly, were wishing for their destruction.

A destruction she had already brought about for Karen – in the same way, with a fake suicide note as cover – as well as the man she had married.

No – the abortion and the matchmaking and all the rest of the slights and insults that Jean claimed were nothing to do with her problems. Her problems ran much deeper. She was insane. Sarah didn't have the exact diagnosis, but she didn't need it to know Jean was seriously ill.

But smart, nonetheless. She could keep Sarah here as long as she wanted. People had been imprisoned in houses like this one for decades, and this situation was even worse, because in those cases there were people out looking for them when they disappeared. In Sarah's case, no one would be looking for her. There would not be any point; she had left a suicide note detailing exactly what she was planning to do, all of it entirely credible given what Jean had been up to.

What would happen to her? Would she last? Physically? Mentally? How long before she lost her mind? How long before she beat out her own brains against the wall?

She had no idea. And she did not want to find out.

In fact, she was *terrified* of finding out.

14

Sarah's mouth was drier than she had ever thought possible, and she was gripped by an incessant thirst. Since Jean had put her down here she had eaten and drunk nothing, and she was now feeling the effects. She needed to drink, and soon.

She had, though, a more immediate problem.

She had to go to the toilet. What had started as insistent urges had become painful cramps and were now a more or less constant ache in her bowels, an ache which was powerful enough to overcome her revulsion at the thought of what it would entail to put an end to it.

She took a deep breath and moved as far as she could to her right. When the chain was taut she squatted, hooked her hands in the waistband of her pajama pants and pulled them down, then moved – to use an expression much more delicate than the reality – her bowels.

The relief was welcome, but the stench was overpowering. She considered taking off an item of clothing and covering the feces with it, but that raised another problem.

She was getting cold.

What was she going to do when winter came? Winters in Maine were harsh, temperatures falling below freezing for days and weeks on end. She would need more clothes, or a heat source.

Except for the fact she wouldn't be here then. She would find a way out. One way or another, she would find a way out.

It was another few hours – Sarah had no idea how many – before the door opened again and Jean came in.

Jean looked at the pile of feces. 'Wow,' she said. 'So little Miss Perfect's shit *does* stink, after all.'

Sarah looked at her, blinking. 'Can you clean it up, Jean? Please. Or I'll do it. Give me a plastic bag and a scoop and I'll take care of it.'

Jean ignored her. She tapped her forefinger against her lips. 'The problem with this bomb shelter is that it was never finished,' she said. 'They didn't put in the plumbing or the electrics. Maybe they ran out of cash, or the Cold War thawed. Anyway, I didn't come down here to talk to you about the plumbing.' She lit a cigarette. 'I came to let you know the big event happened. Ben told the kids. Miles and Faye, anyway. Obviously, Kim is too young to understand. Honestly, I think Faye is, too, but that's beside the point.'

Sarah let out a gasp, which turned into a sob. She pictured Ben sitting on the couch, one arm around Miles, Faye on his lap, saw the confusion on their faces, watched as it turned to shock, then disbelief, then tear-streaked agony.

'No,' she said. 'Please, Jean. I don't want to hear any more.'

'They didn't take it well,' Jean continued. She shook her head. 'But how do you tell your kids about this kind of thing? You have to explain it calmly – Mommy's gone away and won't be coming back – and then start to help them deal with their grief.'

Jean picked up the cigarette packet from the corner of the room and lit up. In her other hand she held a half-drunk bottle of coke. It was all Sarah could look at.

'He didn't tell them it was suicide,' Jean said. 'I suppose he will, later. He just told them you were dead.'

Sarah closed her eyes. This might not have been Jean's original plan, but she couldn't have stumbled on a better way to torture somebody. It was the worst possible situation for a wife and mother to be in: knowing her family was suffering unnecessarily but being unable to do a single damn thing about it. It was like watching her children run blindfolded toward a cliff from behind a soundproofed glass window.

'Drink,' she said. 'Please.'

Jean threw the bottle of coke to her.

'Here you go,' she said.

Sarah untwisted the cap and sipped it; she was not a soda drinker, but in her thirst it was delicious.

She noticed that the smell of the smoke from Jean was masking the stench from her feces; if she had her own it would help block it out entirely.

'Can I have a cigarette?' Sarah said.

Jean raised an eyebrow. 'You?' she said. 'You smoke?'

'I used to,' Sarah said. 'A bit. In college. It's been a long time. I think I can still remember how.'

'Wow,' Jean said. 'Look at you. The minute there's a lick of trouble, you reach for the smokes.'

A lick of trouble? Sarah thought. She was hardly reaching for the smokes because someone had told her her thighs looked big in a new pair of jeans. She was locked in a psychopath's basement, a psychopath who happened to be her oldest friend.

If ever there was a pass for smoking – and draining a large glass of neat vodka, along with some prescription opiates – this was it.

'Sorry to let you down,' Sarah said.

Jean shrugged. 'No skin off my nose,' she said. She took

341

out a cigarette and rolled it across the floor to Sarah. Then she tossed the lighter to her. She was keeping her distance; even though Sarah was chained to the wall she could still grab her, and Jean did not need to risk that.

Sarah picked up the lighter. It was a Zippo. It was inscribed: *To Jack, Love you always, Jean*. Jesus. She still used – without any qualms – the lighter of the man she had killed.

Sarah lit the cigarette and inhaled. The smoke caught in her throat and she coughed, her body rejecting it. Everything about it was foul: the acrid taste, the sensation of her body rejecting a poison, the malign glow of the tip of the cigarette. It was amazing anyone got started.

After a few drags, though, her body remembered that she used to partake, from time to time, and she managed to keep the smoke down.

It was a small victory.

'Jean,' she said. 'What happens now?'

'You stay down here,' Jean said. 'And I keep you updated on what's going on. How the kids are doing. How Ben and I are getting along.' She grinned. 'We can compare notes, after I fuck him. And then, when I've decided it's been long enough – probably when I've fully taken your place with Ben and the kids, maybe moved into your house – you'll get your choice. Starvation, dehydration, suffocation. One, two or three.' She shrugged. 'The thing is, there's no need to hurry from my point of view. You can't go anywhere, and as far as the rest of the world is concerned you're already dead. Only I know you're down here, Sarah, so to all intents and purposes you're mine to do whatever I want with. You're nobody now, Sarah.'

'I'm still a person,' Sarah said. 'I'm a human being, Jean. A mother. A wife. A friend. I have the right to— '

Jean's voice rose to a shrill shout. 'You don't have *any* rights. Down here you are *mine*. So what if you think you

342

have a right to this or that or the other? There's only me, Sarah, and I don't give a rat's ass about your rights, which means they don't exist. Funny, isn't it? Something we think of as so fundamental – our so-called human rights – can vanish so easily. So get used to this, you second-rate bitch: I can do whatever I want to you and it doesn't matter. You don't exist anymore, Sarah. You're gone. The world is moving on without you, while you're down here, a non-person who no longer matters.'

'Jean,' Sarah said, her chest tight, her breath short. 'Don't you have any shred of feeling for me? I'm a human being, Jean.'

Jean shook her head. 'No,' she said. 'You're nothing, Sarah. Don't you see? You're already dead. This is just your journey to hell.'

15

Ben lay on the bed he and Sarah had bought together. To his left, Miles slept. Faye's head was on his chest. It had taken a long time to get them to go to sleep, Faye especially. Every time he had felt her body relax, heard her breathing lengthen and deepen, she had jolted awake.

But now she was – thankfully – asleep.

He felt a surge of anger at Sarah. It had been the same pattern all day: one moment utter grief, a void at the thought of life without her, and then rage. How could she have done this? She could have talked to him. He would have found a way to help her. There were ways to deal with this kind of thing: medication, hospitalization, therapy.

And she, a doctor, should have known it.

On his bedside table his phone buzzed. He picked it up; a text message from Jean.

Hi. Tough day, huh? I made some meals for you for the week. Stuff you can reheat. Can I drop them off?

Jean. What a superstar. If anyone had anything to get depressed about, it was her. She'd had a hard life. He knew it didn't work like that; depression was an illness. But still. She'd had more than her fair share of bad shit happen to her and she simply got on with it.

And she'd been amazing since he'd come home to Sarah's note. She had her own kids to look after, but she found a way to make time – and now food – for him and his kids. Thank God for her.

He texted back.

Sure. I just got the kids to sleep so now is perfect.

He slipped his arm out from underneath Faye and stood up. He went down to the kitchen – he paused outside Kim's room and listened for any noises, but she was asleep – and poured himself a glass of wine – a small one. He'd drunk way too much whiskey the day before, which was not a habit that was going to establish itself. He was not going to become a drunk because of this. His kids deserved better. Sarah might have given up on them, but he wasn't going to.

He sat on the couch. She was gone. His wife, the mother of his kids, was gone. She would never walk into this room again, never come to the couch and sit next to him with a glass of wine and tell him about her day.

He'd called Ian Molyneux who had come to take the note. He'd been a sympathetic cop, not a cop who thought Sarah would show up sometime. Ben could tell Molyneux was thinking, *I've seen it all before and I pity this poor bastard, pity him because his wife is now another sad statistic in the column marked* Suicide.

Ben closed his eyes. It was hard to believe.

A few minutes later there was a knock on the door. He opened it and let Jean in. She was carrying a tote bag full of plastic containers.

'Hey,' he said. 'Thanks for coming.'

She walked into the kitchen and unloaded the bag.

'There's a pasta Bolognese,' she said. 'Some chili. Fish pie. A meatloaf. All stuff you can freeze and reheat.' She gave him a sad smile. 'Comfort food.'

'Thank you,' he said. 'I truly appreciate it. This must have taken hours.'

'My pleasure,' she said. 'I got a sitter this evening. She's with them now.'

Ben felt for his wallet. 'Can I pay for her?' he said. 'You shouldn't have to.'

Jean waved his offer away. 'It's fine,' she said. 'It's the least I can do, given what's happened.'

'Then please let me offer you a glass of wine.'

Jean nodded. 'Thank you.' She gestured to the kitchen table. 'But you sit down. I'll get it.'

'No,' Ben said. 'You've done—'

'Sit *down*, Ben,' Jean said. 'Take a moment to relax.'

Ben smiled. 'OK,' he said. He sat on one of the kitchen chairs, his elbows on the table. 'Thanks.'

Jean poured a glass of wine and sat at the end of the table, at right angles to him. He thought he detected a faint smell of cigarette smoke on her, but then it was gone.

'I still can't believe it,' she said. 'It doesn't seem real.'

'I know.' He felt tears come to his eyes. 'This could all have been avoided, Jean. That's the worst thing about it. If only she'd talked to me about it.'

'I'm not sure she knew herself,' Jean said. 'I can't remember the name, but I don't think she even knew what she was doing.'

'Dissociative fugue,' Ben said. 'Which makes me feel worse.

346

Rachel told me that might be what it was. I should have done something, Jean. I feel so fucking guilty.'

'It's not your fault,' Jean said. 'I don't think there's anything you could have done. And I'm no psychologist, but I'm pretty sure feeling guilty is normal.'

'None of this seems normal. I don't know how I'm going to get through it. I mean, the kids. Fuck. It's going to be so hard for them.'

'They'll get through it,' Jean said. 'People do. My kids did. I won't say it was easy, but they did it.'

Ben looked at her. 'Thanks,' he said. 'It helps to know someone else went through the same thing. And made it.'

'And I'll be here for you,' Jean said. 'Every step of the way.' She put a hand on his forearm. 'Whatever you need, whenever you need it, say the word.'

She stood up picked up his wineglass.

'Another?'

'A small one,' he said. 'I don't want to lose myself in the bottom of a bottle.'

Jean went to the fridge. She refilled the glass and put it back on the table.

'There you go,' she said. She put a hand on his shoulder and squeezed. 'You'll get through this.' She moved behind him and dug her thumbs into the muscles and the base of his neck. 'Wow. Your shoulders are tight. It's no surprise, I guess. I worked as a masseuse, back in the day,' she said. 'At the Sebasco Resort. One of my many summer jobs. Let me work on you for a few moments.'

Ben leaned forward. 'That feels good,' he said. 'Thanks.'

He started to close his eyes. The pressure was – for a moment – a relief. As he relaxed, there was a creak from the stairs.

'Hello?' he said.

'Dad?' It was Faye's voice. 'Dad? I can't sleep. I want Mom.'

Ben looked at Jean. 'I need to go,' he said. He gestured at the food. 'Thanks again.'

16

The click of the lock. The crack of light, unbearably bright at first, then, as her eyes adjusted, Jean's silhouette.

She would have recognized it anywhere. The shape of her head, her narrow hips, the way she held her elbows slightly raised, as though preparing to defend herself. It was a body she had seen thousands, maybe tens of thousands of times. Utterly familiar.

She'd thought Jean – the person – was just as familiar, but it turned out she wasn't.

It turned out she didn't know her at all.

Jean closed the door and switched on the headlamp. Sarah turned her head, dazzled by the beam.

'Please,' she croaked. 'Turn it off.'

Jean clicked a switch and the light went from white to red. It was less dazzling, but it painted the room in a sinister hue.

'Here,' Jean said. She was holding a bottle of water and a sandwich in a Ziploc bag. She tossed them to Sarah. She still did not want to get too near to her captive. It was a wise decision; she obviously had experience. Sarah wondered whether it extended beyond Daniel and Paul. 'You need to keep your strength up.'

Sarah ignored them.

'Eat,' Jean said. 'You'll fade away.'

She was right. Sarah was starving, and felt the onset of a fever, but she didn't want to show it to Jean. It made no practical difference, but it felt good to defy her in whatever small way she could.

In fact, it made all the difference in the world.

'Maybe I'll take them away,' Jean said. 'If you don't want them.'

Sarah's hand twitched out; it was a convulsive, involuntary reaction at the threat, but she managed to pull it back.

Jean laughed. 'You can pretend you're not going to wolf them down as soon as I'm out of here, but we both know it's only for show.' She shook her head. 'Pathetic bitch. This is typical of you. It's why you're in this situation in the first place. You don't know what *matters*. You think your little show of defiance is important, but it's nothing. *Nothing*. That's the difference between people like you and me, Sarah. Like me and the rest of the world, really. I see things for what they truly are. You don't.'

Sarah didn't reply. She didn't need to; Jean's grandiosity, her high self-regard, her sense she was different, better, than other people was characteristic of a certain group of people.

It was characteristic of psychopaths.

'Anyway,' Jean continued. 'Don't you want to know how Ben's doing? I went to see him.'

'No,' Sarah said. 'Don't tell me.'

'Come on now, Sarah,' Jean said. 'He's your husband! He's in distress! And you don't even want to know how he is? What kind of heartless bitch are you?' She shook her head. 'The truth is, he's well rid of you.'

Sarah looked away. She didn't want to hear this; it caused a physical ache in her guts.

'He had the kids in bed. It was tough. They're very upset and it was hard to get them to sleep. I promised to help with them. Be there for them.'

Sarah gave a low groan. She pictured Jean with Miles and Faye and Kim, holding them, saying soothing words to them. She retched.

'No,' she said. 'Not my kids. Please, Jean. Leave them alone.'

'They'll need me,' Jean said. 'Their mom is dead. How can you deny them a woman's love?'

'You're the last thing they need,' Sarah said. 'You're the last thing anyone needs.'

'I don't think Ben agrees. He was very tense, Sarah. Very angry at you. He doesn't understand why you did what you did. I agreed; suicide is such a selfish act. We sat in your kitchen – at the small breakfast table, you know it well – and I poured him a drink. He was grateful of the support, I could tell.'

Listening to this was torture. The image of them, sitting together in her house, in the home she had built with Ben, discussing her suicide, Jean shaping her husband's resentment, stoking his anger; the image was like a scene from a nightmare, a nightmare when you have to watch some awful event unfold but are powerless to intervene.

'I stood up,' Jean went on, 'and was starting to rub his shoulders, loosen them up – they were very tense, he's more muscular than I expected – when Faye woke up. He had to go and put her back to bed.' Jean sniffed. 'It was a shame we were interrupted.' She leaned forward. 'But it was a good start, Sarah. A *very* good start. This will be quicker than I thought.'

She turned to leave.

'Anyway,' she said. 'I'll keep you informed of my progress. And you might want to make sure you take a look at the food and water. Lights out in a second. You need to remember where they are.'

And then she was gone.

17

'How are they taking it?'

Diana, Ben's mother, sat in the front seat of the car, her hands resting in her lap. She had a pained expression on her face. Ben had noticed the way she winced when she bent to climb in, and if he knew his mother at all, that was a sure sign she was in agony.

He'd told her she needn't come, but she'd insisted. He'd asked about flight restrictions for people in her condition; she said she neither knew of any nor cared to know. How, she asked, would the airline know unless she told them, which she had no intention of doing?

'Not great,' Ben said. They were with Jean, Daniel and Paul while he came to the airport to pick up his mum and dad. It was only an hour round-trip, but even then he didn't feel comfortable leaving them. Miles had hardly spoken since he'd told him Sarah was dead – he hadn't mentioned suicide, not yet. He'd stuck at *Mom got sick* – and Faye alternated between tears and outbursts of violent, uncontrollable rage. It wasn't necessarily aimed at him or Sarah; it could be anything. A lost toy, a ripped page in a book, food she didn't like: all of them could send her spiraling into a fierce anger.

It was going to be a rough road.

'It's to be expected,' his dad said, from the back seat. 'It's a terrible loss for them. For all of you.'

Ben pulled out of the airport and headed for the Freeway. 'I can't quite believe it,' he said. 'I wake up every day and remember. It hits me like it's the first time I've heard about it. And I can't believe I didn't see it coming. I should have done something.'

'I'm sorry, darling,' his mum said. 'It's tragic, it really is. But it's not your fault. Suicide is so terrible because the victim isn't the person who dies. It's the ones they leave behind.'

And that, Ben thought, *is the worst thing about it. I can't believe she did this. And I can't stop hating her for it.*

At home he pulled into the driveway. He walked around the car to open the passenger-side door. He put his hand around his mum's waist and helped her out. He felt the bones in her hips; she'd lost a lot of weight. He hadn't realized – she had dressed in such a way it didn't show – and it was a shock to realize how ill she was.

The front door opened and Jean stepped out. She walked down the steps.

'Mrs Havenant,' she said. 'So lovely to see you again. I only wish it was in better circumstances.'

His mum stumbled; Ben caught her. She was pale, her eyes wide open. She nodded, barely seeming to notice Jean, then took a step past her into the house.

'Are you OK?' he said.

'I need to sit down,' she said. She looked at Ben. 'Would you be a darling and put the kettle on?'

Ben nodded. 'Let's get you settled,' he said, and helped her to the kitchen. He sat her on the couch and went to fill the kettle. His dad came and stood by him.

'Can I help?' he said.

'It's OK,' Ben said. 'You take a seat.'

A few seconds later, Jean came in. 'Thanks for taking care of the kids,' Ben said. 'Where are they?'

'In the basement,' she said. 'Best place for them!' She had an odd, almost mocking, smile on her face; probably, Ben thought, she was uncomfortable at seeing how frail Diana was.

'OK. I'll get Mum her tea and then I'll bring them up.'

As soon as he saw Miles's face, Ben worried he'd made a mistake letting his parents come to stay. He was fine with his granddad, greeting him with a hug as usual. He and his granddad had always been close, partly because Roger had always shown him a lot of physical affection, which was not how he had been with Ben and his brother. Like a lot of men of his generation he had not grown up in a world in which men hugged each other, their kids, even their wives. They didn't even really admit to any emotion; the most he could remember from his dad was an occasional, *That was a bit irritating* or *I have to say, I was quite put out*, both of which could be the reaction to someone stealing his place in a queue or burning down the family home. It wasn't so much *Keep Calm and Carry On* as *Keep Calm and Mutter About Your Mild Displeasure*.

It was Miles's reaction to Diana which was the problem.

He had just lost his mother, and here was his grandma, reduced to little more than a skeleton. He turned and glared at Ben, then walked out of the room. They listened to his footsteps climb the stairs.

'Damn,' Ben said.

Diana watched him leave. She put her hands on the arms of the couch and levered herself to her feet.

'Stay put,' Roger said. 'I'll go and talk to him.'

'What are you going to say?' Ben said. 'I think it might be better if I go.'

'It's OK,' Roger said. 'I'll tell him the truth. There's no easy way around this.'

When he was gone, Jean came into the kitchen with Daniel and Paul.

'I'll be on my way,' she said. 'I need to get these two fed.' She put her hand on his upper arm and squeezed. 'You're lucky to have such wonderful parents,' she said. 'They'll be great support. This'll be hard. But we'll get through it.'

Ben put his hand over hers. 'Thanks,' he said. 'And I appreciate your help. I'd be nowhere without you.'

Jean smiled, and then looked at Diana.

'Goodbye, Mrs Havenant,' she said. 'It's lovely to see you. And I hope you enjoy your stay. As much as you can, in the circumstances.'

Diana looked at her, unsmiling, her hands palm down on her knees.

'Thank you,' she said, finally. 'I will try to.' She paused. 'And no doubt we'll have other opportunities to chat. I suspect we'll be seeing plenty of you.'

'Maybe,' Jean said. 'I'm always happy to help. Let me know what you need.' She gestured to Daniel and Paul. 'Time to go,' she said. 'Say goodbye to Ben and Mrs Havenant.'

Daniel and Paul waved shyly, and Jean led them to the front door. Ben followed them. He thanked Jean again, then closed the door behind them.

Back in the kitchen he poured another cup of tea for Diana. He handed it to her.

'The doctor doesn't recommend drinking tea,' she said. 'But I don't see how it makes a blind bit of difference. I'm past the worrying stage now.'

'How bad is it?' Ben said.

'A bit worse than it was when you were in England. More painful. But I'll cope.' She flicked a finger in the direction of the front door. 'That's Jean, correct?' she said. 'Sarah's friend?'

'Yes. She's been great.'

'Are you close to her?'

'Sarah was. I am too, at least in the way you're close to your spouse's friends.'

'I'm not sure I know that way,' Diana said. 'I'm not sure anyone does.'

Ben shrugged. 'I dunno,' he said. 'But it is what it is.'

'Dunno?' Diana said. She smiled. 'You know, there was a time when that would have really irritated me. But those days are long gone. There are more important things to worry about. I only wish I'd learned it earlier.' She shook her head. 'All the energy I used being angry at such things. If I'd channeled it into something else – Christ, I could have moved mountains. So don't make the same mistake I did. Focus on what matters.'

Ben felt tears on his cheeks. He bent over and kissed her.

'It's OK, Mum,' he said. 'I love you. I always have done.'

When he stood up, she was crying too.

18

Jean held a bottle of water in one hand. It was unopened and Sarah couldn't take her eyes off of it; since Jean's last visit she had been consumed by a violent, raging thirst. Her throat was dry and her tongue was large and swollen. She had a deep, throbbing headache.

'Water,' she said, gesturing at the bottle. 'Jean. Water, please.'

Jean ignored her. In the other hand she had a cigarette; it was the second she had smoked since she had come into the shelter. She was pacing the room, sucking down the smoke and shaking her head.

'What a *bitch*,' she said. 'What a fucking *bitch* your mother-in-law is. I can't believe you tolerated her.'

'What did she do?' Sarah said. Jean had been repeating what a bitch Ben's mom was since coming into the room; Sarah wanted to get her talking so they could move off the topic and she could get her hands on the water.

Jean paused and turned to face her. 'She walked right past me,' she said. 'I was waiting at the house with the kids and she got out of the car and walked *right fucking past me*. Like I wasn't there.' She shook her head. 'Arrogant, stuck-up British bitch.'

'She can be a bit much,' Sarah said. It was an effort to speak, the words rasping out of her parched mouth. 'You know she's ill. Maybe she was tired after the trip.'

'Doesn't fucking excuse it,' Jean said. 'And then, when we were in the house she was just as bad. Made some fucking comment about *I imagine we'll be seeing lots of you*. Like I'm forcing myself on them. She's evil. *Evil*. I can tell she doesn't like me.'

She's always been a good judge of character, Sarah thought. *Plus it's a little ironic you're telling me – the woman you've locked in your basement before killing – that my mother-in-law is evil.*

She said nothing though; Jean did not look in the mood to be contradicted.

'The good thing,' Jean went on, 'is she'll soon be dead. Dead and in the cold, hard ground back in England. A place I fucking hated, by the way. Small and petty and full of people who pretend to be nice to you when you can tell they're looking down on you.'

This feeling of people condescending to her was at the heart of Jean's anger, Sarah saw. She hated being ignored or overlooked, as with the matchmaking.

Jean contemplated her for a few seconds. 'Well, it doesn't matter anyway. What matters is, Diana will be gone soon. And Ben will be all the more vulnerable for it. From the way she looks, it could happen any time.' She took a drag on the cigarette; the end glowed in the darkness. 'I wonder if there's any way I could help her along. Some kind of drug I could put in her tea? It can't leave a trace. You'd know. What could I do to the bitch?'

Sarah tried to swallow but she could not produce enough saliva. 'I don't think I can help you,' she said. 'I can't think of anything. Nothing easily available.'

'Right,' Jean said, her voice heavy with sarcasm. She shook

her head. 'Of course you can't. Then maybe I'll use bleach. Kill the bitch that way.' She started to pace again. 'You know,' she said. 'When I look at her, I see you. She's you, thirty years from now. Rich, arrogant, a fucking know-it-all who got everything given to her but doesn't realize it. I'm sparing the world from having to deal with another Diana by killing you. And I'm sparing Ben and Miles and Faye and Kim.' She nodded. 'Yes. This is a mercy killing. Mercy for *them*.'

Sarah didn't care. A new wave of thirst had rolled over her and all she could think of was the water. She watched the bottle swing in Jean's hand.

'Jean,' she said. 'The water. Could I have some? I'm really thirsty.'

Jean turned to face her.

'Oh,' she said. 'So now you need my help. You won't help *me*. You won't tell me what I could use to kill your fucking British bitch of a mother-in-law, but I have to give *you* what *you* want.' She leaned forward. 'That's exactly what I hate about you, Sarah. The fact you think you can get whatever you want but you don't have to do anything in return. Well, you can go fuck yourself.'

She lifted the cigarette to her mouth and took a deep drag, then blew the smoke out in a large cloud. She pressed the glowing end of the butt to the bottle and pushed.

The plastic melted and, with a fizz, the cigarette went out. Jean tossed it on to the basement floor and held the bottle in her hand. The water streamed out on to the floor.

'No,' Sarah said. 'Please, Jean, no.'

Jean dropped the bottle.'

'Lick it up,' she said. 'Like the dog you are.'

Then she left, closing the door behind her.

On her hands and knees, Sarah scrambled forward as far as she could. She felt ahead of her in the darkness for the pool of water. It was rapidly seeping into the concrete. She tried to brush it closer to her mouth, but all she managed to do was disperse it.

Desperate, she lifted her hands to her mouth and licked what little moisture there was off them; it tasted dusty, but at least her mouth was wet for a few moments.

And then she lay down, her forehead on the concrete floor, and cried.

19

Ben opened the front door. Jean was standing outside with Daniel and Paul. She was holding a crockpot; Daniel had a tub of ice cream and Paul was cradling a packet of cookies.

'Mac 'n' cheese,' she said. 'Comfort food.'

'Thanks,' Ben said. 'Hopefully, Miles and Faye will eat it. They've barely touched any food for days.'

And food wasn't the only problem. Faye was still waking at night in tears and Miles was, if anything, even more withdrawn. He looked gaunt, and ill.

'Where are they?' Jean said.

'Watching TV,' Ben replied. 'They've been watching it a lot. I don't have the heart to try and stop them. Whatever takes their mind off Sarah is OK by me, I guess.'

'Can we watch?' Daniel said. His gaze fluttered up to meet Ben's, but then he looked back at the ground. He'd always been shy, as long as Ben had known him; *painfully shy*, Sarah used to say. Not that there was anything wrong with shyness, but in the case of Daniel – and his brother Paul – their shyness was almost fear. It was hard not to feel some sympathy for them.

'Of course,' Ben said. 'You go right in there.'

Ben walked over to the TV room and opened the door. He knew from prior experience that if he didn't Daniel and Paul would stand outside, waiting to be invited in.

Once they were settled he followed Jean into the kitchen. She was setting the crockpot down on the counter and smiled at Roger.

'Hello, Mr Havenant,' she said. 'An American classic. Mac 'n' cheese.'

'Sounds delicious,' Roger said.

'It's pretty basic,' Jean replied. 'But the kids tend to like it.'

'I'm sure they'll love it,' Ben's dad replied. 'Thank you for making it. Someone has made food for us every night this week. It's very nice to feel like the community is lending their support.'

'Jean organized it, Dad,' Ben said. 'It's called a Meal Train.'

'Well, it's very welcome. Thank you, Jean.'

'It's my pleasure.' Jean looked at Ben. 'Do you want to eat now? Or wait?'

'I think the kids are quite settled,' Ben said. 'Maybe leave them for a while?'

'OK.' Jean took the lid off the pot and stirred the contents. 'We could go for a walk. It's a lovely evening.'

'I don't know,' Ben said. He hadn't been out of the house or away from the kids since he'd picked up his parents from the airport. 'I'm not sure about leaving the children.'

'I'm here,' Roger said. 'And your mother's upstairs with Kim. We'll be fine. You go.'

'Are you sure?' Ben said. 'I'm happy to stay.'

Roger nodded. 'Go, Ben. Your mum and I have done it before, remember?'

363

Yes, Ben thought. *But she was in somewhat better health then.*

'Go on,' Roger said. 'Get some fresh air. You'll feel a lot better.'

'Right,' Ben said. 'Thanks.'

They walked to the Town Commons, a series of trails leading through a pine forest. Shafts of light shone down through the trees and Ben felt the warmth of the sun on his face. He inhaled the scent of the pines and it reminded him there was pleasure in the world.

'Thanks, Jean,' he said. 'It's good to be outside.'

'How are you feeling?' she replied. 'You doing OK?'

'I'm mainly focused on the kids,' he said. 'I spend most of my time worrying about them. When I don't I swing between disbelief she actually went ahead and did this, anger at her, and guilt I didn't find a way to stop it. That's the worst part. The feeling I'm to blame somehow.' Tears welled in his eyes. 'And I miss her. A lot.'

Jean walked beside him. 'I feel the same,' she said. 'I should have seen this coming. I think everyone who knows her will feel the same.' She linked her arm through his. 'I feel bad saying it, and I know it's probably not my place, but it's so damn selfish.'

For a moment Ben felt like telling her not to speak that way about Sarah, but he didn't. It *was* selfish, and Jean had as much right to be angry at Sarah as anyone did.

'Don't feel bad,' he said. 'You're only telling the truth.' He pulled her closer. 'And you can say whatever you want. You're the only other person who really knows how this feels. We're going to have to get through this together.'

Jean unlinked her arm from his and stopped. She turned to face him, then opened her arms and hugged him.

'Thank you,' she said. 'I needed to hear that.'

He hugged her back; it felt good to have some human contact. 'It's good to talk,' he said. 'I feel better for this. We should make sure we do it more often.'

'Deal,' Jean said. 'Anytime you want.'

20

Sarah had no idea how much time had passed since Jean had burned a hole in the bottle of water with her cigarette. The image of the water pouring out on to the concrete floor had kept coming back to her, each time more tortuous and more realistic than the last. On a few occasions she hallucinated that Jean was there, doing it again, and she caught herself crying out *no, stop, don't waste it.*

But there had been no one there. Just the thirst. And the knowledge that if she didn't drink, she would die. She tried to calculate how long she could go on, but it was pointless. A person – depending on their individual physiology and condition – could survive, at maximum, a week without water. She didn't know how long it had been since the last drink, so she had no idea how long she had left.

And it didn't matter. The thirst obliterated any other feeling.. She was nothing other than thirst. She was defined by it.

She lay on the floor, hot then cold, shivering then feverish. Eyes open or shut: it made no difference. There was nothing to see. There was nothing.

Nothing but the desire for water. Cool, fresh water. Water

gurgling over rocks in a mountain stream. Rain falling from the skies. A glass full of ice and lemon and beautiful, life-giving water.

She felt her grip on consciousness loosen. She was aware, in an abstract way, this might be the end. This might be death.

But she didn't care. She craved its release.

She came to and there was a light.

The headlamp.

Jean.

She shifted on the floor, and blinked. How long had she been there, watching?

'You're alive,' Jean said. 'I was starting to wonder. I didn't want to check you in case you were playing possum.'

Sarah didn't reply; words would have been impossible. Instead she searched for the shape of a bottle in Jean's hands. Nothing. She could not see through the glare of the headlamp.

'Looking for this?' Jean said. She squatted and rolled a bottle toward Sarah. It hit her outstretched hand and she gasped.

It was cold. Wet with condensation.

A drink.

She peered at the label. Gatorade.

She let out a groan and twisted off the top.

It was the most delicious thing she had ever tasted. No gourmet meal could come close. She felt the cold liquid hit her stomach and it tensed, threatened to retch.

She'd let it settle. Take sips.

But fuck it was hard. All she wanted to do was gulp it down in one go, wallow in the glorious relief.

She stopped herself. Took a sip. Took another.

Then she looked at Jean.

'Thank you,' she said, her voice barely audible.

Jean shrugged. 'It's not out of the goodness of my heart,' she said, and gave a laugh. 'Not at all. Mainly I want you alive so you can hear about what's new in my world.'

Her tone was conversational, an old friend sharing her latest news over coffee.

'I think,' Jean said. 'I think he's falling for me.'

Sarah shook her head. 'No,' she said. 'Never.'

'I wouldn't count on it. We went for a lovely walk together yesterday. Diana and Roger looked after the kids. *All* the kids, mine included. It was almost like we were one big family already. Magical.'

Sarah tried to block out the sound of her words. She sipped more of the Gatorade.

Jean lit a cigarette.

'The beauty of it,' she said, 'is I'm going to get back at Diana at the same time as I destroy you. She's going to be the one who makes it all possible. It'll be when she's looking after the kids that I get my chance, you see. Without her – and his ineffectual father – he'd never leave them. No one else is trustworthy enough – me aside – and so it's *perfect* she's here. Little does she know that her last meaningful act on this earth will be to make it possible for me to steal her daughter-in-law's life.'

Sarah looked away. She had no choice but to hear this, but she didn't want to watch Jean's triumphalism as well.

'It was a poignant occasion,' Jean said. 'We strolled through the Town Commons. Bathed in the evening sunlight. We linked arms, talked about you. How we missed you, but how we were both so angry at you for doing this. I'm going to make sure I stoke his anger, by the way. An angry man will justify many things to himself. For example, he'll think fucking me is justified, because his goddamn wife went and killed herself and he's mighty pissed at her. And then, at the end, we hugged, and promised to be there for each other. Lovely, no?'

'Can I have a cigarette?' Sarah said. She didn't want a cigarette for the cigarette itself; any object would do so long as it was outside of her and the darkness. She needed something to make her feel like she still existed.

Jean tossed the packet across the floor. Sarah picked it up and took out the Zippo and a cigarette. She struck a flame and lit it, then inhaled. She listened as the tobacco crackled and burned.

The smoke was harsh against her dry, damaged throat and she coughed. She put the lighter inside the cigarette packet and slid it across the floor to Jean. It stopped by her sneakered feet.

Jean didn't look at it. Without a word, she turned and walked out of the door and up to the house.

21

Ben sat on the couch, Faye on his lap. She was asleep. It was 5 p.m. on a Friday and he would normally not have wanted her napping then as it would rule out any chance of her going to bed at a reasonable time.

But this was not normally. Faye had not slept more than an hour or two since he had told her Sarah was gone. She would fall asleep around nine, and then, by eleven at the latest, she would be in his bed, wriggling and restless. He didn't mind; it wasn't like he was sleeping much himself, but it upset him to lie there and watch his daughter jerk awake with a cry, snapping out of some nightmare.

He held Faye tight, relishing the warmth of her body and taking comfort in the fact she was at rest, at least for a few moments. As he looked at her, there was a knock on the door.

He didn't move. He didn't want to disturb Faye. Whoever it was would either try the door and let themselves in – which was common in Barrow, if you knew people well – or go away. There was nobody else to answer the door: Kim was out on a walk with his dad, Miles was playing a video game in the living room, and his mum was asleep in the guest room.

He heard the sound of the door opening.

'Hello?' It was a man's voice. Ben tensed. He didn't recognize it. 'Anybody home?'

He covered Faye's ears. 'Who is it?'

'Ian. Ian Molyneux.'

The cop. Sarah's high-school friend. Ben had often wondered whether there was a history between them; he'd never know now.

But the fact he was here suggested there might be an update. Ben felt a flicker of hope; he snuffed it out. This would surely be a routine follow-up to Molyneux's first visit.

'Come in,' he said softly. 'Faye's sleeping.'

Ian walked into the kitchen. He was in his uniform, dark circles below his eyes.

'Hey,' he said. 'How's it goin'?'

'Not great,' Ben said. 'But getting better.'

Molyneux shook his head. 'I'm real sorry, man,' he said. 'I still don't believe it.'

So no update then. The hope went out for good.

'I know,' Ben said. 'It's hard to take.' *A candidate for understatement of the year,* he thought. *But what was he supposed to say?* He gestured at the fridge. 'Want a beer?'

Molyneux nodded. 'Thanks. I'd love one. Been a long day. Big pile-up on 295.' He opened the fridge and took out a bottle of Geary's IPA. 'You?'

Ben shook his head. 'No thanks. I'm steering clear for the moment.'

'Wise man,' Molyneux said. 'So. I came by to check in, but also to fill you in on the search.'

'Find anything?'

Molyneux sipped his beer. He shook his head. 'Nothin'. But then if she went swimming in the ocean – well, the tides are pretty big in the Casco Bay. The body could be anywhere in the Gulf of Maine. I'm sorry.'

Ben couldn't quite come to terms with the fact he was having this conversation, but he supposed it was what happened when your wife drunk a bunch of booze, took some sleeping pills and swam into the black night of the ocean.

'OK,' he said. 'Keep me posted.'

'I will.' Molyneux sat back in the armchair. 'This is the second time I've had to deal with this.'

'Really?' Ben said. He wasn't really interested, but Molyneux seemed to want to talk, and he didn't know how to tell him politely to leave.

'Yeah. There was another woman who did the same thing. Left a note, and drowned herself in the Casco Bay. We never found her body, either. It was Daniel and Paul's mom. Jean ended up marrying her husband, Jack.'

'Right,' Ben said. 'Of course. I knew their mum had killed herself. I didn't know the details.'

'It's uncanny,' Molyneux said. 'Very similar. Their mom – Karen – disappeared. It was some time before we found out what she'd done, though. She must have hidden out for a few days and then done it. Someone found her clothes by the ocean, along with a note.'

'And then Jean married Jack,' Ben said. 'Which didn't work out too well either.'

'I know. She's a saint, that woman. Bringing up those kids on her own. She's had some tough times. And the family she grew up in?' He shook his head. 'We didn't know at the time – we were only high-school kids – but the more I hear about her old man – well, let's just say there's a reason her brother quit town as soon as he could and never came back.'

'Was he— was there abuse?' Ben said.

'I don't know for sure. But I think a lot went on in that house we'll never know about. I met the father a few times. He was a strict man. Serious. I did hear one thing, though, from Howie Davies. He bought the house when Jean's old man passed away and he wanted to rent it out. We were having a beer at the time and he told me the basement had some weird shit in it. Chains and things. He thought her mom and pop were into some of the kinky stuff. If you'd met 'em you'd never have guessed it. He was a mean bastard and his wife gave as good as she got. So maybe it was something else. Maybe involving the kids.' He shrugged. 'But who knows? At least Jean seems to have got out of it unscathed.'

'She's been great since Sarah – since Sunday,' Ben said. 'Making food, taking care of the kids. I'd have been lost without her.'

'Jeanie,' Molyneux said. 'Always been that way. Do anything for anyone.'

'She's great,' Ben said. 'Really wonderful.'

Molyneux nodded. He got to his feet and finished the beer. He put the bottle by the sink. 'OK,' he said. 'I'll let you know if I hear anything. You'll know as soon as I do. And if I can help in any way, let me know.'

'Thanks, Ian,' Ben said. 'I appreciate it.'

'I'll see myself out,' Molyneux said. 'Have a good evening.'

Ben listened to him leave. It was amazing the secrets small towns contained, the things going on right under people's noses. Who knew what had happened in Jean's childhood home? Who knew what was happening at this very moment in other parts of town?

In his arms, Faye stirred. Her eyes fluttered open.

'Dad?' she said, confused and sleepy. 'Dad? Is Mom here now?'

Ben felt tears spring to his eyes.

'No, darling,' he said. 'Not now she isn't.'

Not ever, he thought, and the tears came.

22

Saturday felt worse than the rest of the week. It shouldn't have: it was the same pattern. Sleepless night, Miles and Faye delicate and emotional, Kim oblivious. Ben had tried to get everyone to go for a walk by the river, but first Miles, and then Faye had refused. When they started screaming on the front porch he gave up and let them go back to watching TV.

He felt like a failure, but he wasn't sure what else to do. There was no manual for dealing with this. He put Kim down for a nap, and called Jean.

'Hi,' she said. 'What's up?'

'I'm fucking this up,' he said. 'I don't know what to do with the kids.'

'Have you talked to anyone about how to approach it? A counselor?'

'Not yet,' Ben said. 'You think I should? I'm not sure the kids are ready.'

'I don't think it's ever too early,' Jean replied. 'But you could talk to someone alone. Find out when they think Miles and Faye should get help, and what kind of help is available. You could try Rachel?'

Ben looked out of the window at the backyard. A tall pine – he'd often worried about it coming down on the house in a storm, but it seemed the least of his problems now – swayed in the breeze.

'OK,' he said. 'I will.'

Rachel picked up on the second ring.

'Ben?' she said. 'How are you? I'm so sorry about Sarah.'

'We're doing all right,' Ben said. 'In the circumstances. That's why I'm calling. I think I need some advice. I was wondering if you have a minute?'

'I have as long as you like. Would you prefer to meet in person? I could come to the house?'

'Maybe next time,' Ben said. 'But for now we can talk on the phone.'

'OK. Go ahead. And Ben – I hope you don't think I've been ignoring you. I was planning to get in touch but I didn't want to intrude.'

'It's fine. We've been pretty raw all week.'

'I can imagine. So how can I help?'

Ben paused. 'It's the kids,' he said. 'I've tried to be there for them, but I'm not sure it's enough. I need to know what I should be doing to help them get through this.'

'Being there for them is a great start,' Rachel said. 'It's what they're going to need more than anything. But there are some things you could do, some things to watch out for.' She coughed, then carried on. 'The main thing is to listen to them. Let them explain their feelings. Sadness, anger, resentment, grief: whatever. Let them talk it through, then explain the feeling – if not the situation – is normal.'

'There's nothing normal about any of this.'

'I know. But their responses will be. And they need to know that. And then, when you've listened and explained and talked it through, don't dwell. Do something with them.

Start an art project, or read a book. Move them through the feelings.'

'At the moment they mainly want to watch TV or play computer games.'

'I think that's fine, in the short term. For a while, you're going to be in survival mode, Ben, so it's a case of whatever works. But as you process the grief you'll be able to manage to do some of the things I mentioned. And don't forget external help. There are organizations who specialize in working with children who've lost parents.'

'Do you know any?'

'I can find out for you. And they can be tremendously helpful. They have places you can take the kids where there are people to talk to, scream rooms where they can scream and punch bags and let their feelings out. That kind of therapy is a bit outdated, these days, but it works.' She coughed again. 'How *are* they doing?'

Ben glanced at the TV room. 'Miles is very withdrawn. Faye is devastated. Kim seems quieter than usual, but I think she's too young to really know what's going on.'

'Don't forget her in all this,' Rachel said. 'Grief can affect very young children – even infants – in ways we don't fully understand. But I'll ask around and get back to you with the names of some specialists in this area.'

'Great,' Ben said. 'Thanks. I think we're going to need help. I mean, we can't even have a funeral. There's no body.'

'You could have a memorial service, to say goodbye?'

'We will,' Ben replied. 'I need to get around to organizing it.'

'How are you doing?' Rachel asked. 'This must be very difficult for you.'

'Honestly,' Ben said. 'I don't even know. I'm so preoccupied with the kids, I haven't thought much about myself. But when I do, I go from sad to angry to fucking irate that Sarah did this to us.'

377

'Unfortunately that's normal with a suicide,' Rachel said. 'In the same way as your kids' reactions are normal. You have to work through it.'

'I know. But it doesn't make it any easier.'

'You need to not dwell as well,' Rachel said. 'Find some activity to take your mind off it. Let your subconscious process some of this stuff while you occupy yourself with something totally different.'

It was, in theory, a good idea. The problem was he didn't know what could actually stop his thoughts returning over and over to Sarah and what she had done.

'I'll try,' he said. 'Thanks.'

He put the phone down, glad they had talked, but aware, suddenly, of how long this was going to take and how difficult it would be.

And of what a godawful mess Sarah had left him with.

23

In the end Ben went for a long walk. It didn't work – all he did was veer from anger to sadness to grief. He found it hard to notice what was around him; at one point he passed a man out walking his dogs – Florence and Truffle, he called them – and it was only when the man looked at him with an expression of concern that he realized he was crying.

When he got home, he opened the mailbox and took out the mail. He hadn't checked it for a few days and there was a thick bundle. He walked into the kitchen and put it down on the counter. He could deal with it later.

Diana was sitting on the couch, reading a book. She looked up. 'Would you make tea?' she said. 'I'm rather thirsty.'

'Sure.'

'How was the walk?'

'Good. It didn't exactly take my mind off anything, but it was worth it for the exercise.' He filled the kettle. 'I can't help feeling angry at Sarah. It makes it all so much more complicated.'

'Yes,' Diana said. 'It is a very difficult situation.'

'At least I have Jean. Apart from all the practical help –

the meals, the childcare – she's been through it herself, so she knows how I'm feeling.'

'Really?' Diana said. 'She's been through it? In what way?'

'Her husband died. Jack. It was a car crash, so not exactly the same, but she had to deal with her own grief as well as her kids'.' He poured the tea. 'And they're not her kids. Biologically.'

'Yes, Sarah mentioned that once. What happened to their mother?'

'She died. In fact, she committed suicide. A long time ago, now.' He brought the mug over and handed it to Diana. 'She drowned herself.'

'And then Jean married the man she left?' Diana sipped the tea. 'Right away?'

'I don't know,' Ben said. 'I've never asked. It's not the kind of thing you bring up.'

There was a long pause. 'You don't think it's a bit odd, do you?' Diana said. 'She would marry a man whose wife—'

'I don't think they were married,' Ben said.

'Not quite my point. This man's girlfriend killed herself and then Jean married – or got together – with him. And now another person has killed herself, in the same way.'

Ben frowned. 'Mum,' he said. 'What are you saying? Jean had something to do with these suicides?'

'I'm merely pointing out the coincidence.'

'Sarah was in a bad way, at the end. You didn't see the worst of it. It's not a surprise, Mum. If it was, I'd agree, but it all makes sense.'

'Ben,' Diana said. 'I'm sure you're right. But stranger things have happened.'

'And besides, Jean was her *friend*,' Ben said. 'She'd have no reason to hurt her.' He sat next to Diana and put his hand on her forearm. 'I know you're looking for explanations,' he said. 'But I don't think you're on the right track.'

He looked at his mum. He could see she doubted him.

'And don't say anything to Jean,' he added. 'I don't need to piss her off. Not now. OK, Mum?'

Diana gave him a long, level look. 'OK,' she said.

24

The door opened and Jean stepped inside.

How long had it been this time? Days? Hours? She couldn't be sure. She couldn't be sure it wasn't minutes; time had lost all meaning. She knew she'd slept, at some point, but for how long?

And the thirst was back. Worse, maybe, than before. But somehow she didn't mind. She'd accepted she was going to die. There was no way out of this. Nobody was looking for her. Jean had seen to that. The story of how she had got here was complicated, but the ending was simple.

Jean had won.

And she no longer cared. It was only a matter of time before this was over, and time didn't matter anymore. All she cared about was Ben and the kids, about what Jean would do to them.

Would they end up down here, in the dark, unaware they were chained up in the same place that their mother, who they would grow up believing had killed herself, had been held captive? Would she eventually kill Ben as she had Jack?

Or would Ben resist her? See through her? Steer clear of her and find someone else?

That was all she could hope for now. Hope Ben and her children – whom she loved so very, very much, whom she would do *anything* for – would avoid the fate of Daniel and Paul and Jack and Karen and who knew who else.

But that was all it was. Hope. There was nothing she could actually do about it.

'So,' Jean said. 'Here we are.'

Sarah looked away. She could feel the bad mood coming off Jean in waves.

After a long, tense pause, Jean spoke.

'Your *fucking* mother-in-law.'

The words hung in the air.

'What?' Sarah said. 'What about her?'

'She wants to talk to me. She called me and said she wants to come over and have a chat.' Jean spat on the floor. 'That was the word she used. *Chat*.' She put on a British accent. 'I'd like to come and have a chat.' She spat again. 'Fucking bitch.'

'It doesn't seem so bad,' Sarah said.

'I know what she wants,' Jean said. 'She wants to warn me off her son. I saw it the day she arrived, when she blanked me. She thinks she's *above* me. Thinks her son is, too. Well, I'll show her. I'll show the bitch.'

There it was again. The resentment at being looked down on. A force which had cost two – at least – lives already, and which had been hidden all these years.

And which was all the more powerful for that.

'So I told her to come over,' Jean said. 'I put on my best helpful little Jeanie voice and told her to come on over.'

'Is she coming?' Sarah asked.

'Yes. At eight. Tonight. In an hour, in fact. I might even murder her. Or put her down here with you. Say she never showed up. And after a while, when you're both dead, I'll take you out like the useless trash you both are.'

Sarah still didn't reply. So this was it. This was the end.

'You're probably ready for it now, right?' Jean said. 'Given up all hope? It makes no difference, of course, but I'm interested.'

Sarah looked at her feet. She had nothing to say. Diana would be right there. And she could shout, she could scream, she could rattle the chains, but it would be pointless. Diana would not hear. She could not get her attention. Could not let her know her daughter-in-law was alive and down here.

She blinked.

Unless.

Unless there *was* a way to get her attention, a way Jean hadn't thought of.

'No answer?' Jean said. 'Never mind. I haven't bothered bringing you water today, by the way. It seemed a bit of a waste.' She turned to go.

'Jean,' Sarah said, her voice a rasp. 'Are you not smoking?'

'No. I don't want the bitch to smell it.'

'Could I have a cigarette, though? Dying wish?'

'Why not?' Jean said. She picked up the packet of cigarettes from the floor and threw it over to Sarah.

Sarah took out the Zippo and a cigarette. There were only four or five left. She lit it, and inhaled deeply. She blew out the smoke.

'Better get out of here, Jean,' she said. 'You don't want the smell on you later.'

She closed the cigarette packet and then slid it across the floor. She pushed it hard, so it reached the wall.

She didn't want Jean to pick it up.

Jean looked at it. Sarah held her breath; for a second she thought she was going to pick up the packet and then it really would be all over. But she didn't.

'Yes,' she said, backing away from the smoke. 'I'd better go. I'll have one later.'

Sarah looked away. She heard the door close, and was back in the darkness.

But she was smiling.

Because in her hand she held the Zippo lighter.

And to her, it was more than a lighter.

It was a *key*.

25

Ben pulled on a pair of jeans – black, Sarah had hated them
– and a T-shirt. Miles and Faye were watching television;
Kim was downstairs in the kitchen with his parents. He
wasn't hungry, but he felt he should make some dinner, so
he went to join them.

His dad was reading to Kim on the couch. Her favorite –
Hairy Scary Monster.

'Where's Mum?' Ben said.

His dad hesitated before he answered. 'She went out,' he
said, an evasive tone in his voice.

'Went out? Where to?'

'Erm,' his dad replied. 'I'm not sure.'

'Dad,' Ben said. 'Where did she go?'

'I think she may have gone to see your friend.'

'Which friend? Jean?'

His dad nodded.

'Dammit,' Ben said. 'I asked her not to interfere!'

'Ben,' his dad said. 'Don't worry about it. Your mum wants
to feel like she's doing something. It'll be fine. Trust her, OK?'

After a pause, Ben nodded.

*   *   *

While he boiled water for pasta, Ben picked up the pile of mail he had left on the kitchen counter. There was the usual assortment of flyers and junk mail, bills and circulars.

And there was another thing.

A large manila envelope addressed to Sarah.

He slit it open with his fingernail and tipped it up. A sheaf of papers fell out, and a business card fluttered to the countertop. He picked it up.

DONNA MARTIN, GRAPHOLOGIST.

He straightened. This was the report she'd mentioned. He picked up the papers. On top was a letter. He started to read.

Dear Mrs Havenant,

As promised, here is the report on the handwriting samples you sent me. There is a lot of technical detail, but as I said, the main findings are easy to summarize.

You provided a sample of your handwriting, as well as some other samples to compare to it. I have included them with the report. Without going into details, I can confirm they were not written by the same person. To clarify: you did not write them. Someone forged your handwriting – and it was a skillful forgery.

That person was not, however, the same person

Ben stopped reading. He went back and read it again.

Without going into details, I can confirm they were not written by the same person. To clarify: you did not write them. Someone forged your handwriting

He looked at his dad, looked at Kim sitting on his lap. Listened to the sound of the TV. He let his mind clear so that what he had read could sink in.

Sarah had not written the letters.

Someone else had. Someone else had forged the letters, the postcard, the note in the book.

And the same person had no doubt created the fake Facebook account, and sent the emails, and all the rest of it.

And *all the rest of it* included the suicide note, which meant – and he realized he'd been a bit slow in getting to this – the suicide note was a forgery, too. And if it was a forgery, then Sarah was alive. Or, at least, if she wasn't, she had not killed herself.

She had not *killed herself.*

Someone else had. Or *had* they? Maybe she was alive, and being held captive somewhere.

Ben put the letter on the counter. He needed to call Ian Molyneux, to talk through who could have done this. Who would have wanted to.

But as he picked up the phone, his mum's words came back to him, the words she'd said when he'd been telling her about Jean marrying Jack.

You don't think it's a bit odd, do you? Diana had said, and then, *this man's girlfriend killed herself and then Jean married – or got together – with him. And now another person has killed herself, in the same way.*

Ben took a deep breath.

It was more than a bit odd. He no longer needed to call Ian Molyneux to discuss who it might be, and he did not have time to.

He walked toward the front door.

'Dad,' he said. 'I have to go.'

His dad frowned. 'Where to?'

'To Jean's house.'

26

An hour.

That was when she had said Diana was coming.

Sarah didn't think she'd be there too long; she wasn't even sure she would be there at all. But it was the only chance she had.

So, one hour.

Three thousand, six hundred seconds.

Add on six hundred – another ten minutes – to give her time to arrive.

She'd started counting as soon as Jean left.

One thousand, two thousand, three thousand. Each one a second closer to Diana's arrival.

And to her last, best, *only* chance.

She kept counting, forcing herself to focus on the numbers. It took enormous concentration to stop her mind wandering, to stop herself imagining what was going to happen. Once or twice she almost lost count, but then, eventually, she was there.

Three thousand, six hundred seconds.

Then she went back to zero, and counted the last six hundred.

And then she got to work.

27

Ben ran along the path that led to Jean's back door. He had walked it many times and it had always seemed very short. Now, though, it seemed to stretch on forever. Eventually, he walked out of the trees and into her yard.

The kitchen lights were on, the house warm and inviting. Now he was on his way there, it seemed more and more unlikely Jean had anything to do with this, but he had to find out.

Because even if she didn't, then *someone* did.

Someone who had hacked Sarah's digital life and taken – possibly – her actual, physical life.

Because, of course, if the suicide was faked, then there was a chance she was alive.

Ben pushed the thought away. If it was Jean, then it was likely she had killed Karen and faked her suicide, too, and if she had done that, there was every reason to suspect she had done the same with Sarah.

He didn't want to hope otherwise. He couldn't face the disappointment if he was wrong.

But he couldn't stop himself. Not fully. The hope crept in around the edges.

As he crossed the yard, his run became a sprint.

28

Sarah struck a flame on the Zippo. It danced in front of her eyes, illuminating the basement. She looked around. It was a shame this was one of the last things she would see.

It was odd. This had once been a place of sanctuary, a place where people could seek safety in an extreme situation, but Jean's insanity had changed it into a torture chamber. Well, Sarah was about to turn it into something new again.

A tomb. *Her* tomb. She was resigned to dying. What she was planning would kill her, but if she did nothing, she was dead anyway. At least this way her family would know the truth.

Death may have been all she had left, but at least this was a better death than the one Jean was planning for her.

Best of all, it would piss Jean off no end.

She looked at the wooden door. She knew it led upstairs to the main basement.

Where there was a smoke alarm.

A few years back she and Ben had paid for the smoke alarms in their house to be serviced and updated. The electrician had put some in the basement and explained they should have dual sensor alarms, which would pick up fires that came up quickly and with minimal smoke as well as those that smoldered.

She had told Jean, who had had the same ones put in.

Sarah pulled off her socks. She held one to the flame and watched as the fibers shriveled and melted and then caught alight.

When it was fully lit she threw it toward the door. It hit the wood and slid down to the bottom.

She did the same with her other sock, then pulled off her pajamas and lit them.

When they had been added to the pile, she sat back and watched.

It took a minute or two, but the flames gradually moved from the clothes and began to lick up the wood of the door.

And as they did, smoke filled the room.

Thick, choking smoke.

It wasn't the smoke that would kill her, though. It was the lack of oxygen. The fire would suck it all up and she would suffocate, well before the smoke or the fire itself killed her.

But it was an outcome she could accept.

Life was about doing your best, and this was the best she could do.

29

Ben turned the handle of the back door and pushed it open. The house was quiet, the only sound the ticking of the mud room clock.

He walked through the mud room into the kitchen. It was empty.

There was no one in the living room, either.

He turned to the stairs. Surely Diana wouldn't be up there? But unless she wasn't here at all, then there was nowhere else she could be.

And then he smelled it.

The faint whiff of smoke.

It couldn't be.

He sniffed.

It *was*.

Someone in the neighborhood was probably having a fire. He moved toward the stairs.

The smell seemed to be coming from the kitchen. And it was getting stronger.

He crossed the living room and walked back the way he had come.

And then he saw it. The door to the basement was open.

30

As the flames took hold, Sarah took shallow breaths. She knew it was pointless – there was little oxygen left to conserve – but the instinct to survive as long as she could, despite the futility, was one she couldn't overcome.

She closed her eyes.

If these were her last moments she was going to enjoy them as much as she could. She was going to fill them with love and joy and happiness.

There was a theory that nothing existed outside the mind; the only reality was the one inside your head. It was a persuasive theory; there were thousands of optical illusions which tricked the brain into seeing things that weren't there or missing things that were.

Well, whether the theory was right or wrong, she was going to create her own reality inside her head. She was going to be the author of the last few scenes of the movie of her life.

She pictured the lake they had visited earlier this summer. Remembered holding Kim in the water while Faye and Miles splashed around her and Ben stood on the shore, holding two bottles of beer as the sun slowly set behind him.

She remembered the moment Miles was born. The moment

when the midwife handed her a tiny, blinking baby and she thought *Oh my God, I'm a mom* and she looked at Ben but he was bent over, sobbing with joy and relief and wonder.

She thought of Christmases past and the Christmases to come. And she thought of Ben finding her body down here and learning the truth.

And then she heard it, dimly.

The beeping of the smoke alarm.

She hated alarms, normally. Hated the loud braying.

People kept them in working order, though, because as everybody knew, smoke alarms could save lives.

She would have bet no one had considered they would be useful in *this* situation, though.

And this time she thought, *Good, I'm glad I hear the alarm. Because it means it worked.*

What it couldn't tell her was whether Diana was at the house. She could have come and gone, or canceled and not come at all.

Sarah would never know, and she was fine with that. This was her only shot and she had taken it. She was at peace.

As she slipped into unconsciousness, she smiled.

31

As Ben stared at the basement door, the alarm went off.

The *smoke* alarm.

'Mum!' Ben shouted. 'Mum! Jean! Are you there?'

He heard footsteps coming from the basement. After a second or two, Jean appeared. She was holding a fire extinguisher.

'There you are,' Ben said. 'I smelled the smoke. I'll call 911.'

'It's fine,' she said. 'It often does this. It's faulty. Go home.'

'Then why the fire extinguisher?'

She didn't reply. She just stared at him, eyes wide.

'Where's Mum?' Ben said.

'Who?'

'My mum. She said she was coming here.'

'I don't know.' Jean moved to block the stairs. 'She's not here. Now leave. I need to get this alarm sorted out.'

'Jean. I read the graphologist's report. It wasn't Sarah. Someone was forging the notes.'

Jean's mouth fell open into a fake 'O' of surprise. She put her fingers to her mouth. 'Gosh,' she said. 'What a shock.'

There was a strange light in her eyes, and Ben saw she

had somehow changed, was a person he almost did not recognize.

'Jean,' he said. 'Was it you?'

She let out a sound that was part laugh, part shriek. 'Me? Little old me? You don't think I'd be smart enough to do *that*, do you Ben? No, such a thing would take some kind of a genius, and I'm just silly little Jeannie.'

It *was* her, Ben saw, and he realized there was something very wrong here. There was no more time for talking. He had to get into the basement.

He charged forward and past her; as he started down the steps she lunged at him and pushed him hard in the back. He stumbled, then tripped and fell, bumping down the stairs. He landed heavily on his left shoulder and grunted in pain.

He looked up and she was standing above him, the fire extinguisher raised above her head. She swung it down toward his face; he scrambled out of the way of the blow and grabbed her ankles. He yanked them toward him and watched as she toppled backward.

He pulled again and she fell. Her head banged on the hard wooden steps and she was motionless.

Ben grabbed the fire extinguisher and walked into the basement. He looked around; the smoke was coming from one corner. He walked over. There were stairs leading down to a door. Some kind of shelter – from bombs or tornados – he guessed.

And next to it was a body, the head surrounded by a pool of blood.

A head wearing a scarf.

'Mum,' Ben said. 'Oh, God, Mum. What did she do?'

He knelt down and felt for a pulse. There was nothing.

'Oh, God,' he said. 'Oh God, no.'

And then, from the stairs, he heard the crackle of the fire.

He looked down the stairs. At the bottom was a door. And it was on fire.

A secret door. A door which might lead to a place where someone could be hidden. He aimed the fire extinguisher at it and pulled the trigger.

32

Sarah didn't need the doctor to tell her she had pretty serious smoke damage to her lungs, nor that she might suffer from shortness of breath and other breathing difficulties for the rest of her life. These were obvious diagnoses from both the symptoms she had and the situation she'd been in.

She didn't care.

She was happy to be alive. Happy to be able to have a doctor give her any kind of news. Happy to be at her house, surrounded by her husband and kids.

Ben had come down in the nick of time. He put the fire out and let the smoke clear the room, then went upstairs to get the key to the chain around her neck from Jean.

But Jean was gone.

In the end he found some bolt cutters in her shed and used them to free Sarah, who was barely conscious. Not long afterward she was in an ambulance, breathing pure oxygen.

She found out the next day – when she woke up in hospital – that it hadn't been the only emergency vehicle on their street. Ian Molyneux showed up in a cop car, lights blazing.

He was looking for Jean.

He didn't find her. None of the cops did.

She also found out that her mother-in-law was another of Jean's victims. She must have smelled the smoke too, and gone down to take a look. Jean had struck her repeatedly with the fire extinguisher.

In the hours since she'd come round, Ben had sat by her bed. He would have lain next to her, but there was no room. If Miles wasn't hugging her, Faye was. And if Faye wasn't, then Kim was.

As they sat there, the door opened.

Roger came in. He was pale, his face lined.

'Roger,' Sarah said. 'I'm so sorry.'

He nodded.

'She saved my life,' Sarah said. 'If it wasn't for her, I wouldn't be here now.'

'I know,' he said. 'She was a tough old thing, Diana. I'll miss her.' He bent over and kissed Sarah; he had the musty smell of an old man and Sarah had a sudden glimpse of his future, alone without his wife.

'But the truth is, she was dying anyway,' he said. 'And she would have traded what time she had left for this a hundred times out of a hundred.'

'Roger,' Sarah said. 'Will you stay with us? For a while?'

'I don't know,' he said. 'I wouldn't want to imp—'

'Dad,' Ben said. 'Don't even say it. Stay.'

Roger nodded, and the beginnings of a smile touched his lips. 'All right,' he said. 'I think I will.'

'Good,' Sarah said. 'We'd love to have you.'

Ben looked at her, and then at his dad, and then at the three children lying beside her.

'I'm going to miss Mum,' he said. 'But I'm not going to waste what she gave us. We're going to make the best of everything from now on. We're going to take every opportunity we have to love each other and to be the best we can be. We owe it to her.'

Sarah nodded, blinking away her tears.

'It's strange,' she said, 'to be saying this after what's happened, but I feel like the luckiest woman alive.' She kissed the top of Kim's head, felt the softness of her hair against her lips. 'And I think we're going to be OK,' she said. 'After all this, I think we're going to be just fine.'

A Year Later

A sailing boat bobs on a mooring off the coast of Oregon. It is small, but big enough for a single person to live on.

It is also anonymous. It can move from bay to inlet to island to beach, and stay there, unnoticed. One more boat owner taking advantage of the dog days of summer.

It is nearly time to head south for winter. Pilot the boat down the coast until it arrives somewhere warm. San Diego, maybe. Or Mexico. Baja California is nice.

Yes, it is time to go. Winter in Oregon is not a good place to be in a boat this size. Plus, it is easier to live cheaply in a warm place. The woman sitting on the bow knows that well. She learned it the winter before.

But before she goes she has to fix a problem. She picks up a remote control and turns some dials. Next to her an electronic device buzzes into life and rises into the air, lifted by four rotors. Suspended underneath it is a camera.

It is called a quadcopter.

The woman watches it fly over the water toward a house on the water's edge.

A house where a woman is at home alone, a woman who has been puzzled by some unusual recent events. Phone calls with no one on the other end. Calls from banks telling her she is approved for a loan she did not apply for. Calls from doctors asking why she did not show up for her appointment.

And today, an invite to a charity luncheon. A charity she has supported in the past.

Except there is no luncheon.

There is only the woman who will kill her.

And when she is dead, the woman on the bow of the boat will make an escape south to warmer climes, where she will start working out her next move.

For she has unfinished business. And she has thought about it for the last year. She has made plans and discarded them and made new plans and discarded them and made yet more plans.

But none of them have been good enough.

Until now.

Now she has a plan, a plan which she will consider and refine until it is ready.

And then she will return.

She will return to Barrow, Maine.

She will return to the scene of her only failure. And she will put it right.

But that is for another day.

Acknowledgements

There are many people without whom getting *Copycat* from idea to book would have been difficult – if not impossible – as well as a whole lot less fun. They are, in no particular order:

Barbara, Jessie and Tahnthawan, whose generous advice at many different stages was – as always – eye-opening. I am fortunate to have such insightful and willing readers whose judgement I can rely on.

Marcus Deck, for his advice on the medical aspects of the book as well as his broad-ranging literary criticism.

Becky Ritchie, who is everything I could wish for in an agent. Her guidance on many different matters is invaluable.

Sarah Hodgson, and all the people at Harper who worked on the book. I am humbled by their diligence and creativity – from editing to marketing to cover design to publicity – and couldn't think of a better home for my work.

KILLING
KATE

There's a serial killer on the loose.
And the victims all look like you...

A serial killer is stalking your home town. He has a type:
all his victims look the same. And they all look like you.

Kate returns from a post-break-up holiday with her girlfriends
to news of a serial killer in her home town – and his victims all look like her.

It could, of course, be a simple coincidence.

Or maybe not.

She becomes convinced she is being watched, followed even. Is she next?
And could her mild-mannered ex-boyfriend really be a deranged murderer?

Or is the truth something far more sinister?

AFTER
ANNA

The real nightmare starts when her daughter is returned...

A girl is missing. Five years old, taken from outside her school.
She has vanished, traceless.

The police are at a loss; her parents are beyond grief.
Their daughter is lost forever, perhaps dead, perhaps enslaved.

But the biggest mystery is yet to come:
one week after she was abducted, Anna is returned.

She has no memory of where she has been.
And this, for her mother, is just the beginning of the nightmare ...

KILLER READS

DISCOVER THE BEST IN CRIME AND THRILLER

Follow us on social media to get to know the team behind the books, enter exclusive giveaways, learn about the latest competitions, hear from our authors, and lots more:

 /KillerReads

 /KillerReads